Tom Dooley

Tom Dooley

AMERICAN TRAGEDY

Bill Brooks

FIVE STAR

A part of Gale, Cengage Learning

GALE
CENGAGE Learning·

Farmington Hills, Mich • San Francisco • New York • Waterville, Maine
Meriden, Conn • Mason, Ohio • Chicago

LIBRARY OF CONGRESS CATALOGING-IN-PUBLICATION DATA

Names: Brooks, Bill, 1943– author.
Title: Tom Dooley : American tragedy / by Bill Brooks.
Description: First edition. | Waterville, Maine : Five Star, 2016.
Identifiers: LCCN 2016024368| ISBN 9781432832278 (hardcover) | ISBN 1432832271 (hardcover)
Subjects: LCSH: Dula, Tom, 1843 or 1844-1868—Fiction. | Triangles (Interpersonal relations)—Fiction. | Murder—North Carolina—Wilkes County—History—19th century—Fiction. | Mountain life—North Carolina—Fiction. | GSAFD: Historical fiction | Biographical fiction | Love stories
Classification: LCC PS3552.R65863 T66 2016 | DDC 813/.54—dc23
LC record available at https://lccn.loc.gov/2016024368

First Edition. First Printing: November 2016
Find us on Facebook– https://www.facebook.com/FiveStarCengage
Visit our website– http://www.gale.cengage.com/fivestar/
Contact Five Star™ Publishing at FiveStar@cengage.com

Printed in the United States of America
1 2 3 4 5 6 7 20 19 18 17 16

This one's for Joshua, who fills me with pride.

HISTORICAL NOTE FOR TOM DOOLEY

Tom Dula was a young, twenty-two-year-old ex-Confederate soldier born and raised in the Appalachian hill country of North Carolina, in Wilkes County. He was one of three brothers who fought in the war. Before he became a soldier, he'd become intimately involved with Ann Foster, a neighbor girl, when she was just fourteen; the pair were caught in bed by her mother, which may have precipitated in Tom joining the Army when he was seventeen.

Both of Tom's brothers were killed in the war and Tom had suffered several wounds in his three years of fighting. Upon his return home, he again took up with Ann, now married. Much is lost to history and time, but by most accounts, Ann's husband, James Melton, knew of the affair, and so did others. Ann had two cousins, Pauline and Laura, whom Tom is reported to also have had affairs with.

Legend has it that Tom fell in love with Laura and the two had planned to run off and get married, but on that fateful morning, Laura's body was found murdered, stabbed to death and put in a hasty grave of leaves and twigs.

Tom, fearing he would be blamed for the murder, ran off to Tennessee. A man named Grayson helped capture him and returned him to North Carolina.

Tom was arrested for Laura's murder, and Ann Melton, her cousin, was arrested too. Tom subsequently testified in a written statement that Ann had nothing to do with it. Tom was tried and convicted and sentenced to hang.

But, was Tom Laura's killer? Or could it have been Cousin Ann who killed her out of jealousy? Could it have been Ann's husband who wanted to get rid of Tom? Or might it have been Colonel Grayson, who was reported to have a love interest in Laura and feared she would run off with Tom?

The former governor of North Carolina, Zebulon Vance, defended Tom pro bono because he believed that Tom was innocent.

It mattered not. Tom was convicted of the crime and sentenced to hang but won a second trial on appeal only to lose.

A local poet, Thomas Land, wrote a poem about Dula shortly after he was hanged and it became a ballad sung in the hills. Eventually it was recorded as a song for the first time in 1928. In 1958 the folk group The Kingston Trio recorded the song and it sold millions, making the ballad known around the world for the first time.

The people and events of this story are true, but obviously some of the situations and dialogue are fiction by the author.

★ ★ ★ ★ ★

BOOK I

★ ★ ★ ★ ★

CHAPTER 1

I am Elizabeth, daughter of Swain.

Mute.

Widow.

Poet.

My lover was hanged. I never whispered to him the words I had for him in my heart. I never felt his touch on this flesh of mine that ached so for him. He came to me only in dreams and we made love in dreams. It was a long time ago.

Billy, the town drunk, the schoolteacher, whose pitted face ravaged his self worth, married me. He was not my first choice. I was not his. But fate works strangely enough and Billy and I would have been married forty years last winter except the influenza killed him in the autumn. He shuddered and breathed his last as leaves tumbled from their stout oak limbs and gathered for a final carnival along the ground, or fell madly into the river and swirled away. Billy himself had grown like an old leaf that had browned and withered. We would have been married forty years exactly on Christmas day.

But the one you marry isn't always your truest love. Tom Dooley was my truest love and he was hanged without ever knowing the depth of my heart's song for him. For I was the sweet, sad daughter of the tavern-keeper Swain, and had an affliction that debauched my beauty.

My father was a profane man with profane friends. I was his only child. For he cursed the woman who bore me and took no further risk of being the butt of profane jokes from his own kind.

My mother, whose name was Muriel, left us both shortly after it was learned that I could not speak. Why or what the exact circumstance of her leaving had always been unclear. My father cursed her mightily on many nights—drunk and cursed of spirit—for her abandonment, not so much of me but for himself. His profanity climbed the stairs and crept under my door and found me shuddering with dread at this odd thing I was that caused him and her so much anguish as to put them asunder.

Mute, dummy, dopey the other children called me. *Poor thing, devil's child, witch's brew* were some of the names I heard fall from the lips of the elders who saw me. *Purty little piece* spoke the eyes of the men who drank in my father's tavern and would have me, afflicted or no. For in spite of my affliction, or maybe because of it, such men seemed to desire me. And many of these men who my father knew and consorted with and drank with at the tavern would overlook well enough my affliction, given the opportunity to take me into some dusty backroom, or place me on a bed of moss in the woods and grind into me. So I steered clear of all men for that very reason—knowing that there is no affliction a woman can possess that will stanch the desires of certain men when they are overcome.

I grew up cursed and without true love, but still I dreamt of it. O, not the common kind of love any girl can have if she's willing and desperate enough. For many of the men and boys of Reedy Branch would just as easily and quickly stick themselves into a knothole, or a calf, or each other if no girl were available. But it isn't love you'd be getting, and never love for the reputation you'd earn by performing such lewd acts with those jugheads.

It was Tom whom I fell first and truest in love with the day I saw him return from the war. And even as I watched Ann Melton rush up to him and boldly kiss him on the mouth—though she was by then a married woman—it never stopped me from falling in love with him. And to that love I owe voice—his, and mine—a voice of written words and not those that fall from the lips like petals from a wilted rose.

It is now winter again, and I've decided to add my own words to the letters and notes of my lover written by him as he wasted away two years in jail before he went to the gallows.

O, I went each day to see him, and to write down what he told me, never realizing he was keeping his own diary of the events as well. For, I think he'd come to trust no one completely, so oft had he been betrayed. But if he had known how I loved him, he would have trusted me.

Still, whoever reads the words will not get the story fully. For the story of a single life is never complete but a puzzle with missing pieces. But such a story can be puzzled together enough so that some portrait can be made for others to draw a picture.

That's all I aim to accomplish, to draw a portrait of my beloved—Tom Dooley—a man wrongly or rightly accused of murder. A boy, really, who did not live long enough to marry and have children and grandchildren. The issue of his blood stanched by the hangman's rope. His would-be children, but angels in waiting. The one who loved him truest, his lips never kissed. In the long litany of what might have been in the life of Tom Dooley, add to it our wedding, and children never born, and a future never carved.

My veil is neither long nor black.

The women he had come to believe he loved were not my kind, and surely not his.

Some may have loved him—Laura, surely must have loved him for she paid love with her life. But Ann Melton? No. And Pauline? Hardly. Some of her testimony against him proved less love and more condemnation. She and the mad preacher, Shinbone, disappeared not long after the hanging. Perhaps they are still living together in their own madness amid a crumbling log cabin somewhere in the dark laurels. I've heard rumors long since about them—how a trapper or a hunter would see their ghosts, hear their feral cries in the shadowy hollows of that country. But then, that country is a land to many ghosts and strange occurrences and I don't put much stock in such things. Most likely they are as dead as Tom.

I left that land after Billy married me.

Paris is rainy this time of year.

I teach piano to young girls whose mothers see in them promises of things they cannot see in themselves. Some are startled at first that I can't speak but that I play the piano quite well. I write them a note telling them, *my ears are perfect, even if my tongue is not.* Too perfect perhaps for the rapturous young hearts whose fingers betray their dreams of becoming musical mademoiselles. The discordant, *Tink! Tink!* of their efforts is sometimes as irritating as a toothache.

Between my teaching piano, and selling occasional collections of poems, I manage to subsist nicely enough. My poetry, my quiet life—outside the few hours each day of teaching—my morning stroll along the boulevards, tea in a café—what more could I want, except perhaps to share it with a lover.

No, not even the power to speak do I want as much as my lover returned from the grave, or better still, never sent there in the first place. I've learned to live without a voice but not without love as I would have it. The simple truth is, I have come to like quite nicely not speaking. For everything is learned in the listening of others who talk away their lives, tell their innermost secrets, give away their dreams.

My time is near. I can feel it. It won't be long before I too may be a wandering ghost seen by hunters and trappers. Perhaps

a pair of lovers in some secluded glen, their mouths ripe and stained by the berries and desire while their hearts collide in tender fervor, will see me wandering those hills of mystery. But it is here in Paris where I plan to die. I will never return to Wilkes County—to all that tender terror that went on there.

O, what could be more perfect than to wander as a ghost among the places where lovers meet and give way to unbridled passions—to see them kiss and touch and withdraw one from the other dollops of desire.

O desire, how shall I tell thy story? I shall tell it as well and as truthful as any story can be.

There is a nice young man back in New York who has promised to publish all of what I send him regarding the tragic events that took my lover's life if I promise also to send along my newest collection of poems. Well, I shall just have to do that before it is too late.

My soul is the thrush's beating heart, its ready wings, ready to fly, to fly, to fly.

O, go along there my faithless limbs, and follow the rushing soul to its journey's end.

I'll go along there if you will it . . .

I do, I do will it.

Last night I had this dream of three young troubadours gathered together on a stage lit by electric lights where in harmony they sang:

Hang down your head Tom Dooley . . .

I thought them angels coming to escort me home and searched their faces for the one face I've not seen in ever so long.

But his was not among them and I awoke crying.

CHAPTER 2

Tom Dooley

Tomorrow they kill me. The sun will break clean in a blue sky and folks will bring their kids and butchers will sell candy and it will be the biggest event Statesville's ever seen.

Jeeze Christ, Tom, you're like the circus come to town—better. The show is free!

Wiley chews and spits in a tin cup between his feet. He's got a drooping eye says kept him out of the war.

. . . and bad feet.

You famous, Tom. Most famous goddamn man I ever met. They got reporters come from all over.

Last night I dreamt of a red horse, a sailing ship, Laura in her coffin opening her eyes to gaze at me.

I'm waiting, darling Tom. Join me in this place of darkness, feel the cold in my cold, cold heart.

It sputtered me awake like I was drowning.

What's she feel like, Tom—old sister death waiting right around the corner?

You are a stupid son of a bitch, Wiley.

Shit, I know it.

Grins. Chews. Spits. The brown juice runs down the side of the can and he don't care no more about it than anything.

Need to go to the privy, Wiley.

Piss in that honey pot.

Like to go to the one out back.

16

Shit, Tom, you know I ain't allowed . . .

You go get a shotgun, keep it aimed at my back. I try anything, pull the triggers.

He looks uncertain, as dull stupid men do when faced with a decision.

. . . and cheat the hangman?

You'd be a hero—the man who killed Tom Dooley.

But he shakes his sorry head.

Just like to see a bit of that sky one last time.

You will tomorrow.

Won't have no chance to enjoy it tomorrow.

The muscle below his droopy eye twitches.

Tell you what. You walk me out back, I'll give you my watch. It ain't but a two-dollar watch, but it'd get you a lot of drinks bought after I'm hanged. Got my initials in it.

He is like an ox I'm tempting with a bucket of grain.

Goes and gets the shotgun, unlocks my cage, leads me out back through a thick iron door that screeches when he opens it. Leads me into a courtyard of sunlight. I stop and take a deep, deep breath of all that sunlit air hoping it will warm my cold blood.

Whatcha doing?

Breathing.

Keep moving.

I walk slow, take in the color of the grass, the trees standing higher than the courtyard wall, the sounds of birds, the smell of freedom. But no matter how slow I take it everything passes too quickly and before I know it, I'm back inside my cell.

About that there watch?

I'll give it to you first thing in the morning.

He looks disappointed.

What's twenty more hours to you, Wiley? Why, you got your whole stupid life to live out yet.

He spits out his plug, pulls a twist from his pocket, tears off half, and stuffs it inside his fat cheek.

Silence like after a gunshot settles in.

Twenty more hours, they'll kill me.

This I write in the papers that I'll send to Liza, daughter of Swain—the mute and tender child I learned to love too late. But till then, I'll keep close my thoughts, sharing them only with the ink and paper on which I write.

O, death, why has thou chosen me among all thy choices?
Was my name written in the book of life waiting to be
Pluck'd on this certain day at such and such a time? Or was it
Merely the luck of a bad hand drawn and too poorly played?

Wiley Branch—1st Jailer

He's a pretty boy, Tom is. Too bad they'll hang him in the cool morning. Why such a pretty boy ought to be about doing what pretty boys do. I have thoughts about him, sure. Thoughts I'm shamed to admit to anyone. I always had a taste for pretty boys but it wouldn't do to share it with him.

What little pleasures do I got but these pretty boys. I think of all those pretty boys who went off and got themselves killed and what a waste it was, and how I'd like to have even just one of them to keep safe. I don't know why, I just always felt that way since I can remember. But I keep it all inside me how I feel about pretty boys. Got to.

Look at him sitting there, that pretty hair fallen down over his eyes as he writes on those clean white pages. Pretty as a angel. Tomorrow he might even be a angel. Such a shameful waste. Why I'd take him home with me in a minute.

Hey there, Wiley.

I like the way he talks, the sound of his voice. It don't bother me he calls me stupid or a son of a bitch. I reckon it's just 'cause he knows they're going to kill him tomorrow. I reckon he's got a right to be irritable. So I don't get mad at him for saying such things to me.

I'd like to tell him what a pretty boy he is. But I got my job to keep and I don't say anything to him about any of that, for it wouldn't do no good for him or me. I reckon there'll be other pretty boys come along.

Hey, Wiley, I got to go to the privy.

It stirs something in me. I tell him to piss in the honey pot. I seen him do it before and it stirs something in me. Something I ain't got no control over and I go home at night and think about seeing him pissing in the honey pot and it does something to me.

But he begs me to take him out back. He says he wants to taste some free air one last time. Bribes me with his watch. It wouldn't take that much. Tells me I can keep the shotgun on him and shoot him if he tries anything. I couldn't shoot him.

I couldn't shoot such a pretty boy.

Elizabeth Brouchard

Yesterday a letter came from Tom—the second this week.

Dear Liza,

I will be sending on the papers of my time kept. Things I've recorded since jailed two years now. I've no one else to give them to, and I know how much you appreciate words written. I appreciate as much your letters to me, and having come to visit me as a friend in the Wilkesboro jail when no one else would except my mother and the crazy preacher. You might wonder why I am giving my journal to you and not my mother or other kin. They cannot read or write is one reason. Another is, I wouldn't want them to know some of the thoughts I've been having, some of the accounts of the events that have landed me in this tough spot. Only a woman like you could understand such things. I knew the first time I looked into your eyes that you were someone

I could trust with every little secret. If I have one regret in my whole life, it is that I did not get to know you better—that I allowed myself to be guided more by pleasure than by good horse sense. Had I known then what I now know about you, there would have been no other love for me, no Ann or Pauline or— God, how it grieves me to even mention her name—no Laura. And maybe had I loved you instead of them, there would have been no murder. My papers should arrive to you in a few days hence. I ask that you wait only until my kin have all passed over before you show it to anyone else. Yr. dutiful servant & friend, Tom.

I read it with silent heartbreak, then put it with the others I keep tied with a scarlet ribbon there in the same place I keep my own diary of the events that have occurred. The events of love, betrayal, and murder. For we were all witness to the same events, to the same lives damaged and destroyed, and no one was innocent completely.

Don't ask me if he did it, I dare not ask myself.

But my heart tells me his bones and marrow have no murder in them. Yet I do confess my eyes are cloudy with unrequited love, and love makes fools of us all. Just as it surely must have to the others: Ann and Pauline and Laura: Laura most of all— for she paid the dearest price.

Tom speaks to me about regretting not professing his love for me. And I, who cannot speak, am equally at fault when it comes to such confessions. Nature rendered me mute of tongue, but not of heart. There were other ways I could have exclaimed to him the nature of my love, the depth and breadth of it. But, he loved the others, and I thought it impossible he could love me as well; Ann with her beauty and cunning; Pauline with her naïveté; Laura, with her sweet innocence, or so it seemed. What did I have to compare with all that?

Had I confessed my love in a letter, would that, say, have

been enough to change the events? The words in my heart are like caged canaries fighting to be set free, my tongue the lock that holds them captive. I should have written to him my confession and let matters fall in place, or not. But do words ever alter history of self?

So tomorrow they will kill my love and he will fall into eternity and be as silent as my tongue.

I dread the hours between now and then.

I dread the thought of the day being beautiful, of birds singing, of music and laughter and happy small children and all things I once held as wonderful. For tomorrow will be black, black, black.

And though I have not told him when exactly, I will leave first chance for New York, then on to Paris, and never again return to this place. For love, and the death of love, tear at the heart as nothing else can and I must do something with all these caged birds that flutter around in my heart so wildly, or else go mad. But for the moment, it is better if Tom believes I will be here for him—someone who did not abandon him in life or death.

O, I shall be there when he returns again, just as I was the first time. Only this time, it will be only me, and not one of his false lovers. And I shall go up to the grave where they will bury him and wait until all have left before coming out of the shadows. And I will kneel there beside him and stay awhile. My heart will speak to his heart and he will hear me this time. For angels know what angels know.

And in that cold and lonely place he'll sleep, he'll sleep with knowing he was loved truly.

Perhaps before tomorrow, he will receive my last and final letter.

And, if you are listening, dear sweet Jesus, remember the promise you made: *ask anything in my name and it shall be given.*

Well, I am asking now that you make Tom know I love him.

That I have always loved him.

Tom Dooley

I try not to pray, but cannot keep from it. Shinbone, the mad preacher, tried his level best to convince me of the spirit world and I tried my best not to believe him. For who can believe in a God that allows war and death to those who don't deserve it? And what I've seen, I've seen, and I won't ever forget except by death's grace. Still, I find myself spewing pleas to this ghost called Jesus.

O, Lord, don't let this thing happen to me. Where is there any meaning in this injustice? If you are the embodiment of love as they say you are, then why don't you love me enough to save me?

But time does not stop and the final hour comes closer with each breath and no spirit, holy or otherwise, comes to save me.

I tell myself it is all foolishness, that I am so desperate I will believe anything—that no man is *Saved* until he sees he is about to die and convinces himself of God and God's salvation. All this praying and I don't feel saved at all. I just feel foolish for allowing myself to try and bargain with a ghost.

Wiley shuffles back in again, a letter in his hand, sniffing the envelope.

Smells like it's from somebody sweet, Tom.

Escaping from his droopy eye is a certain suffering that I cannot too long look at.

He hands the letter to me through the bars and refuses for an instant to let it go, making sure that his fingers touch mine. I am the caged dog he feeds more to torment than to keep alive.

He chomps down on his plug, turns his head ever so slightly, and spits, without once letting me escape the gaze of that haughty eye.

Probably that same gal's been writing you right along. She must

*be something real special to attract a pretty boy like you. Something
real, real sweet.*

Then to my relief he goes back out again.

Dearest Tom,

*I hope and pray this letter reaches you in time. I wish you
had given permission for me to come and be there tomorrow.
Well, a part of me wishes that, and a part of me is relieved that
I won't be there. O, this is so difficult to even speak of, but
understand this—I love you. I've always loved you. And I will
always love you and nothing can separate me from your love.
Nothing. I will keep your words close to me, and if you'll permit,
I'll arrange them so that someday the world will hear them and
judge for themselves what occurred here in this place. It is the
one gift I can still give you—to see that your story is rightly
told. I've decided to take up the pursuit of poetry. I know I cannot earn a living at it, not just now anyway, but perhaps
someday I shall. To sustain myself, I'll give piano lessons. Of
course, I'll have to eventually move away. I was thinking about
Paris. What a grand place I've heard it is. We could have had
such fun in Paris, you and me. For you have the soul of a
wanderlust . . . and so do I.*

I have to stop reading because my eyes burn with tears.

It is enough I am loved at all.

It is far more than I could have hoped for: to be loved by this
woman who I gave so little to when the chance was there. Did I
think a woman who could speak and whisper her desire for me
better than one who could not? Surely I did. And surely I am
the worse for it. I allowed false hearts to conquer me, to capture
and cage me. And look at me now.

For love is the greatest of these, the ghost said.

I will read the rest of Liza's letter in a little while. I will read
it in small bits and digest every word and let it settle into my

blood and transform me, if anything can, and make me whole and ready for the thieves of righteousness.

For steal my life they surely will.

But sweet Jesus, let them not steal my soul.

CHAPTER 3

Tom Dooley

The husk mattress shifts beneath me, whispers like a thousand tiny voices whispering my sin.

A square of winter light beckons me from the far end of the cabin. Panes of frosted glass separated by a cross of wood.

The cold breathes my name.

Tom.

I remember an early morning like this one along the Rappahannock. Me and the boys. The river cold black. Cooking coffee. Grass full of frost. Me, a drummer. Ghosts across the river. Fear settled o'er us. Each day more of us missing until we were hardly more than a ragged blanket of God's unmaking.

Beat the drum, Tom.

Ann stirs beside me, one arm across my chest. Over in the corner sleeps Melton. Hair sprouting from the blankets: a bramble of startled gray. She calls him husband. He calls her, *wife.*

Beat the drum, Tom.

I slip from bed, from Ann's slumbered embrace, and pull on drawers, shirt, boots, quiet as I can so as not to disturb Melton, Ann, the world.

The room's only hope is the frosty light falling long through the room. Fire in the stone hearth burned out sometime during the night, sometime between the throes of Ann's desire and Melton's regret. Melton's heart is grown cold as those ashes, my own nearly so.

An old squirrel rifle leans in the corner where morning light has tiptoed, climbed its stock and barrel. I make a silent journey to the door.

I was a soldier once, a drummer mostly, but knew how to go quietly about so as not to disturb the dead. I was full of pride most days: proud to be with the boys and proud to be one of them. Me and the boys gathered by the river, cooking coffee, chewing tack, talking, laughing, being shot at, being scared. Look at me now. Some around here call me a *backdoor man*.

O pride, where have thou fled? To a rusted cage of thy own hand's making.

Ann lies in the bed like a wilted flower I've torn from Melton's garden. But his hands knew not how to raise the lily and care for it, nor keep it alive with love. Where my own hand was careful, knew the ways of the flower and when ready, how to pluck it. And now our sin is our sin. I am not proud of my easy harvest, but not so ashamed I avoid it.

Beat the drum, Tom.

Ann Foster Melton

Who can tell a wild heart not to beat?

When Tom left for the war, Melton came for me. Rained all the night before; it should have been a warning. Melton rode up on a mule. I don't know who was uglier, Melton or that mule. I should have run and kept on running. But where is a child to go alone among these hills? I had not heard from Tom for months. Not one letter to let me know if he was safe or dead.

Melton's voice was high and pinched like a woman's.

Hidey.

Climb down, climb down, my mother said. Liquor was her curse and she was in its grip then.

Don't mind if I do.

The mule snorted in relief of his weight.

Melton never once took his indecent eyes off me. I felt skittish and thought if I ran and threw myself into the river, that would do it. Even Melton wouldn't have truck with a drowned girl.

Him and mother languished over a crock of corn liquor, sipping and negotiating the price he'd pay for me.

She's young and tender and never once been touched; that oughter mean something.

Still, they's gals all over this valley since the war took off all the able men. You'll have to put a fair price on her. 'Sides, how can you say she's not been touched? She was with Tom Dooley for a time, wasn't she, mother?

If'n you feel such, why you come for her, *if they's gals so plentiful and my child here is so tainted with another man's love?*

I guess I always had an eye for her.

She'd make you a good wife, give you all the young'ns you could muster. Jus' look at the hips on her.

I'd go twenty dollars, that oughter do it.

Twenty dollars! Why you can't buy you a good mule for no twenty dollars, much less a fresh young sprite such as her.

They haggled over me like I was a nigger.

What Melton feared was true—if he bought me, he was buying used goods. What he wanted to get so bad had already been gotten. Tom got free what that old fool Melton was willing to pay cash money for. And others got it free too—long before Tom even, and long before Melton. I'd rather have married the mule.

But soon enough the negotiations were finished and I packed what few clothes I had into a carpetbag and climbed on the back of Melton's mule, my arms around his bony ribs while mother counted out her fifty dollars and never even said a word of farewell.

Melton proved hard on me. Tried to wear me out that first night. I bit inside my cheek and stood it and when he rolled off me, I vowed he'd have no more of me unless he beat me and tied me to the bed. He did that too, 'bout every time. I fought him like a wild cat, clawed at his eyes and scratched his face. But mostly it did no good; I'd end up with bruises on my legs, back—everywhere. And when he was full mean drunk, he'd smite my face and blacken my eyes.

Tom don't know the half of what I've had to put up with. He fought his war. I fought mine.

O, I begged Tom not to go and leave me to other men such as Melton. I begged him from the very first. But Tom's head was filled with glory, he said his eyes saw the far shining seas and distant places and that he heard the beat of the drums and my love couldn't hold him. Nothing could, he said.

I gave myself to him, all that he wanted and all that I wanted and wherever he wanted. It didn't matter to me, I had no pride when it came to Tom Dooley. Some men are like that, they make you throw away your pride, they make you want to do anything for them, to keep them. And so that's what I did. I did anything I could to keep him.

Tom Dooley
O, I was well warned the price I'd pay by leaving, by sallying forth to the march of drums, the rattling sabers, the screaming lead.

O, proud soldier, march with thee and recline thy head upon thy tunic

& weep with thee on summer's eve as we count our score of boys dead,

Whose eyes pale as distant stars hold no longer hope or glory! Hear them

Sigh their constant warning and take heed all ye not yet gone to

faraway places
That in a blink and nod you too will join them still there on that
unholy ground.

Our first time together and before I went off, was in a corncrib not far from Melton's cabin.

Melton aims to marry me, Tom.
He's old, old.
Can't we run away together?
Don't ask me to know your heart before I know my own.
Then he, or another, shall have me if you will not.
Then I reckon he will, if you let him.

She sobbed away while the thunder gods summoned me. O, the war was a jolly thing. We played soldiers until came the death upon us. Then our jolly notions fled and left us only with ragged wounds and frightened hearts.

As I unlatch the door—its leather hinges barely protest—and step foot forth into this new world, I think of those days—how far away and rousing they were. But here in the silence of frost in the grass and trees that are stark and white and cool as the lips of a corpse, those days are hardly even a dream to me. Melton's old horse stands frozen, snorting steam. It reminds me of the steam-snorting deer that would drift down from the woods to scavenge corn in the morning silence before battles were pitched—O, what was it, two, three years ago? Louis taking aim, bringing a velvet doe to its delicate knees at a distance of a hundred yards—yelps with glee, *Yahoo, boys, we'll eat good tonight,* the camp gathering. And for a time it seemed hardly war at all, for we could hear the Yanks at night across the river calling out feverishly:

Trade you baccy for some deer meat, Reb!
Trade you a pocketknife for some of that corn liquor!
Trade you my galdurn gal for some!

But not enough to go around for them and us both: one

skinny little doe. Feed the Federals and they'll damn sure kill you the next day Sergeant Carnes warned. We shout back and forth, them saying how they'll get even with us in the morning and us saying how they should come on over and get a kiss from Betsy Bore. Laughter. Silence. Dread like cold creeping into our bones.

A night like long sorrow lay o'er us, our blanket of truth.

Come the morning we fight like hell, try and kill each other, then retreat and go somewhere else and fight again. Half them dead, half us—left there on the battlefield for the bottle flies. Bloated dark corpses upon memory's pages.

O, but that was back then and time becomes confused and I don't trust it, I don't.

Outside Melton's cabin the world seems foreign. The tree-sloped mountains gleam like the frosty beards of old men in repose. Ribbons of smoke curl up from the black creeks. It seems as though God himself breathed down upon the earth a hasty cold breath in his retreat from here.

The grass crunches beneath my boots as I walk to the privy. A chill more unbearable than the morning air touches the back of my neck. I know Melton is watching me through a circle of frosted glass wiped clear by the heel of his hand. I don't care. I don't care.

The dewy scent of Ann clings to me like a nosegay of dead flowers.

Is it drums I hear there beyond the far mountains?

James Melton

What sort of dozen fools was I to marry her, knowing she loved that damn Tom Dooley and would never give him up? My own family was quick to ask and scorned me for marrying the *shrew witch*!

But marry her I did . . .

For better or worse . . .

Isn't that the vow we make before God?

I know they laugh at me down at Swain's. They laugh and whisper and talk behind my back about how it is a man could let another man fornicate with his wife.

I'd kill any sumbitch I caught putting the horns to my woman!

I'd cut off his nuts and boil 'em up good and feed 'em to my dog!

Old Jim's got himself a real tart. Why I wouldn't mind having a go at her myself since she seems so willin' to give it away!

But they ain't none of them knows what it is to love a woman so hard and mightily he'd do anything, put up with anything to keep her. And who among them has a wife looks anything like Ann—the most beautiful woman in all the valley and all up and down Reedy Branch, whose beauty extends all the way to the far mountains and beyond? Not a damn one of them! They don't know anything about beauty. They live their lives in the most unbeautiful way and they do not read and wonder at things beyond what they can see with their own eyes and taste with their own mouths. They do not dream of beauty nor sleep with it close to them. So, how would any of them understand me, or anything about what I'd put up with to keep even a very little bit of Ann's beauty close by? Let them talk. It is a thing beyond me, out of my hands, not of my doing. I'll bide my time and pray God strikes a bargain with the devil and rubs Tom out, for all our sakes.

Tom Dooley

We marched, the boys and me, and bivouacked, and lay out under the stars and under the rain and under the snow, the seasons eroding us with the certainty of time passing. And I beat the drum for them and they told me stories about their gals back home. They told me about their Mams and Paps, and their longing burned a hole in my heart.

Some could read and some could not, and those who couldn't, asked me to read the letters to them and some asked would I write for them as well.

Read it for me will you, Tom, but over here where the others can't listen in.

And I would read letters that arrived to my best comrade, Louis, of such things as crops and weather and of a wife's heart broken and full of longing. Sad sweet things put into words oft stained by teardrops that would smudge the fine blue ink.

Dearest Louis. Oh, how terribly I miss you. It is like a piece of me has been torn out leaving a deep hole where my heart once resided. The baby is doing well, had the colic last week but fine now. The cow stopped giving milk and now I must go to the Carters for it. Night is when I miss you most, for it is the loneliest hour here in our bed and time feels endless and unbearable without you here beside me. I miss your hand upon my . . .

Oh, stop reading, Tom.

And I would hand him over the letter he could not read for himself and he would take it and fold it carefully and put it inside his breast pocket and go off to mourn. Louis, a strapping strong boy of the most handsome countenance and who I'd seen do a thousand brave deeds. But his eyes would fill with tears at the thought of home, at the thought of his darling Minnie and darling babe, Louisa, named after him. And oft I would hear him in the night mewing like a sad kitten and crawl into his blankets with him, for I was just as lonely.

I think he is out there waiting for me still.

In the silence of the privy I can hear the frost crackling as though the world is splitting in two. I finish what I came for and step out again and the sun behind the blind-eyed sky is sharper now, piercing through to warm us all again and bring us all fresh hope.

I see a shadow behind the cabin's window, behind the circle

Melton made now frosted over again. I'm sure Ann has awakened because of Melton's movements about the cabin and is lying still, feigning sleep. They are a couple wordlessly bound, their marriage one of silent, aching hearts. Ann calls me the *healer* of her heart.

James Melton

Look at her there sleeping as though struck dead by love, her bed still warm where he did lay. I want to take the old gun and shoot her, him, myself. Maybe someday I will if it does not end soon. He steals a little of her beauty every day. Takes it with him when he goes and never brings it back when he returns. I go and lay down next to her, feel the hollowed place where he lay and listen to her sleepy breathing. Her beauty shatters inside me like sun-warmed ice. I wish his name had been on the death lists posted down at Swain's, that I'd gone there one day and read the name: *Tom Dooley. Kilt.*

But it never was, and I never read it, and then one day he was back, a hero of sorts, as if his returning wasn't bad enough.

She does not move next to me. I wait, but she does not move.

Tom Dooley

Three years, nine months, twelve days since the first time we fornicated. Why I remember this exactly I can't say, except the war has made me conscious of every minute of my life.

I close my eyes and see again that sunlight that came through the slats of the corncrib as Ann wriggled beneath me, her body warm and damp with the fever of desire. The taste of her breath was sweet in my mouth. We fucked urgently on the cobs of the previous season's harvest, our weight shifting, pressing them down.

Won't you run away with me, Tom, before old Melton can get his hands on me?

A corncrib on a hot summer's day is a stifling place, the bed of cobs rough as shifting rocks under us. But comfort wasn't the quest, and first desire is the strongest of all desire.

Oh, Tom, I can't bear it, the thought of Melton and me this away. He's old and has big horse teeth and smelly breath. He looks at me with his starved eyes. Save me from him, Tom.

It was my first time, but desire is its own teacher. She held my cob in a grip so sweetly painful I thought it would burst open but for her holding it so firmly.

Farther out in the fields we could hear men cursing their mules to plow with vigor the hard unyielding earth, the oaken handles blistering their hands, the unfortunate blades striking buried rock. Their labor a chorus to our pleasure. And being naïve in such matters I asked cautious questions.

Have you done it with other boys?

Oh, Tom, I love only you.

You seem to know your way around these matters.

I've dreamt this day for a year, of what I'd do to you and what I'd have you do to me.

I held fast to her slender hips as she worked over me. The first touch of her wet sex against the tip of my cob was like fire. It was beyond what a body can imagine, especially the body of a boy not yet tested by love or war.

Oh, goddamn mule, pull along there! Gee, haw! Pull along there!

We looked between the slats.

Is that Melton?

Laughed.

Then in small slippages she settled onto me until there was no more she could slip down or me push up.

Tom, Tom. Oh, my sweet, sweet darling.

The first words of lust spoken to me by anyone.

And there in that hot corncrib with the silage dust floating in the air and sticking to us, my heart fluttered like a starling trapped in barn rafters.

The ring of plow blade striking hidden rock sounded crisp as a church bell.

Oh, goddamn mule, whoa up there!

The field hand's curse a condemnation?

Don't let old Melton have me, Tom. Don't let him have me this away.

And as she bared her teeth in sheer pleasure, I thought of the boys and war and becoming a drummer, knowing my hand would not fit a rifle, that I had no murder in me. And as the bony prominences of her hips knifed into me each time she rocked to and fro, I came to realize that without the pain there can't be no sense of pleasure. And even as my blood percolated within my flanks and I felt as if I were being split in two, I thought of places beyond the mountains I wanted to go.

Don't let Melton come do this to me, Tom. O, don't let him have me!

Curse you old mule! Curse ever goddamn hard acre of this ground!

Laughter and curses, the long *hee-haw* of protesting mules, then collapse in a sighing breath, her weight o'er and upon me fully, heavenly, as though an angel fallen from the sky lifeless.

Ann Foster Melton

O, a girl never forgets her first time and she never wants her fellow to forget his, and though Tom was not my first I was mighty careful to give to Tom all the pleasure I'd learned about being a woman before my Tom came along. The others meant nothing to me—no more than a scraped knee.

He asked me if I was his first and I couldn't disappoint him and tell him that he wasn't. What's a small white lie when it comes to such thing? My first was Billy Dixon, of all folks. Billy twenty years old, and just returned from Raleigh where he earned a teaching certificate. Billy with his poor pitted face so awful no girl would freely go with him for such matters, offered me three dollars to let him do it and I did. O, the money was nice, but it wasn't the whole reason I let him. The thought of what it was to fornicate with a man had consumed me since I had witnessed my uncle fornicating with my aunty while staying with them on a visit. I was ten years old, and the sheer strangeness of watching them on that hot, hot day as I lay in the cool dark loft of their barn and looked down upon them, caused my skin to itch in a funny way.

O, Dora, I've got me a need.

Not here, Hiram. What if the children were to come in?

Surely they won't. I seen them all go off toward the swimming hole together. Come on now, let me have at it.

She struggled with him, but laughingly so. He turned her around and bent her over and lifted her skirts so that her bare arse was exposed to him and to my eyes. I watched as he unbuttoned his trousers and took out his swollen cob and pushed it into her like you'd see the animals doing to one another. At first she didn't say anything and he didn't either, except for little grunts he made. But in a short bit she began to moan and he said to her:

Yes, yes, yes. You like it now don't you, Dora? You like it ever bit as much as me. Tell me you do, gal. Tell me now.

I do . . . I like it.

I held my breath, afraid they might hear me, and pretty quickly he finished and replaced himself and she straightened her skirts and they went back out into the hot sunlight together. My cousins numbered seven so I was sure my uncle and aunty did it quite a lot.

So when Billy Dixon approached me after class one day—I was one of thirty or so of his students—and asked me to let him and offered me the money, I did. *I always sensed something womanly in you, Ann—not like the other girls.*

His talk swole my head.

It hurt quite a lot, but he finished quick and told me to go clean myself up and gave me the three dollars. I told myself I'd never do it with him again. But the hurt didn't last so long and neither did the money and I let him do it to me several more times for the same amount. Then too, there was my cousin— one of those seven of my uncle and aunty's. We went back to visit, and I let him do it to me there in the same barn, making him do it to me in the same manner I'd seen his folks do it to each other. And by then I'd gotten some pleasure from it. Then I met Tom and told Billy I wouldn't let him anymore and if he ever said anything, I'd tell my ma and she'd tell the High Sheriff and he would come and arrest Billy and put him in prison. And that was that, for I promised my heart only to Tom and aimed to keep my promise.

Tom Dooley

The lovely Louis was shot and killed at Malvern Hill, the bullet gone through his tunic and through the letter I'd read him three weeks before. His blood stained the words of his sweet wife's longing, the baby's colic, all the rest. I took it and let it dry in the sun, then folded it as carefully as he had done and built a toy boat and tied the letter to it, then sent it down into the current of a stream whose name I did not know. It would either find a resting place or it would not, and stood and watched it sail out of sight.

Sail away with thy memories of truest love, and with thy memory of what was lost here on this day.

Beat the drum, Tom, beat the drum.

The boys and me buried Louis and the others under clouds of acrid smoke and venomous thoughts. Another soldier asked for Louis's shoes and I would not let him take them. We fit over Louis's shoes. He bloodied my nose and I his and Louis wore the shoes to his grave. For what the soldier did not understand was the kinship between Louis and me. For, in spite of his having a wife and me a sweetheart (Ann), there were nights when the loneliness and fear were too much to bear singly. So we shared what we could to sustain us for another minute, another hour, another night. And in the morning we marched like soldiers, fought like men, and kept what secrets we owned to ourselves. Why I think of all this just now, I can't say. Except perhaps that love is love and love is often strange and immeasurable.

I walk away from Melton's cabin, the frost breaking like glass underfoot, the hoary mountains turning slowly to a deeper darkness under sun's growing strength. The chill in me eases a little. I walk toward home, toward the empty cabin I have built where I will lay me down and think of what life has yet in store for me. For since the war, I've learned not to make plans.

I walk away remembering, too, Ann's words that first time there in the corncrib, her voice heavy with exhaustion, whispering to me even as she fell into sleep:

Marry me, Tom. Make a decent woman of me before old Melton can . . .

But I did not marry her, and of decency I know so little it seems. And now Melton has her, and I have her, and silently we share, the three of us, this triangle of whatever you would call it. But love isn't one of its names.

I look back only long enough to see my boot prints in the frost and wonder if the little boat with Louis's bloodstained letter ever found a safe harbor.

Beat the drum, Tom.

Elizabeth Brouchard

O, such strange details, written down on bits and pieces of tattered paper—like a tattered heart long after the love is all fled and we become whole again. Details you'd never suspected my eyes would see—you who played your roles so well under heaven's assemblage, directed by gods and minions of gods and moons and stars.

Tom: The Good. Ann: The Horrid. Melton: The Cuckold. A cast of fools.

&
Then
There
Was
Me
Who
Brought
The
Final
Curtain
Down.

CHAPTER 4

Tom Dooley

Grayson stands in the midmorning air listening as the broke-through sun shatters the frost till it lies wet and dewy. He is brushing his prize horse, a stud named Hero. A Tennessee Walker that stood sixteen hands tall with bright clear eyes that look round toward me when I come up the road and past Grayson's farm.

Morning there, Tom.

Hidey, Mr. Grayson.

He looks down the road whence I've come with a grim mouth of recognition that the nearest place is Melton's.

You're out awful early, Tom.

I still have the night's feel of Ann's warm body in my blood, the taste of her mouth in my mouth.

Early bird gets the worm, they say.

Yes, I've heard it said.

Fine-looking stud you have there, Mr. Grayson.

Best in all Wilkes County. Fast as a bullet, why nothing can outrun him.

I heard stories of Grayson killing a man over such a horse, but no one knows much about him round these parts. He drifted down over the ridge from Tennessee, spitting distance from here practically. Calls himself The Colonel and others who know him do too. He's asked me some about the war, knowing I was in it.

Three years, eh Tom? Long time for a boy to fit a war.

Every time I think of it, I remember Louis: the flower of blood staining his tunic, his tender hands trembling, his yearning sobs. Seems that war's been over for eons, but it's hardly been a year. I never ask Grayson why they call him The Colonel, and did he fit in the war himself. Most men I know don't like to talk about it except in dread and regret. And them that do, mostly didn't go, or mostly ran at the first shot.

Grayson brushes long strokes over his stud's back and haunches until its hide gleams like polished oak.

Winter's about to set in, Tom. Why you can taste it in the air. Tastes bitey, don't it?

Ann has by now probably arisen and washed herself clean of me, and serves Melton his breakfast of hominy and ham with blackstrap molasses poured over everything. His warm wet eyes probably watch her as she sets his plate in front of him, his hand wanting to reach out for her to pull her to him and ask things of her she can't answer.

How come him and not me?

Yes, sir, Mr. Grayson, you can taste the air. And on I go toward home.

Ann Foster Melton

I awake and find James next to me on the bed. He is shaking. I quickly dress and go to the window and look out. There, in the frost, I see Tom's boot prints leading away toward the ridges. James snuffles on the bed, the blanket pulled up to his chin, his eyes peering over the hem at me.

He's long gone, that Tom of yours is. Not even the decency to say goodbye to you. That's what you want in a feller, someone that will use you up and skedaddle first light?

O, his words are bitter.

If you can't stand it, why don't you do something about it?

What would you have me do, kill him? Maybe you? Maybe all of us?

I ache for Tom, ache for his touch, ache for his mouth on my mouth. But all I see are boot prints in the frost.

Tom Dooley

Soon I come to the little schoolhouse, a drift of smoke rising up from the stone chimney, the din of children, of lessons to be learned, of song singing—a clattering of high voices rattling around like pebbles in a pail. Billy Dixon is inside standing in front of the clutch of faces, ramrod straight in his worn black suit, his pocked cheeks huffing and puffing the lessons he is trying to impart: *Shakespeare,* the *Holy Bible,* poems about *Mariners*—multiplication tables and how many rods in an acre. Their little skulls trying to take it all in, tongues lolling, eyes shiny like buttons, their limbs restless to play.

This same Billy Dixon who, comes the night, drinks at Swain's to escape whatever sorrow ails him, cursing his lot in life, bemoaning all manner of travesties. I've heard him. I've sat in the tavern and watched him damn his own life and slobber his heart out to anyone who would listen. Once I went out back of Swain's to relieve myself in an alley and saw Billy down on his knees in the mud, his head up under a slattern's dress. I could tell it was him by the checked trousers he always wore. And I felt sorry for him listening to her cries of false ardor for him as he worked away at her.

Oh, Billy child, oh, Billy . . . you're such a good lad there . . .

It was after that he confessed to me he had no true friends and wondered would I be one to him. I didn't know how to answer, but over time allowed I understood the lonely heart of a man, and told him about the war a little but not overly much. It seemed to break him down some to have someone to share thoughts with. But it turned him into a stray cat that once you set out a bowl of cream for comes round again and again. I had no heart to turn aside his offer of friendship. I never thought of Billy back then as my own true friend. That came later on.

Billy Dixon

I'd see Tom in Swain's most nights. He'd sit to himself and drink and it seemed to me he was as lonely as I was. So we had that in common: our loneliness. But we had something else in common too. We had Ann in common, only Tom did not know of it, unless she told him, and I doubted that she ever had. For she threatened me with the High Sheriff was I ever to say anything about our relations. Tom did not seem to me a man who was very worldly in spite of the fact he'd been off fighting in the war for three years. He seemed a simple, shy young man with no more in common with most of the folks in Happy Valley than myself. So I took to him because of our alienation, and maybe I took to him a little because Ann had taken up with him even though she was married to Melton and maybe there was a little bit of me that wanted to know what secrets he held to get women to love him like that.

So I bought us a round and forced my company upon him. And when he did not reject me, I told him of my troubles—about women mostly.

Listen, Tom. I'm cursed with this pitted face. No decent woman will have anything to do with me.

He suggested I give the Widow Weaver a try, her husband having fallen under the wheels of a wagon that broke his neck the winter previous. He suggested that she wasn't too old or alarming in looks for me, and that I might make a handy father to her three youngsters—me being a schoolteacher and all.

Tis hard for a widow with children to find a good man considering all the good men who never came back from the war, his argument went. There was something somber and distant in his voice whenever he spoke about the war, even just a little.

O, I know, Tom. I know it. But I've given the Widow Weaver a chance and she refused me. Even though Happy Valley is bereft of eligible men, she will not have me.

The one I saw you with that night . . . out there in the alley . . . what about her?

Flo? O, hardly would she make a proper wife. I paid her four bits for the privilege of going under her skirts, so desperate was I for relations. She'd do it with anybody for as little as even a twist of tobacco. You won't spread it around you seen me with her, will you, Tom?

No, no.

In the span of a few drinks, we became friends, I think.

Tom Dooley

And so I paused there for a little while, listening to the children reciting their numbers for a man whose loneliness they might never know, realizing that as children go, they more likely laughed at him behind his back and called him made-up names.

For a moment I felt the need to go to Billy and tell him of where I'd just come from, tell him what it was to sleep with a man's wife in one bed and him in another there in the same room. I wanted to ask Billy if, being a man well educated, he could tell me what it must be like for Melton to lie there in the stony silence of his soul and listen to his wife carry on with another, all the while knowing that she would only give herself to her husband under physical force. Something she told me happened more than once.

I'd never give myself to him willingly, Tom. It was understood right from the start. I fight him each step, claw at his eyes and face until he forces me down . . . That's the only way he has me.

I didn't like to hear of it, of course. It made me angry enough to want to kill him. But I know what it is to kill a man and it ain't easy, no matter what the circumstances. I'd seen my share of kilt men in the war. And if you've not seen a body with a chopped-off hand or a torn away leg amid a field of harvested corpses, then don't tell me about what it is to kill a man.

O, I hate to keep thinking about it, but every little thing keeps coming back to me at the oddest times. I listen to the children and remember that among us boys was a good elder who prayed over us and said were anything to happen to us, God would understand and forgive us our sins and take us into his heavenly kingdom. He said that God understood the mortal plight we'd been placed in by our country and so on and so forth. He was a Scots and rolled his R's and was later shot by his own troop who mistook him for a Yankee spy as he made his nightly visitations to the boys.

I'd rather go home than to heaven.

This, Louis told me tearfully one sodden night when the rains fell so steadily the cold and dampness nearly drove us mad.

So would I, dear friend, so would I.

Do you think it's wrong, Tom?

What?

What we've been driven to do?

The war, the killing?

That, but the other, too?

I still feel sometimes his tender hands under my tunic.

Sure it is, but who is to say if we'll even live beyond tomorrow's morning coffee? And if'n we don't, then who is to say for certain there is a heaven or a hell, or if God is in charge of it all, or if nobody is?

And as his hands explored the tender places as he spoke of his lovely Minnie and how she'd do such sweet and tender things for him and how he would for her.

O, how I miss her, Tom. When a man cleaves to his wife, no man can put that asunder.

Yes, yes, I know. And she must miss you just as terribly, Louis.

His sobs were of tenderness lost.

But when life turns on us and tears us away from those we love dearest, tears us away from everything good and decent and makes the world around us so terrible . . .

In the night we could hear the thunder, like cannon, rolling o'er us, or was it the other way around?

Sometimes he called out her name—*Minnie . . .*

I'm ashamed now to admit it, but Louis and I shared what human things the war allowed us in those cold dark times under blankets soaked in rain and snow, and we shared what we could on warm summer evenings when we'd sneak away from the encampment to be alone and hear unnamed rivers slip their banks.

The sudden cessation of the children's voices causes me to look down at my worn boots. What terrible shape they're in.

Melton is a cobbler and I will need new ones soon. Would it be too much to have Melton make me a pair—would it only add insult to injury? There is no other cobbler throughout the entire valley.

The hoarfrost has burned out of the mountains, and now they stand darkly blue and brooding down upon the valley and me and Billy, Ann and Melton, and all the rest.

Ann was there at the station when I left, sturdy-limbed and hopeful. And she was there again when I marched home, this gaunt thing with all hope snuffed out. She said she hardly recognized me.

I can never forgive you, Tom, for letting Melton have me.

Had I know the terrible price I paid for the adventure, I would have not gone.

O, Tom, these years have been terrible for us both.

Then you married him?

I had no choice.

You could have waited, run away and hid yourself?

If not Melton, surely then another like him, dear sweet Tom. All that stayed behind were the lame and the old and the niggers.

But you had to know I'd return.

We read the death lists, but some told that not all the dead got listed. And after two years of not hearing from you . . .

Well, I forgave her for her impatience. For that is what lovers do, forgive each other even in the face of lies and deceptions. I was too weary to care much and even a lie told well seemed to me equally as suitable as the truth told badly. As I stood there by the vine-snaked fence, Raymond, the daft colored man, came up the road and paused, staring toward the schoolhouse. He used to be the Irishman's man, but quit along with the other few slaves in Happy Valley when the *Proclamation* came down. I don't know that he wanted to quit, but when the Irishman died, he dint have a choice. Daft and childish he stood there, his lips blubbering in effort to speak.

I likes to hear the childun sing.

They weren't singing, Raymond. They were reciting their numbers.

I knows it, Mr. Tom. But sometimes they sing and I like to hear 'em.

I could see the welts along his arms and across his bared calves exposed below his too-short trousers. I could see the welt around his neck. Welts like black snakes. Put there no doubt by a black snake whip.

You better keep moving, Raymond. Someone might get the wrong idea you standing outside the schoolhouse.

He grinned broadly in his innocence, not knowing that I understood about how some men in the valley would equate Raymond's presence in the vicinity of little white children, little white girls most especially. But when I said again how he should move along, he nodded and went on down the road. I think he worked some for Grayson now.

The schoolchildren's voices were raised again and I went on down the road. Pauline was sitting on my front step when I arrived home again. She looked up with those brooding eyes so unlike those of her cousin Ann's.

Where you been, Tom. I've been a-waiting.

Stayed at Cecil's the night. Helped him build a hog shed and we drank after and I fell out there on a pallet.

It was a lie. But I didn't figure I owed any truth to Pauline.

I've been a-waiting for you, Tom. Came early this morning, soon's I could get away from the tavern. Mr. Swain doesn't like me to be gone from him. I told him I was sick with female troubles. He said, go on then, come back 'round soon as you're feeling better.

I took her face in my hands in spite of my indifference.

You look half starved. Don't Swain feed you?

He takes advantage of me, Tom.

But don't he feed you?

I won't eat his food.

I led her into the cabin and closed the door behind us shutting out the bright morning, Ann's passion still running like a fever in my blood. I placed Pauline before me and began deliberately to undress her. I had no heart to take her, but she was there and we both knew why she'd come to see me. So I took her like she wanted me to.

O, Tom. O, Tom.

Tears of joy or tears of sorrow, I cannot say, spilled from her eyes.

I shouldn't take advantage of you like Swain does.

Love me, Tom. Love me hard as I love you.

You're just a little sad thing, ain't you? Like a little sad flower growed all alone.

Yes, call me that, Tom. Call me your little flower.

With great exhaustion I took her and she did her best to satisfy me. And later we lay still with the day waning toward the

48

noon hour ushered in by the harsh caw of ravens somewhere.

You ought not to have come here today, Pearl.

Pearl was the pet name I'd decided to give her. Pauline sounded like too old a name for her.

I wanted to be with you, Tom. I wanted to be with you like this. And I'm glad I come, ain't you?

You know I can't see you regular. You know about Ann and me.

I know. I know all about you. I don't care, though. I just want you to love me, Tom.

It can't be nothing regular. Just so you understand that.

I don't care. I don't care if it ain't regular. Just once in a while, Tom. Just once in every little while.

We slept and woke again and she lay herself atop me and kissed my mouth in an unschooled way until she roused my cob again and we fornicated, but this time there wasn't anything new in it for me and I finished quick and told her she had to go.

I stood in the doorway and watched her go up the path back toward Swain's. She turned and waved as she neared the road and I waved back knowing she had taken some of my pride with her, had carried it off and would never give it back.

Beat the drum, Tom.

Pauline Foster

O, how I loved Tom. But he never loved me. A girl can tell if a boy loves her or he don't. But I pretended he did, and I thought if I were to go to him often enough and give myself to him freely, he might come around to loving me. He might.

And so I went that frosty morning to see him acting all pitiful and telling him things about Swain, how he treated me. And that was the first time we did it—Tom's pity turned to passion and mine did too and we did it there on his pallet. But I didn't care. He could have done it to me a hundred times and I wouldn't have cared. I know he loved Ann and she loved him. And I knew she was jealous and would come after me if she found out. But knowing how jealous she was just made it that much more pleasurable to me—to take Tom from her, even if just for a little while and make him mine. I wasn't the pretty one of us cousins. Ann was the prettiest. Ann got ever thing she ever wanted. And I know things about her Tom don't know. I know she did it with Billy Dixon for money and I know she did it with my own brother one time when she'd come for a visit. Did it in my daddy's barn. Said she'd seen my daddy doing it with my mama and it give her the itch to do it too.

Ann can be awful cruel and incautious.

And maybe what I did in giving myself so freely to Tom was to get back at her a little. I wanted to steal the thing she loved. And maybe in the stealing, something got stole from me, too.

Elizabeth Brouchard

O, I read these things and they cause my heart to flood with ache. And I ask myself why I read them at all . . . For haven't I had life's fair share—my life with Billy, a long and uneventful marriage that was in its own right kind enough, gentle enough, did not demand too much of me or feast on my heart in the journey?

So why agonize at the doings of the now dead as I read their tales?

Billy I can understand—his undoing was his homeliness. Ann's and Pauline's and Laura's were just the opposite. And Tom's, well, Tom's was his easy enough charm and natural inclination toward the gift of self.

Love's hunger I understand—but not all spoken in the name of love is love.

But desire instead. A hungering desire that feasts upon the tender hearts unsuspecting.

O, were it to have feasted on mine as well, be it love or desire.
This I declare—*Elizabeth Brouchard.*

Chapter 5

Tom Dooley

There, on the river rock, flat and white as a biscuit. There where
the jewel green water washes along the muddy, root-exposed
banks—where leathery turtles sun themselves, their ancient eyes
closed to the warmth—is where I first met you, you who would
escape me, love, ill-fated ends.

O, how I hated Swain, for he was a detestable man in every
respect a man could be detestable, and I thought anything is-
sued from him was detestable as well. But having caught a
glimpse of you that day—there on the rock, stretched out as you
were in such an innocent way, I could not find anything detestable about you.

I had cut through the woods to reach the river, it being such
a hot day I thought I would go for a swim. This was before Raymond was found drowned and attached the name *Death* to the
river. Billy Dixon talked often about the river being the mother
to our valley.

*For, she is life itself to this whole valley and all of those of us who
live in it. Look how she gives herself to the crops and the dry haunted
mouths of the thirsty. Look how she flows, has always flowed long
before any of us arrived here—and will keep right on flowing long
after all of us are gone.*

Billy could grow maudlin and spew words freely, most
especially when he was drunk. But I liked to hear him talk of

such things, talk of this valley and the things in it like they were alive.

But beware, Tom, she will take life too if you don't respect her. In the rainy season she floods and will snatch little children and the foolhardy who'd try and cross her. Never cross a raging woman.

You mean river?

River, woman, they are all the same. She just does what her nature is. She is woman and as faithless as any.

I admit I didn't always understand Billy's meaning. But I understood how he could think of the river as a female. I liked to think of the river as a female too. And maybe Raymond did too, and maybe that's why he gave his life to it when he couldn't have the woman he was promised. I don't know. It's only a guess and a wild one at that.

The sun burned terrible hot that day, left the body feverish so that only the woman river could cool it. I heard her whispering voice as I came to the edge of the wood and started across the little fallow field that lay between wood and river. The field had once been beautiful and full of sunflowers with yellow faces and brown eyes that watched over everything. The sunflowers had been planted by O'Leary, who owned the bicycle shop. His only boy, Samuel, had gone off to the same war I had. And in the absence of a son, the Irishman had planted the sunflowers and nurtured them and talked to them like they were his sons. You could see him some days standing out among them under his straw hat, his water can in hand, his lips moving. But when I returned from the war, the sunflowers had disappeared and the field lay fallow, as it now stood.

Billy Dixon told me this story: When O'Leary's son was killed—shot through the throat in the war—and he read the boy's name on the death list down at Swain's, he went the next day and scythed down the sunflowers, then poured coal oil over the ground and set it afire and spent the rest of his days drinking hard and cursing his field. This, until some men found him one day sitting dead in a rocker on his porch, a pocket pistol clinging to one dead finger. The porch faced off toward the field. He is buried here under a large ancient rock with his name and that of Samuel's, chiseled into it by an unknown hand.

The once alive and lovely things of this place have all grown fallow, Billy Dixon said when he told me the story.

Elizabeth Brouchard

I often went to the river on warm days and contemplated what my life had to do with this place where few read or wrote or dreamed of faraway places, as I did. I liked the river because it was always moving on to someplace new and I wanted to move on to someplace new as well.

So when the weather was especially warm, as it was on that day you and I first met, I had stripped off my clothes and found a nice rock and lay watching the river. O, it was my way of being free and natural as God intended all creatures to be.

How long you had watched me before I noticed you I can't say, and I don't care. If it had been any other but you, I would have been frightened, horrified, ashamed. But there was something between you and me from the very first that gave me no shame where you were concerned, no guilt, no second thoughts.

You seemed as gentle as the river, as restless—and I knew your spirit and mine were kindred. I know it still.

Tom Dooley

And there before me was this field that made me think of how unhappiness had seeded itself in a place where a man had once stood with his water can talking happily to his sunflowers. It made me even more want to wash the grit from my skin and feel the cool water wash over me, and feel new again—reborn.

It was when I started across this field that I saw you lying on the rock, your back to me, the long length of it tapering down to the swell of your hips. Your legs were long as a colt's and your feet dainty. I knew who you were by the color of your hair. Thick and reddish as a burning bush, no other girl in the valley had such hair.

I thought about turning around, going a different way and not disturbing you. It seemed mean spirited to intrude. It seemed little enough to leave you alone considering how hard it must be for you to live in this place, hearing what folks said about you—how mean and cruel such talk could be; some of them so stupid as to believe that because you couldn't talk, you couldn't hear. And much of the talk was cruel and pitiless, especially at the tavern (but never in earshot of your pap, Swain), and I didn't like hearing it.

Imagine a gal like that, not being able to say whether she liked the cob or not.

Har, har.

Better for you she wouldn't say and tell everyone about that little cob of yours and how it wasn't doing her no good.

Har, har.

Might be a real bonus to have a woman around who'd not be yapping all the time, do this, do that.

Har, har.

Silence is golden, don't you know.

Har, har.

I bet I could make her say something I was to get aholt of her.

Har, har—

You turned slightly as I stood there debating what to do and lifted your face toward the sun. I could see that your eyes were closed and I could see the roundness of one small breast, its nipple pink as the tip of a tongue, and I felt ashamed watching you thus. I ordered myself to leave. I didn't want your sweet peace troubled by looking into my greedy eyes, and yet, I could not make myself go.

I stepped back into the woods a little ways and found a good-sized limb and broke it so that it cracked loudly enough to alert you someone was coming. I could see you start, reach for the dress lying nearby, and slip it on as quick and clean as new skin. I coughed and came loudly out of the trees and stopped long enough for you to see me, then waved slightly and walked across O'Leary's field to the river.

I feigned surprise to see you.

Hidey.

You nodded and seemed about ready to run.

O, don't worry none about me, I just come to have a swim. Powerful hot day, ain't it?

You nodded again.

I didn't mean to disturb you. You want, I could go on down aways. You wouldn't have to be bothered any by the likes of me.

You had eyes that were green as the river, and though you weren't beautiful in the way Ann was, you were pretty enough to make me want to stay there talking to you even though you didn't say a lick.

Listen, I know you can't talk, and I surely didn't come down here to be yapping and carrying on. So just never mind me, okay.

I saw a book with worn red covers lying at your feet.

You were reading.

You nodded you was.

I enjoy reading some myself. Pleasant day like this is, seems a good place to read as any.

There sure wasn't nothing of Swain in you I could see. Your pap was big and gruff with hair like a horse brush and gray piti- less eyes like I seen once on a Confederate officer who ordered some of his own boys shot for running from a fight. Surely you'd gotten those green eyes from your mother who everyone knew did not exist—for Swain was a rowdy bachelor and I never heard any rumor about your ma or where she was—dead or run off. I tried best I could to make small talk with you.

Your name's Liza, ain't it?

Nod.

Mine's Tom Dooley, pleased to meet you. I stuck out my hand and waited for you to take it. And when you did, your hand was as thin-boned and warm as a sparrow's body.

Then you withdrew your hand from mine and reached inside the pocket of your dress and took out a pencil and with it, leaned and picked up the book and began to write in it. Then you showed me what you'd written and I saw that the book wasn't a book so much as a diary you'd written in. There on the opposing page was what looked like a poem, but I didn't read it out of respect. Instead I read what you wrote.

I know who you are. And I'm glad to meet you too, Tom.

I told you how glad I was glad to make your acquaintance.

Then we just stood there for a time.

Elizabeth Brouchard

When I touched your hand, so rough and strong a hand it was, my breath caught in my chest and I couldn't breathe at all for a full moment.

You seemed as shy as a schoolboy in one respect, as bold and curious as a puppy in another. I liked you immediately, and the thought raced through me that you had seen me naked and that I liked the fact you had. We sat there by the river awhile and you told me about yourself, about how you liked the river and hated the war and that someday you wanted to go all the way to the ocean and become a sailor and maybe a fisherman and I asked you why.

You looked at my written question.

O, I don't know rightly. I guess to cross that big water and see what's on the other side. I guess too, a feller could earn himself a nice living being a fisherman if he had a boat and knew where all the fish were. Sounds silly, I know, me never even having been that far or seen anything but rivers.

I wrote that it wasn't silly at all and that I someday wanted to go to Paris.

My turn to ask you why?

I wrote that I couldn't explain it fully, it was just a feeling I had in me, that I wanted to just go somewhere with lots of people and wide boulevards and visit museums and write poetry.

That sounds like a fine dream to have.

I wrote:

Without dreams, who are we, truly?

You laughed, said you thought it was a fine way to think. I wanted you to kiss me. I wanted to kiss you.

Yes, I was aware of your involvement with Ann Melton, and I'd heard rumors about other girls as well. I allowed that it was because you were still young and restless and probably starved in some ways from having been away to war for three years. It didn't matter who you loved or did not. Not in that moment it didn't.

For in that moment, we were just two dreamers with dreams unmet and with all our lives yet to be lived. I thought anything possible for us—even love.

Tom Dooley

I told you I'd like to be your friend. You wrote you'd like to be mine.

Let's shake on it.

You smiled and shook my hand again and I liked the way you did it so boldly.

Had I realized then how you felt toward me, everything might have turned out differently. But I didn't know and I couldn't begin to know what you truly thought, for I saw you as something fragile, like a beautiful glass bird in some rich man's house that fellows like me aren't allowed to touch. I was afraid that if I did touch you, I would break you and you would be forever ruined.

And even if you had written: *Kiss me, Tom*—I like to think I wouldn't have. I'd like to believe that there was one pure thing in me that would not have violated such innocence.

It felt good to sit and talk with you of dreams and not feel I'd somehow ruined you like I had Ann and Pauline, or that I had ruined myself. And it was equally good to simply sit with you and watch the river and wonder where it was going and which other rivers would join it along its journey, and which ones *it* would join.

It was as much fate for you to come into my life that day as was everything else that happened during that season of sorrow when the beauty and the tragedy of my days unfolded in ways I could not foretell, but are perfectly clear to me now.

Let's shake on it.

We already did, Tom.

Let's shake on it again.

Elizabeth Brouchard

And the time seemed swift and uncertain—like the current farther downstream where the river widened and grew deeper before it plunged over boulders and swept into the great unknown.

What did we known then, Tom Dooley, that might have saved us each our uncertain fates and keep the hangman sleeping in his warm bed undisturbed by assassinations?

O, we knew nothing, nothing at all.

For if we had, I would not have let you go so easily that day.

I would have leapt with you into the river and let it carry us to the deep uncertain places. And if we were to die, then we would have died together, clinging to each other. But if we were to live, then no river or uncertainty could have had us.

CHAPTER 6

Tom Dooley

Grayson trots his Walker up and down the road like a rich man, like a man who has nothing better to occupy his time. Pauline was there waiting for me when I returned from the river. I always had a hard time refusing a woman her needs.

She hums an old song born in these mountains long before any of us as she buttons her dress. The sun shines down on the valley so it looks like a picture of what heaven is like. I feel marked by a hand greater than my own. Pauline slinks like a cat from the side of the bed and comes to stand behind me there at the window.

That's Mr. Grayson, ain't it, Tom?

That horse probably cost more than I'd make in two years.

I'd steal it for you, Tom. I'd steal it and ride it to Wilkesboro and sell it for a hundred dollars and give you every red cent.

You best not be stealing any fancy horses, Pearl.

Why I'd steal ever horse in the valley for you, Tom.

She had the heart of a child, the head of one, too.

I reckon I can make do without any stole horse money.

She nibbled my ear hungry like and ran her hands down along the front of me until she found my tired cob.

You won't do it with anyone else but me will you, Tom?

I watched until Grayson passed out of sight, heading down toward Melton's. I wondered at the devilment he might stir up and try and stain my name with. Grayson wasn't truly one of us, wasn't born here in this valley and lived his whole life here like the rest of us. To me he was just a damn outsider with a fancy walking horse.

You best be getting back, Pearl.

I want to stay here with you forever. I want to hear you call me your little flower.

Someday maybe, but not today. I got me a passel of work to do.

I kissed her childish twisted mouth and watched her walk off toward Swain's tavern with her head hung down. I knew Swain would lay into her soon as he got the chance. Her fate was cast and so was mine. All our fates were cast from the very first day, writ across heaven's slate by gods and angels with nothing better to do.

What little comfort she found in this sorry life, she seemed to find in me. And even though she knew about Ann and me, she pretended not to and talked her childish talk of being forever and faithful lovers. I played her game because it was easier than not playing it.

Pauline Foster

I'd go to Tom's every chance I got. Swain would worry me and worry me and every chance I got I'd run off to Tom's and away from Swain's pestering hands. I know Tom didn't love me truly. But I pretended he did and for a little while I didn't have to think about my life—being Swain's pleasure, the fact Tom loved Cousin Ann, the fact I wasn't ever going to find a love of my own and that she could have any love she wanted.

I hated her for that. So I went to Tom's and I gave him what every man wants, what no man can resist. I made it easy for him and he took it and took it and I was glad he took it. I thought it would save me sooner or later, making it so easy for him, that Tom would come to love me more than Ann. But it didn't save me, and Tom never loved me like he did her and nothing was going to save any of us. And maybe that's how Laura felt when she fell in with Tom—that he'd save her, that love would save her. But whatever happened, love didn't save her. If anything, it killed her. And now she is naught but the thing sin and time has stripped of flesh and blood—a ruined thing, and he is ruined because of it and so is Cousin Ann.

But I didn't have a hand in it. And those who say I did are liars.

Tom Dooley

Soon as Pearl had gone out of sight, I set about splitting wood.

I worked hard all the morning splitting the wood I'd cut for weeks before. It felt good to bring the ax down hard and hear the crack of the wood being cleaved in two. It felt good in the way hard work will, made my muscles warm and tighten into hard knots and raised a sheen of sweat across my chest. There was still a deep anger in me I hadn't gotten rid of because of the war and the fact my friend Louis lay buried in a hasty grave so far from his dear Minnie and darling babe. I knew that his grave was by now grown over with wild onions and bull thistles—eternally lost, as though he never existed in the first place. And I wondered about all the other boys left in unmarked graves grown over by wild onions and bull thistles. I felt anger that we'd fit that war over what came down to nothing at all. It was a ruinous event, and ruined us all in one way or the other.

So I split the wood, brought the ax down hard, as though each chunk was a politician's head and I'd killed nearly the whole dang congress by the time I was finished.

I was sitting winded and tired when I saw what at first I thought was Grayson coming back up the road on his Walker. But then soon enough I could see it wasn't Grayson at all, but another man and the beast he was astride wasn't a Walker but a mule with a tail that swung round and round like a crank handle.

The stranger stopped and stared down at me. I stared back.

Black hat and coat. Black trousers and shoes not in any better condition than my own.

Friend.

He tipped his hat.

I nodded.

Can you tell me if God lives in this place?

I looked around.

If he does, I ain't seen him lately. This place here belongs to Tom Dooley.

Can you tell me if God lives anywhere in this whole valley?

I thought about Melton and Ann and Pearl and Billy Dixon and all the rest of the folks who I knew lived in this valley. A faithless lot at best, me included. I thought about the way we lived, me and Ann in Melton's bed, him in the corner; Pearl and me sneaking around under Ann's very nose. I thought about Billy Dixon with his head under a slattern's skirts for the price of a drink and to soothe a lonely heart if only for a little while. I thought about the blacksmith, Dillsworth, and what they say he did with his own daughters—Nirvana and Rose, with their broad flat faces and crossed eyes and how blood mixed with its own don't ever come to nothing right or righteous. I thought about the way we all seemed so cut off from the rest of the world, protected, or held enslaved, depending on which way you looked at it, by the brooding mountains. So I told the stranger how I didn't see God in none of it.

If'n he did live here once he hasn't been around lately.

The man shifted in his saddle, an old McClellan, and rubbed a hand between the mule's ears. I saw a US brand on the mule's haunch.

Then I come to the right place, brother.

For what?

Why to bring the Good News.

Meaning?

Lord, brother, haven't you ever heard of the Good News?

If you're talking about the Bible and what it has to say, about what's right and wrong and preaching and raising all sorts of holy hell, then I reckon I heard of it.

His skin was the color of the moon.

Name's Shinbone. Tyree Shinbone. I come to preach the Good News.

That Army mule sure don't look like it's got any Good News to it.

The gift of our Lord Jesus.

There's a lot of folks around these parts wouldn't mind a nice gift like that.

He scratched his neck, the collar around it dirty white, stained piss yellow from sweat. I could see by the busted veins in his sun-fried cheeks, he knew the bottom of the bottle.

God rains on the just and the unjust alike.

I took him to mean we were all in the same boat, God doing the paddling.

You been to the war, haven't you, Mr. Dooley? I can see it in your eyes. Such hard hurtful eyes for a man so young.

I figured he must have known a thing or two about war himself, for he sure didn't wake up one day and that mule was in his bed with him, a gift from God. That mule looked stole as anything, and he a deserter.

You want to set a spell, preacher?

Mighty grateful for the opportunity.

Tyree Shinbone

O, I told such pretty lies and I could see Tom believed them every one, for he was a gullible boy even though the war set hard in his eyes. He wasn't but twenty or twenty two years old judging by his apple cheeks. And I was a stranger who thought it best to tell pretty lies if I was to get on with the people of this valley. So I feigned a drawl and talked in the vernacular of these people in order not to set them on edge and set them against me. Call it a sin if you will to lay claim to things in your past you've never experienced. But in this case, I saw each pretty lie as merely a brick set down on God's road to salvation.

So I told Tom I'd fought in the Confederate Army under J. E. B. Stuart and we'd whipped Yanks from Virginia to Tennessee until we got whipped ourselves. And that I'd stole the mule off a general after I'd run him through with my bayonet. O, such pretty lies they were, and I told him others as well:

My pap killed himself. My ma died of heart troubles. My sis ran off to New Orleans where I eventually found her. She was there whoring herself to whatever Cajun would pay her. I got hard into the bottle and all the other sins a man can get hisself into.

That's a hard story.

You bet it is.

Where's God in all this?

That's a fine question.

And he looked at me with those hard eyes and swallowed down his compassion and I liked him right off and saw him as a potential recruit for God's army. O, that I could have saved him from such a hard fate as would come.

Such innocent beginnings assure us not of sorrowful endings.

Tom Dooley

The preacher pulled a bottle of mash from his saddlebag and offered me a pull and took a pull himself. We ended up pulling all the mash out of that bottle by the time the sun set low over the blue mountains.

I best get on.

Where you aiming for?

Why, right here in this valley.

They ain't no work.

I work for God.

Bringing the Good News?

Exactly.

I ain't heard none of it come out of your mouth so far and don't know a soul who'd pay a dime to hear it.

You come look for me on Sunday in some meadow or field and you will.

I watched him ride off. Seemed sober as a judge in spite of pulling all that liquor out of his bottle. He rode like a man with a lot of stories in him and I didn't believe much of what he'd said so far. The sky was by then the color of a rose, the mountains the color of crepe, and silence came skulking into the valley like an unwanted visitor.

The taste of that preacher's liquor got me primed on thinking how I might just find my way down to the tavern that evening, then take a walk up to Melton's. Ann seemed dear to me just then, dear and fragile and easily broken between the desires of Melton and me. But Ann was strong, stronger than any of us and I knew she wouldn't break, and if she did, it wouldn't be easily. So I made up my mind I'd take a walk up to Melton's one more time, and maybe when I was finished, I'd tell Ann I wasn't coming no more and she might just as well settle up with Melton and see her way clear to a predictable future. In one ear I heard Ann calling, in the other, the land beyond the mountains that runs clear to the sea. I was being pulled in two directions.

And lest I forget you, Liza. You whom I barely knew but who haunted my spirit anyhow. You, a fragment thus far in my life, the scent of sweet flowers blowing on the breeze.

But before I could get cleaned up to go I had another visitor: Old Melton himself, as though he knew I'd be making a trip up to his place that evening.

James Melton

I don't know what got into me that particular evening to make me harness up the horse and wagon and take a trip up to Dooley's. Maybe it was the way Ann had been acting all that day: agitated with me and pacing the floor and saying bitter spiteful things to me. Or maybe it was I was just getting tired of being talked about behind my back by the other men whenever I'd go down to Swain's or the mercantile. Or maybe it was I just needed to touch my wife again like a husband is supposed to. But whatever it was, something sure got into me, and next thing I knew I was at Dooley's.

Tom Dooley

Tom Dooley!

Melton didn't bother to climb down off his spring wagon. Just sat there for a long time and glared at me in the gloaming. He didn't act like he was going to say anything, just sit there and stare at me. So finally I said something first.

It ain't exactly the way I'd have it, Melton, for it to be the way it is.

I wished you wouldn't come around no more.

I reckon Ann has a say in it as much as you or me.

She's my wife, Dooley.

I know it.

That ought to stand for something, even in this depraved valley.

I don't see how it can change, unless she wants it to. If I don't go there, she'll just come here.

Oh, goddamn, Dooley, don't you see how things are? Don't you hear what folks say about it all—about me, Ann, you?

I felt murder in my heart.

It's nothing against you, Melton.

Sure it is. It's ever thing against me. Ever time you lay with her it's against me.

I'm sorry, but that ain't the way I see it. You knew I was seeing her before I went off to war. You knew she loved me, or had to think she did. You knowing it should have been a warning it might start up again once I came home. I never planned on any of this.

Neither did I. Neither did I . . .

Melton hung down his head as though suddenly fallen asleep. All the color had bled out of the sky. A whip-poor-will trilled in the darkness.

Go on Melton. Git home. Git home. Ann's waiting. Ann's waiting.

I heard the clatter of his iron-rimmed wheels in the far darkness, the slow steady pattern that sounded like a sad heart trying to sustain itself.

Last thing he said before he shook the reins over the horse's back:

It'll come around to you someday, Dooley, this sin you started. It'll come around, and when it does, I'll be there to see it. There ain't no God if'n this sin of your'n don't come around to you, Tom Dooley.

I told myself I'd not go to Melton's that night no matter what. But I did go. And I kept going back again and again clear up until Laura's murder.

Elizabeth Brouchard

Even these intimacies Tom told me.

Keep the words true, Liza. Don't let others tell lies on me.

I made him a promise.

I'll keep the words true, Tom.

&

I've kept the words true and nothing hid, unless from me it was hid, for where is the real truth in anything?

CHAPTER 7

Tom Dooley

Grayson had been right about one thing: winter in the air. Snow came without warning during the night, soft and silent as death. It came over the ridges, snagged in the trees, clouds and clouds of it like a white army marched quietly down the slopes and into the valley until it lay over every rock and branch and living creature. Creeks ran like black veins in the snow. The mountains disappeared. In a single night, the world had changed.

I felt Ann shivering and arose, slipped from the bed, and went to the window, and the little piece of sky I could see was red—a smoky red, not bright like blood. I slipped back into bed with her.

It's snowing.

What?

It's snowing.

She lay there shivering against me; two blankets weren't enough, my body wasn't enough. Melton snored softly.

It's early to snow.

I know it. Could be a sign of a bad winter.

Oh, Tom, don't say things like that. I'm freezing.

She pressed her back against me and I could feel the blood in me stir. I pressed against her so she could feel my stirring. She lifted her nightdress and brought one leg up and I moved between her legs and felt bad doing it, but couldn't help myself. Seemed like I was completely powerless to resist her, and

70

completely powerful when I was taking her.

I put my hand over her mouth so her little mewing sounds wouldn't wake Melton. He knew everything of course, but sleep was a refuge for him and I didn't want to torture him any more than he was already by being bodacious with Ann—especially after his visit up to my place. I wasn't afraid of him; I just didn't want to make little of him in the doing of what I was with Ann.

She thrust back against me, took me into her body, and held me there with her legs clamped now. She had powerful strong legs, not like Pearl's that were thin and without strength like branches of a willow. It wasn't the only difference between them.

Melton snorted and turned over in his bed; I could hear the leather laces of his bed creak and thought sure he'd come awake.

Don't be careless now.

I won't, Tom.

Go gentle with it.

Yes, yes.

We whispered while we fornicated as though it were a great secret we couldn't let Melton in on. But of course he already knew everything and it was such a foolish game we all played with one another. It didn't take long to quench our desire and we lay still as the dead after. Soon I could hear Ann's little sleep breathing, her body limp next to mine.

I left early that morning before anyone awakened and trudged through the snow hoping the wind would blow and cover my tracks so it wouldn't remind Melton that I was there. Perhaps he could convince himself that I hadn't come the night before. It had been late and he was already half into the bottle. So maybe with a little trying he couldn't be sure whether I'd arrived or had just dreamed drunkenly of the possibility. I told myself again that I wouldn't return, that if Ann wanted to see me, she would have to come to my place. But Ann was a strange stubborn girl set in her ways about certain things.

My love is sharp as a knife for you, Tom. But I won't act like a slattern and trudge up to your place just 'cause you think it might look better to folks. It's my house too—not just Melton's. I earned ever stick and rock in it.

Knives are dangerous things, Ann.

They cut and they cut. And I'd cut him if he was to try and stop me and I'd cut you if you proved unfaithful.

So you see, even if I had wanted to end it with her, I couldn't be sure she wouldn't have done something fatal.

Ann Foster Melton

O, those cold, cold mornings of wanting when Tom left my bed, left me there with James who would come round afterwards and paw at me and try and get me back into bed. I'd fight him, but sometimes there was no fighting him off and he'd take me, and it wasn't like we were fornicating at all, but more like he was wanting to destroy me with his hard rough body and I would hurt for several days after.

You give it to him, by God, you'll give it to me as well!

It wasn't always that way, for lots of times, he just left me alone, went and cobbled his shoes and tended to himself. I guess I should feel lucky it wasn't always that way, but those days it was hard on me and made me only want to be with Tom all the more.

Tom Dooley

I came to Shinbone's camp: a tent, a stump, a rusted bucket, the mule tethered to a stake. Shinbone stood in the glorious cold shaving his face in a mirror of water in the bucket. The mirror caught a piece of sun and part of his face and I tried to pass unnoticed but he stopped shaving and called me into his camp. It was O'Hearn's fallow field. I reckon Shinbone figured he could raise more than a little holy hell on that patch of ground.

Welcome to my church.

I looked around.

Most churches I been in have walls and a roof.

This is the church of the living waters. Don't need no walls or no roof either.

A body could freeze before they got through the singing parts.

He bared his teeth and laughed.

They'd not freeze for all the fire and brimstone I'd rain down upon them.

And what if they weren't sinners?

Then they'd know the loving warmth of the Savior.

I know something else could save a man on such a cold day as this one.

What might that be, Tom?

Some liquor to warm the bones.

His mule brayed and the sound carried out as far as the mountains in that clear crystal air. A patch of snow fell from the upper part of the balsam and landed softly. A jay cawed sharply and the mule flicked its ears.

Jays are quarrelsome creatures.

Yes, sir. About like some women I've known.

You're a ladies man, ain't you, Tom? I could tell the first time I laid eyes on you. But beware: there are Jezebels all around just waiting to snare us. The wanting of a woman will ruin a man quicker than anything.

You might be half right on that one, Parson.

He motioned I should hunker down awhile. I said I best be getting on.

Sit a spell. I could use the company. How'd it be was I to try my first sermon out on you?

About like taking a whipping, I reckon.

He laughed hard.

Could you stand it some better with some blackberry wine to warm you?

Break it on out if you got it, but I can't stand being too long in one place.

Tyree Shinbone

I figured it no accident that Tom came 'round to see me. He wouldn't let on he was looking for salvation—he wasn't the type; few men I ever met that had the Confederate blood in them were the type to admit very much of the heart and what the heart needs.

I pitched into my best sermon, let him have it with both barrels—figured long as he was drinking my wine, he had an obligation to hear me out.

Tom Dooley

Shinbone produced a bottle, took a pull, then handed it to me and commenced preaching all about how Eve tempted Adam to sin, then took on the concubines of King David and so forth. Ranted about how an excellent wife was the crowning glory of her husband, but one who brung him shame was like a rotting in his bones.

It was as though he knew about the triangle of Ann and me and Melton and was trying to burn my soul up with shame over it, trying to warn me about the price I'd pay. He ranted until he was near out of breath, then pulled some more on the blackberry wine, his nostrils snorting steam in that aching cold air.

He smote open his Bible and began to read in a loud voice:

Those whose hearts are perverse are an abomination to the Lord.

Pull of wine.

Keep away from the flattering tongue of a seductress.

Pull some more wine.

A harlot reduces a man to a crust of bread.

Pull.

He who goes to his neighbor's wife shall be burned!

I could see that blackberry wine wasn't doing either of us any good and was about gone altogether by the time he let up some. I stood and said I had to go. His glare burst forth from under the brim of his black hat; a droplet of blood stood frozen on his cheek where the razor had been too keen.

It's the worst kind of sin there is, Tom—to covet thy neighbor's wife.

I balled my fists in anger. Who was this stranger to tell me anything! Outsiders!

Come here to pass judgment on us when they didn't know a thing about us—Shinbone and Grayson.

Talk like yours can get a man a bloody nose, Preacher.

Not my words, but His!

He pointed a bony finger skyward.

Hell, you'll be a long time awaiting God in this place. More likely you'll freeze to death in the waiting.

I was over the next ridge quick enough but could still hear him shouting down the devil with his high and mighty preaching. Calling my name, God's, Satan's.

I made steady journey back and forth all that winter to Melton's, but avoided Shinbone's encampment. Once or twice when the weather let up, Ann came to visit me in spite of her oath that she never would. I was always a little concerned she'd come unexpected trying to catch me with another woman. I worried about her finding out about Pearl and me. Not so much for my sake as Pearl's.

Why you so jumpy, Tom?

Nothing, Pearl, thought I heard something.

Listen.

I don't hear nothing.

Neither do I.

Go on back to sleep.

Kiss my eyes closed, Tom.

One day I found a circle of small footprints outside my window, and the next trip I made to Melton's, Ann was there alone, sulking.

I seen you was over to my place.

Wasn't, neither.

Saw footsteps about the size of yours.

Why'd I be over to your place?

Come to see me, maybe. Come for some loving maybe.

I don't reckon I have to walk near three miles to get some loving. All I'd have to do is let the word out and I'd have men lined up outside my door.

Yes, but you wouldn't let the word out. I know you better than that.

You think you know ever thing there is to know about me, don't you, Tom Dooley?

We quarreled like that until she come out with it, said she heard a woman's voice inside my cabin. I said it was Pearl's, that she'd brought me over a jug of mash to feed the cold I was battling.

Her jealous eyes clouded.

Cousin Pauline?

One in the same.

I'd kill her if I thought you and her were . . . I'd kill you too.

For the first time I realized Ann was right, I didn't know everything about her. Fact is, looking into those angry temptress eyes, I suspected there was a whole lot about her I didn't know and might never know.

Kill me, huh? I don't care for that kind of talk, no sir. Best I get on back to where I can close my eyes and not have to worry about somebody sticking a knife in my ribs.

Just maybe you should.

I slapped my hat back on my head and turned to leave but Ann grabbed me and turned me round and mashed her mouth on mine, and the next thing you know we were giving in to our mad passions. For it was like that with Ann and me; one minute we could be arguing over any little thing—her jealousy, or how I should steal her away from Melton—and the next she'd have me pulled on top of her and I'd be glad she had.

Ann Foster Melton

Tom did everything in his power to make me jealous. But what he didn't understand was the depth of a woman's jealousy, and how much it wounds and wounds. I suspected he was fornicating with Cousin Pauline. I was more mad at her than him—for men are weak and can't control themselves, but women are controlling and know how to turn a man's head and get a man to do their bidding. I wanted the truth, I wanted Tom to tell me with his own lips that he and Pauline were fornicating. I knew if he told me, I'd do whatever I had to to get her to quit going after him. Pauline was a slattern, everybody knew it. After they hanged Tom, she went off somewheres up in Tennessee and had a nigger baby. I wasn't surprised to hear of it. I wasn't surprised.

Tom Dooley

Melton didn't come home that afternoon, and I was just as relieved he didn't. I was glad not to have to have him in the room with us, nor worry what went through his head and feel my own sin try and swallow me alive soon as the passion burned out. That's when the sin hit me hardest, soon as the passion burned itself out. That's when I'd promise myself I wouldn't go back. All the long walk home I would set my mind to stay clear of Melton's. I told myself I had Pearl, even if she wasn't as pretty as Ann, at least she wasn't a married woman. And there were other unmarried girls I could have had if I wanted. Plenty of them. The war had left the whole valley thin on eligible young men. I'd ask myself what did I need another man's wife for? I'd curse myself for shaming myself, and shaming old Melton. I'd promise myself after every visit that it was the last time I'd see her. But then the hours would pass into days and sometimes a whole week, and I'd feel the hunger for her come gnawing at me again. I'd hear her seductress voice whispering in my ear, whispering things that would make any man weak to her, and I'd get myself on back there, Melton or no.

If only I had ever thought there'd have been any chance for you and me, Liza, I could have washed all this sin away and made myself something proud for you. I just never gave it a real consideration—that you'd see anything in ol' Tom Dooley. Never did.

Ann lay naked next to me, unashamed of her nakedness, me unashamed of mine.

We're like Adam and Eve. There's nobody exists except us in times like this, Tom.

I reckon.

I'm the one who loves you truer than anyone.

You're pure temptation.

Not me, this.

She took my hand and placed it on the damp nest of her sex, her womanly scent strong in my nostrils. I was weaker to her than to anything or anyone and she knew it. She was pure temptation. I told her about Shinbone.

There's a preacher come to the valley.

I'd say he's come too late to save the likes of us, Tom. We're our own salvation if anybody is.

He preached to me the other day, when it snowed, after I'd left here that last time.

I never knowed you to be the kind that'd take to preaching.

It wasn't something I planned.

You feel the need for saving, Tom? You feel the need to have some preacher save you from me . . . from this?

She moved my hand, opened her legs wider.

I feel the need for something.

And I know just what that something is.

I stayed that afternoon with her, until the hour got to where we had to light candles and an oil lamp. She looked different in the shadows and the dancing light, looked like a spirit, wicked and destructive. Maybe I wasn't in my right mind, but I thought she spoke in words I couldn't understand as she made me take her again, all the time talking crazy words that made no sense.

Next time I came to Shinbone's camp, I stopped and said I wanted to ask him something. He was sitting on a blackened stump the fire had swept over when O'Hearn burnt down his field. He had a scarf wrapped round his neck and was smoking a pipe. A Bible lay open across his knees. He hardly looked up when I approached.

You've been walking the far way 'round, avoiding me ain't you, Tom?

I reckon so. You making out any good?

The sheep are all lost in the wilderness and have not yet found their way home.

In other words, nobody's come.

They will.

I couldn't see how a man could live as Shinbone did. How it was he hadn't starved to death or froze or had the bears set on him, him with nary a dog to warn him, was a wonder to me. Maybe his god was watching over him after all.

I told him what happened with Ann, only didn't mention her by name, just told him the gibberish that come out of her mouth.

Tongues, Tom. This person you're talking about was speaking in tongues.

Tell me what would make a body speak in tongues.

His eyes glittered and maybe it was the firelight caught up in them, or maybe it was something else made them glitter so.

She got the holy spirit come over her.

Could be the devil, couldn't it?

Could be, I'd sure like to meet her, Tom.

That's ain't possible, you meeting her.

He gave me a knowing smile.

With God, all things are possible. Don't you believe it so?

Hell, I don't know.

I thought of poor Louis whose embrace saved me from so much madness and wondered why it was God would let a Yankee shoot a sweet boy like him through the heart when he had a wife and child depending so heavily on him coming home again. That Yankee didn't just kill Louis that day, he killed Louis's wife and baby. And he killed a little of me too. That Yankee's ball should have found me if anyone; I never had nothing waiting on me like Louis did. Whatever thoughts I had of the possibility of God ceased that day Louis got shot. They ain't no God would let such a thing happen.

You got some thoughts on all this, Tom?

I think some folks just get crazy from trying so hard to believe in something outside themselves. Onliest thing a man truly has to cling to is himself.

Come closer to the fire, Tom. Come into the light so I can show you something.

And when I did, Shinbone showed me his hands. His palms were marked with wounds.

What you think of them there?

Looks like you got shot through and through, both hands.

No. I never got shot.

Then what happened?

Jesus is what happened.

I got to get on.

Wait and I'll tell you a story about these hands.

It ain't something I care to hear.

It might make all the difference to you, Tom.

Sorry, Preacher. I got me some place to go.

He stood there in the fire's light, his marked hands beginning to weep blood. It sent something dark through me and I left him standing thus and headed off into the gloaming.

Now I wished I'd stayed and heard his story about how he got them wounded hands.

Elizabeth Brouchard

Do you, Tom? Do you wish you had stayed and let Preacher Shinbone tell you the story of his hands? Or was it merely a dream you dreamt, a vision of things to come? Tell me true, Tom, and I'll write it well and tell it true and everyone will believe.

But the hour has long passed to answer such things. And in his place stands silence.

Outside the children play in the park, chasing after one another with gaily colored streamers of red and blue while their mothers sit on a bench and tell each other small secrets of what it is like to be a married woman, to have gay children, to live such a sweet and simple life.

And I, here at my window, with the summer evening's light falling across the page, watch the children in the park and wonder at their fate.

Thy hand writes the true words of lives lived and lost, of hearts shattered, of worlds now gone and yet to come.

I, Elizabeth Brouchard, daughter of Swain, mute, poet, sit and write the words and watch the children playing.

CHAPTER 8

Tom Dooley

Pearl ran away from Swain's, came to me for refuge.

You're all I got that's decent to me, Tom.

What he do this time he's not done before?

Oh, don't make me say, Tom. Don't make me tell of it.

Winter was hard on us by then. Worst anyone could recall. The oldest man in the valley, Mr. Racine, claimed he was a hundred and one years old, said he'd never seen a winter like it.

Worst I seen wasn't close to this.

Pearl shook with fear.

You can't make me go back, Tom.

Never said I would.

The problem was, I couldn't have her move in with me and I couldn't send her back to Swain, for I knew what such terrible fear was like, the kind that would cause you to shake like you had a fever and promise God anything if he'd save you. It's been my experience, he never would.

I held her all that day and into the night, the snow falling constantly until it felt like the weight of it might crush us all.

Finally I got her to speak about what it was that Swain had done to frighten her so.

He sold me off, Tom. Sold me off to that daft nigger, Raymond.

She took to sobbing as my arms held her.

He sold you off to Raymond for what purpose?

To be his woman, to go and live with him and cook and clean for him and lay with him.

Why would he do something like that?

Money, Tom. Swain would do anything if there was a dollar in it. He told Raymond he could buy me for forty dollars.

Where would somebody like Raymond get that kind of money?

She was like a beaten child, sobbing so hard she couldn't speak.

Did Raymond . . .

No, Tom, I wouldn't let him. God no! I'd end up with a daft colored baby and then what would I do?

I'll go have a little talk with Swain soon's the weather clears.

Don't tell him where I am. He'll sure come and get me and give me over to Raymond. He won't want to give him back his money.

She was cold with fear. The snow fell hard.

Pauline Foster

Maybe I lied some to save my skin, to save my sanity, to keep Swain from using me so hard day and night. I didn't want but one man and that was Tom. And if I had to lie some to get free of Swain and to get Tom to love me, then tell me what's wrong with that? What's wrong with a girl wanting love and doing what she has to do to get it?

Tom Dooley

The snow was the only thing that kept Swain from looking for Pearl. The snow kept everything bogged down. And all a body could do was what a body could do and Pearl and I were constantly intimate with each other while the weather stayed rough. I had no fear about Ann finding us because she couldn't travel, either. The wonderful thing was the great silence that befell the valley and lay along the ridges. There was unspoken beauty to it all and it was a wondrous thing to see the land rumpled in pure white and the sky as blue as glass, the snow sparkling like sugar. The trees stood black along the slopes, and the creeks ran wet black, and not a thing moved nor took flight. The world had become a dream.

As I stood staring out at it, I wondered if the winter had killed the crazy preacher, if come the thaw he'd be found froze to death, his ranting forever silenced. Crazy old bastard that he was, and yet, somehow I worried over the thought of him suffering too.

One especially brutal cold night I dreamed of Louis. It was an intimate dream. And sometimes it was Louis I was intimate with, and sometimes Louis turned into Pearl. Other times it became Ann. I remember we were in a dark place together, a stranger's house with no light except the light night gives and I was talking to Louis.

I thought you were dead, that that Yankee shot you and we buried you. I even took the letter Minnie sent you from your pocket—it was stained with blood—and I made a small boat and tied the letter to it and let it go drifting on the river current.

No, that must have been a dream you had, Tom. For you can clearly see I ain't dead.

Far off I heard the cannon thunder, then the crack of brutal cold working against the wood walls.

I've missed you, Louis.

He came to me and put his arms around me and laid his head on my shoulder. I kissed his forehead tenderly. But when I opened my eyes it was Pearl I was kissing and she became a flame of fire that set my clothes ablaze. I ran out into the snow and threw myself headlong into it, the cold and the flame both burning my skin. Then Louis was holding me, his tender hands cradling my head.

You killed me, Tom. Your love killed me. It was you and not Minnie I was thinking of when the Yankee ball struck me. It was you I was thinking of in those last moments as my life bled from me. Not Minnie, Tom. It was only you.

Louis, Louis.

And as he lowered his mouth to mine, he turned into Ann and I could see the knife blade flash in her hand just as she brought it down toward my heart. I started awake from the dream and found it was just me and Pearl there in the bed. She was fast asleep. And when the snow stopped falling, I walked to Swain's.

You can't sell something you don't own.

You don't know nothing about it, Dooley. You bring her back.

I have to, I'll call the High Sheriff on you.

You want her all to yourself. Her and all her kin too. You want ever damn girl in the valley because you think you can have them just because you feature yourself some sort of hero, some sort of jackleg lothario. But to me you ain't shit. You're just another briar-hopping ridge runner what will end up with a head full of bug juice and no account.

What's right is right, say what you will. War's done over now, Swain. Slavery's done over too.

I'm coming for her, Tom Dooley. I'm coming and when I do, better be nothing stands in my way.

Swain Brouchard

O, I've a true time of it, trying to make due with what I have. It ain't easy, this hand I been dealt. Ain't a bit easy. You, of all people know the story, so why ask it again? O, that thing about Pauline? Don't believe a damn bloody word. She's a liar and a slattern. And so was Tom Dooley. I gave her work when no one else would, when her mother lay sick and nearly dead and the only work that girl could expect was to take men out back for two bits a throw. And she sure did plenty of that, before I took her in and gave her honest labor. I gave her shelter and a square meal and paid her two dollars a week. But I guess she forgot to mention any of that.

Sure, sure, that nigger Raymond came around, but I wouldn't let him drink inside. He'd come in and buy his liquor and take it outside and drink it and I reckon that's how he struck up with Pauline, maybe seeing her take men out back. I can't say as a fact, but I heard tell she took him out back a time or two and charged him twice the going rate 'cause he was a coon. But it don't concern me, least it didn't till Tom Dooley showed up here one damn winter day—that winter before he murdered Laura—and started in on how I had no right to sell Pauline off to Raymond. I told him how it was.

Sell her off? Why I ain't sold nobody off to nobody, 'specially no goddamn nigger.

Well, you better not, either.

So I told him to get shed of my place, and if I, by God, wanted to sell that slattern off to Raymond or any damn body else, it wasn't none of his business and if he thought it was, we should go outside and take to fistfighting, because there ain't a feller in the whole of this valley going to tell me what I can or cannot do—especially no murdering son of a bitch like Tom Dooley.

Hell, he wouldn't fight me. If he had, I would have broken his damn head in. That's all I got to say about it.

Tom Dooley

I then went on to Grayson's and spoke to him, said I wanted to talk to Raymond.

You leave off on him, Tom. He's not full right in the head.

It's just something I need to say to him, something I need to clear the air about.

You cause him to quit me, you'll have to take over his work until I can find a new man.

I won't have nothing to do with his quitting you, Mr. Grayson. He quits, it won't be because of anything I have to say to him.

*Go on, then. Be quick about it, Raymond's got plenty of work
ahead of him.*

I found Raymond down at the river cutting blocks of ice.
Steam rose off his head. He had maybe thirty blocks of ice
stacked on a sled. He stopped cutting when he saw me, smiled
that daft smile of his.

Hidey, Mr. Tom.

Raymond.

He rubbed a spot behind his ear.

*Want you to know that the contract you made with Swain to buy
Pearl . . . Pauline, well, that's no good. You best go and see if you can
get your money back.*

He didn't stop grinning, but you could see the change in his
eyes.

*I don't understand, Mr. Tom . . . I paid Mr. Swain forty dollars
. . .*

*Plain and simple, Raymond. You can't just go around buying and
selling folks. 'Specially white folks. It's illegal, and what Swain did
was illegal and he knew it was. So nobody's blaming you for this.
But was you to take up with a white woman, even one Swain'd sold
you . . . well, they's folks around here would hang you for it, or
worse.*

He didn't say anything, but the grin melted like some of his
ice was melting on the sled from the sun glancing off the world.

*Mr. Swain say I give him forty dollars, I could have her. I gave
him forty dollars.*

Where'd you get forty dollars from, Raymond?

Saved it. Been saving it for a long time, Mr. Tom.

You didn't steal any of it?

No, sir.

*Best you go see Swain and ask him for your money back. That's
all I have to say. I'm sorry it turned out this way. I know what it is
to get your hopes set high on something, then have them fall through.*

I walked back to my cabin, pausing now and then to catch my breath, for the snow tugged at my legs like a desperate thing trying to pull me down. It seemed like the snow was so deep and beautiful and pure it didn't want anyone trampling on it and ruining its beauty.

The only time I looked back as I climbed the slope away from the river, I saw Raymond setting on the ice sled, his head in his hands. I could almost feel his grief rising like the steam of his labor from him. I told Pearl what I'd done and she wept and kissed my hands and said she'd make me an uncommon wife, that she'd cook and clean and give me children, all that I wanted.

No, that's not why I done it and it ain't what I want, Pearl.

What then?

You can't stay with me.

But surely you love me, Tom, or you wouldn't have gone to Swain and Raymond and told them it was all wrong what they done to me.

I went because it was the right thing to do, because nobody has a right to buy and sell a body.

You didn't go out of love for me?

Not that kind of love.

She looked as forlorn as Raymond had. The world was at once a beautiful and sad place to be.

Her female troubles came and we had no relations for several days and I was just as relieved we didn't because it gave me time to think on a solution and what I came up with surprised even me a little, but it seemed the right thing to do and so I went to Melton's and spoke to Ann.

I told Ann the story of what Swain had done and how Pearl had come to me, but I didn't tell her of our intimacy. At first she seemed suspicious, then disinterested.

What you reckon I should do about it?

She's your kin, Ann.

I know you and her been carrying on . . . you come thinking you'd trick me.

If nothing else, hire her to work for you and Melton. Wouldn't it be pleasant to have someone cook and clean for you? You probably wouldn't have to pay her much over room and board.

I won't have her in my house, especially since I know what you and her did.

It's a lie. We never did a thing, except I gave her what anybody would: shelter and consideration, the milk of human kindness.

Damn liar, Tom Dooley, that's what you are.

Look at it this way: with her here you won't have to worry about her and me being together. You'll always be able to keep an eye on her, make sure she ain't up to nothing.

That seemed to do the trick. Ann moved close to me.

James has gone to the tavern.

I can see he has.

It's been almost two weeks since I seen you.

I've counted the days too, Ann.

You still ache for me, Tom? My cousin Pearl hasn't taken all the ache out of you for me?

Don't be foolish.

Then show me she hasn't.

So ours was a bargain struck, no better or no worse, perhaps, than that of Swain's with Raymond, or that of Shinbone with the devil. But this time when I lay with Ann, it felt different. Something was missing that had always been there before. It was like a crack you see in the ice when the weather turns and it starts to thaw and you're standing out on it. You know it won't hold you for long. That soon it will shatter and you'll drown if you stay on it.

So when I left her, I left dispirited because of this new feeling that had begun in me. I knew it would never be the same way between us, and yet I also knew that I would keep going back until whatever ice we were standing on finally broke completely.

A purple dusk was settling in over the valley by the time I passed Melton on the trail.

I wanted to tell him I'd gone to his place for a rightful reason, that what I done was to save poor Pearl, somehow thinking I would feel better if I told him this. But I could see by the beaten look in his eyes he wanted no truck with me, or anything I might have to say. He had it already set in his head why I'd been up to his place even though it wasn't totally true—just some of it was.

In a single day I had made new enemies: Swain, Raymond, and if Raymond left the valley, certainly Grayson. Meeting Melton on the trail only reminded me of how easy it is for a man to make enemies without half trying.

All I ever wanted was to live a happy, peaceful life.

Elizabeth Brouchard

These things you tell me, Tom. These happy and sad moments of your affairs that you have me record in—call it the *Book of Life,* if you will—I listen to with my own heart nearly breaking under the weight of your love for others when all the while you should have loved me.

But what is done is done and my love bears the burden of your burden and though your words wound me quite often, I shall put them on neat little lines where they will appear clean and unstained—bereft of sorrow. And so many of the words will make a sentence, and so many more a paragraph, and more still, an entire story.

Call it the *Book of My Life,* or, *Tom Dooley's Folly,* or whatever you will, for it is your words I write and none of my own.

O, hand, bear not rancor nor judgment nor
Prejudice for loving wrongly. Sustain
Thee in love's sorrow and give thy heart
Gladly away to him that never lov'd you,

But to him, whom you lov'd too freely.
For love is not to be bartered for the price of love.

I confess I saw us once in a canoe going slowly down the river together, the sun through the trees and arabesque upon the water, the river's cool wetness kissing my trailing fingers. You played the fiddle for me there in the stern and sang of the future, said, *We'll ride this boat clean to the sea, Liza—you and me together and nothing shall ever catch us.*

But it did catch us, Tom.

It caught us and held us tight in its talons, you around the neck and me around the heart and squeezed and squeezed until there was nothing left.

Chapter 9

Tom Dooley

The winter lay long o'er us, and I made my trips back and forth to Melton's even though Pearl was there now, working for Ann, cooking and cleaning and being a servant to her. Melton had cleared out a small shed and chinked the logs and put in a stove fluted out through the wall at the south end. The only other comforts were a bed, a chamber pot, a small piece of broken mirror over a shelf, water pan, and hairbrush. I came there one Sunday when Ann and Melton had gone together to town on a rare occasion.

Oh, Tom, it's almost as bad as Swain's, how they treat me.

It can't be, Pearl. Leastways nobody's taking advantage of you like Swain was.

Ann's so bitter toward me most the time. She accuses me of trying to steal you from her. James averts his eyes, but sometimes I catch him staring at me.

You understand how it is between Ann and me, don't you?

I always knowed. I just pretended like I didn't, but I always knowed.

That's just the way it is, Pearl. Nothing's going to change I can see.

That mean you ain't ever going to love me again?

Depends on what you call love . . .

She asked me what sort of love I saw ours as. I told her if I came around and Ann was there it would be me and Ann, but if

Ann wasn't there, then it could be the two of us.

You mustn't ever let Ann know. Were she to find out, she'd pitch you out in the cold.

Oh, Tom, I don't know if I can bear it, this sort of love.

It's this way or nothing at all.

Then I guess it'll have to be what it is.

She took my hand and led me into the small cramped quarters. I could smell the earthen floor, the tang of wood smoke—the odor of the living.

Cousin Ann will be gone the whole morning, won't be back till this afternoon.

Then we best not waste any more time.

We undressed and lay on the narrow bed and Pearl placed her body atop mine and I could smell her skin, her hair, her oniony breath. She took my cob and put it between her legs and I didn't try and stop her. Ever since that day Ann accused me of being with Pearl, I had a stronger hankering for Pearl. There was something mean in my wanting Pearl out of spite for Ann, mean and dishonest and I admit to it now. I ain't proud of what I done. Don't think me a prideful man for certain things I done.

It was over quick as it usually was. We lay there for a time, tight together on that narrow bed, not saying anything.

Can I ask you something, Tom?

I allowed as how she could.

Why do you love Cousin Ann when you know she's married and you could have just about any gal you wanted? Why take up with a married gal?

It's not something I chose to happen, it's just something that is. We can't always choose who we love and who we don't. Ann and me were lovers before the war—before old Melton came along. His coming along didn't change anything.

We heard the call of geese—a wild far-off call that meant spring was returning soon, bringing with it a whole new season.

Winter's about faded and I'm glad it is.

There's something so mean about winter, Tom.

I placed my hands upon her, ran them down along her bare limbs, along the spine of her back, her skinny arse, between her legs. She lay like a child and allowed me to feel her body and I felt greedy. Knowing I could do anything with her I pleased made me feel greedy. I don't think there is anything I could of thought of or done to her that she wouldn't have let me. That's a powerful thing, to know a body will let you do whatever you will.

Tom.

What?

She got on her hands and knees and put her hindquarters to me.

My cob grew hard again.

I like it when we do it this way.

I took her like that, on her hands and knees, like two barnyard animals. I told her I liked it that way too. I'm ashamed to tell you such things, Liza, but if I'm going to tell it truthful I've got to tell it all, the good and the bad so people won't think I'm lying, think I'm trying to come across as some saint or something. But I am sorry if it wounds you to hear it.

Elizabeth Brouchard

Between us is a woven door of steel—black and cold and unyielding. His voice comes through the small spaces, sometimes weak with shame, as it is now as he tells me of his consort with Pearl. I can see his eyes watching to make sure I write it down.

In this regard he is naïve—the way he tells of it so freely to me who loves him, as though such lewd details will hammer away all deception. But instead, they hammer away at my heart. But what am I to do, if not listen? For love does not run away when the truth of a lover is exposed. Love does not stick its head in the sand and pretend that the lover's history is all a fairy tale.

Is it better to know or not know? That is the lover's quandary.

O, I listen to him tell me these things and it aches worse than anything, for I cannot save him from the truth no more than I can from the fate of a jury's decree.

I understand, Tom, why you must tell every little thing. Does it trouble me that you do? Yes. Does it cause me to flush with embarrassment? Yes. But you are what you are and Pearl and Ann are what they were. Nothing will change any of it, the truth or a lie, for the Great and Holy Judge shall judge us all in the end.

Tom Dooley

When I left Pearl that day, I took the long way round back to my place out of concern I'd run into Ann and Melton on the trail. Still, a part of me wanted to crow about the fact I had two women I could visit anytime I wanted, the fact I was free and young and alive and not dead like dear Louis and a thousand other boys I knew. I had about everything a man could want. But I knew if I crowed too loud, or crowed in front of Ann, she'd pitch Pearl out, or maybe worse. So I kept it to myself and walked through the quiet woods and felt not the presence of life anywhere.

My cabin always seemed more empty each time I returned from Melton's and it did this time too. I thought I'd go to the tavern, but first I'd check on Shinbone and see if the winter had killed him. I don't know why I felt any obligation toward him, but I did. I thought I might invite him to come with me to town, test his mettle so to speak.

I found him in the same little clearing, his tent pitched, sitting on the blackened stump of his "church" reading his Bible. He looked shrunk some, his skin the color of candle tallow.

I see the winter has come and nearly went and you're still here.

He looked up, the wind fluttering the pages of his big red book.

I suppose if God had not wanted me here, Tom, he'd have took me this winter. She was a hard one and I had dreams about angels and old Satan himself fighting over my bones, but now I taste spring in the air and new life, don't you?

I sniffed, said I didn't smell or taste much of anything but allowed as to how the weather changed often and quick in the mountains and spring could come one day and be gone the next.

You don't believe in a whole lot, do you, Tom? Don't hold many hard convictions?

I allowed as to how that was so and asked did he want to come to town with me.

Why that's a sparkling idea.

I was a little surprised he didn't take time to think on it before accepting.

He washed his face in a bucket of water still with a skin of ice on it, broke it with his fist and splashed water up on his cheeks, and combed his hair with his wet fingers, then wiped a thumb across his teeth and rinsed his mouth with the same water.

I could use some stores and a fat meal of cooked hog.

He seemed happy as a child to be going.

We walked along together and I noticed he had a limp.

You hurt yourself?

Oh, had it since the war. Got it at Gettysburg. Sometimes the damp makes it worse.

You were at Gettysburg? So was I.

Why, you don't say. I wonder who killed the most Yanks, you or me?

I tried not kill more'n I had to.

Me, either. Hopefully God will forgive us our duty.

He laughed and his laughter seemed to reach the mountains

and skitter along the ridges.

Why'd you join, you believing so much in God? Don't it say something about you not killing in the Bible?

I was a fool for Glory, proud and vain, is what I was. What about you?

I was a drummer, mostly, but they was times I had to fit my hand around a musket just to save my own skin.

I know it. It was a terrible time, the war was. Woe that we should ever see such again.

We didn't stay long on the subject of war.

The tavern was full of men I knew and they looked 'round at me and Shinbone and some said hidey and some did not. The air was smoky and sour as unwashed drawers. I stood Shinbone to a glass of regular whiskey and he stood me to one, pulling a coin from a small deer-hide purse heavy with silver dollars.

You best be careful flashing that big money around.

You think?

Somebody's liable to bash you over the head for it. Been lots bashed over the head for less.

He didn't act worried. I wondered where he came by such a poke.

Here's to the saints, Tom.

He held his glass momentarily aloft, then knocked it back. He made a pleasant face.

She's got a good bite.

You ain't like any preacher I ever met.

No, sir.

Drinking and all.

Jesus turned water into wine. I reckon if he was opposed to drinking, he'd not done it.

Don't know as I ever read where he drank any of it.

I ain't read anywhere he didn't. That's the thing with the Good Book—it ain't always about what it says, a lot's about what it don't

*say. Most folks figure if it ain't writ down Jesus did this or did that,
he didn't do this or that. Me, I look at it from the other side.*

That's some good reasoning, I reckon.

We found us a small table set toward the back and took up
residence and nobody seemed to care one way or the other.
Some of the men acted as though they were conspiring, for they
spoke in whispers, their mouths close to the ear of their listener.
I thought of Louis, how he and I would sometimes whisper our
feelings in the cold night so the others around us couldn't hear
our soul's secrets.

*He tried to do right, didn't he, then got killed because of it, your
Jesus?*

*Yes, sir, that's some of why they did him like they did—they
couldn't stand no change, nobody telling 'em different than what they
knew all their lives. But change is bound to come whether a body
likes it or not, and change ain't always the worst thing that can happen to you.*

It seems to me that the good always get the short end of the stick.

*Seems like, Tom. But that shouldn't keep a body from doing what
he knows is right, what he believes in.*

*I tried to do a right thing here lately and all I did was make some
new enemies.*

Swain came over and looked at Shinbone, then at me.

You ain't welcome here, Dooley.

Shinbone put another of his shiny silver dollars on the table.

*My friend and I have come to drink and eat. You serve victuals?
Or should we take our business elsewhere?*

Swain's eyes fell to the money.

Beef and potatoes is what we'll have, and more liquor.

All's I got is smoked pork.

*Smoked pork it is then. Throw on some beans with it and corn-
bread.*

Swain left with the money stuck to his fingers.

That one of your new enemies, Tom, or is he an old'n?

New.

In spite of misgivings, I was starting to take to Shinbone. He had a generous heart to go along with his good nature. He ate like a wolf. All the while Swain stood off behind the bar conspiring with another fellow.

Shinbone talked around spoonfuls of his food.

My guess is you got woman troubles, Tom.

You figure rightly, preacher.

I'm guessing that's the reason you got you some new enemies is on account of a woman.

It was a little spooky the way he seemed to know my mind.

About the only thing worth fighting about in these mountains is either a woman, a dog, or a patch of ground.

Tom, that's about the only thing men fight about ever where. Clear back in the Old Testament days, men fought over the exact same things—women especially.

You ever had one?

Had several.

Then you understand.

Of course I do.

I'm about tired of setting in this place, ain't you?

We went outside and the evening sky was bruised blue and black like somebody had hit it with a big fist. The air was cooled considerable and I thought about going back to Melton's. Being with Pearl earlier had made my blood hot for Ann. I thought of her and Melton gone to town and back, how maybe they talked some and Melton told her how he couldn't stand it, my coming around. I guessed that maybe she argued with him over me and told him she'd not have it any other way. And I guessed that saying a thing like that would set him off and he'd force her into his bed and later they'd both feel bad over it.

Shinbone stopped and pointed to the sky.

Dog Star.

I looked up.

Calling us home, Tom, me and you.

I ain't getting your meaning.

Someday you will. That's our heavenly home up there.

Yours maybe, not mine.

I'll pray for you.

Hell if'n I need it.

Hell if'n you don't.

I watched him go on back toward his camp. Watched until the darkness swallowed him, then went back toward my place instead of Melton's. I figured we could all of us use a little peace.

Whoo, whoo said the owl.

Whoo—whoo—whoo?

CHAPTER 10

Tom Dooley

Tom!

Tom Dooley!

A bullet pierced my neck, in the dream it did. I was just sitting around the camp having a fine cup of barley coffee with the boys, laughing and telling stories, when something sharp snapped through my throat.

I heard the boys, saw their peering faces o'er me, heard their groans of disbelief.

He's kilt.

Bleeding out, nothing can be done.

Drummer boy's been shot!

Farewell, ol' friend.

Louis took a scarf, a lovely white scarf his darling Minnie had sent him to remember her by, and tied it round my blood wound.

Hesh, hesh, sweet Tom.

I could see the sun fracture in his eyes—all my breath stole. He placed his mouth on mine and took the last of my air into him.

I came awake in a fright, fighting for life, covers all damp from sweat. The cabin as quiet as a coffin. Then I heard the voice calling my name.

Tom Dooley!

Moonlight crept across the floor and the foot of my bed and

was climbing up the near wall. A pair of eyes stared and stared. There in the ghostly light a glass painting of my pa. He was a vain man and had it done in a Knoxville studio one time when he was there gambling and chasing sporting ladies—this Ma told me, anyways.

Goddamn you, Tom Dooley.

Voice from outside, angry drunk. I pulled on a pair of drawers, considered the small pistol I kept on the night table by my pillow. It had been Louis's—an old cap and ball, black powder Colt Dragoon. But it's bad luck to shoot a man in the night—everyone knows it is.

The voice outside my cabin was rising and falling in a crazy singsong way. From the window I saw Grayson sitting his Tennessee stud, moonlight in its marble eyes.

Stepping out, forgoing the pistol after all, I stood there on the porch.

Kinda late ain't it, Mr. Grayson?

You owe me, Tom.

Owe you for what?

That love-starved nigger. He up and disappeared.

None of my doing.

Sure as hell was.

Grayson swayed there in the saddle, thought he'd fall off and bash his brains out on the hard ground. In a way, I wished he would, but then I'd get blamed for that too most likely.

It's a free country last I heard, Mr. Grayson. I reckon the niggers can go where they want same as anybody else.

Don't sass me, Dooley. Don't make light of a serious matter.

I need my sleep.

I saw the shining barrel of a revolver in his one hand, a bottle of whiskey in his other—both equally fatal in the hands of the wrong man.

Shoot me, what good's that do? It don't bring your man back.

It might give me a deep amount of satisfaction to shoot you. It might give a lot of folks in this valley a deep amount of satisfaction if you wasn't around any longer.

Still won't get you your man back.

Maybe not, but somebody's got to take up his slack.

You figure me?

That's the way I figure it.

Your figuring's all wrong.

A bank of clouds drifted over the face of the moon, and made the world feel like a sad and lonesome place, like a cemetery of night. I saw the shadow of Grayson shift. Wasn't all that sure he wasn't ready to pull the trigger on me, send me to perdition. Maybe if he did I'd see Louis again. I wondered if death gave you wings so you could fly to wherever it was the dead went. Wings seemed somehow unfitting.

You do what you got to, Mr. Grayson, I'm going back to bed.

The clouds swam over the face of the moon, drifted silver light over the land, lighting Grayson up like a ghost. He turned his stud around three times in a tight circle as if to prove something, then started off toward his farm, the Walker kicking out its front hooves in a jolly little trot. He seemed a clownish pathetic thing, Grayson did.

I sat on the step of my poor little porch and breathed in the dank night, grateful I had not been killed by a drunk man. Of all the poor ways I could think to die, being killed by a drunk man seemed to me the poorest.

Colonel Grayson

I blame Dooley for most of the troubles in this valley since his return. He's stirred up things plenty. Came down to my place and talked to my hired man and the next I know, I got no hired man. I did some asking around and what I heard was there was some trouble between Dooley and Swain and the girl who worked for Swain, Pauline Foster. I don't know rightly what it was except Dooley and Swain had a falling out over it and after, Dooley came round and talked to my man Raymond while he was down to the river cutting ice. Next day Raymond went missing. They found his body in the self same river that spring. Drowned.

That's the sort of troubles I'd lay at Tom Dooley's doorstep. Raymond was a happy child till Dooley came and talked to him.

Tom Dooley

It was that very morning after Grayson came drunk in the night when Ann arrived at my door, her eyes fierce as a copperhead's.

You come by yesterday, didn't you? When I wasn't there? When it was just you and that little tart there alone. I don't even have to guess what you two were up to!

I came to see you.

Her breathing was little sharp daggers of anger. Morning was rising over the ridges, the sky a ragged gray—too early for quarreling with any woman.

I warn you this, I catch you with her, I'll . . .

Then from now on, you come see me, you walk that miserable trail to my place.

She went wild from jealousy and tried to scratch and claw me and I had to catch her up and hold her. And the more wild she became the more I desired to possess her. She fit me and I held her in my grip and kissed her mouth hard until she bit my lip and drew blood. I threw her across the bed and she cursed me.

You white nigger bastard.

Is that what Melton calls me? Is that what your lovely husband says I am?

I fell atop her and kissed her again, harder this time, the bitter salt of my blood smearing her mouth, her tongue licking at it. My cob rose stiff between my legs and I pressed it between hers, through the folds of her skirts until I knew she could feel it.

You want every woman but me. You had me, now you want every woman you ain't had, including Cousin Pauline. I know you already had her, I know it ain't enough you have us both!

She shoved her hand down between us, grabbed my cob. It felt like she was trying to tear it from my body.

Don't!

I will!

I rose from her enough to tear open her capote, to get at the buttons of her dress and tear them as well, tear and tear until her breasts fell free and lay full and white with their hard brown tips alert.

Her glare lost none of its viper intensity. She hissed. I lifted her skirts. She tried to claw my eyes. I pinned her wrists.

I don't want her in me!

She won't be in you. I'll be in you.

She bucked and fit, lurching her hips upward into me, tossing her head wildly, her sunny hair a sweet tangled nest that hid half her face.

If you do this, I'll say you raped me.

Go ahead say it. Everybody knows about us.

I'll say . . . I'll say . . .

But even as she fit and protested and cursed my existence, she parted her legs for me to enter her. It was like a crazy game, of course. We both knew it, understood it. She wanted me to take her, wanted me to force her to give herself to me, to prove somehow that I wanted her worse than I wanted any other woman.

Fuck me, Tom.

Yes, I'll fuck you.

She could swear as well as any soldier when she wanted.

But our love was like that of two angry angels wrestling each other. We churned and struggled as though locked in mortal combat. Our minds and bodies were crazed and delirious. Whatever wild spirits were inside of us wanted to get out and enter the other. She tore at me and I tore at her, and when we'd finished, we lay exhausted, two spent souls who had fit for their lives, both so defeated neither cared if they lived another day.

Tom?

Yes.

Do you love me?

Yes.

Would you kill for me?

It was an odd question, even for Ann, who could be so volatile I was sometimes afraid to close my eyes on her.

I'd like to think I'll never have to.

But if you had to, would you?

Ann, you are as precious to me as my own blood but you're asking me something I can't rightly answer.

Oh damn you, Tom Dooley.

She cursed me still, for I could not give her what she wanted. I did not know what she wanted. I told her about my midnight visit from Grayson in order to change the subject.

You should have kept clear of that whole business. I wished now that I had not listened to you and let you talk me into taking her in. You see what happens when you try and have a generous heart, Tom?

I thought about Raymond, about how even a daft creature such as he could feel a crushed heart. But then love isn't a thing that requires very much thinking. Love just is and it doesn't matter whether you're daft or not.

Ann Foster Melton

O, is that the way he told the story? It isn't true, not a word of it. Yes, I went there on that winter morning. But I went out of

106

kindness, not jealousy. I'd heard he was sick with a cold and I brought him some broth and biscuits. He was wild crazy about some incident with Grayson, how Grayson threatened him or the like. I'm not exactly clear. I tried to calm his anger, but instead he grew angry at me and when I tried to leave, he wouldn't let me. Instead, he . . .

I told him while he was doing it that it wasn't what I wanted, that I'd tell my husband if he didn't stop. But he wouldn't stop and threatened to kill me if I told anyone. I don't know what got in to him, what it was that changed him so drastically from a friend to a fiend. When he finally let me go I was too scared to tell anyone, even my husband, what Tom did to me. And I never did tell anyone until just now.

O, I know you loved him, Liza Brouchard, like we all did. I know you would have been a fool for him like we all were if it wasn't that he ignored you and chose others in your place. But be glad that he didn't set his ways for you—be glad you escaped his snare. You, of all of us, was the lucky one.

Tom Dooley

With Ann and me it was always like a storm, and after the storm passed, everything was calm again and I told her my thoughts about not wanting to stay in the valley any longer and she listened like she was interested.

I was thinking maybe of going over the mountains.

Where over the mountains?

I don't know. Just I look at them sometimes and I feel like I should go and see what's over them.

I thought you been all over them mountains, Tom. Didn't you go over 'em when you joined the Army and fit in the war?

It wasn't the same thing as it would be now.

Good God, Tom. You talk like a wild man sometimes.

I was thinking how maybe a new start might be just the thing.

I wouldn't have no enemies over the mountains. There'd just be strangers. I wouldn't have to compete over the love of a married woman. I'd gotten hungry to go over those mountains once and now I was getting hungry to go over them again. And when I mentioned these things, Ann grew restless and questioned me and I was near afraid I'd stirred her up again.

You wouldn't leave me, would you, Tom? You'd take me with you if you was to go?

Yes, I reckon.

I don't know if I'd taken her or not.

You won't find no woman good as me over them mountains.

No, probably not, just strangers.

You won't find no woman who will do this . . .

O, but she had her ways of twisting my head round. Her sunny hair lay gathered across my loins as I felt the warm wetness of her mouth try and stir my cob to life again. I lay there staring up at a spider's web, lovely and delicate, woven between the roof beams. There waiting in the eye of the web, a fat sleek body of a Black Widow like a watchful dark eye waiting for the proper opportunity. And from below I could hear Ann encouraging me.

That's it, Tom. That's it.

I closed my eyes and near choked on the sweetness of it all.

Elizabeth Brouchard

The storm was always in you, Tom. Always raging and raging. And into your rage you gathered the rage of others—& Melton, Pauline & Grayson—and caused them to storm like a hot wind until everything blew down and was left in tatters.

And now your rage has blown itself out, and like the sea that suffers under the storm, the waters are all calm again and there is no trace of you, no sign that you've ever been, except for one:

My tattered heart.

CHAPTER 11

Tom Dooley

Winter died without a whimper, and next anyone knew, the dogwoods were blooming and the mountains were whispering a warm breath over us all. Ann came several times to visit, but mostly I went to Melton's to see her. And when it wasn't Ann I was visiting, it was Pauline, for I couldn't seem to quit either. I thought soon enough, things would work themselves out the way they were meant to without me having a direct hand in it. After all, I reasoned, why should a fellow have to give up things of pleasure in a world so filled with sorrow?

On the first truly warm day when the sky was the color of a polished pan, I found Billy Dixon asleep on my porch. He was lying on his side, his shoes under his head, his legs pulled up like a child. I don't know how he got there or when. At first I thought he might be dead, but then I saw his ribs bellow. A string of spit hung from his mouth.

Wake up there, Billy.

No movement.

Said it again, then I took a dipper of rainwater and sloshed it down on his pale, pitted face.

Wha . . . wha . . .

You acting like a stray dog, Billy.

He popped right up, the cold water like a slap. Knuckled his eyes.

Hidey, Tom.

Hidey.

He looked around.

How'd I get here?

You tell me, we'll both know.

Oh hell, oh hell.

Somebody's hound bayed up the valley, bayed and bayed and bayed. Billy looked 'round, eyes wide.

Hear that. Means somebody's dead.

Means just some old dog's hungry.

No, sir, Tom, means somebody's gone and died.

Ain't you supposed to be down at the schoolhouse?

His gaze drifted west toward where the mountains were taking on the shine of the sun along their dark sleepy slopes, and in the meadow beyond the creek where the schoolhouse stood.

I'm not feeling so well, Tom.

You don't look it, neither.

The baying stopped. The valley fell silent. A hawk scoured the east ridges for breakfast. It was turning into a nice morning. I went inside and poured Billy a tin cup of hot coffee and saw the tatted handkerchief lying on the pillow, an embroidered *A* for Ann. She said she'd always want to see it there whenever she came to visit.

So's you won't ever forget me, Tom, or what is yours for the taking.

It floated like a leaf when she'd dropped it.

I half thought of giving the thing to Billy along with his coffee.

Go on, take it, Billy. Take it and go to her and win her heart and take her away from me and Melton. Take her out of this valley and far away.

We sat and blew off the heat of our cups and sipped the bitter chicory. Billy said it was about the worst coffee he had ever had and I said if he didn't like it he could march on into the village and see if he could find some better for the same price.

I didn't mean any offense, Tom.

None taken, Billy. What about them kids, won't they all be waiting for you down at the schoolhouse?

He felt around in his pockets.

I lost my watch somewhere last night.

You might check up under some slattern's skirts.

Oh, hell.

I reckon it ain't but eight o'clock.

I'm all blank about last night, Tom.

Hard liquor steals a man's brains.

We watched the sun crawl all the way to the peaks of the west range—Grandpa's Knob and Bearhead Knob and Sweetheart's Gap—till everything was golden. Then the valley itself filled with buttery light that came creeping right up to the steps like a cautious old hound and licked the toes of Billy's feet.

You think God has a hand in all this, Tom?

Hard for me to believe in God, Billy, after what I seen in the war. I don't know how any God would let men do such things to one another. And tell me this, what sort of God would give some men regular brains and others made of mush?

You mean fellows like Raymond.

Make him colored and daft all at the same time. That's a hard way to start out life you ask me, might as well made him a dog—he'd have it better if he was.

Some things just are, Tom. God's a great big mystery.

Maybe so, but I ain't got time to figure it through.

Billy drained the dregs of his cup, made a bitter face.

What do you think ever happened to Raymond?

Hard to say—but wouldn't be hard to figure why he up and left.

I told Billy Grayson blamed me for Raymond's disappearance.

These fellows round here take things like that serious, Tom. They still got a lot of the old ways in them. I don't reckon no war is going to change what's in their bitter hearts.

I fit that war, Billy. Grayson and some of these others seem to have forgotten that.

But why'd you fight in it, Tom? To keep the niggers as slaves?

Fit it 'cause I wanted to be a drummer and I wanted to see what was over them mountains. I dint fit it for no other reasons. I just fit it, Billy.

Not because you wanted to keep the niggers owned?

Hell, why would I want to do that? Onliest slaves I know about is fellows like me and you, Billy. We all slaves to the rich man, men like Grayson and them. They get het up and start a war over somethin' or other and make others do their fighting just like they make fellas chop their cotton and chop their tobaccy.

Billy laced on his shoes, stood, and stomped a bit trying to get the feel of them right.

The old bitch we call Mammy South is dead, ain't she, Tom?

No, she's not dead, Billy, she's just different than what she was.

These fellers want to still take her to the dance.

The dance was over the day Lee gave up his sword.

Yeah, but these fellows ain't so easily swayed—they're bullheaded. You can't beat them for nothing. They'll still be fighting the war for a hundred years.

He looked blighted; his cheeks fire red from all the drinking.

I guess I better get on down to the school.

Billy Dixon

Tom was a good ol' boy, a true friend. Sometimes I'd go into Swain's and drink till it felt like my liver was drowning and I'd fall out on Tom's porch on my way home again and he'd find me and not say a word about it and bring me coffee. We talked about the war and how it'd changed us, changed everything, it seemed. I never went off to the war and if I had, I'd been killed sure as anything. But maybe that wouldn't have been so terrible considering how everything was the poorer for us Southerners.

You understand that, don't you? How it might have been easier had I not lived to see the things I did in our little valley? We called it Happy Valley—everybody did, that was its name. But it wasn't Happy. It wasn't ever happy I can recall.

Tom Dooley

I guess it was around noon on a fine spring day when they found Raymond. Fish Bailey and Otis Dillingham found what remained of him snagged in a tree that had long ago fallen into Celebration Creek, struck down by lightning nobody ever saw.

They came into the tavern and announced it.

We found Grayson's nigger.

Yassir, found him in Celebration Creek.

Anybody seen Grayson today?

No, no.

Well, somebody ought to go tell him where his nigger is.

Everyone stood looking at one another, nobody volunteering anything.

Hell, somebody ought to go. That whole section of the creek will be ruined somebody don't drag him out.

It was decided that Fish Bailey and some of the others would take a wagon and a trace chain down and drag Raymond out of the creek. Otis Dillingham made a concession to ride up to Grayson's and tell him the news.

Somebody remarked it was just as well, what happened to Raymond. Some fellas laughed and some didn't.

I heard you tried to sell Pauline Foster to him, Swain.

Like hell I did.

Tried to sell her to that nigger?

Why the hell'd I'd want to go and do a thing like that for?

Knowing you, you'd see that little slip as money walking around.

Goddamn your sorry soul. Hesh such talk as that or I'll brain you.

It's just as well what happened. He hadn't kilt hisself, somebody else might have done it for him.

How you know he killed hisself? How you know he just didn't fall in and drown by accident, or maybe somebody done it for him?

Don't make no difference, does it?

No, I reckon it don't. Dead is dead.

How about a round on the house, Swain?

How about kissing my ass?

I'm sorry to have to say these things, Liza, to tell these things to you, but I was there and I heard it all and I went out of there and kept walking until the feeling I had began to ease up, the worst of it, anyway. I found myself standing at the schoolhouse fence, the voices of the children singing a child's song.

. . . I likes to hear them sing, Mr. Tom.

I heard Raymond's voice. I saw his happy dark face too, and for a moment it blotted out the sun. I recalled when I went out to speak to him about what Swain had done to him, the deception, and how his happy dark face turned sad. I reckon Raymond wasn't much older than myself, though nobody knew how old he was, he may have not known himself. I thought what a short unhappy life he must have lived, except maybe his mind wouldn't let him know all the unhappiness. Maybe in that way, his mush brain was a blessing and not a curse.

I stood and listened to the children singing, and when they stopped, the whole world fell silent.

I went on home and got down my fiddle and played "Four Cent Cotton," and "Loch Leven Castle," and "Going Down to the River." But after that last one, I couldn't play any more and put the fiddle up thinking I might not ever play it again, for its music was mournful and sad as a widow's wail. And Raymond's desire for Pauline must have been like a moth's, beating its wings against the candle flame trying to get at something he couldn't possess. I reckon Raymond wanted love like everybody else. I reckon a daft brain don't make a difference when it comes to things like wanting to love and be loved. And I reckon he surely must have known he was dying and would never ever know love when he swallowed the first mouthful of creek water.

I went later that evening up towards Melton's, but dallied along the trail until the valley gathered in the darkness for I didn't want to visit Ann, but wanted to visit Pearl instead.

When I arrived I stood there in the brambles a hundred yards from the cabin and watched as figures passed back and forth in the yellow window light inside of Melton's. I reckon it was just past supper and Pearl was cleaning up the dishes. I then went round and entered her little shed and undressed and climbed into the small bed. I felt hidden from the world, hidden and waiting for something to happen that would dispel my lonesome mood.

I lay there for what seemed like a long time and felt exhausted and wanting to sleep. Next I knew Pearl was in the bed beside me, her wet kisses waking me from my drowse.

Oh, Tom what a surprise to find you here.

Hesh, hesh.

I took her fast and swift, hearing her sharp little grunts beneath me as she bore my hunger and I didn't care if I pleasured her or not as long as I pleasured myself. It was a mean spirit that had me in its grip, and afterwards she didn't say anything for a long time and I didn't either.

Her bed suddenly felt a terrible place for me to be.

Don't leave me, Tom.

I was already half dressed and couldn't explain it, what had taken hold of me. She tugged at my shirt to try and keep me from pulling it on and I yanked it from her grip.

Let me be, Pearl.

115

But why, Tom? Why?

I raised a hand to strike her, but let it fall helplessly away. To hit her would have been meaner than hitting a dog because it wanted to lick you. So I told her why I was the way I was.

They found Raymond in the creek today.

She didn't say anything.

Maybe somebody killed him and threw him in to make it look like a drowning, or maybe he threw himself in because he couldn't stand living no more.

She ran her hands over my chest like she was still hungry for me, like she hadn't heard a thing I said about Raymond.

It don't bother you, does it?

I'd rather he be dead than to marry up with a nigger.

He wasn't going to harm you, Pearl. He didn't know any better. Swain put a dream in his head and he thought it was real. He was just daft.

Why you care, Tom? Why you care what happened to Raymond? He's just a . . .

I put my hand over her mouth to stop the word. I didn't want to hear it again. I'd heard it all I wanted to hear it during the war and after, down at the tavern, and I didn't want to hear it come out of Pearl's mouth again.

I got to be going, Pearl.

She started to cry.

I didn't care. I left out of there with her still crying and walked the dark trail back to my place and had to go by Celebration Creek and the very spot where they found Raymond and I could hear the water whispering in the dead branches of the lightning-struck tree. It was like the water was whispering of the conspiracy to the thing that had held him so dear so that he might be found at all.

I lay abed alone, every desire and lust and dream I'd ever had, spent.

I kept hearing Pearl's condemnation.
Hell, he was just some poor damn . . .

Elizabeth Brouchard

O, I know, Tom, I know. The spiteful aching words falling off of hateful tongues can do such damage and destroy every little thing of God's grace & of *man*. Hateful words can be a fire and a plague upon our lives and souls and mark us such we cannot ever be again what we were born as: sweet, innocent little selves that ran about with happy heads and unblemished hearts.

Is that what happened, Tom? Did the spiteful things said, the terrible things done, undo you? Did they, Tom?

But, O, if you'd let true love into you, Tom—if you'd been as a single window letting in the sunlight, how it might have saved you and bound up your wounded heart and all the bleeding places.

And so these words I add to the others, yours and mine and those of Ann & Pearl, Melton & my own father—Swain.

& I must remember that they are only words and not stones upon which my house is built, nor stones that once slung, will kill me.

Sleep well, Tom. Sleep well.

& I will too.

Chapter 12

Tom Dooley

Grayson would only pay five dollars for Raymond's burial. Shinbone said he'd oversee the spiritual proceedings, no charge. I told Grayson I'd dig the grave and he could keep his almighty money.

Fine, you owe me anyway for putting crazy thoughts in that boy's head.

I owe you nothing. Him maybe, but not you.

Grayson laid the money on Shinbone's stump alter.

Never let it be said Jim Grayson don't take care of his obligations—and rode off on his fine stepping horse.

Shinbone and me dug the grave together and lowered Raymond in it wrapped in tarp and without benefit of even so much as a coffin.

Doesn't seem right, not even a pine box.

His is just an empty vessel, Tom. It won't matter. Few years from now even the pine would be rotted away. We just turn back into what we once were—dust. It don't matter.

Shinbone and I sat atop the mound of earth we'd dug for the grave, winded and uncertain what had changed in the valley, but knowing something had. A bird I don't know the name of but whose wings were tipped with yellow lighted on the branch of a white oak and sang and sang.

Seems it ought to rain on such occasions, not be such a pretty day, not have birds singing.

I looked at the sky; there wasn't a cloud anywhere.

Maybe sunshine and pretty birds singing is exactly what's needed.

Shinbone looked at me.

Let me say a few words, then we'll finish this sad business.

Go ahead, you seem to be the one with all the words.

Shinbone nodded, started in.

The Lord is gracious and full of compassion. His tender mercies fall on all things great and small, like welcome rain upon the tongues of the thirsting. He upholds all who fall, and raises them up again. He gives everlasting life to those who believeth in him. Lord, we pray you raise up poor Raymond's spirit to your heavenly kingdom, that your mercy washes away whatever sins he may have committed. He was just a daft child didn't know any better for the acts he may have committed. But in your almighty grace, you make him any man's equal. Amen.

Those were fine words, Tyree.

We are all brothers in death, same as life, Tom. Death just declares it final.

I know it.

I could not help but think of Louis there in the wilderness the night before he was shot. We were near eat alive by mosquitoes and near starved and practically dead of thirst and fatigue. And we knew that we'd be in for a terrible time come the next day. We'd about lost all hope of anything good ever happening to us again. Louis shivered through that terrible night, whispered his fear in short hard epithets.

I'm scared, Tom. Scared I'll be killed.

We took pieces of paper and wrote our names on them and where we was from and pinned them to our shirts so when we were killed, others who'd find us would know who we were— had been—and not just black-faced corpses.

Don't be afraid, Louis. Dying's just dying, that's all it is.

I want to see Minnie and my baby again. I want to hold them

119

and tell them how much I love them and that all what's happened to me in this war ain't what I truly am. Nothing against you, Tom, but I feel pitiful and weak and sinful when I think about what's happened.

I understood completely.

I know, Louis. I feel the same. I don't know what this war's all about except I know it ain't about us and fellows like us. It's about something else, but I can't say what rightly.

O, Tom, do you think all this time God's been watching down on us, seen everything we did, knowed every thought we've had?

I don't think God would get within a mile of any of this. What kind of God could watch what we're doing to one another—us and them Yanks—and not put a hand to stop it? If such a God be, then he is laughable and crueler than any officer I ever knowed.

All through the night we listened to our fate: men moving about, the crack of a limb, the rattle of a tin cup, a cough. Then silence, then more movement. We heard the Yanks on the other side settling in, getting ready for the coming fight, restless as we was restless, scared as we was scared. We was like doves cowering in the night, waiting for the morning slaughter of the huntsmen. And Louis breathing hard, confessing, afraid as I'd ever seen him—as though he knew tomorrow was it for him.

I just can't no more, Tom.

Me, either.

If we die tomorrow, our souls will be stained forever with our sin.

We ain't dying tomorrow. You'll make it home to Minnie and Louisa and I'll make it home to my people and that will be the end of it and we'll grow into fat old men with lots of grandchildren and that'll be all she wrote.

But Louis's fear had put a darkness in me and I hoped if we were killed, it would be early and that we'd not have to fight the whole day only to be killed in the twilight hour. I always thought I'd want to die in the morning, not in the evening—not beyond the supper bell. I wanted to hold Louis and make him know it would be all right, that we'd be safe, but I couldn't bring myself to do it. I knew whatever had been between Louis and me had forever changed us, but I didn't regret it no more than I regret having lived or dreamt or hankered for the far mountains.

Shinbone stood with the wind fluttering his hair into stringy brown ribbons.

We're the unwanted, Tom, you and me and poor fellows like Raymond there.

I began shoveling dirt down in the grave, the clods striking the tarp-wrapped body with dull thuds.

If we are, then it was your God who made us the unwanted, just like he made Raymond a mush brain and Grayson a high-stepping man and all the rest of us what we are.

O, don't say it, Tom.

It's true, ain't it? He made us all—the good and the bad. We ain't none of us had no choice in the matter of what we are, what we become. If sinners we be, then sinners He made us.

Shinbone began to shovel too. I don't think either one of us wanted to think any more about death, best to cover it up and get on with the matters of the living.

Tyree Shinbone

Tom was a fellow I admired much for his unfettered ways and free spirit. But he held no truck in the Lord I could see. The war ruined him, ruined his thinking, and I can't say I blamed him for being godless in his thoughts. For some, like myself, such a terrible event will cause a man to cleave to God, but for others, it will only alienate him. Tom was like that, alienated from all godly thoughts.

I believe there are good men who are godly without knowing or thinking that they are. I believe Tom Dooley was one of those men. I believed it then, and I still believe it, Miss Brouchard.

Tom Dooley

Shinbone told me he admired me for my unfettered ways. Said things I didn't fully understand the meaning of. I think some of it was he may have been going crazy even then and nobody knew it, especially not him. We finished up our burying and sat a spell in the warm sun and I listened to Shinbone carry on.

We're the unwanted because we represent the truth, Tom—fellas like you and me.

I don't represent nothing I can see.

Surely you do, just as I do. I tell them what they don't like to hear and you go about your way without care what they think of you. You're honest in that, Tom, and honesty is an unwanted thing with most men. I reckon there is plenty of them who would like to go about as unfettered as you.

I wanted to deny there was anything in me anyone would admire. I know I tried to always do right by others, never wanted to kill anybody in that damn war. I just wanted to be left alone is all.

Shinbone sighed. *I look at you and oft wished I was as unfettered myself. But I'm fettered to the Lord, Tom. He's got me buckled down.*

I don't know a thing about it.

Surely you do, and I suspect the reason is because you have faced death and realize there's nothing to it, no reason to be afraid. You've seen the face of the shining God a time or two already.

I ain't seen the face of nothing.

Why I've seen it myself—that's how I know about you.

I suggest you leave off with all the God talk.

I wish I could, Tom. I wish God hadn't burdened me with this heavy load.

Oh, Jesus Christ, Shinbone. You don't want it, leave it. Go on and cross them mountains and don't come back.

I can't. I am bound to the Word. I can't leave it, Tom. I can't.

I thought they were blisters, when after we'd finished shoveling the dirt o'er Raymond, I saw Shinbone's hands again. The palms were bleeding like last time he'd showed them to me before at his camp—wounds in the palms. I wanted to ask him about those hands of his, but by then he had a look in his eyes like he wasn't there. I just walked away, leaving him by the grave, and went to Melton's, my heart full of anger.

It was that day that I met my true fate—Laura Foster.

Elizabeth Brouchard

You had eyes of love for everyone but the one who loved you truest. Laura was the prettiest of the lot. Pretty and sweet and not plain and naïve as Pauline, or beautifully tart like Ann—but sweet as a fresh persimmon and you could not pass her by without a taste.

O, I know the story well enough, but tell me again how you fell so madly in love with Laura Foster and how such madness transpired, by your hand or another's, into murder?

Was she as simple and sweet as she appeared, clinging like a persimmon to the greenest branch of life, airy and ripe for the plucking, Tom? Or did you take her too soon from her airy loft? & when you took a taste of her, was it sweetness you tasted or the bitter poison of life itself?

Tell me true and I'll record it true, for all around us is false rumor.

Tom Dooley

I don't know, I don't know.

&

was she took or was it me?

&

did the stars all fall from the sky that night?

CHAPTER 13

Tom Dooley

The day I met Laura Foster, Melton stood talking to a man over the back of a horse. The man wore faded coveralls, a gray felt hat mapped by sweat. He was barefoot and sorry looking. I thought maybe he had come to buy a pair of shoes from Melton—him being the valley's only cobbler. The man was about Melton's age I guessed, forty, fifty years old. Hard to tell with mountain men, for they have the age of earth in their faces. The horse was a fine-looking black Morgan, maybe, with white socks; its eyes were dark as smoked glass. It wasn't a wagon-pulling horse, but was nonetheless harnessed to a wagon loaded down to the axles with furniture and trunks and even a spinning wheel.

Melton stopped talking to the man when he saw me approach the cabin. His eyes got on me and stayed on me. The man he was talking to swung his head about and looked at me as well. He had a briar patch of red whiskers and a face near long as his horse. His fists were balled in the pockets of his coveralls. I reckon he was about one of the poorest-looking mountain men I ever saw.

He paid me no more attention than he might a chicken that had wandered into the yard. He leaned and spat tobacco juice and turned back to Melton. Droplets of brown juice clung to his whiskers and he didn't bother to wipe them away.

I hear tell you might have a patch of ground to lease.

Maybe. Who'd you hear it from?

Feller in the tavern.

Swain?

He didn't say his name, I didn't ask. I come out here to look at it.

You aiming to raise cotton, maybe some tobacco?

No, sir, cotton's too damn hard a raising, and so is tobacco, and 'sides, I couldn't afford no hands to pick it if I was to raise either.

Then what you need a patch of ground for?

Hogs, maybe.

Hogs?

The man looked about in all directions. He studied the land, the hills, the buildings, everything in sight like he was reading a book.

It looks like a right good place. Better'n where we come from.

Rocky in some places, clayey in others. It's hard to find flatland, unless you get you a piece of river bottom.

River bottom's too dear. I reckon hogs is a good thing to raise. Hogs don't get et by bole weevils and don't get ruined from too much rain, and you don't need no flatland for 'em either. Hogs eat about anything, snakes, slops, whatever. Hog meat is dear.

Hogs, eh? Well, I don't know about no hog—stink is bad.

I went on in the cabin. Ann was sitting at the table and another young woman sat opposite her. Pearl was at the stove stirring something in a pot. All three looked at me when I entered. The room smelled of cooking and of woman.

Ann didn't allow I hardly take off my hat.

Why, Tom, what are you doing here this time of day?

Her eyes flashed like dry lightning when she saw I was taking notice of her guest. So did Pearl's.

I was just on my way to town and thought I'd stop and say hidey.

I just couldn't let it pass, so I introduced myself when I saw Ann wasn't about to.

Name's Tom Dooley, ma'am.

Mine's Laura Foster, and hidey, Tom. I'm another cousin to Ann and Pauline here.

You sure favor these two. But truth was, Laura was prettier than either Ann or Pearl. Ann was a beauty but in a hard way, whereas Laura was younger and bright-eyed and it was her brightness that caught my attention most. And I didn't make any pretenses about it. For I was, as Shinbone had called me, *unfettered* in my ways. But Ann picked up on my unfettered ways and spoke up.

Excuse us, Cousin Laura. Tom, would you mind stepping out back with me a minute?

I followed Ann outside through that little back door Melton had cut in, he said for the purpose of escaping a fire in case there was one at the front. Melton was a mighty practical and fore-thinking man. Once outside, Ann lit into me good.

Damn you, Tom Dooley. I saw the way you was looking at her.

Where'd you want me to look?

It ain't enough you got me and Pauline to rut around with, is it?

You know there's nothing between me and Pearl.

Pearl is it? I know you'd probably do it with a heifer given half the chance.

No, ma'am. Them heifers fall in love too easy.

She didn't find any humor in me and went to slap my face but I caught her by the wrist and told her not to act so dangerous.

She ain't staying, so no use you getting any ideas about her.

It's just as well. I'd hate to have to fit you ever day of the week over your crazy notions about me and some woman or another.

The anger made her taut as a spring and caused her cheeks to flush a shade of primrose. Ann was a strong gal and I had trouble holding her still when she got like that. She pushed up hard against me until I felt the length of her taut body. She pushed until she knew I was feeling her like that, like the way she got when we was ravenous with each other. O, I hate to tell you these things, but I must so you'll understand the way things were. I'll take all the blame you want to heap on me, for I was unfettered and maybe too much a fool—mistaking desire for love and all those things I didn't understand until now.

We spat and argued some but Ann knew me too well.

You like to get me this way, don't you, Tom? You're the only man who could ever get me this way and you know it and that's why you do it.

I could see the corncrib, sunlight drifting through its slats. I could smell the hot must of the corn and remember the bone-hard way they felt when we first laid on them that time of our beginnings. And shelled, the cobs were the color of dried blood. My own cob hard and hot with her pressed up against me, her body taut like that, hard in a way a woman is seldom hard.

I ought to make you take me over to that corncrib right now, do it like we did that first time.

Don't be a fool—your husband is round the other side talking land with a man.

Go ahead, Tom Dooley. Go ahead, take me here and now. Take me in front of Melton and Laura's daddy and Pauline and Laura her damn self. Let them all see how you take me, let them see it and envy it!

She took my hand and slipped it under her skirts until my fingers touched the warm hardness of her thighs. I felt the heat of her drift down on the back of my hand when it brushed up against her sex. O, I'm ashamed to say such things now.

She was the devil and the devil is a powerful wicked thing when it comes in the form of a woman. But I mustn't blame it all on her. It was a lot of it me too.

We're both the same you and me, Tom. We're both willful and wretched.

I didn't come here for this.

Then what did you come here for?

Hell, I don't know anymore.

You put murder in my heart when I think about you and other women, Tom.

Such crazy damn talk!

I pulled free and pushed her away from me. She hissed like a cat and tried to come at me again, but I held her off.

I got to get on.

You coming back this evening?

Might. Might not.

Maybe I should find me a man who is more regular in his wanting.

Maybe you should. I hear Billy Dixon's in the market for a gal.

Oh damn you, Tom Dooley.

She slammed the door going into the cabin. I felt as if I was standing on the edge of something deep and fatal. I wanted to leave her as much as I wanted to take her. I wanted to punish her with my desire. I wanted to steal her pleasure and keep it as my own. She was like a slow poison in my blood I knew would kill me, but a poison I wasn't sure I could go without, much like a starving man will eat putrid meat knowing it will kill him but he can't help himself.

Ann Foster Melton

Tom came sniffing round the day Cousin Laura and her pap showed up at our place. Came round like he had an instinct for any new pretty gal in the valley. He was cocksure of hisself and I think he tried his best to provoke me as often as he could. He liked me riled in order to shame me, in order to show his power over me. O, he had power over me aplenty and he knew it. And I was powerful crazy over him and he knew that too.

That's the trouble when a woman loves a man so much, he steals her power from her. She can't control herself, her mortal thoughts nor desires. I did things for Tom Dooley I wouldn't have done for any man.

But before you think it, before anyone thinks it, I never murdered Laura or nobody else for him.

Tom Dooley

On my way back round the cabin, I passed by the window again and looked in and saw Laura Foster sitting there alone while Ann was standing by Pearl at the stove, giving her every what-for judging by the way she was waving her hands about. Then, as though she knew I was there, Laura turned her head slightly until her eyes met mine through the green glass and we just looked at each other. She smiled and I smiled back.

I went on back round front, past Melton and Laura's pap talking about land still. I went past them for Melton's benefit, so he could see I was leaving. His eyes trailed after me and I could almost hear his heart rejoicing that I was leaving.

Go on, Tom. Go on the hell home and don't come back.

I figured someday if things with Ann and me went on long enough, he'd go mad and kill me. His love for Ann would surpass my own and it would steal his soul, like it had stole mine, and he'd go mad and that would be all she wrote.

In a way, we were all mad from something.

I was mad with desire for Ann, and Melton was mad with hatred for me, and Billy was mad with longing for any love he could find. Ann was mad for me, and Grayson was mad with loss over his field hand, and Pearl was mad with loneliness and Shinbone was mad with the holy spirit.

Then there was Swain who was mad with greed and an old recluse who was mad with lust for his own daughters. There was the war that had been mad for the blood of young men and young men mad for the war.

The world spun and spun with madness until we all were dizzy.

Elizabeth Brouchard

Tom, do you think it was all this madness that drove you to it?

I wasn't driven to anything.

But you're here in this place with darkness looming o'er you.

It wasn't my doing put me here, wasn't my hand in it. But it was fate—that untrustworthy old bitch.

But surely you had to know that you couldn't just go on and on the way you were—that things couldn't just go on and on the way they were.

I can't say.

You can't or won't?

A body knows what a body knows.

Then tell me what you know for certain; don't leave me to believe things that aren't true.

Those mountains looked more dear to me that day. I saw them as a fortress, something to keep me in or keep others out. I'm not sure. I should have gone on back across them right then, that very day I met Laura Foster. If I had, I wouldn't be here now. My whole life would be different.

And you and me, well, there might have come something of us, don't you see, Liza?

Did you love her true? Did you love Laura truer than the others?

Love's a slippery thing. It changes. First it's one thing, then another.

What you've written in your journal, and what you've had me write—it all sounds like love confused with something not close to love at all.

My words don't seem my own when I look at them. They seem writ by a hand other than mine. I read them and they don't seem my own.

But surely they are your words, Tom.

At times it's like there's a power taking over my hand, guiding it to write the words. I just let it. I can't say if the words are always true or not.

The sweet dove flies without thought to its wings or how it is able to soar. Perhaps the words in you are like the wings of the sweet dove, Tom.

Maybe so.

This lattice of iron between us is hard and cold and cruel. Was your love for Ann like that, Tom? Was it that way for Laura near the end?

O, don't ask me such things, Liza.

I watch you pace and limp beyond the lattice of iron.

The dampness hurts my feet. I got my feet froze that first winter during the war.

I bet you wish you had them stuck in sunshine.

I bet so.

Do you wish me to write about your feet as well?

Tom Dooley

I woke in the woods somewhere on the trail between my place and Melton's. I don't know what happened, I guess I must have fainted for lack of eating anything for several days. I had lost my appetite for no understandable reason. I woke and smelt the mossy ground there in the woods where old trees lay in rot and the shade was deep and cool. There was something comforting about lying there, hidden from the world. I didn't want to get up. I wanted to just lie there and become part of the land, my roots grown deep in the black wet loam.

Would you like me to read you something I wrote the other day about my time in that old war?

Yes, read it to me, Tom.

The weight of my words are trapped here inside this book.

The weight of it feels about like the weight of a heart if you was to hold one in your hand, I reckon.

July 14th 1863. We have arrived in Fredericksburg and given the task of watching over captured Yankees. The colonel has passed down orders to the officers who have passed them down to the sergeants who have passed them down to the privates:

Shoot any prisoner who tries to escape.

Me and Louis confer and both agree we couldn't shoot an unarmed man just for trying to run away home, even if he is a Yankee. Louis asks me what should we do if one tries to escape on us. I tell him just to look mean and wave his big musket around and I'll wave mine around. And if one actually runs, we'll fire over their heads and let them skedaddle. So that's what we do for several days until everybody gets used to the idea and sees it more as a sport than anything.

Each day a few of them die and have to be taken out to a field and buried. Louis and me are sometimes put on the burial detail and dig and dig until our hands grow blistered.

Louis asks me why it is I think some of them die like they do during the night. Heartbreak, maybe, is what I tell him. For I don't know myself why they do.

One fellow we come to like quite well: a blue-eyed boy named Hank who always has a smile, even though his ribs show through and his feet are in terrible condition because one of ours had taken his shoes.

Hank tells us he's from Michigan. Calls himself a Wolverine. Says a wolverine is the *fightingest creature God ever made* and asks if we had them in the South. He and Louis argue over whether a wolverine is a meaner fighter than a badger or the other way

Wolverines is the fightingest! Hank argues.

Badger! argues Louis.

No, sir. Wolverine.

You don't look so full of fight.

No, sir, I sure don't. I guess you got me on that one.

Louis and me take a liking to Hank and sneak him some extra Johnny Cake when we could and he showed us a photograph of his mother, who had sorrowful eyes.

What happened to him, Tom?

He died like a lot of the others.

I use the book sometimes for a pillow, my head resting on words I must have wrote but can't remember doing so.

And in the book are names of those you loved dearly and those you lost—Louis and Hank and others . . .

And now I've lost even my own life.

O, Tom, the words seem so bitter even in their beauty.

Better from my lips than those of strangers.

O, that I could kiss those pale, pale lips just once.

Liza, my heart beats your name.

CHAPTER 14

Tom Dooley

What words are there to rightly tell how it was between Laura and me? No words I know can paint a true picture of the feelings I had nor describe the fire that burned through my blood, the way it burned up every defense, every logic, every reason. It was a storm of fire that swept o'er me. It left me weak and helpless as much as some battles I'd fit in the war had. Only the lucky or profane seemed to survive such things.

But I didn't care if I survived them or not. From the very first, when she turned and gazed at me through the green window glass, as though I was looking at her through water, I could not stop thinking of Laura Foster. I knew I had to have her.

Her pap leased a patch of land from Melton that lay the far side of Bald's Gap. Far enough from Melton's, I reckoned, that I could go visiting Laura out of sight of Ann's watchful eyes. I had no choice in the matter but to go, I was full of this awful hunger for her. It was the feeling poets write about, I guess. It was the feeling I got when I'd listen to Louis's tender words as he spoke of his Minnie. It was a feeling like watching the sun lift over the mountains where each time is like seeing it for the first time.

It was the feeling of being drunk.

And *it* wasn't nearly the same feelings as I had for Ann. What I felt for Ann was raw in wanting to possess her more than to love on her—a *right now* feeling that could come on me sudden like a storm. And once I got my satisfaction the feeling fled me just as sudden and I had no more interest in her. It was nearly the same way with Pearl. Only with Pearl I was able to take what I wanted so easily without protest and without consequence it made me lazy and without care about myself no more than about her. With Pearl, it was like stealing from a child, and with Ann it was like trying to steal from the devil—I knew there'd always be some sort of hell to pay. It was only afterwards, as I lay in Ann's bed or Pearl's, that I felt bitterness close around my heart like poisoned vines that would strangle. This bitterness would leave me feeling I'd sinned as much against myself as I had them. And in the case of Ann, there was Melton to consider as well, what I was doing against him. Seven sins from Sunday it felt like. Even though Melton and me were not friends of any sort, we were still men and understood what men understood about one another and understood how easy it is to ruin a man's pride. I felt marked and unclean each time I fornicated with either Ann or Pearl.

But Laura was like a refuge for me, a safe place where I didn't have to sin anymore against myself, or others; I could feel clean and unmarked by starting anew with Laura.

And when I went to see her, my spirit felt light and airy like a fast fiddle tune that made my feet want to dance and dance. And whilst my feet were dancing, my heart acted like a quick bird that sought to fly away, its wings thrumming in my chest for release.

So I made up my mind that once I went to courting Laura, I'd end it with Ann and Pearl. And the mere thought of ending it was like weight off my shoulders, a mountain water washing the sludge of corrupted blood from my veins.

I even stripped naked and went out and stood in the rain and scrubbed my scalp with a bar of lye soap and scrubbed my flesh till it felt like new skin again. I turned my face to the sky and let the rain fall upon my closed eyes and upon my tongue until I nearly wept with the joy of it all. I felt free for the first time since the officers announced to the boys the war was over, that we was free to go home.

O, I know how foolish it must sound to you, of all people, Liza, to equate the two—love and war. One offers death and the other life.

Word of the war's end took our breath away. Some of the boys went about stunned, disbelieving, their gaunt faces like the living dead, their eyes no longer to see hope's horizon. Others danced a jig; their arms interlocked, and sang joyous songs. And some simply sat on their blankets and wept.

Hell, she's finished, boys!

Lee surrendered his sword.

No! No!

We been whipped!

Lord almighty!

Beat the drum, Tom. Drum the men to order.

But there was no order anymore—the flesh and the hearts of the boys had been freed and they could be whatever they wanted to be and do whatever they wanted to do. No one could give them any more orders. We were as free as the niggers most of us never owned nor hardly even knew anything about.

I beat the drum and the men sang Dixie but their hearts weren't in it like they once were. Their pride had become as ragged as the raggedy flag we'd been following for nearly three years. And when I struck the last drumbeat, we straggled off, leaving behind us a great silence.

Goddamn, goddamn.

And I walked away from the camp and away from the others amid the smoke and dust, knowing I'd left my shadow some-where on the land. I walked off and stood upon a small ridge and looked down at a river whose name I did not know snaking lazily under a blood-red sun as it had always done. A river without any valor or defeat to it known, I thought, a river without any regret. A river that had washed away all the blood in it.

Looking down on it, I imagined a little wood boat with a letter tied to it floating away to a far-off dream where Louis waited for the rest of us to join him. *Someday, someday.*

We'd fit the whole damn war for nothing it seemed to me. For that river was as it had always been, and the hills were as they had always been and the sky was as it had always been. Whereas Louis and thousands like him were dead for a vainglorious notion that nobody understood except the generals and politicians. We died in ragged lines, blown apart by shell and ball and sometimes chain. Bayoneted and shot and burned alive. Our hands and feet and torsos decorated the lands from Virginia to Tennessee. Our bones fertilize the earth still, and for a hundred years more. The only thing that had changed was us boys and a colored man's right to go where he pleased—all the rest remained as God had made it.

The deer and bear and birds will return, but we never will.

The trees and grass will grow up again, but we never will.

Our lost sweethearts will find new love again, but we never will—those of us left behind the shattered walls, the shorn fields, the tattered woods, never will again. *Goddamn, goddamn.*

Elizabeth Brouchard

And while you were gone, there was this empty valley of a place, Tom. This valley grown bereft of youth, and it seemed we'd grown old almost overnight—old and out of balance with young women going about with empty hearts and nowhere to place their love, except for the old men and lame and useless who would take advantage.

But surely our sorrow was not the same as yours.

Our burden was not as great or tragic.

And when you and a few of the others did return again, it brought once more hope to this place. So it seems so unfair that the seeds of hope returned, never blossomed into what might have been. And you did not blossom, Tom. Instead you were let grow to seed and trampled and pulled out by the root.

And all your youth and all your beauty could not save you. And now, even love cannot save you. For if it could, I would kiss your sweet tender mouth and free you from this cell and nurture you all the rest of my days with love. My love would be balm to your injured soul. My love would be music to your ears. My love would be the rich dark soil for you to take root in again and grow and blossom.

Grant to me, Glorious Father, this right to save him.

Tom Dooley

Yes, surely the journey was long and twisted and all out of shape. And life's truest hope did not lead me to you, sweet Liza. For the war had turned my head all around and left me insensible and foolish and not afraid of death or the consequences of living. So let me tell you how it was, how it was, how it was.

Relief at first that she was over, and then gladness seeped back into us because we were still alive and able to know such things and home we went, bereft, defeated, but alive, sighing relief, but too, our hearts heavy with guilt to be alive still.

And in my long journey I had time to think about it all and conclude that there are never any tomorrows, just the now. And it was this very thinking that led me to dance in the rain for the joy of thinking of Laura Foster as the skies burst open. For to me, she was my second chance at life—a true and honest life without sin or guilt.

It was as though God hisself brought her to me, for when I

opened my eyes, she sat her pap's horse there in the rain and said:

I never saw a naked man dancing in the rain.

The rain had left her hair to hang in dark tangles about her face. Her wet dress clung to her as if she was shedding her skin. She seemed a woman born of water, risen straight out of Atlantis—or some mermaid I'd read about that prowls the seas, but here she was among the mountains.

You must think I'm crazy dancing around like this.

She didn't say a word, just sat looking at me.

The rain beaded upon her sweet face.

Aren't you afraid you'll catch your death?

No, ma'am, I'm afraid I'll catch my life if I look at you much longer, or have you look at me, thus.

That's an odd thing to say.

You wouldn't think so if you knew what was in my heart this very moment.

Why don't you tell me what's in your heart, Tom Dooley.

The way she said my name was like hearing the church bell ring down in the glade on Sunday morning, or a warbler singing among the pines.

I feel plum foolish standing here thus before you.

Then maybe you should invite me in out of the rain and clothe thyself.

I think that's a fine idea.

Inside my cabin, I rubbed dry and she sat before the fire and I said it would be she who caught her death if she didn't get out of her wet clothes.

I think a gentleman would offer to assist me.

I've been accused of many things but never called such a name.

She smiled and lifted her wet hair from her neck and I took the buttons of her dress starting at the top and undid them. I brushed her bare shoulders and back with a dry towel and she inclined her head exposing her nape and I kissed it gently.

Her dress fully removed was heavy and dripping and I hung it before the fire on a drying rack, then set about helping her remove her underclothing, peeling it from her, exposing more and more of Laura Foster to eyes that craved to see her thus. I couldn't help but compare her in my mind to those cousins of hers, Ann and Pearl, for there were similarities, but none that mattered to me.

She took my face in her hands and kissed me, her mouth so terribly tender I lost all thought of Ann and Pearl or any other woman I'd ever known. Of course I did not think of you, Liza, in that way back then. For if I had, there would have been no Laura Foster, no Pearl, no Ann. But then I know you might find that hard to believe considering the circumstances as they are. But if you think it a lie, ask yourself what good would it do me to lie about such things now?

Elizabeth Brouchard

O, even if it is a lie, Tom, I choose to believe it. For I did not present myself to you in such a manner as to give you indication of my availability, and even if I had, there is nothing to say you would have taken notice. Girls with tongues as sharp as Ann's or Pearl's or Laura's, tongues that could whisper sweet promises, what would you have seen in me with a tongue so dull and useless?

I knew that Laura was prettiest of all the Foster girls, and Ann so wildly beautiful. What chance would I have stood against their beauty? And with my muted tongue, what chance would I have stood to win you?

None, none at all.

Tom Dooley

O, I wish you would not write of such things to me now that nothing can be done about it. But still, I'm glad you do. For,

even though I gave myself to others, I will go to my grave knowing that if I could do it all again, I would give myself only to
you.

Go on with your story, Tom. I didn't mean to interrupt.

Well, on that rainy day, the fire crackled in the hearth & the
flames leapt against the blackened stone & steam rose from her
wet clothing. I kissed her as passionately and yet as delicately as
I knew how. I didn't want to frighten her. But she wasn't
frightened at all.

Cousin Ann warned me about you.

Hesh, hesh, sweet girl.

*I want you to know, Tom, that whatever you are, whatever you
were before I came here, doesn't matter to me.*

I've been waiting for you all this time.

She rested her head against my chest as softly as a child
would and I held her tenderly as I would a child:

You must promise me one thing, Tom.

Anything.

*That if I give myself to you, if I give my heart to you, you won't
mock me, you won't tell the others and see me as a thing to play with
for your amusement.*

I began to promise, but she put her fingers to my lips to stop
whatever promise I was about to make.

*Think carefully, Tom, before you speak. Don't steal from me the
only thing I own that is yet precious. I'm not sophisticated like Cousin
Ann, and I'm not a fool like Cousin Pauline. I'm a common girl
with common dreams, don't take advantage of me, will you promise
me that?*

And even as I promised she trembled in my arms; I thought
from her being cold and wet, but she said it was really because
her heart was fearful of being ruined by loving me.

There can't be any ruin in love. Tell me how.

If I give my love to you and you leave me, if I become your lover

141

and you become a stranger, then it will be ruin, Tom.

There was no doubt in my mind that I had loved her from the first moment our eyes met. But to prove to her that I loved her and would not ruin her, I refused to take advantage of her when I knew I could possess her in front of the fire.

Instead I wrapped her in a blanket and dressed in dry shirt and trousers and fixed a meal of mush and biscuits and slices of salted ham and black coffee sweetened with sugar.

We talked as we ate, our desire cooling temporarily, as she told me about her life and her pap and how they'd left Iredell County because her pap was forever restless and it was the fourth or fifth place they'd lived in the last several years. I asked about her ma; she said she didn't know that much about her, that her pap never talked about her.

All he ever said was, that one day she just up and left us.

I told her about me, about my adventures in the war—some of them, anyway—and how happy I was to have come home again whole, but that lately I'd gotten a restlessness in me—*like bugs crawling on my skin*—and was thinking about going over the mountains, maybe going all the way to the ocean.

You sound like daddy.

I'm not shiftless if that's what you mean. I'm just a plain curious fellow.

Oh, I know you are, Tom. I seen it in your eyes that very first moment. I knew you were different than the others.

You known other men intimately, Laura?

I've had beaus that pursued me. I been asked to marry twice and refused. But no man has known me in that way you speak of.

O, my heart sang with joy, for every man wants a woman untouched by another man—a woman unfamiliar with intimacies.

But answer me this, Tom. Suppose I had been with other men, would it make a difference to you now?

I told her that nothing would matter to me—but was I sure? O, I can't say that I was. So I told her what I thought was the right thing to say instead.

All that matters is just what I am now and what I'll be when I'm with you.

The sound of rain makes me sleepy, Tom.

I carried her to my bed and laid her on it and lay down next to her and she watched me in that curious way she had of watching me.

It's okay if you want to have me, Tom. I made up my mind riding over here. If you want me, it's okay.

No. I don't want you this time, Laura.

O, why not Tom, don't I please you?

You please me fine. I want to think about it a little while and keep thinking about it until I can't stand thinking about it.

I thought how easy it had been the first time with Ann, and the first time with Pearl and the first time with a lot of girls in the valley. I didn't want it to be that easy between Laura and me. I wanted it to be special, take my time with it, let it simmer in my heart.

I feel so sleepy.

Close your eyes.

I watched her sleep until the rain stopped and when it did, she opened her eyes and kissed me and kissed my hands. It stirred the passion in me all over again and I was tempted to take her there in the stillness that's left behind when the rain stops. But I held off, and holding off seemed to increase the pleasure, knowing that the time would come soon and I wouldn't need to hold off any longer.

I took great pleasure in watching her dress. It was all I could do to keep from stopping her. I walked her outside and gave her a foot up onto the back of her pap's horse.

Come court me, Tom. Come court me proper and make me feel as special as I do this very minute.

I'll come. I'll come soon and court you.

And someday maybe . . .

Yes, someday maybe we will . . .

O, don't say it, Tom. Don't say the words just yet. Let me keep them like little gifts in my heart until I hear you say them to me someday.

I touched her foot and off she rode toward the bald & beyond the bald, fingers of silvery clouds laced the evening crimson sky. The cicadas had started up and sang an evening song and the sun threw its last red rays up against the gloaming like a fiery breath. Above the bald a lopsided grin of moon stood smiling down on the lower valley that was already grown dark. I felt alone, more alone than ever, standing there—alone but happy as I'd ever been.

Perhaps if there had been a gypsy-telling woman in the valley she might have told me of the ill fortune that awaited us, Laura and me. She might have told me about you, Liza, and how you would have saved me from all this. But as it stood, I could see nothing in my future but unbound joy and went inside and took my fiddle down and played and played such happy songs my heart near burst. I played and the cicadas became still and listened, and so did the moon and the evening stars. I played so hard because I wanted the sounds to carry across the bald and have Laura hear the happy music.

Your love for her makes me weep.

My love turned into tragedy.

& Murder entered into it?

I cannot say, for I do not rightly know.

Elizabeth Brouchard
Postscript:

Are you yet the brightest star that appears in the blackboard sky, the tip of Sagittarius's arrow aimed at all the cherubs' hearts, dear Tom? Or, were you that shooting star I saw that streaked so bright for the span of a breath, then vanished?

Each day extends the distance between now and then— between the rain of Paris and that time when you strode, nay, strutted, through the lush green Yadkin Valley with a heart full of love and promise, never seeing the dangling rope, nor hearing the hangman's nervous cough.

I am both blessed and cursed by this fading memory.

Both blessed & cursed.

★ ★ ★ ★ ★

BOOK II

★ ★ ★ ★ ★

CHAPTER 15

Tom Dooley

He says his name is Winston Newbolt and that he's a reporter for the *New York Herald.* He smells of whiskey and cigar and wants me to tell him about the events. He sits outside my cell and scribbles notes for an hour at a time. But lest he tell it wrong, I've taken to keeping my own account, writing it all down as best I can on sheets of foolscap brought me by one of the ladies from the Society of Friends. She says the society is made up of Quakers. She is motherly. Her name is Polly Boots. Funny name, Polly Boots. I've written her name down so those who read my account won't forget who was kind to me and who was not. Polly is a spinster, has a sister who is a spinster too.

Can I bring you anything, Tom? A Bible perhaps?

Some foolscap and a pen and ink. No Bible.

So you can write your folks, people you love?

Yes.

The weight of a Bible has a certain comfort, Tom.

Have you met the wild preacher, the one called Shinbone?

She shakes her head, not sure of what I'm talking about. I don't tell her the true reasons I want the foolscap.

I can pray with you, Tom. I can write things for you if you can't write them yourself.

I learned to write some . . . well enough for what I have to say. Pray? I don't know about all that. I tried my hand at it during the war and it didn't seem to take.

Well, you wouldn't hold it against me if I was to pray for you and the others were to pray for you, would you, Tom? You wouldn't think of it as meddling?

No, ma'am. Pray all you want.

I write things down as they come to me, not in any order, just as they come to me. Sometimes I have dreams and wake up and write them down when the moon is bright enough to see by. If not, I try and remember the dreams and write them down when there is enough morning light. I can't always remember them, though, just the terrible ones.

I keep the foolscap under my pillow and the ink bottle and pen in my shoes under the cot. Time passes more easily when I write instead of just sitting here and thinking of all the things that have transpired in the last season. I call it the season of my sorrow. For that's what it has been right enough, except for you, dear Liza. The year began with such promise, with Laura's arrival in the valley. It began as a season of joy and ended as one of sorrow.

I like the sound the pen makes as it scratches across the page. I like the feel of how the paper resists the nib, then gives into it. I like seeing the words being born out of the pool of indigo ink. I write slow and careful because I like getting lost in the wet black curves and lines. From me, these things flow, from a place I didn't even know existed these things come forth, these thoughts and words. And I am amazed at what the words say when I've finished, for I never know ahead of time. My hand is blind.

I read the words over whilst I eat my meals: breakfast of pone and black coffee, dinner of mush and pone and black coffee, supper of side meat and hominy and black coffee. I read and eat slow to make the time stretch on and on—these precious moments in which I can escape my captors, my judges, my executioners.

I even write about the reporter, how he stays close to the shadows, becomes hardly more than a strange voice without face, without hands or arms or body—just a glowing tip of a cigar. He comes in the evening and sits on a stool in the shadows and smokes his cigar and asks me to tell him of the events of the murder.

How'd it come about, Tom, all this nasty business? Who were your co-conspirators? Was it a ménage à trois? *I've heard that it was.*

I told him I didn't understand what he meant? He called himself a Brit, but said he worked for a newspaper in New York City.

He wrote it down on a piece of paper—that strange phrase—and slipped the paper to me through the bars.

It means a love triangle, Tom. The phrase is French.

I looked at those strange words and thought, my god, there's a whole other language out there in the world I'll never get to know more about.

The French have such lovely phrases for their sordid deeds.

I don't know how to answer him, nor even know if I want to. He is very patient and persistent without being pestering. He wears a straw hat and a black suit—what I've seen of him in the light—and a gold chain across his waistcoat that I suspect has a fancy gold watch attached to the end. I saw reporters in the war, most of them scurrilous drunkards. Newbolt isn't like any of them. He seems like a man who would hate war or anything loud and rebellious. Curious, but cautious.

As Newbolt waits for me to tell him of the events, his breathing is like the purr of a large tomcat accompanied by the dry sound of his cigar burning to ash.

I can't say for sure what it was or wasn't, Mr. Newbolt, what or how this trouble began. I still ain't figured it out completely.

Take your time, Tom. I'm here for the duration.

151

The duration?

He sucks deeply on the cigar, patient as an old tomcat.

I don't know how to tell it right.

I'll help you, lad. Just say it in your own words. That's always best, you know, simple words.

You don't seem like a fellow who would admire simple words.

Oh, I do, I do indeed. I'm not like most of my countrymen. What good are fancy words if no one can understand their meaning? Like, ménage à trois, eh? Fine example.

He chuckles and I hear water dripping somewhere.

They say you were quite a war hero, Tom.

I stuck three years, got captured twice, came down with the rickets once, the scurvy once, the shits a dozen times. You call that a hero, I guess I was one.

It went like that between us each time. Newbolt sitting in the shadows smoking his cigar, asking questions in that educated manner, scribbling, me trying to keep a close hand on what I said and didn't. It wasn't just my life at stake in all this. Poor Laura was already dead, of course. There was every possibility they'd hang Ann as well as me, and maybe Pearl too. So you see, Liza, it wasn't just I wanted to save my skin the reason I didn't tell him everything. I wanted to save theirs too if I could, in spite of everything that happened.

Shinbone came regular to see me too while I was in Wilkes-boro. He, for one, never asks me if my hand was in murder.

God knows the truth of what happened, Tom. I don't need to be asking you those sorts of questions. Righteousness shall prevail.

If it is righteousness, why am I here, Tyree?

Who can know the ways of man or God, Tom?

Sure not me.

He brings me hard candy, a checkerboard to pass the time, his philosophy on the nature of things.

You were both were star-crossed, Tom, you and Laura. Like Romeo

and Juliet but without all the family feuding.
They must live in the next county, for I never heard of them.
You never heard of them! Har! Har!
Shinbone's laughter climbs the cold, stone walls of my prison.

Tyree Shinbone

O, I could not help but feel akin to poor Tom—a brother in the spirit, only he did not know it, would not accept any godly delegation. So, we played checkers instead and talked little of the lord and the soul's salvation. He simply wouldn't have any of it. And what sort of Christian would I be to shove righteousness down a dead man's throat? So instead I spoke of things he might take to:

Love and death seems to go together, Tom. It's the death of one or both of the lovers that makes love more bittersweet. Why most great works of literature tell such stories—that's why they're great works.

Jesus Christ, Tyree, I don't need to hear of such things. Move your man.

Tom was a righteous enough checker player.

Tom Dooley

Each visit, I learn a little more about Tyree Shinbone. Things come out of him I don't expect, like that whole business about Romeo and Juliet. He confesses over the weeks of coming to visit that he's well read, that half the things, maybe most he's told me before were lies. He don't know why. He tells me he was educated in Pennsylvania. He tells me that his daddy made a fortune in the railroad business and his mother was a debutante, as if I knew what that was. I wanted to ask him how he went from being a rich man's son to a tramp for Jesus. But I held off, figuring he'll get around to it if he wanted me to know. He's always been damn mysterious. But it never did stop his philosophizing about all manner of things. And for all I know everything he's revised might be damn lies as well. Still, listening to him lie is better than staring at these walls.

Your story is timeless, Tom, and we are timeless, folks like you and me and old Romeo and Juliet. I think God just made some of us to be timeless. A hundred, two hundred, years from now they'll still be telling of you and Laura Foster, just like they still tell of Romeo and Juliet.

Who the hell cares? I won't, will you?

Shinbone's eyes can get as blue as winter ice, his hair a tangle a rabbit couldn't free itself from. I guess he can't be more than ten years older than me, but he looks to be old as Moses.

I think Tyree Shinbone was going crazy even then. He'd talk of this and that and a lot of it made no sense. But he brought me candy and the latest news:

They say Ann's a raving bitter shrew.

They still got her locked up then?

Well over a year, Tom, same as you.

And what of Pearl?

Shinbone kept his own consul when it came to word of Pearl. Fell silent as though struck by an anvil.

And Melton? What do you hear about Melton in all of this?

He just stays out there at his place wild as a goat.

And Grayson?

Why concern yourself over Grayson?

He's the one led them to me, laid all this at my feet.

Grayson's gone back up to Tennessee the way I hear it.

He was rational at times, and I thought he might be trusted. But now I can see that I could trust no one but you, Liza.

The trouble began early, soon after Laura and her pap had settled in, the suitors came calling. Among them: Grayson, Swain, Billy Dixon, Sam Pie, and George Hare, about every unattached man in Yadkin Valley wanted to court Laura. I came over the bald not long after Laura found me dancing in the rain. Came to court her proper, win her heart, her passion, her everything. I brushed off an old suit and had Barter McClee cut my hair. Barter, you know, cut hair and was the undertaker. *I bet you buried plenty in your time.*

Snip, snip.

Lost count, but I buried about everybody come to this valley and died. Men, women, children.

Snip, snip.

Don't it bother you, working with the dead?

They don't complain. I used to be a tax collector. Lord, how folks complained.

Snip, snip.

I seen plenty of dead myself. I'm still bothered by it.

We all just vessels to carry our spirits around in, Tom. Once the spirit has fled, we just empty vessels is all. I just bury the vessels of what people once was.

Cut that hair good, would you? I aim to go a courting.

I'll do her.

Snip, snip went his shears.

I gathered wild flowers from the meadows: loblolly, firewheel, Sweet Betsy, trout lilies, oxeye daises, lady slippers. I gathered the flowers under a sky swept with mare's tails and tied the stems together with a piece of bright red ribbon I bought in the mercantile from Mizrus Boots. It looked like I was carrying a rainbow in my hand.

That's a right enough pretty ribbon, Tom.

Thank you, Mizrus Boots, it's for someone special.

Mizrus Boots was the sister of Polly Boots, who came to visit me in jail and bring me the foolscap and pen. Her name was Lydia, I think.

I'll bet your buying it for that new gal whose daddy leased land from Mr. Melton, I'm guessing.

Yes'm. Her name is Laura.

She's a cousin to Ann Melton and Pauline Foster, ain't she?

Yes'm, she is.

Pretty girl from what I hear.

Yes'm, pretty as this piece of ribbon.

I wondered, looking into Mizrus Boots's happy old eyes if she'd ever knew the love of a man in her time. It seemed impossible to believe that such happy women as she and her sister would not at one time or another known a man or two along the way. Seems to me you can't know happiness without having known some kind of love or another.

Pardon my rambling ways, like I said, I just write this as it comes to me.

I took the ribbon and started for the bald.

But when I came over the bald and started down the other side, I saw Grayson's walking horse tied up outside. My heart turned to stone. I reckon they were all inside the little cabin together, Grayson and Laura and her pap. All I could think about were those times I'd gone to Melton's and the three of us were inside together, and how it never stopped me and Ann from our intimacies, the fact Melton was there. Maybe it wasn't stopping Grayson either—him a man of money and means; maybe his high-stepping ways had won her over. Surely they would have won her pap over. Maybe she got a look at his fancy horse and fine clothes and realized what a mistake she'd made with me. Why else would Grayson be inside? Hell, I threw those flowers to the ground, ribbon and all, and walked on back to my place.

My mood made me think of mournful times. I could see gray troops coming out of the mist—their muskets carried high—a line of ghosts. And I could hear mournful fiddles playing, too.

Beat the drum, Tom.

I could hear the rattle of drums drown out the mournful fiddles and watch as the gray line began to stagger and fall and disappear under thunderous black clouds that rolled over the beautiful land of farmers, tinsmiths, cobblers, sweet children.

O, I see Laura's face now, even as I write of these things. I see her there on the wet cold walls of this my eventual tomb. Her voice calls out to me day and night.

Tom, Tom.

She holds out her hands to me and I move toward her, for I want to have her hold me and take away the stain on my soul. But when I try, she fades away and there is only this silence. I think this silence will be like the silence of lying in my grave.

Elizabeth Brouchard
This madness wore the mask of a commoner
&
seduced you, Tom,
took way your foolish heart
&
sold it for the price of folly.
For, you thought
that youth was everything, and everlasting
&
the day would not be seen when you drew your final breath.

But rest there now in earth's bosom there by river's glory. Rest, rest and watch the sun come and go for a thousand years and tell me if you can, how one's bones feel turning to dust after the heart's long been silenced.

CHAPTER 16

Tom Dooley

O, I thought I'd eliminate the competition one by one, and first on my list was Billy Dixon. I thought as a somewhat friend, he'd see the light the easiest and if he didn't, I'd make him see it. So not long after I'd seen Grayson's horse outside Laura's cabin, I went to see Billy.

Billy Dixon!

Half drunk, he came to the door of his squalid little cabin, for he was no better off than any of the rest of us, even though he was more educated and had gone a year to college in Raleigh.

Get out here, Billy, we need to talk.

Tom?

Goddamn right.

The last of the plum evening light was draining out beyond the ridges. Peepers had begun their evening song from down in a marsh beyond the cabin. On hot evenings, the marsh stank of muck and critters that had crawled in there and died, or got done in by other, larger critters. It was a dark place I never liked going.

Billy stood with his braces hanging down, his shirt off, the yellow light of his cabin behind him so he looked more like a shadow than a man.

Tom?

How many times you got to ask? Yes, it's me. Now get out here.

He stood there scratching his head, the liquor in his brain

158

twisting his thoughts. I walked up closer to the porch.

That damn roof's about to fall in on you, Billy.

He looked up, then back at me, squinting in the dim light.

You come all the way here to tell me about my porch roof?

I came all the way here to tell you Laura Foster's spoke for.

Why, who's spoken for her, Tom?

You damn fool, I have.

Off to the west I could see lightning snake through the darkening sky, but too far off to hear any thunder.

Why, Tom, I thought you and Ann were . . .

Were what? Ann's a married woman.

Hell, Tom, everybody knows about you and Ann.

You don't know a thing, Billy. You only know what you hear and you take that as the gospel. I'd think an educated man such as yourself would be above rumors.

You saying it's not so?

I'm saying stay the hell away from Laura. You can go after any gal in the whole valley, any in Wilkes County for all I care. Why you can go all the way to Watauga County if you've a mind to, but Laura's spoken for.

Shit, Tom. Shit.

There wasn't a soul in Wilkes County more surprised than me when Billy come flying off his porch and hit me a good one in the jaw.

Billy, what the hell you doing?

I'll fight for her, Tom. I'll fight you or anybody.

It was about the worst fistfight I ever was in. Billy hit me and I hit him and we continued that way until neither of us could raise a fist or draw a breath all the while the dark closing in on us. We lay there with just a bit of buttery light falling on us from inside Billy's cabin. Our faces were bloody and our lips busted and more blood still leaking from our noses. My mouth tasted like salt and copper pennies. We coughed and spat and tried to get up and finish the other, but neither of us could, so we just lay there wishing we'd die or get better quick.

Where'd you learn to fit like that, Billy?

At college. I was on the boxing team.

Hell, you must have been the A number one champ.

No, I was the worst one on the team.

Then I'd sure enough hate to get into it with the champ.

Me too.

An owl hoot from a nearby tree sounded like a question nobody had an answer for.

I'll come back after I heal up some if I have to.

You come on ahead, I'll be waiting for you.

You'd rather take a whipping than leave her alone?

I'm the loneliest fella in this whole county, Tom. I reckon I'll take what I have to for love or even something like it.

We lay there quite a spell. The stars appeared in the sky and we lay there looking at them.

That there's the Big Dipper, Tom.

And that's the Archer, Sagittarius.

Grayson's after her too, you know.

I know it.

And so is Swain and Sam Pie and George Hare and about every fella who ain't married or wished he wasn't.

I know it. Laura's a damn fine-looking girl and I aim to have her for my own.

You going to fight them all?

I have to I will.

We were finally able to get up but neither of us had the heart to do any more fitting that night so we drank the rest of Billy's liquor instead and got well enough oiled so as the cuts and bruises didn't hurt near as bad. The jug empty, Billy tossed it into the dark.

You that set on her, I won't go round her anymore, Tom.

Hell, I know you're lonesome, Billy, but they's plenty of other gals.

He shook his head and some of the cabin's light fell on his face and I could see his eye was swollen and I could see his pitted cheeks and he looked gruesome. I felt sorry for him because I knew it was hard for him to get with girls. I knew it was why he took to paying for the privilege of shoving his head up under the skirts of tarts. I felt damn sorry for him.

You know something, Billy?

What?

That Pauline's a nice gal.

The one who works for Ann?

Pauline's her cousin, Billy.

What're you saying?

I'm saying she's a nice enough gal and she don't have a beau.

I think maybe I got a broke tooth.

I brushed off the seat of my pants, tucked in my torn shirt, and stood with an ache in my ribs while a star shot clean across the sky.

It's your choice, Billy. I was you, I'd get myself over there before someone else does—Sam Pie or George Hare, one of them.

Hell, I might, Tom.

You ought to.

Maybe I will.

I feel like I've fallen down a flight of stairs.

Same here.

See you 'round, Billy.

See you 'round, Tom.

And that's how I squared it with Billy Dixon. But I can't be sure. Laura's secret was unknown to me and in the end, I guess we all had secrets needed keeping.

This I write in my accounts, these things about Billy and me and Laura and the others so that you'll know, Liza, that it wasn't only me who had such an interest in her, but it was only me they blamed for her death.

Elizabeth Brouchard

O, Tom. If only you could have looked into the future and saw that Billy wasn't to stay lonesome forever. O, what little fate's ironies accompany us in our journey through the living land, surrounded as we are by the unknowable truths like airy threads attaching themselves to us all. We dance like puppets, twist and turn and bow at the puppeteer's command until he tires of us and cuts the strings and we all fall down.

How strange thy journey, how bittersweet thy destiny.

Billy Dixon

Yes, Tom and me fought like wildcats over her. I won't deny it. But thinking back on it after so long, I can't see why either of us fought a single minute for her. It was Tom who came out on the short end of things, and it is this I regret most. But no one loved her hard as he did, and no one made as much a fuss over her as he did.

But then you know, Liza, that young men are foolish men— the most foolish of all God's creatures—dumber than oxen— and I wasn't immune from such foolishness. Not then I wasn't. This I confess this to you now.

Tom Dooley

The jailer brings me my meals. He shoves the plate under the bars and waits till I take out my spoon and fork from my pocket. He has a big belly, short legs, hair stiff as straw. Never combed. His name is Augustus Keyes.

Keyes is a right proper name for a jailer.

You got me there. I don't reckon my daddy ever thought the family name would end up in a place like this.

May be more to a name than we know, name like Keyes, you turning out a jailer.

Yessir, may be. You want an extra slab of side meat with your hominy, Tom?

Side meat or shoe leather?

Keyes brays like a mule, but he's a good little fellow and I put his name down in my accounts as well. He has a wood leg to go along with everything else. I asked how he come by it.

Chopped it off by my own hand.

Hell of a thing to do—was you mad at yourself over something?

Wasn't intending to.

Had to hurt something awful.

Like you wouldn't believe.

He says he chopped it off whilst splitting poplar chunks— laughs, says any damn fool ought to know a leg from a poplar stump.

Supper is like every supper, just like breakfast is like every breakfast and dinner like every dinner. Everything is the same in this place. I ache in my bones for something new, just as I'd once ached for Laura. To pass the time and not to think of Laura I palaver with Keyes over supper.

Tell me all the details about that chopped off leg.

I was just splitting wood is all, same as I'd done all the time.

How old was you?

I was near seventeen, eighteen, maybe.

Must be something to go through life with a chopped off leg.

You don't want to know.

I guess I don't.

You going to eat that side meat?

I see the hunger in his eyes, tell him to go ahead and have at it, offering him a biscuit to eat with it. He sits on a three-legged stool while he eats. I'm thinking: *four wood legs and one of flesh and bone;* with that many legs a fella could walk all the way to Egypt.

Darkness creeps up the stairs and in through the window. It

comes in silent, the darkness, and gets close on a man and I ask Keyes to light a lamp and he does and it gives some comfort. Then he goes down the stairs to his quarters, his wood leg thumping, and closes the door behind him and slides the bolt with a scraping sound, a sound of something final and everlasting. The cold silence seems to rise up through the stairwell, ooze out of the walls. I sit on my bunk and think about how the days seem to go so slow and yet so quick at the same time, and realize that the passing of each brings me one day closer to my eternal end.

I think of young men dying young, and think of dear Louis.

The really good thing about Louis's dying was it came quick, unexpected. We were rushing forward in a charge, these ragged boys that we were. We probably looked like we were grinning but we weren't. Into the rattle of the muskets of Billy Yank we charged, into the spitting tongues of flaming death. The lead balls buzzed round us like a thousand angry bees, and when they'd strike something—flesh or bone—there'd be this flat hard slap of a sound. And whatever boy they struck, it would drop him. Some cried out and some did not. The dead would lay like they got hit, their eyes half open, only the light gone out of them, their hands clutching musket or air. The dark stains of their wounds percolated up through their shirts, their pants, all the while their open mouths grinned.

Still, onward and onward we charged in ragged lines that became more ragged as we fell out and stumbled forward, holding our breath for as long as we could, expecting the stinging kiss of death.

Slap. Slap. Slap.

Oooh! Aiyee! Oh goddamn!

The boys toppled like young trees in a bitter wind.

&

Louis turning in that last fatal moment to look at me as he

mouthed the words—*We'll make her, Tom. We'll cross this field, and I'll keep marching, all the way home to see my darling wife* . . .

And I started to yell back—*We'll make her, Louis, nothing can kill us, we're timeless*—when the ball struck him. *Slap!*—like that. And I watched him topple facedown into the grass, then roll over slow, thinking he'd get up again. But he never did. Instead he lay there a moment blinking, his beauty undisturbed except for this small bloody bubble over his heart with nothing else to mar him. He never said what it felt like to die. I never got a chance to ask.

I hear Keyes clumping around on his wood leg downstairs in his quarters, a gut full of side meat. Probably bitter still about his chopped off leg. Some bastards are just luckier than they know.

Augusta Keyes

O, I never yearned to be a keeper of caged men. Before I lopped off my leg I dreamt of being a prizefighter. I was strong and willing and knew a fellow could make himself a nice enough living fighting for purses at county fairs and such. I'm built strong all over, even my legs—it was no small feat for me to chop one off. No small feat (feet) ain't that a joke somehow? My pa wanted me to be a lawyer and I could have been that too. And I was engaged to a pretty lass and could have married and done well. But hell, something simple as a glancing bit of steel changed my whole *history*.

Tom Dooley's the most famous fellow I ever kept, and a fine decent fellow to boot. In another time and place, we might have been friends. I might have challenged him to a boxing match, or a foot race. We might have swum in the river and went to the dances and dated beauties.

In another time.

Tom Dooley

Newbolt comes at his usual hour—right after dusk—and I'm almost glad for the company. He is fragrant with the smell of onions, cigar, and whiskey.

Tom.

Mr. Newbolt.

He takes up the stool Keyes sat on, its legs farting against the stone.

How are you this evening?

How well is a man in my condition supposed to be?

Yes, I suppose you've a point there, lad.

We play out the silence with each another. Out of anguish the silence causes, I tell him the story about the fistfight with Billy Dixon that time; he seems to enjoy it, scribbling notes, asking a few questions. I flower it up some: how Billy and me fought for the better part of an hour busting chairs over each other, tearing up his place, busting out windows with each other's heads and so forth.

Newbolt takes to it like a cat to a bowl of milk.

I've heard it said that Southern men have rather short fuses and are not given to threats but are quick to defend their honor. Would you say that's true, Tom?

Well, I sure never expected old Billy to jump on me, if that's what you mean.

But jump on you he did.

Yes, sir. I guess we Southern boys are somewhat hot tempered.

And would you say it was this hot temper of yours that led to the final trouble with Laura?

You're forgetting something, Mr. Newbolt?

His heavy breathing awaited my answer.

I wasn't the only hot tempered boy living in these ridges when that there final trouble occurred.

Point taken.

He struck a match and it flared and the light danced in his small dark eyes as he suckled the end of his cigar, then shook out the flame with a snap.

I'll tell you something else too.

Yes, Tom.

It ain't just the men in these parts with hot tempers.

I could hear him scribbling away in the shadows.

Go on, Tom. I'm listening.

Winston Newbolt

O, I'm not at all surprised at the embellishments of Tom Dooley. He was a plain-spoken fellow, but still, even the plain-spoken ones are likely as not to throw a little sugar atop a story if you act like you're willing to buy into it. But for the most part, I confess that I found him rather sincere when it came to denying his role in the murder of Laura Foster.

He seemed to me to be truly affectionate of the poor girl and quite grieved at her death. But then his grief may have been out of guilt as much as out of anything. I've never yet interviewed a jailed man who proclaimed his guilt, and like as not, I never shall.

Still in all, I much liked him and was a bit sorry to see him go to the gallows.

Elizabeth Brouchard

Someone once said to me: *Every hundred years, all new people.* O, it was said in jest of course over aperitifs at the *Café du Monde,* and we were all a bit delirious in our youth and libertine ways. Death seemed so remote there in the fullness of our lives, a distant unimaginable thing. And how many times have I heard someone say, *If I die,* as though there were any question about it.

Tom and Laura and the others are all dead—as dead as Shakespeare and his *Romeo & Juliet.* And so is Billy, and so, too, is love I suppose; at least for me. But now, when I read over the notes and letters it makes them seem not dead at all. And when I give into memory, they are all alive still.

In a hundred years there will be all new people to replace us all, and a hundred years after that, and a hundred years after that.

But in a hundred years, there will still be the same memories of all the old ones carried in the new hearts—and they shall never perish.

Let not their words perish. Let not their stories go untold.

I've done what I can to see that it is so.

CHAPTER 17

Tom Dooley

Moon walked through the valley and I followed along behind it.

Ann.

Silence.

Ann.

A shuffling inside the cabin.

Ann.

Door opened on creaky leather hinges.

Where have you been, Tom?

Been gone. He in there?

No, gone to town, gone to the tavern.

Silence.

Well, you coming in?

No.

No?

I ain't coming in.

Then what are you doing here?

The moon stood smiling down at me, at this tragic thing I'd become inside my heart. Full of wanton lust uncontrolled—weak as the weakest sinner. I had no say in my own doings is how I felt.

But surely Ann knew my soul better than I knew it.

I don't know why I come. I was just following the old moon.

Damn you, Tom Dooley. You come to try and break my heart, break my spirit is why. You won't have me yet you won't leave me alone, either!

Her hand fell sharp and flat against my cheek, stinging it with resentment. I'd vowed not to see her again—vowed it a hundred times—but with my heart heavy from seeing Grayson's horse that morning down at Laura's, I felt a need for some untold revenge: if Laura was going to see Grayson, then I'd, by God, see Ann. O, it was such foolishness I know, but that is how crazy bone jealousy can make you.

Elizabeth Brouchard

Your unrequited desire for Laura led you to Ann.
Yes, I guess that's a fancy way of putting it.
Your raging jealousy of one turned into lust for another.
Made me as blind as drinking bad whiskey.
You needed to prove something.
Yes.
And such love and jealousy and rage are born of a sickened heart, but such I think I can understand. But it was not true love, Tom. For love has no room in its house for jealousy and rage.
O, I know it don't, Liza.

Tom Dooley

I had convinced myself I was just going there to tell her I was finished seeing her; that I was in love with Laura. Maybe I wanted to make her mad as me, jealous as I was jealous. All the way there, following the moonlit path, I schooled myself in the language I'd use to tell Ann we were quits, to hurt her with.

But once the door opened and you saw her and she told you Melton wasn't there, your heart aching away for Laura the way it was . . .
It was the slap that done it, Liza, strange as that sounds.
It set you off. It stung your passion, your anger, your jealousy.
O, I hate telling of it, but it lit a fire in me, burned up all my resolve.
Tell of it fair and true, Tom. Tell of it fair and true.

When she slapped me, sudden like that, my blood heated so quickly I had no time to tame it. I took hold of her and pulled her to me cursing myself for doing so. And she didn't dally, but urged me on.

Go on, Tom, you know you want to. Go on and take what you came here for! Take what's legally Melton's if you want it.

Her words were as much an ache in my heart as the sting in my cheek. Everything inside me seemed to explode. I took her there in front of the cabin, down in the dirt. Are you sure you want to hear of this?

Let what has begun not stop—don't be faint with me.

All right, then. I ripped away what little she was wearing and took her with her eyes full of moonlight. She was like a ghost, like the way Louis was a ghost—both of 'em stuck in my goddamn head.

Don't be faint, Tom.

I took her hard, like we was a pair of dogs. Hard enough to make her cry out, and when she did, that was all it took and my passion flooded from me. I hated myself.

Were you ever going to let her alone, Tom? Or did you think you could make it work, the lot of you—Ann and Pearl and Laura all together, and Melton thrown in the mix—seeing them alternately whenever the mood struck?

O, I don't know. I never thought beyond the moment about it.

Ann Foster Melton

In spite of whatever anyone's told you, little mute child—Tom had a hunger for me that no other woman could satisfy in him. He was a hog for my kind of love. He'd see me and right off start rooting round. Maybe he's told you different. Standing there in the shadow of the gallows, maybe he's told you all sorts of things. But truth is, Tom was a fool for me and I think he killed Laura Foster because he couldn't give me up and she told him she wouldn't tolerate him seeing the both of us. Laura might have seemed pert to some, but she could have a black heart when she wanted to. Maybe it led to a big row between them and with his hot temper and hers to match, he stabbed her like everyone says he did. He always did carry a clasp knife.

You'd probably not know what it is to love someone so hard it's worse than the wanting of life itself. That's the way Tom loved me, more than life itself. I think maybe Laura stood in the way of his wanting to keep loving me. Maybe it made him mad having someone tell him what he could and couldn't have and he killed her because of it. But if you ask me do I know for sure if he killed her? I don't. But a man standing in the shadow of the gallows is liable to say all sorts of things to save himself.

Tom Dooley

That night, there in the yard with Ann, O, I can't tell you how pitiful I felt having done what I done to her—for it wasn't love or anything like it that caused me to do what I did that night. And to make it worse, she was full of vile threats to me.

I should tell my husband that you came here and raped me.

It wasn't the first time she'd threatened such.

And do you think he'd believe that?

He might if I put enough tears behind it. If I clung and begged him to defend my honor, he might take up a gun and find you and shoot you.

Then go ahead, it might be the best thing could ever happen to me. He'd have you all to himself, unless he got so mad he killed us both!

You've changed something dreadful, Tom. You're not the same man I once loved so wildly. There's something mean and niggardly about you. You hurt me inside just now, what you done. You didn't have to do that to me.

It was like being stabbed in the heart to hear her say those things, but they were true. I confess to you now, they were true. I felt so completely lost to myself that I didn't hardly know right from wrong anymore. She was right, I had changed, but she had changed too. And our changing had changed one another.

How much had to do with the fact you loved Laura?

Most of it, I guess. Maybe none of it. I don't know hardly anything anymore, Liza.

Do you think some of what you were feeling was because Ann was the wife of another man, that you'd cuckolded Melton? Was it the cuckolding of another man that made you want to keep on with her?

Yes, I suppose looking back on it, that could have been some of it.

And maybe truth was, Melton liked it in a way too—some men have strange and perverse desires, Tom. Do you think Melton liked it, being cuckolded?

Maybe so. What do I know of such matter, truly?

Your sin and Melton's sin and Ann's sin—all one great sin mixed together, Tom.

You're starting to sound like Shinbone.

Elizabeth Brouchard

My own jealousy of hearing such things did make me a bit self-righteous—I could not help it when I'd heard Tom speaking thus of Ann and Melton, and Laura and even Pearl. Even though he was, as Ann had said, confessing in the shadow of the gallows, and even though I loved him deeply, I still could not ignore such tender sad torments. And sometimes I'd change the subject altogether because I could not bear another moment of hearing him recount his life with those other women, knowing as I did every second the terrible price he was paying for his youthful indiscretions.

Tom Dooley

One evening after you left the jail, sweet Liza, after that time I told you about going to Ann's and practically raping her, I fell asleep and dreamt of Pearl. In the dream Pearl was standing in the Yadkin, the water up to her shoulders, its black wetness swirling around her, rising sometimes high as her chin. I knew it was trying to drown her. She was calling to me—*Tom, Tom. Help me, Tom!*

What is it, Pearl? What's got you scared enough to go stand in the river?

It's Raymond, Tom. Raymond's after me. He wants to cut my throat with a razor.

A shadowy figure come into my dream, a heartbreak of a figure whose face I could not see clearly.

I gonna kill her, Mr. Tom. I gonna kill Pearl for leavin' me like she done. She my woman. Mr. Swain done sold her to me. But she leave me, would rather drown herself than be with me. 'Cause I a nigger, 'cause I daft in the head. I gonna kill her, Mr. Tom.

Come closer, Raymond.

And when he did, I saw his eyes had been eaten away.

She thinks drownin' is the easy way. It ain't. I done drowned and dem big snappin' turtles done eat my eyes out and chewed off my fingers, and the water done come in my mouth so much I couldn't swallow it all.

O, it was the most terrible dream, Liza. The worst I had to that point ever. Then I watched Pearl slip beneath the surface of the water and then resurface, naked and white, her breasts eaten away by turtles. I woke weeping.

& sometimes I awaken and see a shadow of something outside the bars of my cell that causes my skin to crawl.

That you, Raymond?

A tiny scraping sound from the dark. Mice, maybe.

Keyes, you out there?

No answer.

I hold my breath.

Mr. Keyes?

It is so dark it feels as though I'm inside a grave and maybe I am and my heart races until it feels as though it will burst. I gasp and claw for air. I pace and cannot sleep until the first morning light sifts down into the room through the small window above my cot.

Thy little horrors.

Yes, yes, sweet Liza.

Is it guilt or simply fear that strangles you?

Tyree Shinbone

O, I went often as I could to see poor Tom. His health had declined in such short fashion. His sunburnt skin gone pasty, his weight dropped off, his eyes near hollow with fret. He begged me to bring him ink and foolscap. I asked was he going to write goodbye letters. He simply smiled wanly and didn't say but instead declared he needed something to keep his mind and hands busy. So I went to Mizrus Boots and got him the ink and paper and some nibs and saw in her twinkling blue eyes love starved from her for untold time. One can always tell when a woman has been starved from love. And though she was a good bit older than me, I knew I'd bring to her the next time I came a potion that would cure her.

She told me anytime Tom wanted more foolscap and ink to let her know and she'd bring it along.

Tom Dooley

Shinbone arrives with a fresh bottle of ink, foolscap, nibs.

This place is taking all the starch out of you, Tom.

I dream of dead people. It ain't pleasant.

Laura?

Yes, sometimes. But others too.

Have faith.

That's your department.

There is noticeable change in him. His face is shaved clean revealing blistered cheeks. His voice has an airiness, like a fine fiddle playing on a pure warm day.

I owe you for the supplies?

Not a penny.

How was Mizrus Boots?

We prayed together.

There was something in the way he said it made me feel uneasy.

You best be careful, Shinbone.

I could use the company of someone young and fair, Tom. I surely could.

She's a spinster—maybe twice as old as you.

Preacher's got cravings just like spinsters do, Tom.

He laughed and laughed.

Beloved I beg you as sojourners and pilgrims, abstain from fleshly lusts which war against the soul . . . One Peter, Verse 2, Chapter 11.

He grins like a possum and quotes scripture, but I don't know why. I'm guessing he's going mad, mad, mad.

The Lord expects much of us, Tom. Some days I'm not up to all He expects of me. It's been two years since I've had any female companionship. In some ways I'm jealous of you, Tom, your free ways with love.

I told him I didn't want to hear about it. He laughed and carried on anyway. No point in me telling you all the things he said. Stay clear of him, Liza. I don't trust him.

Elizabeth Brouchard

Tom had good instincts. Shinbone went completely mad later. And who is to say what carnal acts or otherwise he committed before his madness claimed him? Would murder be among his forte? I think anything possible.

The young girls come every day for the piano lessons, and their *mamas* go shopping for hats even in the rain. The air of my apartment is filled with discordant melodies by the tiny chubby hands of soon to be mademoiselles. Their hopeful luminous eyes attend with glee their dancing little fingers. O, what does it matter to most of them? They will undoubtedly marry fine young monsieurs and live in luxury and never have to depend on earning their keep as pianists.

See the rain how gently it falls. And the same rain that falls in Paris also falls in Happy Valley upon the graves of dead Tom and Laura and all the others in that mournful place.

And it is just me now, here in my lovely apartment with its tall windows and high ceilings and carpets
& the letters, Tom's journal and my recordings of
the unhappy memory of a
life done too soon.
Play my little darlings, play.

Chapter 18

Tom Dooley

Days that twisted in my gut like tainted food came and went without relief and still I refused to go over the bald again to see Laura. I had an old squirrel gun and I'd look at it and think what it would be like to press the barrel to my head and send myself to wherever people like me end up when they're dead. I wondered if I'd feel an instant of pain before I died, would it be just a sharp, jagged thing that ripped through my senses. I took up the gun several times and tested its heft—it seemed all out of balance to me, much like my life.

But I couldn't do it. My hands could never take another life, not even my own. The war had ruined my taste for blood.

My hands trembled terribly when I put the gun back in its corner.

But, I sometimes think the real reason I couldn't kill myself was because I didn't want any of the others to have free rein with Laura. The thought of her with another man made the ache in my belly seem all the worse. And yet, I refused to go over the bald for fear I'd see Grayson's horse there, or Swain's or Billy Dixon's—or any of the others who were after her. Thinking of their hands on her, their mouths their hungry eyes . . .

O, that your passion was so great for someone worthy of such love, Tom.

O, that it were.

But as it turned out, I didn't have to go to her. Instead, she returned to me.

This time she arrived under a rainless sky.

You're not dancing, Tom.

It ain't raining.

Golly but her smile could melt lead.

You only do your dancing in the rain?

I didn't answer, for I was afraid of my anger, what I might say to turn her away, but glad she was there and too full of pride to speak.

You only do things you like, don't you, Tom? You make promises to a woman, then break them because you changed your mind and don't feel you owe anybody any explanation, including me.

O, she had such beautiful skin—like that of a doll's.

Bisque?

Yes, that's it, I believe.

Tell of her beauty, how it made you weak and willful and willing to do anything.

I snubbed up on her. I wanted her to know I was mad at her for allowing Grayson to come round, knowing he'd try and win her over with his fancy ways, his fine horse and money, knowing I was no match for such. So I didn't say anything for a long time. I wanted her to make an effort to win back my affection and finally she did.

The cat got your tongue, Tom Dooley?

About the onliest cat I know is you, Miss Foster.

What's that supposed to mean?

Means what it means.

Well, she couldn't understand why I was the way I was and I was too damn het up to explain it just then, so I stood there not saying more, for I knew if I did words might come out that could never be put back in. In spite of how mad I was, deep down I didn't want to run her off. I just wanted this madness to go away and to feel like she wanted only me.

She abided your anger; it didn't trouble her that you were so taciturn?

She didn't run off, if that's what you mean.

No, I suppose she did not.

And did I tell you she had sunlit hair and cornflower blue eyes?

I remember her as pretty, Tom.

She stood her ground and I stood mine. I was mighty snubbed.

Ain't you going to tell me what's wrong, Tom?

Then, before I could stop it, it burst out of me like I suppose those pigs did that fellow Shinbone was telling me about—the ones Jesus scared out of that lunatic fellow.

You letting Grayson court you is what's wrong.

Oh, Tom, you don't know a thing about my heart.

I know what I seen when I came over the bald. I seen his horse tied up out front of your pap's and not a body in sight. Reckon you were all tucked inside having a high old time of it.

He come to court me, yes. But I wouldn't have nothing to do with him. Him and Pap sat around talking crops, the weather, pigs. Talking and drinking whiskey.

She laughed then, suddenly and freely as a happy child. O, she could be such a happy child at times. Still I didn't want to give in to her.

What's so damn funny?

How it is you think I'd fall in love with a man old as my pap. You must think me broke in the head. I could have me any man in the valley if I wanted, why'd I want an old one like Mr. Grayson?

There's one man you can't have so easily.

Who might that be?

Me, is who.

You think not?

I know so.

She slid off her pap's horse, come to me then, her eyes fixed on mine. I could feel all my anger just melting away like late snow on the sunny slope of the bald. And when she got close, still staring into my eyes, I thought of that squirrel gun and how I was glad I hadn't used it.

So you believed her, that she hadn't been unfaithful with Grayson?

Yes. I would have believed just about anything she told me. O, I can't tell no more to you, Liza. I can't go on telling it to you.

Elizabeth Brouchard

It is a small victory I claim without wanting to. Surely he sees it in my eyes when he talks to me about Laura and Ann, how it wounds me even though I do my best to remain stoically his friend. But try to tell a heart that loves that it can only be a heart of friendship. I do my weeping alone in the sanctuary of darkness even as I hear the men who visit my father's tavern laughing and cursing through the thick walls—their voices as nearly muted as my tongue, but not so muted I cannot hear the din of their shamelessness, or hear my heart breaking.

Tom Dooley

When you are gone away each day and evening from me, Liza, I write down those things I cannot always say to you, or those things that I've forgotten. I write things that come to me unbidden, like love or rain or sorrow. I don't always know what words I'll write, what thoughts I'll have, what forces move my hand.

The sound of the pen's scratching is a small comfort to me.

O' Daughter of Jerusalem, take thy hands and absolve me.

Bend thy heart to my heart's will, and rain upon me warm kisses.

Let delicate words woo and win me, let me partake of thy fruits.

Of thy passion let me sing, and swallow down the bitter wine of Sorrow so that only joyousness flows between us like blood shared.

These things I write without will or want.

I read the words and wonder if maybe some spirit isn't taking me over, preparing me for the long death. For, where else would such things come if not from another's spirit? Laura's spirit, perhaps?

This too, I remember about that day:

Tom, you're such a sensitive fool. Why I've already promised my heart to you.

But when I came over the bald and seen Grayson's horse . . .

Let's not talk about that old man . . . let's go inside and let me show you my truth.

So inside we went, into the cabin that became our small sanctuary. And once inside, she did everything I'd dreamed of her doing. She did it as though she knew my heart better than I knew it. She pressed her mouth to mine and in the doing I breathed her into me and tasted her tangy thick tongue and nibbled at her lips. She was like sweet music playing over my skin.

Oh, Tom. I wish you had come to court me, but since you didn't, I've come to court you.

Peeling away my shirt, her hungry mouth upon my mouth, my fingers woven in her sunlit hair. *I sing thy song.* She was fresh and ready as ripened fruit and when I lifted her and carried her to my bed, she seemed made of nothing at all; she was pure lightness, the lightness of butterfly wings.

I remember how exactly she watched me as I removed her dress. How exactly her eyes never left mine nor mine hers until we was fully naked.

Is this what you crave, Tom? Am I what you want above all others?

Yes, yes.

Then I give myself to you gladly and without reserve.

Then I sing love's song so all the angels can hear.

The gates of love part for thee, dear Tom.

And my gaze traveled the long length of her, from the small round breasts with their rosy tips to the inward curve of her ribs just above her jutting hips. Down along the length of her legs, firmer than I'd expected, down to her feet delicate as porcelain. I touched my lips to her throat and she uttered tiny pleasures.

And as I kissed her, angels stood guard.

I kissed this place and that, the hollows and the hills of her. My lips suckled her breasts and made their tips grow tender and firm as sun-warmed berries.

I cry out to thee & bring to thee love and promises of love.

Tom, Tom . . .

She was like a woman praying to her Lord—supple and beholden. Her fingers threaded through my hair and she pulled me upwards again and I kissed her fully on the mouth, my thumbs swiping away her tears. I asked her if this was what she wanted, should I stop, leave her be, save our love for another time.

Oh, Tom, you know so little about me. I know so little about you. I cry because I am as happy as I've ever been. Don't stop loving me. Please, don't ever stop loving me.

And I promised her that I wouldn't.

My lips brushed over the delicate valley of her stomach, my mouth resting there for a moment, my hand poised just below on the golden thatch of her sex feeling its warmth rising to greet my palm. I felt safe there with her, told her I did, and she spoke gentle with me all the while.

I am shelter to your love.

You are my harbor from stormy seas.

Rest for a while here in me.

I will rest for a while.

I kissed where my hand had been resting, the tiny golden hairs tickling my nose. I wanted to drink in her scent, never be without it as she trembled and whispered to me. O, I was drunk with her and she with me.

I've never had it so, Tom. I've never let a man do these things to me.

Then I want to be the first.

Then be the first. Be the first man to do these things to me, Tom.

My hunger was greater for her than it had ever been for any woman and I took my pleasure in her, giving her, as she told me afterward, the greatest pleasure she could have ever imagined. And the more I gave her, the greater my own pleasure. The more I took from her the more I wanted to take. And she let me do every little thing to her.

For in thy harbor I am safe, thy love is a fortress against my enemies.

The waters are calm, Tom. The waves have all been broken upon the shore.

Afterwards she lay in my arms seeming hardly more than a child to me, small and warm and vulnerable, but happy. I closed my eyes and thought I must surely be in a dream, for nothing real could be as sweet. And she spoke to me as a lover would speak.

Was I everything you hoped for, Tom?

Can't you tell?

I want to hear you say it.

You were more than everything I expected, Laura. You were more than any man could want.

I want it to always be this way between us.

It will be. I promise you that it will be.

Tom . . .

She wept softly, she said, from the happiness that was in her. Her tears were a warm rain against my shoulder that cooled with time. The delicate way she wept stirred my pleasure for her again. I think somehow she knew it would, for she didn't protest when I positioned her o'er me. She didn't resist when my cob entered her, did naught but close her eyes and arch her back and take me as deeply as either of us could go.

Oh, lovely Prince, how shall I be for thee?

A wanton girl, a daughter of Jerusalem, a virgin bride . . .

And pray thee hear my call and answer it and

Never leave me outside the harbor of your love—

Nor lock the door upon my heart, nor cast me away

From thy sanctuary—I love only thee, Tom. I love only thee.

This I write even though I don't know if she said these words or they were simply words born in my bones that fateful day and are there in my bones still. For, love is a tangled thing that tangles the mind and ruins all reason.

We spent the entire day in each other's embrace and by the time the sun had crossed from the east mountains to the west, we were weak from our passion. I knew that our fates were forever tied together; that whatever happened to one, would affect the other.

Tom, I must go, or my pap will come looking for me.

He will be fearful his lovely daughter has fallen into the hands of someone like me.

No, not that.

Her laughter was like a wren's chirp.

He loves his dang horse more than me and he'd be feared someone had stolen it and come looking for it.

And he'd be disappointed to find you here with me.

He has high dreams of me marrying above my raising.

Go on, then, and marry rich.

O, don't make my tears of joy turn to tears of sorrow—don't ruin it, Tom, this special hour.

I thought of course she was fooling with me, but she assured me that her pap treasured his horse more than her.

He'd trade ten of me for one like Mr. Lee.

That's what he named it, Mr. Lee?

After the general.

185

Then you better ride home fast and stay there until I come for you.

Oh, Tom, will you come for me? Will you come and take me away and make me your wife?

Yes, yes, soon, soon.

I watched her ride off toward the bald, my heart wanting to race after her. I watched her go just as I watched her every time she came to visit me, always worried her pap would discover us whilst coming to look for his horse. I thought often of shooting his Mr. Lee just so he'd quit loving it more than his own daughter.

Now my thoughts and hand are weary and through the small window I see a field of stars, a moon tipped on its side, all against a chalkboard night. The walls are cool and damp, my life is a tomb that shrinks round me, and Laura sleeps alone in a dark grave of desire's doing.

I wish I were with her—and soon enough I reckon I will be.

My solace is, that you will not read some of this while I am still alive, Liza. But if you do, know this: love made me its wretched fool.

Elizabeth Brouchard

O, I've read it a hundred times, Tom. I could not help but reading it. I read it on quiet days when the little mademoiselles aren't here playing the piano. I read it in the dull winter light and sip warm tea with a shawl over my shoulders and wonder what it would have been to have you love me with such passion and desire as you did Laura that day when she came to you, when you were all *snubbed up* at her, your anger and jealousy and gladness all stirring inside you until it became a fire that burned you up.

Following the heat of anger is the heat of passion.

This I know, Tom.

Not by your hand, but by another's.

But it is with regret, love; with the warmest and saddest regret of all regrets that I confess such things to your ghost.

O, but that your hand had been the one and only hand that touched me in my desire. That would have been my fondest wish. And now there is only memory of those things, of those touched and untouched places and my regret is still great, but less so with each passing day.

My love may have saved you, saved us all.

But love so mute has no voice.

And who listens to the silence?

CHAPTER 19

Tom Dooley

Once I had made my vow to marry Laura, I knew I had to contend with Ann. But Ann wasn't the only one—there was Pearl too.

I felt it only fair to tell Pearl straightaway that I loved another and would not see her again. Of the two, she would be the easier to deliver the news to. So I went first to her place. Once arrived and into her little shack she was full of questions.

Who, Tom? Who do you love so that you won't see me again? Is it Cousin Ann? It doesn't matter to me—see her and see me if you must.

No, it's not Ann. But you must not mention to her about this.

Oh, Tom, I will kill myself. I will throw myself into the Yadkin and take my own life!

Like Raymond did? Because he couldn't have the one he wanted?

Oh, how can you mention his name to me? You're so cruel, Tom. This love you speak of has made you cruel.

I'd stood off in the brambles waiting for Melton and Ann to leave together so I could visit with Pearl, and one day they did when the sky was gray and lifeless as flannel. I stood and waited for them to go round the bend toward Reedy Branch. Chickens scratched in the yard and a rooster stood atop an upturned bucket and crowed and crowed.

I waited for Pearl to come into the yard. She had a butcher knife in her hand and I watched as she chased down one of the

188

hens, then sliced off its head, its wings flapping furiously, then tossed it aside. The chicken stumbled and fought the death visited upon it, splattering bright red raindrops of blood over the ground. Pearl stood and waited, the knife in her hand. It looked like a small smile played at her mouth—but maybe it was a grimace.

I came out of the brambles and she started, then ran to me and flung herself into my arms.

I'm needy for you, Tom. Where you been? Cousin Ann and Melton have gone to Reedy Branch. We've all day alone.

I can't, I can't.

This is when I told her I loved another.

What is there for me to live for if you don't love me anymore?

Why, everything. Fact is, I know a fella right this minute who is interested in you.

Some of the gloom went out of her eyes.

Who?

Billy Dixon.

Billy Dixon?

Yes.

That pit-faced schoolteacher?

He talks to me all the time about you, how he'd like to come courting you.

But Tom, I don't want nobody's love but your'n.

All the while she pressed herself to me, held me in her grip, and I admit I was worried a little she might take that big knife of hers and plunge it into my liver, for I've seen what crazy love will do.

I know it, Pearl, but I've met another. Give me credit for my honesty.

O, how could this be? How can you say you met another when you said you loved only me?

She was distraught and I wasn't sure I could calm her. I

knew she'd subside given time, but what I didn't know was if she'd tell Ann. If she did, I had a whole other problem to contend with.

What can I do to make it up to you, the hurt I've carried to you this day?

Nothing. O, nothing at all, Tom Dooley.

Surely there has to be something.

She wept and chattered her teeth and stormed about. I wondered then and there if it was a mistake to tell the truth. I wondered if those we love, or those who love us, ever really want the truth said when it comes to matters of the heart—lies seem life's only real comfort.

It'll do you no good, Pearl, all this weeping and carrying on. I've made up my mind and I come here out of respect for you and your feelings. I could have lied to you, kept carrying on with you and nobody the wiser. But I didn't.

She knelt in the dust meowing and declaring how life was over for her, that she'd never love another, me trying to convince her otherwise but growing weary of such dramatic carryings-on.

Well, I've done about all I can, Pearl. I don't know what else there is to say or do.

I turned to leave, figuring I'd take my chances she'd not tell Ann. But I wanted a little insurance too.

You know if Cousin Ann finds out what we been doing behind her back, she'd throw you out, you'll be without even a bed to sleep in.

I felt bad having to use a threat, but it was probably the truth; Ann would throw her out without an ounce of pity. That seemed to stop momentarily her anguish.

I should plunge this here knife into my heart!

Billy Dixon would sure be sorry if you did.

She was further removed from her distress by the small flattery. I took it as an opportunity for a more gentle approach. I knelt down next to her, took the knife from her hand.

Why love never goes on forever, Pearl. Nothing ever goes on forever, even the most beautiful love. Things change, people change, their hearts change with them. Why even if I'd never met another, who's to say things between you and me would have lasted forever?

I guess I can see some of the reasoning in what you're saying.

Sure you can. Old Billy will love you twice as hard as I ever could. Why, me, I'm just a wild weed. I wouldn't make you a good man. Billy's got himself a fine profession. He'd make you a better man than I would Pearl—give you a home and babies.

She looked at me with her mud brown eyes, the little dark centers like drops of ink.

I'd a made you a good woman, Tom.

Sure you would have. And you'll make Billy a good woman too.

He really talks about me?

All the time. Boy is just pining away after you, day and night. Drinks because he's so lonely for you, Pearl.

Well . . .

You'll see. But you can't say nothing to Cousin Ann about us, it'll ruin everything.

She suddenly lurched for me, threw her arms about my neck, and held on tight, the warmth of her breath blowing on my cheek like summer wind.

Just one more time and I won't say nothing, Tom.

One more time of what?

Of going in the bed with me.

Pearl, I promised to remain faithful to my new love.

O, Tom, become faithful to her on the morrow, but today be unfaithful with me. Just once more before you go, before Billy comes to court me, before you and me can't be unfaithful anymore.

I tried to slip her embrace, to walk away and remain faithful to Laura. You see, Liza, how it was for me? How hard I tried to do the right thing? I tried my almightiest. But there we were alone in the glade, our secret guarded by the wind and pines and the mountains—guarded by the silent sun and silence.

I promise I won't say anything to Cousin Ann if you'll be with me just this once more . . .

And the pleasure of her mouth wasn't completely unwanted.

Afterwards, when I came out into the yard, buttoning my trousers and hitching on my shirt, Pearl, exhausted on the bed, I saw the chicken lying dead—a lump of bloody feathers—where it had finally quit fighting its fate. I wondered if chickens had worries like humans, or if they were just chickens and didn't know anything. Surely they were incapable of thinking about things such as death. I thought I'd rather be a chicken in that bloody moment.

Pauline Foster

He told you I begged him? Now that is a foolish thing. Why should I beg a man who told me he loved another? O, you don't believe him. Surely you don't. Tom can be such a liar when he wants to be. Anything to save himself from slander and shame. He lied about poor Laura, didn't he? He said he never done it. But I heard him with my own ears confess it. I heard him and Cousin Ann saying how they done it because Laura gave them the pox. Gave it to him and them he gave it on to Ann.

O, Tom Dooley is a liar and a sinner and as far as I'm concerned a murderer as well and whatever the hangman does to him cannot repay the pain and shame he's done to all the rest of us. All any of us ever did—Ann or Laura or me—was to try and love him. But you can't love a man who has the devil in him. You can't ever love a man like that.

Elizabeth Brouchard

Once again I hear what others say about you, Tom. I listen and sometimes wonder if I am like them—a fool? Am I a fool, Tom? Has your tongue grown so used to lies that they seem the truth to you? Tell me what it was, Tom, that finally was your ruin, for surely love cannot cause ruin unless it isn't true love. Surely it can't.

Tom Dooley

Shinbone said that plenty of great and lesser men have fallen to the temptations of a woman. He said the landscape of history is littered with such deceits. Shinbone says Laura and me were star-crossed, like Romeo and Juliet.

O, such sweet references. Do you think you were really, Tom?

I don't know. Shinbone said that some of the greatest men in the Bible were victims of temptresses.

But weren't they willing victims, Tom?

O, I know it.

And how could a man less great than a prophet resist such temptation? Is that how you reason it, Tom?

O, I hate to tell you these things. I truly hate it.

After I left Pearl's that day, I'd gone and told Billy Dixon that I'd talked to Pearl and that she was eager for him to come courting. He sat on the front row plank of his little schoolhouse, a stunned look in his speckled eyes.

What'd make her all of a sudden open to such a proposal, do you suppose?

Hell, Billy, don't go looking any gift horses in the mouth.

What'd she want me for, except maybe to tease, have somebody she could reject like you did her?

Goddamn, Billy, you the most down in the mouth son of a bitch I ever seen.

O, hell, Tom.

Just go on and court her. Pick her a mess of wildflowers, stop and buy a ribbon from Mizrus Boots to tie them with. Go at night so she can't see your face if it'll make you feel better.

He sat and squirmed like a schoolboy being asked to recite his lessons. I cuffed him on the back of the head.

*You don't go, old George Hare or Sam Pie or one of them will.
They'll be plowing her field quicker than you can blink. Empty-
headed gals like Pearl don't last long in this neck of the country. Old
George will fill her belly full of babies and Sam'll work her like a
mule.*

Empty-headed and homely, you mean.

It don't matter she ain't the prettiest . . .

That seemed to light a fire under him.

I guess if I'm going to, I better get on over there.

*You sure better. And don't forget them wildflowers. Women go mush
over flowers.*

He was a sight to see, heading out of that schoolhouse. I was
happy for him, damned if I wasn't.

Elizabeth Brouchard

You were both fools, you and Billy. How strange things turn
out. To have heard you say these things to me, to have read your
writings about such things, was like trying to handle a sharp
knife: no matter how I tried to deal with it, it always cut me and
I always bled a little.

Tom Dooley

Door opens and closes—a clatter of iron, the silence that follows after the footsteps have stopped.

I take out my pen and listen for the cooing of the mourning
dove, the ache of the cicada, the thrum of the frog. I wish I had
my fiddle here to play. I wait for the words to come. It goes like
that sometimes. I dip my pen into the bottle of ink and wait and
nothing comes, as though the spirit has fled me, refuses to
speak. Thump of Keyes's wood leg on the stairs as he brings me
a biscuit for supper.

I'd a brought you some side meat, Tom, but it was tainted.

He is a kindly man, what's left of him. Thump, thump, goes
his wood leg. Thump, thump, goes the heart. Thump, thump,

the drum I used to beat but beat no more. My hand begins to move over the foolscap, my eye follows the flow of ink:

Thy love is like summer's heat.

Thy eyes the color of an autumn day.

Thy lips are as cool as winter snow.

Thy heart is full of spring's hope.

Thy promises are like the seasons

That come and go in ceaseless wonder.

My heart is bursting with untold joy.

I call to thee but never an answer.

My hand shakes and I lay aside the pen, for they are not my words, my thoughts, but those of a spirit that abides in me. I can hear her voice inside my head. The ink pools on the page like spilled black blood.

Ann called the house one morning when mist still slept in the hollows.

Tom! Tom!

Laura's pap's horse was tied up outside and surely Ann saw it.

Oh no. Pearl has given us away and now everything will be ruined.

And when I looked out the window and saw her there in the yard, her face a fury and she saw me, she drew a finger across her neck, as though she were slicing off a chicken's head. I started to dress, but by time I came out, Ann was nowhere to be seen—gone back to Melton's I reckoned, to scheme the ways in which she would rain down misfortune on us all.

Ye, who destroy my heart will I destroy his heart in kind.

And ye, who ruin my love, will have his love ruined in equal measure.

Do not tempt the temptress, Tom, for the apple is a poison I offer thee.

My hand trembles and I must hold it steady. More and more

of this black feeling seeps into me and won't let go. I can't explain it proper. And in the night I dream of a smiling hangman who owns the face of Louis.

Hidey, Tom.

Hidey, Louis.

The colonel sent me.

Which one?

Why Colonel Grayson of course.

The hard knot of rope is scratchy round my neck. The fingers that place it there, tender.

The neck I kissed on those lonely nights I now must break. You understand, don't you, Tom?

Then kiss it once more before you do.

The trap below my feet swings free and I go rushing down.

I am jerked taught.

I dance in the air a jig of dying.

The lovely bosom of Abraham beckons.

I am timeless.

Elizabeth Brouchard

And when all was said and done—when things got sorted out. When seasons changed again and again and love sloughed off its skin like an old snake growing older and wiser still—Billy came to me and sought my advice and in his seeking, I saw not so much his pitted face, his uncertain ways, his foolish past, but saw instead the potential of something greater.

O, how these things do play themselves out well.

So that we can hardly tell

What the Gods did send us in love's disguise

to test and ruin us—portrayed us as wise

& lovey as dancing doves through whose wings

the sunlight shows fine bones of deceit and other things.

Rest on, timeless Tom. Rest on.

Chapter 20

Tom Dooley

Newbolt comes to question me again. It is early and he is disheveled as though he's slept in his clothes and doesn't care. He asks and asks me about Laura and murder.

And on the day Laura disappeared, you left the county. Isn't that correct?

Me and half dozen other fellas.

But it was you the finger of guilt was pointed toward.

You write of it how you want to, Mr. Newbolt. I know what happened, and I know what didn't happen. But folks round here already made up their minds I was the one done it.

He strikes a match to light his cigar. In the flare, his face becomes a jack-o'-lantern, a shred of gray forelock dangles over one eye. Morning light has not sought out this place yet and the match flare is like a bursting sun.

I'm tired of answering the same questions.

The search for the truth is a tiring task, Tom.

Let me be. O, let me be.

Newbolt is as worrisome to me at times as was Ann. They both fray my nerves. How I withstood her assaults in the face of everything now, I hardly understand. I remember the time she came and pitched stones at my door.

You're in there with that little whore!

I tell Laura to stay put, to let me handle matters.

Her eyes were full of questions; fear maybe. Who could blame her? O, the fear that must have shot through her in her final moments before the flame of life was snuffed out of her. I calmed Laura as best I could before going out to confront Ann.

Hogsheads of clouds were ganged up along the west ridge of the brooding mountains. Belly-rumbling thunder followed forks of lightning. The air tasted like tin.

Go on home to Melton, Ann. Go on back to your husband.

Not till you bring her out here where I can see her!

It's none of your business.

Ann was dirty-faced, barefoot, and shameless, her hair a bramble, her eyes white with raving.

You've gotten into Melton's liquor. You're drunk as a damn skunk.

Maybe so. But I ain't too drunk to know what you and that little bitch been doing behind my back! And I'll cut your heart out and hers too and feed them to the damn dogs.

It's just something that happened, that's all. I didn't plan on nothing, and neither did Laura.

Oh, goddamn you to hell, Tom Dooley! Goddamn you both.

Maybe He will.

Maybe I'll lend Him a hand in seeing you both go there.

A gray streaky curtain of rain swept in over the spiny backs of the mountains. First along the ridges, then down the slopes, turning them darkly wet before reaching the glade. Ann hardly seemed to notice, stood glaring, her wet hair becoming plastered to her head, her dress soaked through and through. There was truth and a coldness to the air, like a dishonest heart revealed. The whole of the valley was swept with rain. But that cold rain didn't cool her and my attempts to reason didn't cool her.

You'll see, my bastard lover. You'll see not to tamper with a woman's heart.

I never tampered with it. What we had, we had. And now it's finished.

It ain't never going to be finished for me, Tom Dooley. Never!

It never should have gotten started after you married Melton.
Leave it be, Ann. Go on home and let old dogs sleep.

The wetness of her dress became like a second skin, thin and
hiding nothing of what was underneath. I think she wanted for
me to see her like that, hoping she might tempt me away from
Laura.

But when I didn't move to go to her, she lifted her skirts and
showed me her nakedness. I looked away, looked off toward the
blotted ridges, the gray nothingness the world had become. I
didn't want to see her that way anymore. My desire for her was
as damp and sodden as the cold rain. I had no more truck for
her.

I ain't tempted. Nothing you will do will tempt me.
Look at me, goddamn you!

She screamed and screamed until I looked. Her bare legs
were mud splattered, her cunny closed up like a flower against
the chill. Water ran down the inside of her thighs. But nothing
she did or said or showed me could change my mind.

I don't care for what I see.
You cared for it once well enough.
I don't care for it no more.

I knew without looking that Laura was watching us from the
window. I knew how upset Ann's lewd display must have been
for her. But I couldn't help the way Ann was acting any more
than I could help what later on happened. Ann was a woman
driven by mad passions; everything with her was full bore. And
I understood that part of her, it was that part of what made me
desire her in the first place, and it was that part of what made
me want to leave her in the end. I finally understood why
Melton felt helpless to deal with her, why he never took her out
behind the shed and whipped her with his belt or divorced her.
He was afraid of her lusts and how nothing would stop her
from having them. And there in the yard that day I was a little

afraid of her too. Not for myself so much, but for Laura or anyone else that Ann thought was trying to steal from her those desires.

Then I curse you, Tom Dooley. I curse you and that witch whore of yours.

Stop it!

You just keep going around fucking this one and that and you'll get yours. You'll sure enough get yours and so will she!

Silver wires of lightning danced atop the ridge, the surrounding sky blue black. Thunderclaps shook the ground. I started to tell Ann to clear out when a bolt of lightning split a tulip poplar to its roots just beyond my tool shed and turned the air raw.

I heard Laura cry out from the cabin and turned and saw her standing in the doorway.

And when I turned back again, Ann was gone.

What'd she want, Tom? What was Cousin Ann doing with her dress pulled up?

Nothing, she's gone crazy I think.

She's in love with you, isn't she?

She's crazy, that's all it is.

Oh, Tom, I don't believe it—that'd she act that away.

The storm pulled its clever tricks for the better part of an hour, then marched on leaving behind a gloom in its wake. And even after it marched on, I could hear the rumble of thunder and neither of us felt in the mood to make love, so we just lay there listening to the baying storm marching on. Then Laura got up and went to the window and looked out, I thought to see if Ann had returned.

Pap's horse has run away, Tom.

The rope she'd tied the horse with dangled from the tree limb.

You go on home and I'll go look for him and bring him round when I find him.

I don't understand, Tom. About you and Cousin Ann. I thought you said you was finished with her.

You know how she is. She just won't quit a thing. Don't worry none about it. Go on now, start for home, I'll come round later with your pap's horse.

Something precious between us had been broken, left dangling, like that horse rope. I couldn't fix it no matter how hard I tried. I knew that when a thing between a man and woman gets broken, it can't be fixed completely—it will always be a little bit broken.

Ann Foster Melton

O, he was such a craven man when he wanted to be. Craven and cruel and Laura was such a pretty little fool for his lies. Like we all were. And if I'm not mistaken, little mute angel, you are too. I can see it in your eyes. O, you don't fool me with your silence and high-minded ways. A woman can always tell what flows in another woman's heart by the way she tilts her head, the way her eyes glow when the mention of love's object is spoken. You don't fool me one little bit. But you wouldn't be the only fool he's charmed. I think Tom could charm a snake out of its skin, for it takes one to know one, don't you see.

Sure I confronted him about Laura. I let him know he couldn't have us both just because he thought we were such fools. Her, maybe, but not me. I know what you're thinking little mute angel that you are: you're thinking I was a married woman and I was trying to have both my husband and Tom. But I'd run away from Melton in a heartbeat if Tom would have only asked. He never did. I think he liked it that I was already tied to another. He liked coming and going as he pleased without any of the obligation that true love holds.

It was the devil in him, don't you see. For what good man would have another man's wife right under her husband's nose.

Think of me what you will. It don't matter. It don't matter a goddamn.

Tom Dooley

Newbolt questions and questions and questions.

So Laura was suspicious of Ann. And was she also frightened of her?

I reckon she was, but I wasn't going to admit how bad things was, frighten the fragile little thing that she was. As far as being scared of Ann . . . well, Ann could be scary when she got het up over something.

You were the instrument of her anger, you and Laura.

I wasn't the instrument of nothing.

Truth became a weapon.

Suddenly I wanted to smoke a cigar and be fat with freedom.

You have a fancy way of putting everything.

Just searching for the truth, Tom. That's all.

No more now, Mr. Newbolt, maybe tomorrow.

All right, Tom. I'll come round tomorrow then. Sleep well.

Oh, I think of it now and I want to write of it in a way that fixes everything, that does away with Ann and her madness, and the murder and all the rest of it. I want to rewrite the tale so it has a happy ending, one where nobody's heart is ever broken, where no dreams are lost to the terrible days of reality. Promise me, Liza, you'll write it for me if I can't.

In the fury of thy passion, love was lost to thee.

Oh stop it, hand!

Thy bloody passion left thee a broken
Wingless spirit bound to earth eternally.

Oh, goddamn, goddamn . . .

Maids of honor tend to thy bride. Buckle her shoes and
Put fine combs and soft ribbons in her hair

Laura, is that you?

. . . & kiss tenderly thy pretty eyes closed for ere more.

The ink spills upon the page and drowns the words in a black lake from which rises no hope. The ink stains my fingers, my cuffs, as black blood would do were I to bleed it; and I can't wash it from me.

I dream I dance with Laura's corpse in a moonstruck glade.

Tyree Shinbone

Dance with her Tom. Dance and dance and dance.

Tom Dooley

Shinbone is sitting outside my cell when I open my eyes. He has arrived with the morning. He possesses the smile of an idiot.

I feel lost, Tyree. My dreams are torturing me.

God is with you, boy. He is everywhere and sees into our hearts and knows of our sins.

No. He ain't in this place. He is not with me.

How can you be so certain? You claim to know the one thing, but deny the other.

Because this ain't no godly place, because I got me a coldness in my bones. The devil stole my soul in the middle of the night while I dreamed of dancing with a corpse.

You've not had your soul stolen, Tom. If anything, you may have sold it.

I ain't sure no more what's what, Tyree.

He sits, one leg crossed over the other, his eyes full of blue madness.

We fucked, Tom.

What?

Me and Mizrus Boots. We fucked.

A deep ache crawls through my chest, into my neck, my jawbone.

I don't want to hear your ravings, Tyree. Get out the checkerboard or let me be. Let me not think of tragedies, false or real, and do not tell them.

It was when I went to fetch you your ink and foolscap . . .

Stop it!

And I told her how long it had been since I'd been with a woman and she fed my longing with her own . . .

I'll call Keyes and have you thrown out.

She said I mesmerized her with my longing . . .

Keyes! Keyes!

Well, of course one thing led to another . . . man being man and woman being woman. We was natural, Tom. We was natural and what we done was natural. I understand now fully what you went through with Laura and Ann and Pauline.

If not for the steel latticework of the door, I would strangle him.

You see, Tom, the reason I tell you these things is the preacher has no one to confess his sins to and you are the perfect one for me to tell such things to.

I'm not your confessor. Confess to that God of yours if you need to confess at all.

Keyes rattles open the door, his wood leg thumping impatiently.

What goes in here?

I want to be left alone. Will you please get this madman out of my sight?

Let's go, preacher. Leave the boy be.

She was a virgin, Tom. She told me so. She was as tender as ten virgins . . .

I hear the scrape of the wood leg on the stone floor as Keyes wrestles Shinbone out, hear the madman say—*Oh, it was a delicate act, but one well done and now she will not have to go to her grave wondering what the love of a man . . .*

Move along you crazy son of a bitch!

Shuffling, grunting, stumbling. A chair falls, a door slams closed, a bolt is thrown. At last silence, sweet and lovely silence.

I weep for the spinster if what Tyree says is true. I wonder if he raped her or put a drug in her water. I worry he's spoilt her as I'd spoilt Laura. When Mizrus Boots comes to see me the next day I look deeply into her eyes and see only the same happy eyes I always see as she passes me the foolscap and ink to replace that which I've spilled and ruined the paper with.

I can't tell by looking at her if Shinbone has told a lie or not. She doesn't mention his visiting. I think if the madman has done what he said and Mizrus Boots is unwilling to confess it— then it is a secret she keeps for good reason. For maybe it wasn't rape at all, but some form of strange desire that overtook her and caused her to give herself willingly to the crazed preacher. Who can know the heart of anyone, the hidden desires too long unattended?

Take thy love swiftly, without regret. Look not back upon the heart's reason.

Mizrus Boots smells of lilac water, her cheeks are rosy as though recently pinched.

I've been praying for you, Tom. We all have.

Thank you kindly.

Tom?

Yes'm.

No one is completely innocent in the eyes of God, and no one fully guilty.

I just want to be innocent in the eyes of these who would see me hanged.

Through the bars her fingers touch mine, and I wonder had they also touched the mad Tyree in ways more intimate. And if they did, did he kiss them tenderly, suckling each one in a state of hungry passion that clouded her judgment?

Bless you ma'am, for your kindness.

You've become like a son to me. I never married or had children of my own.

Never met the right man?

Yes, I did once, but . . .

For the first time her eyes lose a bit of their happiness.

I need to know something?

Yes, Tom?

Did . . .

Oh, it's best not to talk about it, don't you see.

Are you all right?

Dear Tom, you've worries enough, haven't you . . . don't worry about me. My life has been lived as it has been lived . . . I've no regrets.

She kneels on the puncheon floor and bows her head and prays for me, calling down God's mercy upon me and all I can think about is the mad preacher's hands holding her, taking every advantage of her, stealing away her purity.

I reach through the bars and touch her hair and when she lifts her face to me, her cheeks are wet with tears.

I must go now, Tom. I won't be back again.

I know.

Goodbye, goodbye.

The scent lilac lingers after she's gone and I breathe it in for it causes me to remember Laura, the smell of her freshly bathed, coming to my bed, her skin smooth and warm, her hair damp against my chest.

Polly Boots

Tom had the child of God's heart in him—you could just see it. He was tender and kind and I felt most sorry for him, most sorry. He looked no more dangerous than a caged pup. O, I don't know if what they say he did is true or untrue—given man's wicked nature, who can say for sure. We are all sinners of a kind, one kind or the other. Let he who is without sin cast the first stone. But surely not me. Surely not me.

Tom Dooley

I open the new bottle of indigo and dip my pen in it and let my hand do what it will under the blind guidance of higher gods. I've no say in it.

I call to thee a thousand times, my love.
I answer love's call a thousand times.
Our echoes of love are like thunder in the night.
Our love calls and calls like the hunger of a child.
Call to thee now O' love, call down the silence.
I can't, I can't, for death has stolen from me thy love
& stilled thy voice for evermore and evermore.

Why, hand, don't you write of the beauty of her face, the sweetness of her mouth, the warmth of her limbs? Why is it harder and harder for me to see her face clearly? Each day cruelly steals a little more of my memory until at last I won't be able to see her at all. Why, hand, don't you tell me how she looked?

I do not know.

Elizabeth Brouchard

I read these things now and wonder. What must it be like for a soul to know its end days are arrived, to stand at the edge of the abyss and look into it?

Billy said to me one day, *That poor son of a bitch. I can't even begin to imagine what it was like for him to sit there in that dirty cell and wait for them to come and hang him.*

O, how I wept the night he said it.

We were standing on the shore of the Atlantic Ocean watching the last of day's light play over the water. Farther out steamships came into harbor, came home again from long journeys. And I thought of you and how you'd said you wished you could have become a sailor—how you'd like to have gone to sea.

Do you think he was guilty?

Billy sighed and crushed out his cigar on his bootheel—a habit of his I always disliked.

Hell, I reckon he must have been—they found him guilty twice and hanged him didn't they?

I know he was your friend—but there comes a certain callousness after the fact, a certain resignation that what was done must have been the correct thing. Billy always had a certain fatalism about him. He would not allow himself to believe that innocent men could be murdered for crimes they did not commit. But Billy was a shortsighted man too—believed only what you put in front of him. It got worse the older he got. Like most men, he gave up idealism for practicality. I grew indifferent toward him later on in life because he lost his dreams and possibilities about us, others, the world.

Don't know why you waste time writing poetry, Liza. Who reads poems but the fey and affected, but the dreamers and fools. You'll never make anything of it, I'm sure.

Billy died a stuffed shirt and I hope he met a practical God at the far end of his last journey, and I hope that I do not.

You would have liked the sea, Tom, watching the steamships come and go to and from unknown places.

We would have been such footloose travelers, you and I.

O, the wonders we would have seen.

Tell me if you can—are there such wonders in that world you now reside?

CHAPTER 21

Tom Dooley

Over the bald each day I went and over the bald she came. Back and forth we journeyed in our love, not caring what the others thought or how they'd have us be.

Billy Dixon came round one sultry afternoon, his face glum as anything, half drunk.

How's it going with you and Pearl?

It ain't, Tom.

How so?

She's got eyes for another.

You waited too long to make your move. I tried to warn you.

No, I made it soon enough. But it didn't stick. How's it with you and Laura Foster?

Let me show you.

I took my fiddle and played for him reels and waltzes and jigs. He sat and listened with a forlorn countenance and when I'd finished I said:

That's how it goes with Laura and me—our love is pure music.

O, how I envy you, Tom. You went off to war and came home a hero, then you found love not once but thrice.

Just a fool who got lucky and didn't get himself killed.

And you courted the gals of this here Happy Valley: married, widowed, single.

Not all true, some courted me, and I never courted a widow.

You made them all love you like faithful hounds love their master.

I wanted to tell him maybe all, except for Ann. How I was afraid to let Laura ride home alone after a certain hour, afraid Ann might be waiting for her along the trail. Ann would have no master over her—she wasn't the sort of woman to let anyone tame her.

It's the damn preacher, Tom. That Shinbone. He's a-courting Pearl now.

My ribs ached hearing it. I don't know why.

Why that's a surprise and a half. I thought all he courted was his God.

Well, if so, he's sure keeping it a fine secret from Pearl. For, what they do with one another sure doesn't have any Godliness in it.

A girl like her is easily deceived, Billy.

I reckon you'd know if anyone would.

I played the fiddle low and sweet to try and turn his mood. But instead he drank his liquor hard and stared at the faithless sky.

If you want, I'll go talk to him, tell him stay away from Pearl.

As if that'd do a bit of good. She'd go to him, so taken with him she's become. She'd go out there in that wilderness camp and eat grass if he told her to.

Then I'll go have a talk with her instead.

O, you don't have to take up for me, Tom. What sort of man would I be to let another present my case? No, no, Pearl's a lost cause to me.

No man ever won a woman by having a faint heart. Fit for her, Billy.

Do I look like the kind of man who'd fight another, who'd even stand a chance of winning were I to?

You fit me good and proper, Billy—why my ribs was sore for a week.

But I sure didn't whip you, Tom. What would it look like to Pearl if I was to fight for her and lose?

We sat and listened to the hoppers sawing in the dry grass, to the crickets singing in the dark cool places under the house. A hound bayed from off somewhere far down the valley as the light of day turned to the color of an old silver spoon that needed polishing.

Someone's dead or dying, Tom.

Why's it you have such in your mind every time you hear a hound baying?

I don't know. I've become like all these others—full of witch tales.

How far'd you get with Pearl before Shinbone came round?

Not too very . . .

The dusky sun glowed golden against his pitted face and made him momentarily lovely. I thought of Louis, how lovely a boy was he. I wondered for a time, before that fatal shot that took him if maybe I lost all manliness. But since that day to this, I've had no doubts. For it was Laura I now loved most truly. And before Laura, it was Ann and maybe even Pearl a little—and others along the way. I think that war just made us all a bit funny and queer about ourselves. The loneliness and fear twisted things in our hearts and passions, made what was true untrue. Made us question everything about ourselves. But I'm okay now.

Billy and I drank until that old evening sun went down beyond the ridge.

It doesn't seem real does it, Tom?

What don't?

This life.

Hell, seems real enough to me.

I mean when you stop and think about it, that we're only here for a short time and then are gone again, it don't make much sense. Why so short a life? What purpose do we serve? What's the dang point?

Whiskey turns you into a thinker, don't it?

I suppose it does.

You was smart, you'd march over and take Pearl from that mad-

man and marry her, Billy.

She'd never do it now that Shinbone's got her under his spell.

Shinbone ain't the marrying kind, but Pearl is.

You had at her plenty, didn't you, Tom?

That ain't important what went on between us. What we was don't have a thing to do with what we are. Yesterday's gone and what happened in yesterday is gone too. If we was all perfect, hell, wouldn't it be a perfect place.

Well, I still can't get it out of my head, what all you done with her and what Shinbone's doing with her right this minute, even if she was to go with me, there'd still be that in my head ever time I got up with her—how she'd had other men.

Ah hell, Billy.

I thought for a moment he was going to fit me again, remembered the sting of his knuckles on my jaw. Son of a bitch could hit for a schoolteacher, I'll give him that.

Elizabeth Brouchard

Did you ever tell Laura about Louis, Tom?

Louis is lost history. It didn't matter none about Louis.

The history of the heart is such a tender tale.

Oh, stop it, Liza.

You begged me to desist my inquires whenever I touched a tender place in your soul. But how could I ever know a thing about you unless I asked the most tender things? I only wanted to know the true you, Tom, not the other you that everyone else knew, or thought they knew. You see that is what love is, wanting to know the true other—not the false. And yes it wounds, the things you sometimes say, but wounds heal with time as long as they have the balm of truth to heal them.

Little did I know I would end up marrying Billy. Who could have foresaw such an event? All that love I had for you simply spilled over to another and was lost; for Billy never had the capacity to accept so much love, had never known it before he met me. I'd thought a man like Billy was capable of returning love measure for measure, so bereft of it had he been. But instead, he'd only learned to be cautious, suspect of any sort of love as true, and I never could teach him about me—not the way I could have taught you, Tom. Not the way I could have taught you.

Tom Dooley

After a time of just sitting, listening to the evening come down around our ears, I grew restless to get on.

Well, Billy, what are you going to do?

Go on home, I reckon.

Just let Shinbone have her?

I reckon.

Maybe you ought to go over and knock the shit out of him and tell him to leave your gal alone.

He's a preacher, Tom.

He's a goddamn madman, crazed in the head as a lightning-struck mule.

Billy eyed the sky as though he expected Jesus or somebody to come down like a bolt of lightning and strike me dead. All I saw when I looked up was the Dog Star.

I always thought you and him were friends, Tom.

Whatever gave you that idea?

You talk about him a lot.

I talk about shooting squirrels a lot, it don't make me friends with squirrels.

Hellfire but you're a confusing man, Tom Dooley.

Damn straight.

Billy slept on my porch that night, mouth so wide open, stars could have fallen in it and he'd never even known the difference. He seemed to me as pitiful as some old hound without a

home, just somebody's nuisance of a creature. I hadn't the
heart to chase him off. But maybe I should have.

Newbolt comes a visiting and offers me a cigar and I take it
and he says:

Are you enjoying your cigar, Tom?

I feel like a banker.

There is a certain je ne sais quoi about a good cigar.

Je ne sais quoi! As if I'd know what that meant. He had a flannel mouth brought all the way from New York. It wouldn't hold
rainwater in this valley. I asked him was he married.

Only to the profession of words, dear boy.

Sometimes I set my hand to writing and strange things happen.

How so?

*I write things I hadn't intended, like as though there is some force
inside me taking over.*

The muse, says he.

The what?

He simply blows smoke rings and grins.

The next day after Billy had gone to sleep on my porch, I
went to see Pearl, to warn her about Shinbone and try and get
Billy into her favor.

*What concern is it of yours, Tom Dooley? I recall it was you who
didn't want nothing to do with me.*

Billy's a good fella, aside from his getting into the bottle at times.

Tyree doesn't drink and speaks sweet words a woman likes to hear.

Billy would too you give him half a chance.

It was a moonstruck night and I told her to blow out the
lamp in case Ann was keeping an eye on things.

She's awful peeved with you, Tom. Curses you left and right.

I can't help none of that. I didn't come here to talk about her.

*Oh, Tom, come back to me. I'll give you more than Laura ever
could.*

She took my hand and placed it on her breast, but I pulled

back like it was fire.

*So there you were with her alone, the night full of moonlight . . .
surely you were tempted.*

I admit I was somewhat. I'm just a human man.

I told her Shinbone would only bring her heartache, that he
wouldn't stick like Billy would stick.

*You claim to know a awful lot about what other fellas want, Tom,
but you don't know a thing about me.*

*I know you're wanting to have me right now, that's how far your
loyalty to Shinbone carries. That your way of showing me how much
you're taken with him, putting my hand on your teat?*

She suddenly kissed me hard and bit my lip so that it bled,
then licked the blood from my mouth and offered her tongue to
me to suck.

And did you take her offer?

I pushed her away is what I did.

*That must have taken great will considering everything that had
already transpired between the two of you—your known history with
her.*

*O, Liza, I know I sound like a no account man, but I wasn't
always. There was a time when I was decent and honorable. I never
killed nobody in that war unless'n he was bound to take my life. I
could have killed more, but I dint. Them poor Yank boys was just like
us Rebs, scared and doing only what they was ordered. I dint like
killin' none of them.*

Pauline Foster

Sure, he came to me and begged me to stay away from Tyree.
He tried his best to convince me to take up with old Billy. But
Billy wasn't nothing compared to Tyree. It was like comparing a
stud horse with a three-legged dog. Tyree had been everywhere
and promised to take me everywhere with him when he left this
valley again. Billy didn't want to do nothing but teach in his

little schoolhouse and drink himself into the bottom of a bottle for all I could see. Billy didn't have no fine ways about him. Tyree had been to London, England and back again. Said he'd take me to India with him. India! I guess you could see why I wasn't about to trade him off for no Billy Dixon.

Tom Dooley

Keyes comes with my plate while I wait for you, Liza.

Supper, Tom.

That side meat moving or is it my eyes?

Har, har.

The side meat's gristly, the mush tasteless, the coffee bitter. I've lost all appetite for everything but freedom. I eat as much as I can, slide the plate under the bars for Keyes to pick up when he returns, and take out my ink and foolscap. Go on, hand, write what you will:

The truth is, I fucked Pearl that night. I fucked her bitterly and hated myself for doing so. I fucked her with haste wanting it to be over quickly, before I had time to think and change my mind. I fucked her in a punishing way. But little did she seem to understand, mistaking instead my carnal sorrow for her cherished love.

Oh, Tom, says she. Oh, Tom, oh, Tom . . . over and over until I wanted to scream. I cursed myself all the way home, along the path, past Billy Dixon's place where I knew Billy to be wallowing drunk out of pity for himself. It's so goddamn easy, I wanted to shout, to wake him with the truth of how easy it was to diddle a girl like Pearl. All you have to do is shove it in, Billy. Just shove it in and she'll be yours.

I hated Pearl and I hated myself and I hated Billy Dixon and the whole damn lot of 'em—ever body but Laura. Laura was the only one who could make me feel clean.

A pain in my chest stops my hand. Approaching death? If so,

I deserve it for such black thoughts.

Keyes comes and picks up my tray, eyes the leftovers.

I wasn't hungry.

Hmmm . . . hmmm . . .

I know he will consume what's left, quietly, secretly; he has the appetite of a goat.

Oh, near forgot, this came for you.

He hands me an envelope through the bars, my name neatly written on it.

I can hear the hunger in his breathing.

I didn't eat off none of that side meat, case you were wondering.

Might just put it between a biscuit. No use throwing it to the dogs.

Hell no, better in your belly than some dog's, Keyes.

Okay, then.

After he leaves, I open the envelope and take out the letter inside.

Dear Tom . . . it begins. I can see it is from Ann.

CHAPTER 22

Tom Dooley

The letter is from Ann, its words are like fishhooks in my flesh. Her accusations far-fetched:

You killed her, Tom, confess it. You killed poor Cousin Laura and now want to lay the blame at my feet.

O, God.

They have me locked up day and night. I plead for mercy. If only you'd confess you done it, I could go home. James comes every day and cries and tells me he loves me and that it is all your doing that has put me here. I know you hate us both, but is that any reason to do what you're doing?

Could it possibly be that Ann is right, that I did the terrible thing they accuse me of, that my trembling hand that trembles now as it takes up the pen is the same hand that . . .

They say I will hang, that they will stretch my pretty neck. How could you hate me so much as to let them do it? Your false love is worse than treason, your heart black as rot if you let them hang me.

I cannot force my eyes away from her scrawl of scorn.

You are a god-awful son of a bitch if you let them hang me, Tom Dooley.

Oh, please, please don't let them do it. Please, yr. Ann

P.S.: . . . who loves you still in spite of everything you done to me.

Ann Foster Melton

O, the carnage Tom Dooley wrought on this place and me. He consorted with me right under my husband's nose and he took liberties with Pearl and poor Laura and about any gal who would let him. He had no more morals than a dog and his ways nearly got me hanged. Were it not for dear sweet James—a faithful husband if ever there was one—I might have gone crazy for the worry. Tom put a knife in poor Laura's bosom as surely as he consorted with me and the others. I don't know why he done it other than her jealousy might have drove him to it. And but for a last minute fit of conscience, he would have let them hang me as well.

O, I'll never forgive him for what he did to us all—the carnage of his lust. But I can see in your sweet little eyes you don't believe he done it. Just be thankful you weren't his next victim little mute girl. It could just as easy be you lying in a grave, as it was dear Cousin Laura.

Tom Dooley

Laura and I swam naked in the Yadkin River in those first warm days of that summer. We swam and lay out on rocks and let the sun warm us. I loved to watch her body drop through the air from the bluff above the river. It was like watching a wingless angel, an arc of pale beauty, innocent and free of earth's bonds. And when she pierced the water, she became as an arrow that pierced my heart. In after her I dove and we would unite in the green coldness beneath the river's surface, the sunlight shattering above us. We would cling to each other, holding our breaths for as long as we could, legs and arms entwined, mouths pressed together, then kick to the surface where we'd gulp in great amounts of air, laughing, splashing like otters.

Oh, Tom, Tom, I'm as happy as I've ever been.

The sound of her happy voice thrilled me and I could not imagine ever being without her.

And when we became too warm from the sun, we would go under a large sheltering oak and recline in its shade and there we would make love to the chattering protests of blue jays and squirrels.

One time we fell asleep and awoke again and I saw a pile of fresh horse apples where there hadn't been any before, and knew that Grayson had come upon us and had seen us lying together in our nakedness. O, what thoughts must have gone through his mind seeing Laura, her beauty exposed to his craven eyes? And I wonder did he do more than simply watch? Thinking about him watching us ruined the lovely day.

I didn't say anything to Laura, letting her remain instead sweetly ignorant. And now thinking back on it, I should have gone and threatened him to never come round again in secrecy. But I had no proof it was him and not some other who'd come upon us.

. . . *you are a god-awful son of a bitch if you let them hang me, Tom Dooley.* Ann's words sting as surely as death itself. But then too, she claims to love me and that sting is almost worse than death.

To think of Laura then, a freshet of life, full of love and laughter—and to think of her now, tiny and curled in that small grave where she will forever be silent—this year and the next and the next she will remain thus for all eternity and the thought causes me to wretch.

I dip the pen into the dark bottle. My hand takes on life of its own.

Thy love was spring, eternal spring.
Thy kiss was as new rain upon my tongue.
Into a lovely flower I grew, fed by love.
I waited for thee in vain through the
Same spring as would always be, until at
Last, the winter called death claimed me.

This my blind hand did write sometime between dark and dawn, Ann's letter lying open on the cot like a paper moth, its wings spread wide.

I wonder if Grayson told Swain he saw us that day by the river, and if Swain told the others—Sam Pie and George Hare and Billy Dixon. And did they laugh and make lewd jokes and rub themselves in drunken desire vowing to have their turn at Laura as well, to take her for their own? And did such desire lead one to murder her? Did one of them come upon her that morning and she refused them? O, so much speculation, who can know the truth of anything? You must understand something, dear Liza, about men, something I learned during the war: given the right, or wrong circumstances, there is nothing beyond what a man is capable of, murder included. Brother Cain slew Brother Abel, after all. Perhaps with Laura, lust was the culprit.

You see, things were later said, I later learned, that caused me to wonder.

What sort of things, Tom?

Little vicious whispers, nothing too specific—but the men eyed me when I came and went from the tavern and spoke close to each other and sniggered. But Grayson never did—he acted above it all—like he had his own secret to keep.

You doubted Laura's fidelity to you?

Not at first.

But later on?

O, I don't know, really. It'd be harsh of me to talk down of her now that she's dead. O, I could have fit them all, every last man, knocked them down and warned them to stay away, to stop their talk. But you know how these mountain men are, Liza: they're rough because they was born rough and they have to stay rough all their lives.

Yes, my own father included.

221

They are truly capable of anything. They dote on cruelty when they think they got you. They'll stick a man as easy as a pig ready for the slaughtering. To them, blood is blood, it don't matter none.

But aren't you one of them too, Tom?

I reckon maybe I am. Maybe I'm worse in a way from some of 'em. I went to war and learnt my business and some of them did not. But we've all got the same dirt under our nails, and gaze upon these same mountains and that same sun.

For it is born in each of you, these rough ways, this cruelty when one among you is weak . . . be it man or woman.

You have to be hard to survive in these mountains.

And determined . . .

Yes, determined to take what you want, what you need or else it will take you.

It is life itself you fight for . . .

Yes, life itself.

And sometimes pleasure too.

And sometimes our pleasure too—when it don't come along easy or natural.

Elizabeth Brouchard

O, my father was a cunning man and I wouldn't put it past him to revel in Tom's undoing, to conspire and bare his teeth, become this feral thing that men do become when drinking and lust enters into their heads and their blood runs hot.

But Papa never showed a penchant for any woman other than Mama. I think she tainted his view of all women until he saw them as little more than things to use, like a gun or knife or slave. He had no true fondness of them after *Mama's* betrayal. So, when Tom told me these things I had no trouble believing him, but dared not look back too harshly on a man whose wife had left him all alone to raise a wilted little flower like myself.

I can hardly write of him at all, so mixed are my feelings . . .

Tom Dooley

That out of town newspaperman, Newbolt, wears checked suits. The sort of suit a man might wear in a big city, but not in Wilkes County.

You must stick out like the old Joe's pecker round here.

Har, har.

You mind my asking what a suit like that costs?

It's silk, Thomas. I purchased it in New York City. It cost me forty-five dollars, custom-made. You like it?

I reckon it would be a nice suit to be buried in.

Har, har, I suppose it would. Me, I'd not want to throw away a good suit like this on some stiff, if you'll forgive my indiscretion in saying so.

Hell, Newbolt, I don't understand half of what you say sometimes, but I like listening to you.

Forgive me if my mind wanders—it's hard to stay thinking on one thing too long in this place where the time never seems to change—where I am caged like a pitiful dog.

I went round to each of the suitors and warned them to stay clear of Laura. Of course they thought me just a damn fool—all these older men: George Hare and Sam Pie, and Swain, and Grayson especially.

You might be some sort of war hero to these others, Tom Dooley, but you ain't as much as pig shit to me.

You think you're the onliest one with an aching cob?

It's time for some others of us to start having our pick of the gals round here.

You're just a tallywacking son of a bitch!

Like that it went. They thought no more of me than a shoat hog.

Laura did admit that many men came to her cabin and tossed their favor at her pap, carrying with them jugs of liquor and of-ferings to set him up by paying cash money as if they were buying a horse. Said her pap was playing one off against the other to get the highest price for her. Laura had no say, you see, in who came and went, or who her pap invited in to stay and drink and talk of marriage. He was, she told me, a shrewd negotiator for her favors. She wanted bad to run away with me before she got sold off to one of them.

Pretty gals have always been seen as hardly more than just something to barter for or to sell. Pretty gals have always been just like niggers round these parts, don't you know that, Liza?

And in the eyes of the other suitors, you were the bane in their affairs.

O, your words, even written out, seem as fancy as those of that newspaperman, Liza. But, I guess you're right, I was.

You were their ruin, their poison when it came to girls like Laura and Pauline and even Ann. You won their hearts so easily. Those other men didn't want used goods.

What man does?

None, I suppose. It's a good thing for men that we women don't see it the same way—or there wouldn't have been a man in this whole world would ever have won himself a sweetheart.

You're right as rain, Liza. But listen: Those gals were free to choose whatever man they wanted . . .

But they did choose you, Tom: Even Ann, already married to James.

Yes, and look what it's gotten me, all their choosing.

Elizabeth Brouchard

I know that the hours of long visits, the self-absorbed way you became in your recollections, had an effect on me, my mood, my patience at times. I never wanted to be harsh with you, but there were moments I couldn't help it. My anger grows and grows because you are where you are and because you brought down this house of cards upon yourself. Maybe not entirely, but mostly it was your own selfish and lustful actions that brought everything crashing down, Tom.

O, I know it isn't what you wanted. I know that if you could, you would probably give your life for Laura's. But as it is . . . well, as it is, you might well give your life for her, for no good reason whatsoever. So just ignore my sometime hasty observations, my haste in wanting to condemn you for some things. I don't mean it. Like you, I came to love too much and sometimes my love blinds me and sometimes it makes me feel mean and cruel toward you. Like any woman with a half jealous heart, I want to make you see how you've hurt me with all this talk of other women, other lovers, the things you did for them that you never did for me. I'm sorry, Tom, but if we can't be honest with each other now, when will we ever get the chance?

Tom Dooley

Somebody shot the windows out of my cabin one night, and another time I came home and found evidence of a fire set, but lucky for me, doused by a sudden rain.

The other men conspired to run you off . . .

Somebody didn't want me around.

One thing led to another . . .

It's me behind these bars . . . I don't see nobody else, do you?

Tell me if you ever again confronted Ann before that tragic day of Laura's death.

Yes, many times . . .

She would come around and beg me to take up with her again. She would promise me that she would forgive all if I would vow to her that I would stop seeing Laura. She was a mean trickster and a meaner temptress still.

Why you want her, Tom, when I'd do anything for you?

Facts haven't changed any, you're still a married woman, Ann.

I'll get unmarried if that's what you want.

No, my heart doesn't ache for you like it once did. It's too late for that.

I'll go and pack my things today and move in with you.

No, no. Don't you understand a thing about me?

That was how it generally went between us. She'd plead, and then when I wouldn't give in, she'd curse me and swear to get even. It wasn't enough she already had a man she didn't want; she wanted a man she couldn't have.

Maybe we're all given to such easy temptations, Tom—wanting the thing we don't or can't have—believing we can win such objects of affections by sheer wanting alone.

And when we get it . . .

We don't want it.

O, Liza, how did you get so wise and me so ignorant?

When you are gone in the dark late hour, I hear Keyes's wood leg on the stairs—*Thump! Thump! Thump!*—bringing my supper, smell the fried side meat, and know each meal I eat will be one less I'll get to eat. Keyes has told me they are to take me off to Statesville soon and that can only mean one thing.

Tom, how's she going tonight?

He swings open my cell door and hands in my plate, a fork and spoon, no knife of course, then steps out again and makes sure the lock is turned in place.

He snorts impatiently as though he's got some place to go and I don't know why he stands staring at me as long as he does. I tell him to go on and he does, *thump . . . thump* down the stairs, each step he grunts from that big belly of his he carries.

I eat my supper in silence, not hungry. The room I'm in gets smaller by the minute. I take up my pen again, this time determined in what words I'll write . . . for they are words meant for Ann and I'll force my hand to write them. I'll give Keyes the letter to take to her when he comes to collect my plate:

Dear Ann,

You blame me for everything, say that if I'll confess to Laura's murder that you'll be set free, that your pretty neck won't be broken by the hangman knot. Is that what you want of me, this man you say you love in spite of everything? Is that how you'd see your lover, swinging from the Tory tree? Is it me, or you who should confess? I know I ain't been in my right mind for a long time. I know I'd gotten bad drunk that night and was still so the next morning. But I wasn't alone, if you recall. Your pretty throat swallowed some of that liquor too. My only real regret is that I allowed you back into my life at all. Shinbone calls people like us Star Crossed & Timeless. I think people like us are simply fools guided by our lusts and not our heads. I know that is what it was for me, or I'd not let you turn me back into your fool. I hope that you are the one who is happy now that you see me in this place, now that you have made sure my fate was sealed. But what I want to know is, who were your co-conspirators, or was it your plan alone to see me thus? Without affection, Tom Dooley.

I fold the letter quickly into quarters before I change my mind and tear it to pieces. I don't know where to place the blame, but I know I must place it with someone.

Thy love was false and falsely said
But my ear did hear it as pure truth
And caused me to raise my hand in
Oath of vain servitude to my own death.

Could I, I wonder, dig my way through these stone walls with just a pen and fork and spoon? And could I go beyond those far blue hills and sail across the oceans and come into strange lands that would have me as I am? And if I could, could I leave behind all thoughts of love and Laura Foster? & could I go without you, Liza? For taking you with me would only bring you to ruin as it did the others. O, what devilment I've placed myself in—what a terrible stew!

A gentle rain begins to tap along the outer walls like an

insistent lover. It falls upon the thirsty grass beyond these walls and dances upon the sill. And in my haste to taste its freedom, I extend my fingers as far as I can through the window bars until they are touched by what feels like a dead girl's tears that soon bring my own . . .

I close this for now, Liza, knowing you will read it soon enough and understand I'm not as all cruel as they would have me.

Elizabeth Brouchard

It has rained a thousand days and more since you wrote those words. And the rain has not changed, and the seasons come and go without change. And everything is the same and nothing is the same.

My bed is empty, Billy is gone too and I sometimes wonder if there is a heaven and if there is, is Billy still drinking and falling asleep on your porch, Tom? I'd like to think it so.

I close for now, the young mademoiselles are waiting for their piano lessons.

CHAPTER 23

Tom Dooley

Lawyer Vance comes to see me, a portly brave man whose faith in justice is unflagging.

We ain't lost yet, Tom.

But in his eyes, I see the cause *is* lost. Two trials and two convictions, what hope can remain?

They've only circumstantial evidence, no eyewitnesses, nothing to tie you to Laura Foster's murder but their pitiless hearts and jaundiced eyes—for somebody has to pay, or they will not rest easy in their beds at night.

What about Ann, will they hang her too?

O, let's not concern yourself overly much with poor Ann. I'll defend her.

I want to thank him for his efforts, but if he defends Ann as well as he did me, then surely she will hang. It's not his fault. I had fear and superstition working against me. I had a jury with George Hare and Sam Pie and Swain and Grayson as my peers. My peers! Their slanderous hearts will put the rope around my neck and Ann's as well.

You've done what you could, Mr. Vance. Best you go and defend Ann and try and save her from the rope. Forget about me.

I have appeals in to the courts as we speak.

Twice guilty. How you going to appeal that in people's minds?

I have great faith that justice is blind.

And so are those who sat in judgment of me.

I'm even appealing to the governor for a pardon in case all else fails.

I found Pearl in the meadow with Tyree Shinbone. Found her on all fours, Pearl's bare buttocks exposed to Tyree, his cob long and hard. I'd gone to warn each about the other—a grand scheme I'd worked out to win Billy Dixon another chance with Pearl and to save her from the madman.

But too late, too late—Pearl grunting with each thrust of the preacher behind her.

Sister, let me save you from hell and perdition!

Oh yes, Brother Tyree!

And bring to thee redemption!

Oh yes, bring me redemption.

And rain down fire and brimstone upon thee who is a sinner.

I am a sinner! I am a sinner! Rain down on me fire and brimstone!

I stood off in the brambles and watched and felt anger prickle the back of my neck. My plan had been to tell Tyree that Pearl had the pox, then go and tell Pearl the same about Tyree. I'd had it once myself and knew how terrible it was to get rid of. Left unattended it infects the brain, makes a body go crazy, bluestone is its only cure!

The pox pickles the brain like vinegar pickles an egg.

Maybe that was Tyree's affliction—an infected brain. And now, Pearl would share in it too—his growing madness. And soon it might spread throughout all the valley until everyone was as mad as the preacher.

Oh, it was hard to contemplate—the once sweet and shy Pearl growing mad from a diseased brain. But there she was, on the ground in front of Tyree as he bucked into her delivering his *redemption,* a victim of his lust and hers. I had to go and tell Billy to forget about Pearl, to set his cap for another.

Just as I turned to leave, Pearl cried out and I looked round thinking Tyree had hurt her. But no, they lay collapsed in a heap of smoldering flesh, twisted arms and legs, he atop her, kissing the back of her head as she mewed like a kitten. It was a sad and terrible thing for me to see.

Because you still had some feelings for her?

Perhaps, for even the faintest love is still love.

O, Tom, don't whisper of faint love to me, I beg you not.

When I found Billy, he was sitting with the barrel of a shotgun pressed under his chin. He had his shoe off and was attempting to pull the trigger with his toe. I kicked it out from under him.

The hell's gotten you in such a state?

I seen him, Tom.

Who?

Raymond.

Raymond's dead, drowned last winter in the Yadkin, don't you remember?

No, he was here not half an hour ago. He asked me about the children, asked if they still sang. Then he warned me to leave Pearl alone, that she was his—he'd bought her.

You got to leave off drinking so heavily, Billy.

I swear, I swear, I saw him, plain as I see you now. Are you real, Tom? Or am I seeing me another ghost?

I took him outside and plunged his head in a bucket of rainwater as many times as it took to get him sober, then told him Pearl was a lost cause, that she'd come under Shinbone's spell.

I don't care about nothing, Tom. I'm all lost to myself. I don't care about nothing.

Maybe not today, but tomorrow you'll care again, or the day after.

If true love ain't in the cards for me, what's the point of living?

Love ain't a bowl of soup to feed your belly, it ain't a roof to keep the rain off you. Love ain't everything, Billy. It ain't even half of everything.

Easy enough for you to say, seeing's how you've always had a woman loving on you and you on them.

They ain't none of us got nothing except what we imagine we got. You're imagining you got nothing, so you got nothing. You're all a mess, Billy—headed for an early grave you don't change your thinking.

Piss and damn. Piss and damn.

Billy Dixon

Tom caught me trying to blow my fool head off. It was a fool head I was aiming for, for who but a fool would attempt such a thing over such as Pauline Foster—or any other woman for that matter?

O, I might for you, sweet Liza. I might for you.

Tom Dooley

I left him there with his wet head and miserable notions and figured if he was going to kill himself, he would eventually and nothing would stop him. But I doubted Billy had it in him; it takes a certain sort of heart to take a life, even if the life's his own.

Do you believe in ghosts, Tom? That Raymond actually came to visit Billy?

Yes, I do.

Do you believe Shinbone's madness was spreading throughout the whole of the valley, infecting everyone he came in contact with?

If not his, then somebody's was, for it sure was a madness of one sort or the other.

Like a plague?

Yes, I reckon it was—a plague of madness, for what else could account for the murder of Laura?

Was she so innocent and all the others so guilty?

O, Liza, I can't say. I can't say. Maybe she was as guilty as us all. But the child she carried wasn't guilty. The little babe cannot be guilty . . .

Elizabeth Brouchard

On bright days, the mademoiselles stroll the boulevards of Paris under lovely parasols. I observe their lovely faces and think how different they are than the women of Reedy Branch who, in those infinite days, had hair that smelled of cooking fire, and no beauty to them. O, the mademoiselles of Paris are tall and limber and graceful as cats and not stout and sturdy as hewn logs.

The girls of Reedy Branch dye their lips with raspberries picked in summer's heat, thinking it some sort of beauty. But the mademoiselles of Paris rouged their cheeks and sprayed their necks with perfume. The girls of Reedy Branch hid their desires from husbands and lovers, but the mademoiselles took lovers to their beds while knowing husbands winked and worked in musty offices.

Tom Dooley

A few mornings before she disappeared, Laura rode to my cabin.

Tom, there is something I need to tell you.

I'd thought it would be that another man had wooed her away from me—Grayson with all his money, or Swain with his perfidious lies. I put nothing past those two men especially— I'm sorry to say it to you, Liza, about your own father, my mistrust of him. The others, Sam Pie and George Hare and the rest I knew were just as wanting of Laura's love, but being men of such common stock they couldn't come up with a plan between them to win her from me. Grayson and Swain were a different matter.

If it is to tell me another's won you over, I don't want to hear it. You can get back on your pap's racer and go straightaway home.

Oh, don't be such a jealous fool. It's nothing like that.

Then what is it?

Don't you want to even kiss me first?

So I kissed her and let the sweetness of her kiss crawl into my bones. I kissed her and kissed her and carried her into the house in spite of her protests that what she'd come to tell me was most important.

Later, there is always time to tell me later.

But Tom . . .

. . . and removed her dress and other things.

Oh, Tom . . .

. . . and kissed her honey mouth and nectared breasts and the fine down below her navel until I heard the soft little sounds I'd grown so accustomed to escape her lips . . . and kissed her and kissed her.

This I write with all candor.

Later as we held to each other quietly, a stripe of sunlight lay across the bed. And up from the river blew the gentlest of breezes—like cool fingers seeking us out and caressing us most tenderly.

Now what was it so all fired important that you came here today and kept me from my work?

I said it sweetly, teasingly, for we'd learned to be as children when together—laughing and teasing each other, chasing and catching and dragging each other down into an embrace, playfully, blissfully.

O, Tom, I'm not sure if it's good news or not.

I felt suddenly afraid I'd lose her through this news she was about to tell me.

Go ahead and just say it, Laura.

She gave me a lingering kiss.

I think your baby child grows inside me.

My heart lurches even now as I think of those words that force me to reach for my pen and ink to add to the account of the events that lead to the tragedy.

O what news thou has brought thee of

Events not yet but soon to be, of a changing

Season wherein all dreams become reality

And time itself sifts backward to this moment now?

With such joy I kissed the slight roundness of her tummy, imagining the small fluttering life that must already exist there and she wept when I did so.

Don't cry.

I cannot help it.

I kissed her hands and the prominences of her warm wet cheeks.

She clung to me and made promises of being a good wife to me.

We'll marry.

When, Tom, when?

Soon. I'll need to think it out.

My thoughts of a life together lay beyond the Yadkin Valley, lay beyond the ridges, lay beyond anything I could imagine. I'd need to raise some quick money for us to go far away, but how I didn't know.

I dangled a needle from a thread above my belly.

Whatever for?

To see if it will be a boy or a girl.

And what did the dangling needle tell you?

That it will be a boy.

I should have been happy, overjoyed, but all I could think of was of other boys who grew into men and went off to war never to return. The jellied eyes of the dead, their dark faces turned toward the sun—so many mothers' sons all in a row, scattered like human trash. All began their new life foretold by the dangling of a needle, and I wondered if the dangling needle ever foretold of their youthful death.

Well, a boy is a fine thing to look forward to.

Really Tom? Are you really pleased?

Sure I am. Why every man wants a son, don't he?

He'll have your fine hair and dark eyes.

Oh, I don't know about that; let's hope he looks more like you.

In spite of misgivings, there was a sweetness to the news, and Laura seemed so fragile to me in that golden light as the sun sought its evening rest. I took her gentle into my arms and held her, for I felt greatly responsible for the first time in my life.

My pen scribbles along the page of its own truck:
Listen to thy beating tender heart,
& tell me if you hear it—the heart of an
Unborn king, a fiddler, a riverman, a
Wanderer, surgeon, lawyer or Prince?
For who can know what blood thy blood will
Stir, and what great or terrible deeds
He will perform upon this heaving earth?

A boy, she said it would be, foretold by the dangling needle. You see, she was a superstitious girl who would turn and walk the other way if a black cat crossed her path, and toss salt over her shoulder if a shaker spilled.

She was not unusual for mountain folk. Women especially let themselves be guided by superstition—and who's to say they don't know things most the rest of us can't conceive? For I tell you here and now that I believe things happen round us without our knowledge, that Billy Dixon did see Raymond's ghost, and that I have seen Laura, here in the cell on certain nights when sleep has drugged me just so. And I believe it is her hand that guides my hand in writing of such things—for I have no poetry in me, no words that can match what I see on the page.

So there are strange occurrences and I'm not one to judge them anymore like I once did. I only hope that this other world round me where fairies and unseen gods live who wait to claim me, do so with loving kindness, more so than I've had on this earth and in this life until this very moment—and when they put the rope round my neck.

For what kindness will I find in death

That I've not found in life if not that
Angels exist, and other fantasies?

Keyes stomps up the stairs. I realize it is morning—the last words I wrote caused me to faint and sleep the night. Which morning it is, I ain't sure, but it doesn't really matter so much if it isn't my last just yet.

Tom, how're you this morning?

Ready to walk all the way to those mountains.

Shoot boy, I wish I could let you.

Wouldn't nobody have to know I didn't trick you.

I'd know.

Would it be the worst thing you ever done, letting an innocent man escape the rope?

No, sir, if you was innocent like you say, it'd be a good thing. But I ain't a judge and I ain't a jury, I'm just an old one-legged jailer. It ain't much to lay claim to, but without it I'd have nothing. So if I was to let you go, you'd just be making me into a one-legged tramp.

You give that letter to Ann?

Yes, sir, I seen she got it.

Well, hand me in that mush and side meat, I'll see what I can do with it.

Tom?

What?

She didn't say nothing when I give her the letter.

I didn't expect she would.

Elizabeth Brouchard

The ladies of Paris are like no other ladies anywhere. Their lovers often take lovers—it seems a trend and no one minds. It is everyone's secret here in beautiful *Paree!*

The mademoiselles do not fret over minor infidelities and other betrayals, for they have their parasols and beautiful dresses & lovers of their own, you see.

CHAPTER 24

Tom Dooley

Laura's pap threw rocks at my door until I came outside. He had one in his hand ready to throw it.

What are you doing, Mr. Foster?

I ain't letting her marry a no account long as they's fellas like Grayson willing to pay for the privilege. Swain owns a tavern, George Hare a farm, Sam Pie a mill. What you own? You know how fine it would be to have a son-in-law owns a tavern?

He reminded me of a banty rooster, feisty and small but didn't know just how small he was. His black hair stood up on his head like a rooster's feathers and he had little rooster eyes. He was scratching up my place and I didn't like it one bit.

You best go on now, Mr. Foster. It's my business and none of your own.

By gar, I'll see whose bidness my kin is.

Laura's of age to say who she does and doesn't want to marry.

Marry! Why boy, you got a head chock full of queer ideas, ain't you?

Don't be throwing no more rocks at my door.

I'll bust you in the damn head with one . . .

I'm not trying to rile you, but if they's any busting to be done, I'll be the one doing it.

His face became as dark red as a rooster's feathers.

Don't come round my place no more, Tom Dooley. Don't come

round Laura no more, or you just might end up floatin' in the Yadkin.

I watched him hike up onto the back of his unsaddled horse,
shift his weight until he was balanced just so, then dig his heels
in and race off as though to show me he could handle about
anything—a big fast horse or a "no account" fella such as myself.

*That had to have made you feel pretty badly, being upbraided by
such a man.*

*No. It just made me more determined than ever to get me some
money put together and take Laura off from this place, far from the
men who would try and own her and sell her for the price of a drink.
For, she wasn't a thing to be owned, to be sold off to the highest bid-
der.*

No, of course not.

*Men round here, some of them anyways, feel as though a woman
ain't nothing but a piece of property. Like your pap did with Pearl,
trying to sell her off to Raymond.*

So you made yourself a new enemy in Mr. Foster.

Yes. I was getting good at making enemies without even trying.

*But surely he couldn't have had a hand in Laura's death or you
in this fix . . .*

*No, but the way I heard it, her pap sure didn't seem all that broke
up, either; he was a lot more concerned about his stole horse than he
was the fate of Laura.*

She took his horse that morning she was to meet you.

So they say.

Squire Wilson Foster

I let that fool Tom Dooley know I wan't going to stand for his
taking up with my child. I went out there and raised holy hell
with him for even thinking such notions. But there he stood all
puffed up as though he was the richest fella in the valley, as
though my word didn't count for nothing. He had no respect

for me or Laura neither—if he had, he wouldn't a put such fool notions in her head. It was all those fool notions got her where she is—and got him where he is, too.

Damn sorry thing a man can't raise himself a child and have her grow up and marry into something.

Now all I got is a little old grave to look at and a sorry future when I could have had me a little something for my troubles. Why, about any man in the valley would have given a pretty penny for a pretty gal such as Laura. But no, Tom Dooley saw to it that any such a dream got ruin't. Far as I'm concerned, Tom Dooley is a stealer of other folk's dreams.

Tom Dooley

Pearl came a day or two after Laura's pap had thrown rocks at my door, stating her reason for coming was that Laura had sent her. I could still see her that day in the meadow with Shinbone. For that was how I would always see her—her white hams offered up to heaven as though it was Shinbone's sacrifice to his god of lust.

Cousin Laura sent me to give you this.

She handed me a letter sealed with wax.

Thank you for delivering it.

She dawdled.

You best get on back lest Ann starts to wonder where you went off to.

I don't work for her no more.

Oh, and how is it you're getting by?

I took up with Tyree; he takes care of me now. But then I reckon you already figured that one out.

How would I know what you and Tyree been up to?

Don't play fool with me, Tom Dooley. I saw you that day standing off in the brambles. You got yourself a eyeful of me and Tyree. And you want to know something?

No, I don't.

I was glad you seen us. I told Tyree later how you was watching and he laughed and laughed and so did I . . .

I felt suddenly sad for her. Tyree Shinbone would only lead her to great heartache. Pearl was fragile in a way the others weren't—she was fragile in the head.

How do you mean? She doesn't sound fragile, Tom. She sounds as flinty as the others . . .

She isn't as pretty for one thing. She is the sort of woman men find easy to take advantage of because she's so needy of loving—it wouldn't take much for her to break in the head.

So you found her easy to love yourself?

Yes, I loved her in a way, and still I took advantage of her, and each time I did I felt the sorrier for it.

Because it turned you into the same as the others—the very men you'd come to detest.

Yes, yes, yes.

I told her I wished her the best in her new life and she smiled but without pleasure and her lip began to tremble.

Oh, Tom. I know you must hate me for what I did with Tyree. Don't hate me.

I don't hate you.

I'll leave him if you want me to.

I don't want you to.

I was angry was partly it—the reason I took up with him. You left me for Laura. Then that pit-face Billy Dixon come round saying how you'd sent him; I felt like I was your slops you was offering to any old hog that came along. You made me sad, Tom, your leaving me, you telling me how you didn't love me.

I know it, Pearl. I know you were sad.

She tried to throw her arms around me and kiss me, but I held her off. I had to make a stand, stay true to it or forever be a man without any sort of conviction that was worth having.

Go on now, Pearl. Go on back to Tyree.

Okay, Tom, if that's what you want.

Shouldn't be what I want but what you want.

I don't have no say in nothing, Tom. I'm just a gal given to the lies of men. I'm just a plaything for them to have their ways with. I know I ain't nothing but side meat, Tom. I know it.

And over the rise she went, her head hung low, the wind tugging at her faded dress, the brown flour dust rising and falling round her feet.

She seemed doomed. But it wasn't her who was doomed, but me.

Pauline Foster

Cousin Laura asked me to carry Tom a letter for her. I didn't want to. I was afraid if I saw him again, I'd make a fool of myself. I'd been with Tyree in his camp and I knew Tom saw us one day and what we was doing with one another. I didn't care he saw us at the time—I liked he saw us. I wanted him to hate what he saw us doing. I wanted it to eat his heart out with jealousy, but I guess it never did. I knew the minute I saw him again I wanted him worse than I wanted Tyree. But Tom wouldn't have nothing to do with me no more. I can't say's I blame him. I wouldn't want nothing more to do with me was I him.

I guess I'm sad to hear of him going to the gallows.

I guess I'm sad in every little part of me.

But he shouldn't have done what he done.

Tom Dooley

I opened the letter and read it.

Dear Tom,

Pap has swore I won't ever see you again. And I have swore I would. He got good and drunk and took a belt to me and said he'd see me dead before he'd see me married to Tom Dooley. I told him I loved you and no other and it made him even more het up. He lashed me across my back and legs and tore my dress and said was anyone going to ruin me, it'd be him and not some goddamn no account. Oh, Tom, I hate using such words, but use them to make you understand how strongly he intends on keeping us apart. But I'd rather be dead than to not have you. I will take Mr. Lee and sneak away on Friday morning and meet you by the springs at eight o'clock. Be there waiting for me if you love me. Your darling sweetheart—Laura.

The trap had sprung, I guess you could say, only I didn't know it and Laura didn't know it and no one knew it except the one who'd see her dead. I think of her riding away from her pap's that early misty morning, her hopes pinned on me. Oh, God, how I think and think and think of her.

What's that I hear?

The tolling of the church bells.

Is it Sunday?

Yes, Tom. Look out your window and see how the sun smites the trees.

Winston Newbolt

I knew time was running out for Tom, that soon they'd send him to Statesville to be hanged and my assignment would be finished. I still hadn't gotten any of the real answers I wanted, nor a confession—nor even a complete denial that he had a hand in the young woman—Laura Foster's—murder. I remember one of the last times I went he told me the story of how he'd tried to deceive James Melton into giving him money to run away with Laura. And perhaps he was this time telling the truth. It got so I couldn't tell with him which was true and which false.

Tom Dooley

I had only one place, one soul I could go to in hopes of borrowing some money. There was only one man I knew who had what I thought I needed, but I knew I couldn't get it from him direct. I'd have to go at it another way. I'd have to lie and make myself appear something I was not, and it would be the worst lying I'd ever do in my life.

I took up residence in the brambles outside of Melton's. I waited over a day and a half. Near to dusk on the second day is when he came out and climbed in his wagon and headed toward Reedy Branch, no doubt to Swain's for an evening of drink. A greasy light glowed inside the cabin. I went on over and knocked on the door and Ann answered it.

Well, would you look at what the cat has dragged to my door.

Ann.

What you want here, Tom Dooley?

Came to see you.

She looked beyond me to the gathering darkness.

You been out there waiting, ain't you? Waiting for James to leave, waiting to come see me.

Yes, that's right. I come to see you, for I realize now that I made a mistake.

That so?

O, she acted mighty pious. But I stood my ground, ate whatever little pride I once had—all in the name of love.

Yes, but if you're going to give me grief over it, I'll just go on.

I turned to leave, I had to make it convincing.

No wait.

I won't beg.

Nobody's asking you to beg. Come on in.

So in I went, my mouth full of lies waiting to be spit out.

I prayed for the day you'd come back, and now here you are. I'm so het up with loneliness . . .

Sure, me too. I ain't hardly been able to sleep, eat, do nothing, for the thinking about how it was between us, how much I missed you.

Tell me something, Tom.

What?

Why we doing all this talking when we could be loving in the bed?

I don't rightly know.

And so there it was, me having to do the thing I didn't want anymore to do. I had told myself I would always be faithful to Laura, but now to save her, I had to break that promise. I didn't see no other way around it.

She acted starved for me. The fear in my mind was that Melton would change his mind, turn around and come back and this time rip loose—shoot us both maybe, ruin everything as far as me setting Laura free. I tried to make quick work of Ann's passion; I put the cob to her hard and fast and relentless; I told her lie upon lie about how I loved her and how it drove me near crazy not to be with her like I was now. Her hunger for me only seemed to grow instead of wane; she entwined her limbs around me strong and tight as wild grape vines; clung to me so tightly it seemed that we became one thing, one terrible beast of a thing.

She drew out my strength, tore it from me instead of the other way around, until I almost prayed that Melton *would* change his mind and come find us thus and kill us both—relieve us of our dark ways.

And by the time she was sated, the lamp had guttered out and we lay in that blackness of night and I thought I could make out the shape of her, but really what I was able to see was what I'd come to memorize, like a blind man, in all those days we'd been together. Hers was a familiar landscape to my hands: the broad forehead, the pert nose and wide mouth, the long swan neck. Even the weight of her breasts I knew so well. And the rest of her I knew equally as well—her thin arms, the roughened hands, the ropes of muscles in her legs. She was a ground I'd plowed and planted my seed in so often I dint need no eyes.

Tell me, Mr. Newbolt, has imprisonment changed her much?

It has taken its toll well enough.

All is rottenness.

Everything is just as it used to be 'tween us, Tom. Ain't nothing changed 'tween you and me. We're just who we are and just who we'll always be. We are joined by mother fate and we must never again fight against it.

O, my hand does take up the cause:

Did the urchin god avow to
Set the world afire with
Love so counterfeit that
Lovers deceiv'd could be
Persuaded to purchase
What could not be owned?

Scratch goes the pen across the page—the timeless page—leaving in the nib's wake the wet blue tendrils of words unbidden, timeless, infested in the soul. Laura's hand or mine?

God's?

A dark demented muse?

Nobody's.

I confessed in a humble way the reason I'd come to see her. Confessed it so it sounded like an afterthought, to try and keep the deception alive.

I need money.

Is that why you came to me, for money and nothing else?

No. I came to you because I needed to come to you—for no other reason.

You've been deceitful to me before, why should I trust what you say now?

I've always been truthful with you. I told you about Laura.

But not about Pauline.

Pauline didn't count with me.

You counted with her, and it counted with me.

I arose and walked to the door and opened it and felt the cool winds trailing down from the midnight ridges, felt the cool wet feel of a coming rain upon my naked skin.

There was no moon and the sky was starless and the world seemed perfectly dead to me, and I perfectly dead to it.

O, come back to my bed, Tom. I'll give you money if it's what you need.

I had it in me to walk out into the night and keep walking and never look back.

But your need to save Laura was greater than your repugnance, Tom?

Yes, sir, it was I reckon.

I went back to her bed and lay beside her, and let her warm wet mouth stipple my flesh trying to resurrect my cob in order to satisfy her renewed desire. But I could not raise it and she could not raise it no matter how hard she tried.

What is it, Tom? What ails you?

I owe a lot of money that I must pay off if I'm to remain living in this valley.

To who, Tom?

I can't say. You'll just have to trust me.

Melton's got some, but he keeps it on him, and the rest he keeps hid and I don't know where. But I can find out where and get it for you.

I felt my heart sink like a stone dropped in a bottomless river.

He don't give you none to keep handy?

No.

How soon do you think you could get it off him?

Soon's he comes back, I reckon.

Tomorrow, maybe?

If he comes back by then.

I got to get on home now.

No, don't go just yet—it's been a long time; my need has been building up. Don't go just now, Tom.

And so I stayed and I did the best I could to satisfy her in all the ways I knew how and by the time morning came round she'd fallen asleep and I made my way on back up the trail to my place feeling tired and ruined. When I got there Grayson was waiting, sitting on his stud horse, as though he'd been waiting a long time for me.

Elizabeth Brouchard

The crème of your story is raised to the very top. It is thick and sweet from all the churning, but soon sours when left unattended.

The little mademoiselles play so dutifully the scales

While their *mamas* eat sweets in aromatic parlors

As their

lovers

recline and dream of novel ways to entice them.

Billy bled to death the doctors say from old habits: whiskey consumption, bad diet, tobacco that eventually ulcerated vital organs and left him for me to find in the water closet, down on his knees in a lake of black bile.

Liza, Liza—even God can't save me. A fella knows when his time has come and mine surely has.

He was thirty-nine, hardly in his prime

& I

yet childless.

O, what lovely little songs the lovely little mademoiselles do sing:

Frère Jacques, Frère Jacques, Dormez-vous? Dormez-vous? Sonnez les matines. Sonnez les matines. Ding, ding, dong. Ding, ding, dong.

CHAPTER 25

Tom Dooley

His eyes shone under the broad brim of his hat—a smooth gray felt hat with a black ribbon round the low crown. He was a pretty man the way he dressed: black Prince Albert coat, brocade waistcoat underneath, trousers tucked down inside his bull-hide boots. I half expected he carried a pistol in one of his pockets—men like him usually do. He shone his eyes on me.

I came to deliver you a piece of news, Tom Dooley.

Go on and deliver it.

Comes to my attention through Mr. Foster you be bothering Laura; troubling her with insane ideas of marriage.

What's your interest in all this?

Why that's easy enough. I got me need of a young wife, someone sprightly and pert. Laura fits the bill.

There it was, you see—my notice, delivered by Grayson by way of old man Foster. Hell, like he didn't want to trouble dirtying his hands with me knowing I'd fit him till one of us couldn't stand up no more, so he sent the rich man instead, for the promise of a sprightly pert young wife.

He's playing you off, Foster is. He's double dealing, only you don't know it.

Grayson's eyes shone a little less on me.

How so?

He was here the other day telling me how nice it would be to have a son-in-law owns a tavern. Last I heard you don't own any tavern, but Swain does.

Swain's a lowbrow. Laura wouldn't hardly toss a bucket of ditch water on him if he was afire.

Swain ain't the only one Foster's considering; there's Sam Pie and George Hare too.

Grayson shifted his shoulders and set his jaw a little stiffer. I was hoping he'd fall clean off his blooded horse, that'd I'd gave him a belly full of worms telling him about the others Foster was appraising for his lovely child.

I intend to have her, Dooley.

You and half the other men in Reedy Branch. But none of you are going to have her, for you can't steal a heart already given away.

He heeled his horse a little closer.

Don't be some sort of damn fool. You don't know who you're messing when it comes to you messing with me.

I know damn well who I'm messing with, Mr. Grayson.

You'll never have her.

His words were dark and cold as the bottom of a well. He turned his stud's head toward the blue mountains and rode off and I thought how easy it would be to go inside and get my rifle and shoot him in the back and watch him fall and writhe in the dust and take his last goddamn breath. But I couldn't kill nobody, not even Grayson. I'd lost my taste for killing the day I built the little boat and tied Minnie's letter to Louis on it. I made a vow I'd never lift a hand in the undoing of another.

Meaning you didn't have a hand in Laura's death.

No, sir, Mr. Newbolt. Don't you see how I could never harm even a hair on her head?

Yes, Tom, I think I do. But someone did harm her in the most terrible way.

I know it. Lord, I surely do and it eats me up that somebody could do such a thing.

And did Ann get you the money?

251

Yes, she did in a little while.
You want to tell me about that?

Winston Newbolt

The boy turns pasty when speaking of death. Is it the pallor of fear, the guilt of what he may have done, or is it the long days and nights locked up in a place with too little sunlight?

O, the guilty sing like caged birds to be set free.

But Tom hardly sings at all these days.

Tom Dooley

I can hear Keyes in his quarters thumping around on his wood leg. I can hear the laughter of a tart that sometimes comes to visit him late of the evening when all is settled into night. She is the same tart whose skirts Billy Dixon paid a dollar to put his head under. I think her name is Florence and that she came to the valley with a husband after the war from Statesville. Keyes calls out to her.

Flo, Flo! Come hither, gal!

More laughter, squawks like a chicken with its throat being cut—more squawk than laugh.

Keyes plays the fiddle for her and she sings terribly to it. They laugh and sing and you can tell by the sounds they make what he's doing with her when the fiddle stops and his wood leg takes to thumping against the wall.

Oh, my, Augusta, what a big old scamp you are!

Come hither to me, gal! Let me get good a sniff of you!

Har, har. You old scamp. Do you like these?

Indeed I do, let me have a feel. Why they're as big as mush melons.

Cost you a silver dollar to be touching them, Augusta old boy.

Why, what good is money if a man can't spend it on his pleasure?

Then go on to it, my sweet man, touch and lick them if you like.

Touch and lick them rough and long as you want.

Eventually the light and noise from his quarters is snuffed

out and darkness creeps up the stairs and finds a place to lay its wearisome head outside my cell. Generally the tart takes her leave near daybreak, Keyes's snoring bidding her farewell.

Oh, I think of the gayer times when love was all there was to concern myself over—the love of life and all things worth loving: the love of a woman's kiss, her sweet laughter, a knowing glance wherein a secret is shared. All gone to me now and forever. Darkness awaits me—the eternal darkness of a long death that is forever and without end. I must write of these feelings, let come out what will come out.

What would you have me do, O' silly
God who has made me thus, which I
Have not already done under thy whimsical
Stare, knowing I am unable to be my own
Master, to steer my own ship through the
Troubled seas thou hast cast me on?
Goddamn. Why me? Why me? Why me?

And when I come to my senses again, where Newbolt stood, now stands Tyree Shinbone.

Tom.

Don't tell me. You come to crow some more about you and Pearl, or is it Mizrus Boots? Well, I don't want to hear it.

Mizrus Boots?

Like you did the last time.

You must be mistaken. Why would I say anything about Mizrus Boots?

Oh, hell, Tyree, I'm all confused. Being locked up has messed up my mind.

Have a taste of this.

He slips me a bottle through the bars—peach brandy. It is a small enough comfort in a place that has so few.

Go on, keep it, just don't let old Keyes find it, he'll drink it all up.

You heard any news lately?

Tyree burrows his eyes under his shaggy brows like two little creatures trying to hide from a hunter.

Word is, they're going to move you down to Statesville soon.

To be hanged.

O, Tom. I don't know nothing about what it is they do down in Statesville . . .

Sure, that's where they take fellers to be hanged.

Let's have another pull of that brandy and play us some checkers.

I can't concentrate on nothing. Tyree wins every game easy.

You hear any word on Ann?

They say she's a shrew locked up so long.

Pearl?

Pearl . . . let me think.

She still out to the wilderness with you?

Some. Not steady, though. Comes and goes.

Where she go when she goes?

Melton's mostly. Fact is, I wish she'd stay gone . . .

I guess he's getting his revenge.

I reckon maybe he is. On you and me, and Ann.

Tyree Shinbone

I love Tom as a brother loves a brother. Sometimes I dream I've et his flesh. O, jolly little brother that he is, he screams and screams and fire rages through the woods, and the whole world is burnt up.

I am troubled by my thoughts lately.

Maybe Pearl has given me the pox for I feel queer lately of something—like worms crawling in my veins headed toward my heart, my brain. Her cunny was her only grace and to the grave it might one day take me.

To die mad of the pox—now wouldn't that be something for a preacher man.

All my kin have died rich and well respected . . .

Tom Dooley

It was a Wednesday when I'd gone to Ann's. This was two days before I was to meet Laura at the springs and set off toward who knew where exactly? I had it in my heart to, as I said, go far beyond the blue mountains, go all the way to the sea. I featured us living by the sea, me and Laura and the babe. I had dreams of becoming a fisherman, purchasing a small boat, and everyday head out into the deep waters to cast my net and earn an honest living. I thought of the daily returning, how it would be when the evening light spread itself over the water all golden till the whole world was a sea of gold. I thought what it would feel like to be honest and tired, my boat full of fish. And upon my return, Laura and the babe would be waiting for me on the dock, their faces happy to see me and I would scoop them up and carry them off home where we'd sup and afterwards I'd play with the babe and later lay with Laura in our bed and hear the waves breaking against the midnight shore.

In my mind, I could see the moon a broad white strip on the water.

I don't know why I had it in me to dream such a life, I just did. I think a man can be other things than what he was born to. All I was born to was this valley, these blue unchanging mountains, this restless spirit in me. I'd gone to the harlot war and let her embrace me and escaped her murderous arms. It did not kill me and I figured it was somehow a sign for me to do better things with my life than I'd been doing. A life not fully lived is one that's wasted and no account.

I'd come home worn out with war and listened to the men in Swain's ask me all about it, slap me on the shoulder and ruminate how they'd have gone themselves except they had the gout and couldn't march, they'd had palsy and couldn't hold a rifle steady, they'd had wives and big broods of children that couldn't do without them. I drank their whiskey at first because

I didn't want to insult them by not, and I listened to their questions of what it was like—*the glory of killing Billy Yank*—and muttered as best I could some sort of response that didn't mean anything to me but gave them something more to chew on. Seems like those who didn't go needed the war more than those of us who went. And after a time of being home again, I looked all around me, and everywhere I looked what I saw was men doing the same tired work, or none at all. I saw their slattern women with their faded eyes, their dirt-faced kids, the same scratch land along those ridges, the same rich folks living in the river bottoms. I saw dirt roads going nowhere unless a fella took them. But folks didn't seem to want to go nowhere or do nothing—except for me. I'd seen some of what was beyond those mountains but not enough. O, not nearly enough and I wanted to cross them again and this time stay gone forever.

Tyree Shinbone

Some are born of fire and some earth—but you were born of water, Tom.

I wanted to go to sea and become a fisherman.

Jesus said, Come unto me and I'll make you fishers of men.

I dint want to fish for no men. I just wanted Laura and me to have a life, to take our living from the sea and not depend on anyone.

He fed the multitudes with just a few loaves of bread and a few fish.

What are you talking about, Tyree?

The fish is a symbol of everlasting life, Tom.

Maybe it would have been for me too, had I made it as far as the sea.

I think I can see such oceans in Tom's old eyes.

Tom Dooley

There is a long silence, with just the ticking of Keyes's clock downstairs to interrupt it. Keyes's clock is ticking off the minutes. *My minutes.* For time has become a slippery thing. Each tick is a reminder of how dear and precious my time is. Pen scratches wearily over the page of foolscap:

Oh peek into thy heart, dear Jesus, and tell me where is your mercy now?

Bend low and whisper into my ear what I did to deserve any of this.

What you writing there, Tom?

Nothing, Tyree, just a letter.

You want me to carry it to someone?

You'd have a long journey if I did.

On that fateful Thursday Pearl came and said Ann had sent her for me to come that evening.

What of Melton, will he be around?

Didn't say.

Then there is a chance he'll be there.

She played the daft girl of a sudden, her previous desire for me absent in her dull stare.

Has Tyree ruined you, girl?

No, Tyree ain't ruint me.

Something's sure wrong with you.

Nothing's wrong with me. I got to get on.

I thought her behavior strange, for most generally she was eager as a hound to see me, eager to offer herself to me, to beg me to take her in and save her from all the world and from all of those who would set upon her. But instead, with just a few simple words and vacant eyes, she sallied off back toward Melton's and that was that.

Tom, you're mumbling. It's your move.

I have no heart for games, Tyree.

Should I tell you a story then?

No. Leave me be.

Okay Tom. I'll come round later on, see how you're doing.

Tyree—

Yes, Tom.

Oh, nothing, nothing at all.

I set out that evening on the trail lit by the ghost moon's light. I could smell the river beyond the trees—dank and running slow like it does that time of year. It has the smell of old snakes and turtles and rotted memories. Something of a chill come over me as I smelt that old river. Raymond twisted in the branches of a dead tree, river water running through his nostrils. Raymond's eyes all et by turtles.

Fisher of men—Tyree says. It was George Hare and Sam Pie fished him out; I guess they were the fishers of him.

And when I arrived at Melton's, Ann was waiting for me, drunk and crazed. I saw the madness in her moonlit eyes.

Tom, you sorry fucking son of a bitch!

I should have known she would see through my ruse.

Ann had the instincts of a fox.

Elizabeth Brouchard

Billy changed after you died. It was like something in him died when the news came finally back to the valley.

George Hare brought a newspaper down from Wilkesboro with the article in it:

Elkville Citizen, Tom Dooley, hanged . . . & it went on to tell the grisly details and how more than three thousand folks came to the ***Big Event!***

It told of candy butchers and lemonade sellers and pickpockets and how you stood upon the scaffold and held up your right hand and swore: *This here hand would not harm a hair on Laura Foster's head* & so on and so forth.

My father bought drinks all around and there were cheers and good riddances. For men like Mr. Pie and Mr. Hare finally had the opportunity to make hay with some of the local gals now that *old Tom Dooley was dead, dead, dead!*

Billy found me by the river near the same place where you first saw me, where we first met.

Those pretty tears will fill that river up, Liza.

But I didn't care.

You loved old Tom, didn't you?

How'd you know? I wrote on my slate.

I may look a fool, but I ain't.

And that's how it really started—our courtship, if courtship it could be called. Billy loved you too, and we found comfort in our mutual love and grieving.

I know I ain't no Tom Dooley, Liza.

Nobody said you were.

He took his time reading my words. He seemed to me patient in his thoughts and deeds.

Thing is, I ain't like a lot of these others round here, neither. I got dreams like Tom did. Maybe not as big a dreams, but dreams to move on . . .

What sort of dreams, Billy?

Eventually I taught him to sign so we could speak to each other more easily and without benefit of slate and chalk or pen and paper.

We shared that in common too, our dreams.

We told the river our dreams and it listened. Our dreams were like little seeds that just grew in common ground we'd cultivated without even half thinking.

O, it wasn't love between Billy and me, Tom. It wasn't ever really love. But it had to do because we knew love wasn't ever going to find either of us out.

My love went with you to the gallows—and died with you. My real love, did.

They never mentioned that in the newspaper article George Hare brought with him down from Wilkesboro.

&

They never mentioned how your heart must have felt in those final fateful seconds waiting for the trap to spring. How terrible it must have been for you—the waiting.

CHAPTER 26

Tom Dooley

I love you and I hate you, Tom Dooley.

You've gotten into Melton's liquor again.

So what if I have—ain't you ever heard when two people marry what's one's is the other's?

You sent Pearl to fetch me.

And here you are, you blue-eyed devil.

O, Ann, let's not play so many games with each other. Come out with it, what ails you.

You ail me. You and your lies is what ails me.

I half expected Melton to step from the shadows, a gun in his hand to kill me, a plan of deceit to destroy me utterly and finally—Ann the bait to lure me.

He ain't here, if that's what you're thinking.

I come for the money you promised me.

Stole money, you mean. Stole off the man whose wife you been fucking right along.

I won't stand to hear such, not from you most of all.

Hear it you will, Tom Dooley. The price of lies is dear these days. Are you willing to pay it?

My anger was a hot sickness in my throat, but I knew I must do what had to be done. I'd come too far not to play it out to the end, one way or the other.

Whatever you heard, you heard wrong and I don't understand your venom. Why are you acting like a stepped-on copperhead?

You want that money to marry Laura and run off with her. You thought you'd blind me with your lies, but I know what the truth is and what it ain't.

Where'd you hear such a thing?

Why, Mr. Melton, of course. You remember him, don't you, Tom, my loving and faithful husband who likes to drink at Swain's where all the talk goes about.

I tried hard to think of how anyone would know of my and Laura's plans.

Grayson, do you suspect it was?

Yes, sir, Mr. Newbolt, it was him who I figured. Had to be. Somehow Laura's pap learned of it and told Grayson and he told the others—Melton among them.

So it foiled your plans.

Not quite, but mostly it did.

But, Tom, isn't it possible that it could have also been Pearl? Couldn't she have read the note before she brought it to you that day and told Mr. Shinbone, or even Mr. Melton himself?

I reckon it might could be so.

And out of her jealousy she . . .

Maybe she could have even told Ann directly and Ann was just playing it off as Melton told her.

Such twists and turns it could have come from Shakespeare's pen.

My hands shake now sometimes so terribly I can hardly hold my own pen well enough to write.

Laura Foster, Laura Foster, my heart is broken, twig-like. You, the young bud that never blossomed. Thy fruit never ripened. Like a sapling, the winds of fate have sent you low to the ground and snapped you in two. You will never grow straight and true and skyward. No children will climb upon you and swing from your leafy limbs. No man will ever come with an ax and harvest you for his fire on chilly winter's eve. Pruned in the prime, you have fallen—struck and cursed as the cursed dogwood, but even the dogwood blooms in the spring, where you never will.

Her keening voice comes to me in the night, or is it the wind? All last winter her voice of wind haunted me. I would go and sleep at her grave if I could, let her drag me down into it with her. She lies there alone, her spirit searching for heavenly rest. For I've heard that the spirits of the murdered never find rest until the hand that done the deed meets its own eternal end.

Are you waiting for me, Laura? Are you waiting for the trap to be sprung beneath my feet? Will that calm you, bring you rest? But surely you know it wasn't me who set the snare. Did you turn in that final moment to see whose hand bore the blade, the silver arc cutting thinly through the air?

Ann stood there saying vile things about Laura and me, her breath a vapor of the foul whiskey homemade by a nigger cousin of Raymond's, sold at half the price you could buy at Swain's.

Well, go on to her, Tom, if that's what you're aiming to do. I don't care a mighty goddamn.

I was already in it deep, the lying; one more lie wouldn't hurt Laura and it wouldn't hurt me and might even help us both.

She come to me for help. That's all.

Yes, and I know the sort of help she's a-looking for.

No, not what you think.

Then tell me what it is—this new lie of your'n.

And so I told her the only lie I thought I could and make it seem just pleasing enough to her, but not so much she'd gloat in the misery of it.

And that was?

I even hate to repeat it now.

But unless you do, how will the others know, Tom?

I told her that Laura had come to me saying she was pregnant, but I saw no pity in Ann's wistful gaze. Then I told her it wasn't mine but another's.

Whyn't she go to whoever the pap is? Why'd she come to you, Tom Dooley?

Because the pap is her own pap, that's why. She was riddled full of guilt and shame.

Even with a head full of bad drunk angels Ann gave a start at such news.

Lordy, Jesus! Her own pap?

That's right, only old Jesus ain't the one going to help her—it must be me.

Why you? Why not some other?

Like you, maybe, who wouldn't give her the time of day? Or Swain, who'd try and sell her off to one of those louts hangs round his place drinking all day?

Grayson, what about him? I heard tell Grayson's been going over there courting her. Why wouldn't she go to him?

She's afraid of Grayson. Grayson's as old as her pap and the two of them drink together most every night.

I don't reckon I could have pulled it off if Ann had been full sober. She was just drunk enough, and maybe pleased enough the babe wasn't mine, to buy it whole hog. Hell, I told it so sincere I near had tears in my eyes.

So Ann gave you the money?

Said she would, said she'd not gotten it just yet.

And she never did give it to you?

No, sir, she never did. Instead, what she did was dangle the promise of it in front of me like a carrot in front of a donkey, only the donkey was me. Said I should come back the next day.

And when you went.

Same thing.

And the time grew shorter still . . .

Yes, sir, the time grew short.

Winston Newbolt

So many lies abound in this place, among these people, even I
am not sure what to believe. There is a sincere timbre in Tom's
voice, but the most guilty men in the world can come across as
the most sincere—for what have they got to lose by more lies,
and what have they got to gain by favoring the truth?

O, I can't wait to return to New York, for I've become too
enchanted with Tom Dooley to be faithful to my trade.

Tom Dooley

Keyes calls out in his sleep some nights; calls the slattern's
name.

Flo. Flo!

Shut up, I think. I imagine them together—three good legs
and a wood one lying on the floor, or propped up in the corner
maybe. It's a sorry thing to think about it, but sometimes the
thinking about such keeps me from thinking about other things
much worse.

*By Thursday evening I'd become desperate. Even thought of rob-
bing Melton if I had to. Maybe hide along the road and when he
went by in his wagon on the way back from Swain's leap out and
knock him in the head with a rock and take his poke. But in the end
I couldn't do it. I wasn't any sort of thief. I might have been a lot of
things, but I wasn't a thief.*

*That last night before I was to meet Laura I waited for Melton to
leave home, then crept up to the house. I could see Ann inside, and
Pearl was with her and they were talking close together. I went round
and knocked on the door and Pearl answered it.*

*Cousin Ann, Tom Dooley's here. Real proper announcement, like I
was a stranger to them suddenly.*

Ask him what does he want?

Ann, you know why I've come.

He says you know why he's come.

I don't know no such thing, why he's come.

Pearl started to repeat Ann's words.

I don't need a go-between. Come out here, Ann. Come out now.

Ann appeared behind Pearl; the greasy light caused them to look more like sisters than cousins—twin devils arisen from the flame of deceit.

What you want, Tom Dooley?

You know what I want. I come for what you promised me.

Ann laughed like I'd told her a wicked joke.

Would you listen to him, Cousin Pauline. I swear; Tom Dooley's become so starry-eyed over Cousin Laura he can't think straight. Believes things not yet told or happened.

Pearl laughed a little too, but not as loudly as Ann.

You said for me to come tonight and you'd give me the money.

Why I said no such thing. Whatever money are you talking about?

Their laughter trailed after me into the outer dark as I walked away from that awful place of conspiracy.

Go marry your little she bitch, Tom Dooley. The only thing you'll be buying with your empty pockets is a passel of misery. You'll see. You'll see.

There was something evil on the loose that night. I should have gone straight to Foster's cabin and taken Laura away from that evil place.

But you didn't.

No, sir, I dint.

Newbolt says he must go take care of his sour stomach with a libation. I guess he means a drink at Swain's for that is the only place in Reedy Branch a body can get sound liquor unless you favor the nigger's place, which most white men don't. I would give anything for the freedom to go and buy a drink of Swain's liquor and pour it down my gullet and hear the rough talk of the trade there and have a stranger's hand clap me on the back and ask me about war and women and hunting squirrels. That which I once hated so well, is now the thing I'd wallow in if I had the chance.

But more than this, I would go to the sea, go to the sea, go to the sea.

Dear Mother. I am sending this farewell to you to let you know my last thoughts, no matter when they might come, will be of you. I know I've not written and not wanted you to travel all the way to come to the jail and see me like this. Understand it is the last pride I have left—to be thought of in the light you always knew me and not as a convicted and imprisoned man. I know it must be rough on you to have to hear the mongrel crowd talk about me—to hear that your darling son, Tom Dooley, is a murderer. But don't believe them, for I would not lie to you about such a terrible act. Surely not now, when the die has been cast and I am nearing my final hour. I will send on with this letter a few things: my Barlow knife, two tintypes—one of me taken in Va. when I was in the Army, the other of me and my friend, Louis Stephens, who was killed, a few dollars script, my fiddle. Do with them what you will, sell them if you must to help feed yourself. Somebody might pay you a decent dollar for Tom Dooley's fiddle. For my friend Shinbone says I am timeless. Oh what a terrible time this must be for you. Please don't fret over me. My friend Shinbone also says heaven is a lovely place to be and that he thinks I'll go there if I confess my sins to Jesus Christ. I ain't yet, but he's near got me convinced. Your loving son, Tom.

I blow the ink dry and know the words are forever writ.

That night I dream of Ann.

I see her riding through the woods, her hair snagged with briars—she is riding Melton's dark bay, a fury of muscle between her scratched and bleeding legs.

Ooweee, horse. Ooweee!

The thunderous hooves toss up clots of dirt and I don't know why she's riding so.

The dream shifts.

I see Shinbone dancing naked round a glorious fire. I see

Pearl crawling on all fours. I see Jesus nailed to a tree lift his thorn-capped head and open his eyes until they are staring directly into mine. I see Laura staggering with a pale hand clasped to her bloody bosom.

I awake, but the dream is terrible enough to drag me back into it, again and again.

Shinbone tosses something into the fire causing the flames to flare violently at the darkness. Pearl waggles her pale hams, lewdly winking. The howling mouth of the nailed Jesus matches Ann's howling: *Ooweee, Ooweee!*

I fall from my cot to the hard floor striking my chin. I huddle in a corner, certain I'm going mad, praying that I will before that final hour strikes. The thought of madness seems to me the only refuge. I will myself to stop breathing, my heart to stop beating—but life seems indestructible by my own hand. I cannot do it.

Keyes calls up the stairs.

Tom, Tom, you all right up there? What's all that racket?

I hear only my labored breathing now. The death is in my veins. I can feel it, black and whispering, seeking me out.

Tom?

I don't answer.

Elizabeth Brouchard

These words now are like a scattering of dead birds amid my garden. There, between the roses and dahlias and marigolds, are the fallen sparrows and a stink rises up that cuts off any sweetness the flowers may have offered.

O, Tom, when you fell through the gallows, dropped from this world to that, the sparrows fell with you, fell from heaven without God's knowing it.

CHAPTER 27

Tom Dooley

All night I lay in fevered sleeplessness, listening to the darkness scrape against my windows, listening to the moon tilt in the sky, listening to falling stars, listening to the river thirstily licking its banks.

I could not rest for thinking of the coming morning. I had hardly enough script to pay for travel as far as even Tennessee much less beyond the blue mountains beyond and beyond where I'd promised myself I'd take Laura and our babe to the sea.

I could see her leaving her pap's at dawn—the first light barely risen across the fields, creeping up the slopes of the mountains, that gray ripe dawn that comes on slow and flares up fast once the sun strikes it. Old man Foster would come awake later and find her missing and his horse missing and curse us both, for he wasn't a fool about such things. We'd have to travel fast and steady and make it as far as we could the first few days. Laura would want to dally along brook and field, for she was ever the bearer of a child's heart, full of romantic notions and she would try and get me to dally too.

But I knew Foster was the sort who would see it as his fortune fled, his opportunity to have a son-in-law who owned a tavern where he could go and drink, or one who owned a large farm upon which he could live without rent. He would see his future gone and want it back and come after it with blood in his heart for the man who'd stolen it from him.

It wouldn't take him long to find us if we dallied. We mustn't dally.

I had packed a kit: extra shirt, long drawers, my razor, fiddle and bow and sundry things—those worth owning and needing. Once we reached the sea, I'd become a new man with new things—a rubber coat and boots to keep me dry. Oh, I had such hopes of becoming a new man. I knew no matter how much Foster craved an easy future he would not follow us as far as the sea. Instead he'd suffer his loss in Swain's, drinking and lamenting his stole fortune of a daughter.

Why they even goddamn stole my horse, can you believe it!

And his besotted brethren would lament right alongside him and curse my name, but I did not care, for I cared not for any of them.

Are you feeling better this evening, Mr. Newbolt?

Somewhat, yes. Thank you for asking, Tom.

I wish I could say the same, about feeling better, I mean.

Tell me more if you will about what happened the morning you were to meet Laura.

There is an odor of sickness about the reporter that even the smell of his cigar can't mask. Perhaps it's attached itself to his clothes and he doesn't realize it.

I wrestled with the devil all that night.

And did you win, or he?

He, of course, for see what terrible events occurred.

Scribble, scribble goes his pencil as he takes notes in that little book of his.

This story will age over time, Tom. It will age like wine and be drunk forever.

Oh, I don't care nothing about it, Mr. Newbolt, about it lasting and aging and being drunk. Can't you see none of that matters to me?

Yes, yes, of course. But what is done is done, and we may as well tell of it as well as we can, lest it build into some sort of legend that only flirts with the truth.

Then go ahead and write it how you will.

I did not tell Newbolt that I am writing my own account of the events, or about you, Liza, who comes and helps me with the words. I don't want to give away my last secret, the last thing left to me as my own.

Here's how it went.

I went straight off to Billy Dixon's first light.

Why Billy's?

He was the last resort, the last hope for me to get some money. Billy had been a bachelor all his life and I figured without a family to feed and support he might have saved a little—certainly enough to pay for slatterns when he wanted; and I've seen him spend freely in Swain's. It was an odd co-incidence that when I knocked on his door and he opened it, I could see the slattern, Flo, there in the room in his bed.

He scratched his haunch trying to wake up and his hair was stuck wild on his head; he had some bruises on his neck.

You been wrestling, or what?

He offered me a sloppy grin.

Oh that, and touched his neck.

I need your help, Billy.

Well, shoot fire, Tom, couldn't you come round later when I got no company?

Need it now or not at all. I'm in a fix.

Come in and have a drink.

Yes, sir, believe I will.

The room smelled of violence and sex but I tried not to mind it and instead set myself at Billy's little table and allowed him to pour us each a cup of liquor from a bottle near empty with two or three other empty ones lying about the floor, one chair busted, a curtain torn, a picture knocked off the wall and tumbled in a corner.

Billy cast a glance toward the snoring Flo, then lifted his cup.

A man has to fortify himself against such assaults.

This said with a wink, as though I'd know and appreciate what battles he'd fit the night before, him and Flo. But I didn't care nothing about it other than I was a little glad Billy had gotten over his heartache of Pearl quick enough.

Now what sort of fix are you in, Tom, to be coming round so early of a morning?

I told him I needed the loan of some money. He asked me why. I lied, told him I was in trouble with Grayson and had to clear out of the valley or Grayson might swear out a warrant for my arrest with the High Sheriff.

Why not expose him to the truth of your plight, Tom?

Dint want him to know about Laura. Dint want anyone to know, for the fewer that knew, the less chance they'd track us down.

Go ahead with the rest if you will . . .

Newbolt cuts loose with a loud belch—the escaped air sours the room.

Well, sir, I could see by Billy's look he didn't fully believe me but wanted to badly enough because of the friend I'd become to him, how I'd tried to help him with his romantic problems with Pearl. So I straight out asked him for money.

Boy, I wished I had her to give, Tom. But I ain't.

Why ain't you? You been a bachelor all your life, Billy. Why ain't you got it to give?

That there lying on the bed is a lot of the reason. I've spent most all I ever earned on women like Flo there. I've bought whores since I was of a mind to notice 'em. Man with a face like mine ain't exactly what marrying gals is looking for.

I've a notion to rob her, Billy, take off her what you paid her for last night.

Go ahead, Tom. If that's what you've a mind to do. I won't try and stop you.

My hand was played out and it was a losing one. I gathered what I had left of my pride and shook Billy's hand and went off to meet Laura, knowing she'd probably been waiting by the spring for me nearly an hour already.

And that is where you found her?

Yes, but not like I'd thought I would.

Dead?

Yes, already so.

And you had no hand in it?

No, sir, I dint.

Tell me if you would, what she was like that first moment you saw her.

I close my eyes and try not to see it—Laura, there by the fallen tree, her body reclined, one arm flung over her eyes as though not to witness the terrible act committed upon her—a red flower stain on the front of her dress.

She had on satin shoes.

Such expensive shoes for an impoverished girl. How do you think it is she came by them?

I don't know.

Grayson, maybe—a gift?

My heart raced even as hers had stopped, as though it were beating for the both of us. I kneeled there in the moss beside her and lifted away her arm and looked into her half-closed eyes. For a moment I thought they saw me, but then what might have been was lost. I called to her and held her close, but I knew there was nothing could be done for her. Too often I'd seen such eyes in the war, such dead beauty unmarred except for a single wound. I kissed her cooling lips and they did not kiss back. O that they would and I could have breathed new life into her and cleaned away the stain on her bosom and taken her

273

with me to the far sea.

What happened then, Tom? Did you run then?

What happened was the strangest thing and I don't know if it were coincidence, or what.

Suddenly Ann was there.

Had she been there all the while?

I couldn't say.

One minute she wasn't there and the next she was.

Oh, Tom, what's happened to Cousin Laura?

She did seem genuinely surprised—her face struck with horror at the sight of the still wet bloodstain now covering the whole top of Laura's dress.

Someone's killed her.

Oh, Tom, why'd you do it?

I dint do it.

Surely you must have, for who else would come along and hurt such an innocent girl as Cousin Laura?

Yesterday you'd not a kind thing to say about her; how do I know it wasn't you who did this?

Me, me! Oh, Tom, how could you think such a thing?

I grew suddenly sick and wretched knowing I'd never again hold my sweetheart, that our babe would not see the light of even its first day—that three futures had been ended in the swift stroke of an angry blade.

Ann took to ranting and carrying on and I thought she'd draw the attention of others by the way she was doing so. I grew fearful that if others found us thus, Laura's blood now on my hands, my clothes, they'd think I done it. And surely as I've already told you, Mr. Newbolt, I'd made a lot of enemies just trying to be Tom Dooley.

Can you tell me how she ended up in a grave?

That part I am ashamed of. But mostly it was out of fear and Ann's wild claims . . .

Do not destroy us both, Tom Dooley, with your false accusations. I would not hurt poor Laura for love nor money.

Odd how you just happen by at this self same hour when I was to meet her.

Surely coincidence that I did, for I was coming to your cabin to bring you the money you'd asked me for.

But my cabin is the other way . . .

And felt a thirst and diverted my journey to come down to the springs for a drink.

It all seemed too much coincidence, but still . . .

If not Ann, whom do you suspect had a hand in it?

Your voice has the tinge of suspicion in it, Mr. Newbolt. I already swore to you I'd nothing to do with it.

I'm just trying to learn the truth here, Tom.

Yes, sir, I understand you are and I'm trying to give it best I know how. But the truth can be a strange creature.

I pleaded with Ann to calm herself, that I wasn't accusing her of anything, that I was distraught as she over the event and that we'd do no good drawing attention to ourselves with poor Laura's body not yet cold. I reminded her of a fact or two . . .

Pearl for one has heard you swear vengeance on Laura and me. Don't you think she'd swear to it in a court of law?

This stopped her raving.

Then what should we do, Tom? For we'll both be suspects in this . . .

I don't know, but we mustn't be found this way and we sure can't just leave her thus . . .

And so it was agreed that even though we'd nothing to do with Laura's death, we'd bury her and that I would leave the valley for a time and Ann would remain with Melton as though nothing had happened.

And of this, I am greatly ashamed, for all the scheming did no good, and the deed was ignoble and I question now how true my love for Laura was knowing what I done to her earthly

Bill Brooks

remains—how unceremoniously Ann and me dug her grave and put her in it.

That surely was a hard decision.

I can't talk of it anymore.

I understand, Tom. I'll come back tomorrow.

Oh, I wish you wouldn't. I wish you wouldn't ever have to come back.

He stops writing, closes his little book, and slips it into his pocket saying he'll return again when I'm feeling better.

There is something bursting in me, a great hot stone of something that needs to come out. I take my pen and dip it into the pool of ink. The sheet of foolscap lay blank, waiting to bear its children: words.

Sin, who calls? Thy great voice roars within me.

But I will not answer, I mustn't answer once nor

Twice nor ever. Love's lamp put out, Darkness

Grows all around me. Thy flame Extinguished,

I am lost in darkness—the Stars & Moon provide

Me not enough to light to find My way. Sin's call,

Call no more, for Loveless darkness has claimed me.

My head grows too weary, Liza; I'd just as soon the hangman's noose end my misery as to live yet another moment with thoughts of Laura death plaguing me as they do.

Ann Foster Melton

O, great liar!

It was Tom who suggested we bury her in a quick grave. I wanted to go for help, to bring back a wagon and carry lovely Laura in it to town and see she had a proper funeral, but Tom was against it.

You fool! he warned me.

What was I to do? I thought if I refused, his murderous heart might murder me too, for when a mountain man gets his blood

276

in a boil, there is no telling what he might or might not do.

Jealousy is more dangerous than liquor in the heart of a mountain man.

So I went along, helped dig Laura's grave with a tree limb. We had to bend her legs to fit her in.

Tom Dooley

We dug a shallow grave, Ann and me, and placed poor Laura in it along with a bundle of clothes she'd brought, a poor trousseau, and covered her up with dirt and leaves and twigs and my tears fell upon the grave so heavily Ann cursed and tore her dress out of anguish not for Laura, but for my love for Laura.

Take me, Tom. Take me here and now. Take me atop her damn'd grave. For my flesh is all afire with need and I want you to prove to me you love me and not her.

I was stunned she would suggest such a thing and told her, no, I would not do it.

O, don't you see—don't you understand what odd feelings it sends through me to see you grieve for her so hard? Take me here, upon her grave and prove to me your love. Or, who knows what I might say if this were found out.

It would be a ghastly mean thing to do . . .

Take me, goddamn you—rape me if you must!

Leave me be.

She tried to get me to do it. She exposed herself, lay on the ground with her legs apart clutching at herself, her face twisted into a mask of madness.

And so I ran. I ran away and told myself I could never come back, that I could never stop running unless, or until, I reached the sea.

You wanted the truth, Liza, well there it is . . .

Elizabeth Brouchard

O, Tom, the sea awaits us all. If only you'd listened to it and gone before that fateful hour . . .

Or, listened to the truest heart . . .

I was mute, but you were blind . . .

& deaf.

So all our hearts turned into stones that sank into the waiting sea . . .

& rest there still . . .

O, God, yes.

★ ★ ★ ★ ★

BOOK III
TESTAMENT

★ ★ ★ ★ ★

CHAPTER 28

Ann Foster Melton

All is sorrow, bent and cold like old iron twisted by a force unseen. Why do you come to question me when my hands are without blood?

O, fair sister, Tom told me you were there that day—this from the mouth of your lover. Do you deny it?

Damn Tom Dooley and his lust, and damn his dead lover, for I'd nothing to do with it, this evil they claim.

O, wind, I hear thy name singing
Evermore of love and sweet regret,
Of end days when thy shadow
Creeps into light places and
Brings dark & cold everlasting.
He says you and he . . .

Before the war I took up with him, and after. And in between James married me and tried to wrap me in his withered limbs and squeeze from my heart every drop of loving blood I had in me for Tom Dooley. I should have let him. How better off I'd be.

Tell me true of thy story, for what is there to gain or lose in the telling?

O, the first time words flowed from his mouth like bees from the honey hive. Their sting was sweet.

The way I understand it, this affaire de coeur *did not stop after you married Mr. Melton and Tom came home again . . . I saw him there that day at the station. And I saw you there as well, your arms wrapped round him . . .*

He was a fiddler turned drummer to rally the men and watch them fall—ragged gray soldiers from the sky into hell, I suppose. The hero, the hero, the little drummer boy. I could not help but desire him still.

You always loved him, Liza, you poor wretched mute . . .

Winston Newbolt
You are a fair and pretty lass and I would be a dolt not to tell you those things you ask, Miss Brouchard:

I stood once upon the ramparts of Bull Run and watched the struggle as all the while men in beaver hats picnicked with women under parasols as though it weren't a war at all but a great stage drama, you see—this Civil War that in the end ground the very bones of fair-haired boys, that ate its young. O, they surely were somebody's boys, but they weren't mine.

Blood is blood.

Do tell.

Ann Foster Melton
I wash my privates now with a rag squatting over a tin pan of cold water. How do you think it feels for such a pretty gal as myself, once married to a wealthy man in Reedy Branch, to squat over a pan and slop cold water o'er her privates, lady that you are?

There is hope yet, for Tom has not gone to the gallows and word has it that Mister Vance will be defending you.

O, you turn away & avert your eyes like I'm less than you. But all my life men have looked at me as if I were something they'd like to eat, to ravish, to pass around like a jug of liquor. A woman knows the beastly hunger of men from birth to grave. But I suppose you in your delicate ways, you with your dumb tongue will never know such things. Be glad you don't.

I met him in the spring that year the war started. He had the eyes of a child. But when he returned, he'd left his child eyes behind somewhere, there beyond the mountains in places where the dead were.

But before he went off to become a drummer—on that spring day—his blood was innocent. O, I don't mind telling you about it.

Why I'm off to fit the war, says he, *and wouldn't you do a brave boy a favor by going down to the river with me.*

The river! Why what would possess me to do such a thing?

For the chance to swim and a taste of this fine chicken in my poke and . . .

He had his poke slung over his back and grinned like a possum.

I'm Tom Dooley and live the other side of Reedy Branch and reckon I never seen you round here before this very moment. Why you must be an angel dropped straight down from the sky.

Me, an angel!

I told him my pap and me had just moved from Wilkesboro and we didn't get to beyond Reedy Branch much. But I think he knew whenever a pretty gal set first foot in Wilkes County and he had come to secret me out. Surprised he didn't go after you as well . . . except for, of course, you don't speak a damn word.

Wilkesboro. Well then you're a city gal.

What if I am?

I heard me some interesting things about city gals.

I asked him like what.

Heard they're bodacious.

That's a big old word for a briar hopper.

I know plenty more and I could show you some things even a city gal might not know.

I don't know what you got cooking in that kettle head, Tom Dooley, but I'm a virgin and aim to stay such till I marry.

Virgin! Lord, such talk.

I can confess it to you now, Liza Brouchard, I wasn't—for other boys had had at me before I ever come to Wilkes County. But even you know it wouldn't do a gal no good to confess such doings with other boys, now, would it?

I'm a freeborn child and speak my mind. You like it I do?

I surely do.

So I went on down to the river with him—the first fatal step in the journey of my undoing.

And when we heard the river's song, and stood upon its banks, we saw two shadows cast upon the water, his and mine, as fate would have it, like wingless angels we stood as if anchored to the earth, to this place that would draw us again and again in times of love and hate—where death, too, would come to visit.

And if you'd known then this outcome now . . .

Lord I'd a run and kept running.

That's a pretty dress, do you intend to swim in it?

O, lordy no! My pap would skin me—it was my ma's.

Well, best hang it on a branch then.

His gaze fell on me and never strayed as he shucked his clothes.

Well? You swimming or not?

This, he asked me while standing naked as any boy I ever seen—then plunged like an otter into the green waters of the Yadkin and swam careless.

O, he was as pretty as a god and I swam that day with him, his flesh wet and slippery against mine. And I knew when he kissed me I'd been kissed not by a boy, but a pretty little god.

You thought him a god?

O, he wasn't any true or goodly god, but one that proved false, the sort the Bible warns you about.

Do you read the Bible much?

I have these last two years. Before that, well Mr. Melton used to quote from it in those latter days after Tom came back from the war and I took up with him again. No, I never used to read the Bible or pay no such mind to the recordings of the dead.

Does it bring you comfort?

It makes the time less a numbing thing.

When we climbed out of the water and lay on a rock, he started talking his game again.

I'm going to war, you see. And maybe I won't make it home again, and maybe I won't never love me a gal, and never marry or have me any children.

You expect to breed me, here and now, leave me with a belly full of a child never to see its pap?

Wait . . .

And he went to his poke and pulled out a fiddle and a bow.

Thought you said you were carrying fried chicken in that poke?

O, he laughed like the devil, then began to play for me so sweetly I wept. I wept not for weeping's sake alone, but because his tears encouraged mine, because the sounds he wrought from his fiddle called down the angels.

Then when he stopped playing, this pretty little god with tears streaming down his cheeks came close and laid himself in my arms and begged me to save him from all things terrible.

Like what, Tom?

I ain't no true fighter. My hand don't fit a gun. And someday I aim to earn my living as a fiddler, though I dream of the sea and becoming a captain. But surely if I go to that ol' war, there's ever chance I will be kilt. I can feel the cold death a waiting for me. But I must go help the boys whup old Billy Yank lest I be scorned as a coward.

He said this with such great drama I nearly laughed.

You don't look like the whupping sort.

My heart is full of sorrow, but go I must.

Then let your sorrow come into me, let it abide in me. Let me be the cup you fill your sorrow with. But not here, not out in the open where ever body can see.

Then, where?

I thought and thought.

How about my pap's corncrib?

He near fell over with laughter.

Corncrib? Why, gal, tha's the strangest place I ever heard.

But before you know it that's where we wound up, there in that hot stifling corncrib crushed down upon the dry ears.

It was a long time we lay there watching the world through the slats. I had no heart to tell him it wasn't my first time in a corncrib with a boy, or in a haymow or inside a milking house, either.

I feel a specialness, Tom.

Me too, I swear it.

As though we've been bound by something greater than we know.

That which binds us will never be broke.

It must be God's will.

Surely it must.

But we did not count on murder.

And if they hang you as could surely happen . . .

Then triple murder it will be and the blood of us all will stain those left, and not one soul, living or dead, will be untouched.

Tell me how it came to pass that you and Tom were able to carry on before your husband's very eyes.

Some men are woven without fiber, and for what I did to him, what I allowed in his house, I am now ashamed of. For, he dint have it in him to face Tom down, to take charge of his own wife, to put an end to our sin. I can't explain it, really. Mr. Melton is a good man with weak resolve. Perhaps he thought that if he tried to stop me, I'd leave him and go off with Tom for good.

So he was shy about you and willing to abide in your ways?

He bided his time, thinking maybe I'd wear out on Tom—that ours was a fire would quickly burn out. But it never did, till now.

Did he know about you and Tom before he married you?

Yes, I told him my heart was with another.

Tell me how it came to be that you married Mr. Melton if your heart was given to Tom.

It was in the second year of Tom's absence that Melton came to courting.

I won't lie; I need a wife. You're young and pretty and I'm twice as old and no prettiness to me. But I got land and a house and some other holdings and some say I'm not the richest man in Reedy Branch—not like Swain who owns the tavern. A young gal could do worse than me; marry for something as inconsequential as love and end up worked out by the time she's thirty. Men are scarce these parts now the war has begun—you know it, I know it. I'll give your pap a nice purse if you'll agree.

I have me a sweetheart named Tom Dooley off fighting in that there war, Mr. Melton, and already gave my heart to him.

Suppose he don't come home—plenty won't from what I read on the death lists posted down at Swain's every day.

Why, the boys will whup those Billy Yanks easy, probably be home by autumn.

They didn't come home last autumn. And they didn't come home last winter neither. You could end up a spinster you ain't careful. You're what, about sixteen, already? They'll be plenty widows and single gals looking for theyselves a man like me time this war is through. You want to take your chances, see if this Tom Dooley comes home?

He had a sure way about him; as though he had his whole

life planned out and was going to see it worked through just like he'd planned it. But every day that passed and I did not hear from Tom it seemed to me he had foretold the future of his never returning and Melton kept watering my seed with his words.

And when Tom didn't come home at the end of that second year . . .

I married Melton.

But did you think Tom might return someday, or did you think he was . . .

Dead? His name never showed up on the death lists, but I never got a letter from him, either. Augustus Sweet's boy went off to that war and never came home and nobody ever heard if he lived or died. Some who did come back was missing an arm, a leg, a hand, I wasn't sure I wanted a part man, even if it was Tom. I thought maybe marrying Mister Melton was a sure thing. You knew what you were getting right up front, in spite of his age and shortcomings.

It seemed so. I gave to Melton what was Tom's—the very thing he left behind. That first night we was together was worse than any war in my way of thinking . . .

Come here and rest beside me, sweet little gal.

Melton lay abed and patted the coverlet as the moonlight shone in his eyes like tiny pieces of milk glass.

I ain't ready for that yet.

Sure you are, come on here and rest next to me now, don't make this any harder'n it has to be.

He called me Ivy instead of my name. So I asked him:

Who's Ivy?

Why, did I say Ivy?

I later learned Ivy was his dead wife and all the while that night as he . . . he called me Ivy.

Ivy, Ivy, Ivy.

It was like being buried under a pile of sticks that a muskrat was trying to burrow into. It scratched and hurt and was not tender in any way, and after, I felt dirty as a muskrat.

And so you and Melton were husband and wife for some time before Tom came home again.

A letter finally arrived from him.

Dear Ann . . . the usual of how he missed me, and a list of reasons he'd not written before: marching all the time, sickly, under attack, captured.

James Melton had all but put out the fires that had raged in me for Tom, not with his own fire, but with the coldness of his being. So when Tom's letter came, I felt a new fire burning in me.

O, my pretty little god was safe and returning to me
& in spite of Melton's legal paper declaring me his
Property, I vowed I'd see Tom Dooley the moment his
Pretty little god feet touched again the Soil of Reedy
Branch—the fiddler, the drummer, the once lost love.
And I did see him.

He threw his arms around me and whispered long faithful promises . . .

O, Ann, the journey has been long . . . my eyes have witnessed such terrible things . . .

Hesh, hesh, don't talk of things that wound you, but tell of things residing still in joyous places.

We went to the river, to the very place we'd first went three years before, and he looked at the same water with his now weary red eyes, all the wonder wiped clean from them.

It's exactly like it was, like I seen in my mind all those terrible nights when thunder roared and it rained steel upon us shattering our bones and breaking our bodies . . .

I placed my lips on his lips and stanched the flow of his bitter travail, for I did not want to hear it—the horrible hours stolen from him: *Thy sweet innocence. I lost my fiddle somewhere between here and a fiery woods . . .*

I'll get you a new one.

We stood looking at our twin selves rippling on the water, then his knees buckled and he fell to the grass and I fell with him and gave myself again to him as naturally as if he were my husband and I his wife.

And now you are here in this terrible place.

Yes, now I am here . . .

Look at me little mute sister. Look at me as if I am still the beauty I once was, as though I am still a woman who can seduce a man as I once could so easily, and not as I am, this ragged thing who washes her cunny in a cold pan of dirty water and waits for the hangman to come.

Elizabeth Brouchard

How I both loathe and feel sorry for you, Ann Melton, wife of James, unfaithful harridan, that you are. Your mouth twists with your lies and yet your eyes are full of fear, you tremble as a trapped fox and bare your feral fangs at any who would come near you.

Tell me, how does such a wench win the hearts of men other than by your course beauty? How does any but the most impoverished of spirit man abide in thee?

If such as beauty brings, I am glad I did not have it.

Chapter 29

The Testament of Billy Dixon

The world is an empty place for those of us who know not beauty or wealth, who lack in the social graces—I count myself among these. What do you want to know, dear Liza, that you don't already know?

Everything.

I know this: I was just a poor pit-face schoolteacher where the rest of this valley was concerned, most especially by these mountain fellas.

But not by me, Billy.

O, save me from my friends, for thy enemies I'm well aware.

O, Liza, if only you'd loved me half as much as you did Tom . . .

You knew all along?

From the first minute I see you and you asked about him.

And thus . . .

O, it's late in the game for us, Liza. Too, too late in the game. We've played our hand and all that Tom business is ever so long ago. Let it rest, won't you. Let me rest. (Billy died the following Saturday.)

Tom would have loved you if he had not so much love in his heart already. I'm surprised he did not take up with you. But then to all us fellas, we stayed clear of you because of Swain and because you were . . . well, I'm ashamed to admit, but we all thought of you as afflicted. O, I know it's such a terrible thing for me to say to you after all these years of us being married. Don't let my words sting.

Your words do not sting me as you might think. I've lived my whole life hearing it: mute, idiot girl, dead tongue. Fools everyone, for they thought because a body could not speak it could not hear or think, or even tie its own shoes.

We both know well enough what a cruel world it is. I'm only glad we were able to leave that place and not look back.

But Tom never left it . . .

No, he never did.

Tell me about you and Tom and Pauline.

O, are you sure you want to hear it? What good can it possibly do for me to tell you such things?

I made a promise.

To a dead man.

To Tom Dooley.

Even in death you would not betray him.

Tell me, Billy . . . You and Tom shared her then, before she went over to Shinbone's camp.

Yes. Tom took my case up with her and convinced her somehow that I was a good choice, given the choices she had. This was after Swain had used her and tried to sell her to that poor, softheaded Negro, Raymond.

Why do you think Tom would pass her along to you, having saved her from Raymond?

Because Tom didn't ever love her. She loved him, but he didn't love her. And yet he didn't hate her, either. He was that sort of fellow; if he didn't love you, it didn't mean he hated you. I think he cared about Pauline as you would a baby rabbit or some other of God's creatures that seem defenseless in a world so cruel.

Did Pearl ever tell you of how she felt about being part of a ménage?

She didn't have to. Everybody knew what was going on. Lots of men in this valley felt it was wrong what Tom and the Foster girls were up to. But not because those fellas kept such high morals themselves, or for any more reason than they were jealous. They talked about him something terrible.

O, that goddamn Tom Dooley is hogging all the women round here.

Ain't it enough he's putting the cob to Melton's wife, he's got to put the cob to her cousins as well?

Maybe them girls is all inbred girls, maybe they got the same daddy and they don't know no better.

Maybe somebody ought to take and cut that boy's cob off for him!

Harsh words from harsh men in a place where women with even a dollop of perceived virtue were rare. Such was the situation too because of the war that came and took away the beautiful young lads and made it a widow land, this you know already, Liza—you seen how it was, so many of them boys gone for good. Once the war was quit, there were plenty of women to be had—some with broods of kids, worn-out widows with plain faces and hard hearts, which made the comely girls comelier still; pretty fresh girls like the Foster girls—and you as well, Liza.

The Foster girls were young and lovely and the men that were left were crusty as snapping turtles, some just as vile in their nature . . .

Do you think someone of them could have conspired against Tom, could have led to . . . Laura's death? Who whispers the truth and who keeps it is anyone's guess. The fact was that only Tom and Ann stood accused, only Tom and Ann were in jail. But who can say whether or not pinning a murder on Tom was their pact? Some like Grayson and even your father, well, who'd put it past them? But, show me the hard evidence, I say.

Where were you when . . .

Drunk as Jacob's goat—lying abed with a slattern, Florence Garvey. Tom came that morning to my door.

I could stand some help, Billy.

I knew he meant money. He told me he was in a scrap with Grayson and he needed to clear out 'cause Grayson was threatening to swear out a warrant for his arrest with the High Sheriff. I tried to reason with him, make him see the weakness of his thinking.

O, Tom, Grayson will hunt you down with his dogs if you run. You might just stay and face the music.

No, I can't Billy. I can't.

I told him I'd spent all my money on drink and slatterns, like sad old Flo lying on the bed. He said he could almost rob her, that's how desperate he felt. But I knew it was just talk. He talked of his wanting to marry Laura and how they were to meet that very morning.

She waits now for me, Billy. Without a poke, how can I carve for her a future?

If I could make it so, I'd give you a fortune.

O, I know you would. You've been a good enough friend.

We shook hands and I watched him go off—toward the springs, where he said Laura would be waiting for him. I watched him march off into the golden light that morning brought, and the light surrounded him as though he were one of God's angels lost and wandering. It was no murderer I saw in that golden light—it was just a good boy who'd fallen into trouble.

And that's the last you saw of him until he was arrested and brought back?

Yes. I saw Grayson and George Hare and Sam Pie and three or four others herding Tom like he was a shoat hog between their mules and long-legged horses—Grayson riding up front like a general—chin stuck out, proud that he had captured the murderer of Laura Foster. His pronouncement, not mine. People came and stood along the road and cursed Tom for what he'd done—what they'd thought he'd done, and he never said a word in his own defense. Pauline came by later and told me Grayson and them had caught up with Tom near the Tennessee line. She was shivering, could hardly talk.

You think he did it, Billy? Pearl asked me as Tom was led past.

No. You?

I don't know, honestly know, but could be he did.

You knew him well as me, Pearl.

I thought I did once. We shared a pallet is all. He never loved me. How's I suppose to know what was in his head?

You know him to be decent and kindly, though—didn't he always treat you square?

Decent! He passed me round like I was a liquor jug.

He saved you from Raymond.

For what did he save me for, Billy? For what?

I reckon he saved you for the mad preacher—ain't that who you been sharing a pallet with lately?

You're mad with jealousy still.

I think Tom's got clean hands is all. Jealousy's got nothing to do with it.

After that, she would never speak to me again. I'd see her on occasion in the village, but she wouldn't look at me.

The light is oddly strange at this hour . . .

O, I know it. I see it settling over the roofs of Paris and it leaves me melancholy. Does it leave you melancholy, Liza?

That's the way it always is when it's true. The evening comes on and flattens the light down over everything until it's like a painting . . .

The sky is . . .

Like washed blood and bruises, I know it.

Will you go to the hanging?

What are you talking about, Billy? The hanging took place forty years ago.

I must go and rest now, Liza, will you come and lay with me?

I think I will stay here and read and try not to look at the bruised sky and think of the conspiracies. I think I will stay drunk a week and listen to the madness of ravens. I think I will spend my very last dime on a slattern and write sonnets to her:

O, foul and troubled air that blisters the skin &
Rains bitter ruin that blinds the eye—blessedly so,
That I do not see the wickedness that doth abound
& drip from the dubious hearts of kindred men.
Kiss me with thy bruised mouth and let me taste thy
Honeyed lies for the price of coins I dare not squander.
Tell me sweet tales of unfaithful love & dazzle me with
Thy jeweled faithless smile & gnash me with thy teeth until
I am rendered blood and bone and little else save a spirit spoilt.
You're just an old fool, Billy.
There are worse things than being an old fool.

See how the last light glows almost tenderly, then is gone . . .

I will tell Tom when I see him of your loyalty, Liza.

Billy, I'm sorry I stirred the ashes in your old burned out heart . . .

O, don't trouble poor Tom none with my niggling thoughts—for what good would they do him, or anyone? Who cares, do you think, the thoughts of a pit-face teacher who was lucky enough to have married you, the mute muse of us all?

Had I known that in seventy-two hours you would be dead, darling Bill, I would have not disturbed you with my everlasting curiosity. You were the last true link—that part of the chain of events that keeps me tethered to the long ago past.

Tisn't nothing, darling girl.

O, that I could have loved you better, could have been a better wife to you, dear Billy, could have given you children to dote on, perhaps the past would have long ago faded from memory, wilted in the pages of some old book like a pluck'd rose whose red turns black with mourning.

O, dear Billy, why is it do you think we can never love as fully the ones we end up with as the ones we did not?

Do you in that nether place hear the children singing?

Yes, I hear them dear—I hear them singing.

CHAPTER 30

The Testament of James Melton

Don't come here looking for any sympathy from me. Tom Dooley is a legalized son of a bitch far as I'm concerned, and he got what he had coming to him. Look how he ruined lives and stole futures. O, I've nothing good to say about Tom Dooley, nothing good at all. If you've come here looking for sympathy, you've damn sure come barking up the wrong tree. Why, I'd a put the rope round his neck myself and kick the chair out from under him if they'd let me. The snap of his neck bone would have been music to my ears. And I'd a let him swing for the ravens to come and eat the eyes out of his skull and for every man jack to witness what happens to a legalized son of a bitch.

But you didn't hate Ann?

O, I never could. She was as much his victim as Laura was . . .

And you?

Me. I should have done the right thing. If I had, the state maybe wouldn't have had the expense of hanging him. I guess you could say we was all Tom Dooley's victims . . . those who died and those of us who have still to die.

Could you . . .

I got shoes to cobble and no time for idle talk.

Ann gave me this to give to you.

A letter, is it? All this time she sat silent, swallowing her lies and those of Tom Dooley, and now she writes to me?

She asked me to wait until . . .

Until they hung him, or until I gave a reply? Even in death she wouldn't betray him. It don't matter. And even if I could help, what do I care what happens to her now?

Surely you loved her once . . .

Loved her like the blue-eyed devil she is. Loved her like a backslider loves sin. Loved her like a man eat up with love. But I ain't eat up no more. Man can only take so much. She become like over-ripened fruit to me, ruined from too much ripeness.

Would you like to read it?

Oh, hell, oh, hell! What do I care what she says. I have plenty of my own words if words is what you came here for!

I have broken my teeth on the Bones
Of Love, & feasted on cold desire.
My cheeks are stain'd with ruin's tears
And dark jealousy has set my soul afire.

Look it me, would you? What do you see, but a man who all his life has tried to live the godly way and do right by others. And for this I was repaid with treachery, deceit, and the shame of being a cuckold. Behind my back when I went to town to drink at Swain's I could hear the men whisper and snigger and snort over the infidelities my sweet faithless wife committed under my nose and in plain sight. It was as though I ate broken glass and swallied pepper, the way such talk felt in my guts.

I don't understand why you . . .

Let it happen? O, I could have taken matters into hand. I could have killed Tom Dooley and gotten away with it by law. Not a man in this valley, judge or sheriff or neighbor, would have convicted me if I had. I would have been carried about on their shoulders and called righteous and a hero, and been boughten beers.

But you chose to do nothing.

Because she would have left me if I had. What would I have

gained if I had taken back my honor, my manhood, and lost the very thing I wanted it for in the first place? Tell me what good is a man's pride, his honor, if he loses the thing that causes his heart to beat?

Pride and honor . . .

O, hell, give it over to me and let me read it. Let me read it aloud so you'll know what sort of damn craven fool she is.

Dear James, I have had much time to reflect on the events that has led me to this place—this tiny small place where indignities are as common as the lice that invade my bedding. And for what? What did I ever do to deserve this fate? To you I confess my sins of infidelity, but not murder. I never had a hand in it. Think of me what you will, but I never murdered Laura or anyone. The only thing's been murdered is my freedom. O, I am sorry for my caprices. I am sorry I was so shameless when it came to you, rubbed your nose in my mess. For that I should be punished, but not for this I did not do. Maybe you think, like a lot of others, that sin is sin and I'm getting my comeuppance—if not for the one thing, then for the other. And maybe I am. But if they hang me, then the innocent will be murdered by them that's not fit to judge me. For who among any of them is without some sin? I know if you will go and speak to the judge, if you will protest my case, it might make all the difference in the world—for you were the wronged party as well as anyone—and I would be forever beholding to you. And if not the judge, then hire me a lawyer. And if set free, I will come and be your wife in all the ways a woman can be a wife to a man. I know you are a good man and I have dragged your name through all sorts of mud, but once you see how I can be with you, once the others see it, they will forget, and you will forget all this terrible business. And some day this black thing will be behind us, and the memory of it will be wasted away. Save me, dear husband. Save me if you can. Yr. Loving wife, Ann.

Mr. Melton?

Oh, hell.

It sounds sincere enough . . .

I don't know what to believe anymore.

Surely a person can change.

Oh, hell. I wish you'd leave out of here, gal. I wished to God you'd never come here with your silent ways and slate and chalk and your big dark eyes like one of God's own, sniffing around for sympathy for that damn murderer. Go on back to your pap's. Don't let him find you out. He's no more love for Tom Dooley than any of the rest of us. If he was to find you out, he'd surely take a belt to you, afflicted little child that you are, you've a lot to learn about the human condition. Go on, now. Leave me be. Leave us all be.

CHAPTER 31

The Testament of Colonel James Grayson

I never had it in for Tom Dooley, in spite of what others may have told you. Tom was just Tom and I know there are folks around here who didn't care for him much and there are folks that did. He was in the war three years and that ought to count for something in the book of life and I'm sure that it will when he faces his maker.

He was a drummer . . .

Yes, I heard that he was. Look it that sky, those mountains, the lay of the valley—the way the river flows through it like a vein bringing life blood and taking life blood away. You can see why a man would be hard put to leave a place like this.

Tom has spoken often of wanting to leave it.

Of course he has, look at what he's wrought. Have you gone to visit Laura's grave?

Yes.

Along the pike, not far from where she was found. We dug it up high so when the river floods it won't wash it away. O, she'll never leave this place—Tom made certain she wouldn't.

Would you have shot him without a trial if he had not surrendered?

I would have done what was necessary to see justice served.

Even though you couldn't be sure it was he who . . .

If you don't mind my saying so, Miss Brouchard, but it seems to me you're a bit naïve. I think everybody knows he done it.

Why else would he have run off the very day Laura came up missing? And lest you forget, he was tried and convicted twice for the crime.

But weren't there others who left the day Laura disappeared?

Might I compliment you on your fine penmanship . . . I suppose being mute you've had to learn to develop a fine hand.

But about the others who left that day of Laura's disappearance . . .

Rumors. Something bad happens, the air is rife with rumors. Don't believe everything that passes from the lips of drunk men and gossipy women.

You're not originally from here, are you, Colonel?

No, Miss. I come down from Tennessee originally. Have a place just north of here. Raise blooded horses—Walkers mostly. Raised them in Tennessee as well, but this land down this way always looked bluer and greener somehow.

There was some talk that you had been pursuing Laura's affection . . .

Laura was a pretty girl and I won't deny I had gone a time or two to court her. She was too good for the likes of Tom Dooley, I can tell you that.

But she was quite a bit younger than yourself?

A young woman does herself well to marry an older man . . . a man with experience and holdings and not someone who is young and foolish and just as liable to leave her with a brood of kids and no sound future as he is to go off hunting squirrels. Older men are steady men. Speaking of which, I don't know why it is I never really noticed you before, Miss Brouchard. Has anyone spoken for you? Has anyone asked your daddy about coming to court you?

I've no interest in being courted, and if I had, that man would have to ask my permission, not that of my father.

Of course. Forgive me my assumption. You are indeed a

grown woman now. But think carefully about it—about your future. There isn't much of one for a young woman with ahhh . . .

Affliction I think is the word you're thinking, sir.

I did not mean to . . .

Elizabeth Brouchard

I tell you, Billy, I watched this tall well-constructed man mount his tall and well-constructed horse and there was an aura about him of something cheap and insincere and not quite truthful. Having looked into his unflinching gaze, I'd no doubt that this Mr. Grayson was a man whose heart was carved from ancient glaciers, or that he would stop at little to achieve his aims. I was just as pleased that our conversation was brief and that I didn't have to suffer longer his greedy stare, or hear his condemnation of Tom. And when he rode off, I had only these words in my heart: Goodbye and good riddance, Mr. Grayson.

Chapter 32

The Testament of Tyree Shinbone

I was wondering when you'd get around to me.

I've gotten around to you now, Mr. Shinbone.

I can see that you have. Have they all told you what a madman I am?

There have been certain allusions made.

Has anyone told you you have the bluest eyes?

I am not so easily charmed or you so mad, I think.

You know, sister, I might be able to fix your affliction. Do you want me to lay hands on you and together we'll pray that the Lord almighty will fix your tongue?

Not here for that, Reverend.

Look at the flight of the hawk as she glides along the ridges looking for a mouse, a hare, anything at all that she can eat or take to her roost and feed her fledglings.

I did not come to talk to you of hawks and other wonders of nature either, sir.

O, I know you didn't, I know you didn't. You came to talk to me about murder and scandalous events, of naked haunches aglow in the moon's light and the depth of man's desire and depravity and all manner of sordid things. But you did not come here to talk to me about mending broken tongues or hawks. Tell me, Miss Brouchard, what does a sprite of a girl like you want to know such things for?

I've made a promise.

To Dooley, yes, he's mentioned you, your kind nature. He's told me of your visits to him at the jail. If I didn't know better, why, I'd say he's in love with you. Do you think it's possible for a man with the gallows on his mind to let thoughts of love creep in?

I don't know what is possible or what is not in the affairs of death or love . . .

But surely you know the story already, why come to me? For if I'm mad as they say, then what stock can you place in me, dear sweet child?

The story keeps changing, everywhere I turn, every lip that speaks it, speaks it differently . . .

Because they all know of their guilt in the matter—they're all complicit, you see, in poor Laura Foster's dying.

It wasn't far from here where it happened . . .

Not far at all . . . why you can almost throw a stone as far. Have you gone there yet, seen the little wooden cross, her name burned into it—the wild lilies that have sprung so pale where her innocent bones smolder? I have, and I tell you, it is a sad thing to think of one so fair and pretty lying deep and alone and silent for evermore.

Yes, I have visited her grave where the river in spring cannot reach it . . .

O, they are wise here who bury the dead. They are wise about so many things: when to plant and when to harvest and where to dig a grave. They are wise in every way except the condition of the human heart. Of that, they know nothing at all. For they are hungering, these people. Hungering for things they cannot have, starved for the flesh of Jesus Christ almighty, thirsty for the lamb's blood. They are not the people of Moses—the chosen ones—but rather the ones *not* chosen, the lost tribe of Israel. Listen.

I don't hear a thing . . .

At night you can hear their fiddles sawing and the screeching of tarts. You can hear their laughter as they dance and consort with one another, as they bed each other's wives and foul each other's fair daughters to satiate their craven lust. And as sad as it sounds, theirs is the music of lively reels carried over with them in their blood from the gutters of County Cork and alleys of Glasgow and the slums of London. They are gutter snipes and worse, the jetsam and flotsam of the human condition. No country fair and green as the Emerald Isle or the Isle of Man would have them. They are, to put it bluntly, potato eaters.

And what about you, Mr. Shinbone? Aren't you one of them, too?

I dance the jig and caress the flesh
Like all the rest of them Irish & Black-
Eyed Scots whose fiery anger & poverty
Is like a rock weighted down inside them.
I am dust as they are dust and no better—nay!

You had relations with Pauline Foster. Can you tell me why a man who claims the Lord as his savior would . . .

Indeed, I had her right here in this very place where the Lord hath led me, this but two years since he struck me blind while in the arms of a slattern named Fannie Fright—a tawny tart who made her way from the whorehouses of New Orleans to the best gentleman's club in Philadelphia where my own father introduced us. I suppose you could say dear *Pa Pa* and I were bonded by a sort of proxy incest—sharing her as we often did. This, while my own *Ma Ma,* who was once proposed marriage to by the Prince of Denmark, idled away her time—happy, as it were, with *Pa Pa's* hefty allowance and the constant company of handsome young suitors. So you can see why I grew up feasting on the carnal pleasures—even God is hard put to see me off women. Maybe that is why he struck me blind, and maybe I risk being struck blind again.

Struck blind? Literally?

O, yes, yes, then I heard His voice.

My son, my son, why has thou forsaken me?

Have to tell you, it was a hell of a scare.

But it had no lasting effect?

No, none, indeed. For a time, I forsook all pleasure, lived like
Saint John in the wilderness . . . came to this place because it
seemed to me a wild, unclaimed Eden—a place unspoiled where
I could begin my ministry and wash my hands of the past. But
Pauline was the devil's temptation and the devil proved me
weak still . . .

*(It is a well-known fact that the pox, if left unattended, can lead to
insanity. I wonder if this was the case with Mr. Shinbone. For, I look
into his eyes and see wild haste, and in his voice there is the sharp
edge of something about to slice through all common reality. He
doesn't stand in one place for more than a moment and waves his
arms about and moves around in tight little circles, as though
something is nagging at his heels. Of all the characters I've thus far
encountered in my search for your truth, Tom, Mr. Shinbone is by far
the most unpredictable and insane:)*

Getting back to the events of Laura Foster's death . . .

Well, you see sweet child—did you say your name was Grace?

Elizabeth.

Well you see, dear Elizabeth, the Lord himself commanded
me that fateful day there in Madam Fright's satin bed:

*Go forth into the wilderness and build a temple in my name and
bring to this place the Word, and let those who have ears hear, and
those who have eyes see, and I shall make you whole again, Tyree.*

He called you by your first name?

O, I know it sounds a bit preposterous . . .

Just a bit.

Came here as though led by His very hand.

(How could I bring him round to tell me anything worth telling?

And yet I found myself almost mesmerized by his madness. Could he have been the one who killed Laura Foster? He certainly seemed capable of almost any act—murder notwithstanding. But if this was the case then I knew I must be careful of him, Tom, for he could just as easily kill me.)

I'd like to ask you, Mr. Shinbone, if you think Tom Dooley capable of murder?

Murder! O, well, we're all capable of such a thing—why we're direct descendants of the greatest murderer of them all. Why it's in our blood to murder and to perform other carnal acts. Tom told me himself of the men he murdered in the war—fuzzy-cheeked boys with blue eyes and blue coats and mouths pink as little girls.

(I told myself to simply pretend that I was writing it all down and never leave on that I thought this man crazed. For either he was, or I was. Tom, how could you have consorted with such a man?)

But Tom was a drummer . . .

Surely he was, but a killer of men as well . . .

This he confessed to you?

O, confess it indeed, but even if he hadn't, I could see it in his eyes.

Tyree, Tyree, I killed the weak and halted and strong all the same. I shot them through their tunics and through their privates and through their pretty faces. I watched them blow apart and falter and fall and tumble down.

Who, Tom? Who did you shoot and watch tumble down?

The Billy Yanks, of course. It was our proper duty to kill them. It was God's will. It was manifest destiny—ours, and not Lincoln's little blue boys.

He told me, too, how he and the boys would march past entire fields of dead, their bodies bloated to twice normal and how the stench was so great they grew sick and wretched all over their own shoes, their bile as yellow as the sun on wild daisies.

That is what we did to them, Tyree—those boys whose mothers sent them off with pretty red scarves to tie around their pretty little throats to ward off the winter's chill. But the scarves would not stop our ball. We shot them terrible and turned them into things no living soul could stand to look at or be around—these pretty little blue boys we turned into offal.

O, I told him I didn't want to hear nothing about that war. I told him I'd been there, myself, giving cold comfort to the broken boys.

Why didn't you want to hear of it?

Because, I never was in any war. Because my own life had been one of great privilege—my father having paid a man three-hundred dollars to go and fight in my place—our livery man's son—while I drank good wine and fucked lonely women on silken beds—many of them the wives and sweethearts of those who had volunteered. And it was acceptable to believe that perhaps some of these slatterns' husbands and sweethearts also then did lay among the dead in those fields Tom was witness to, and perhaps himself had shot and killed. It was too raw to listen to him tell of it.

Silence . . .

O, did I say *fuck*? Pardon me madam for my lewdness; it just comes over me sometimes.

So it was your shame that Tom aroused in you by telling you of the war . . .

Shame is hardly the word for what I felt.

And could such a man murder again—could he have murdered Laura Foster?

O, great God, no, I don't believe it. But was he capable? Yes, as any man is capable. As I am capable, as you are capable . . .

(Did he have it right, Tom? Were you capable of such a thing with

all the killing instilled in you by the war?)
O, I can't let myself believe it.

Shinbone rants, and rants ring in my ears still.

Smell how fresh the air is after it rains. It is as though all the vile past is washed away here in Paris where I have only my poems and books of the memories I chose to keep.

I shall soon stop thinking of all this, Tom.

I shall put together the letters and journal entries and testaments and send them off to a friend, a nice young man in New York who has published some of my poetry. And then it will be finished, this sorrowful journey, at last and I can put you to rest, Tom. I can put to rest this love I've had for you and let it be forever still.

It is a journey's end that I eagerly await & one I shall abhor.

Chapter 33

At the Grave of Laura Foster: From the Final Notes of Winston Newbolt, Reporter, *New York Herald*

You cannot speak, can you sweet sister?

You cannot say who did this thing.

You rest here above the river that one can see slithering through the oaks and ash and poplars, slithering like a fat green snake toward some hapless hare.

There, there near that river they have told me of death and lust consuming—yours and Grayson's Negro and others as well. It seems to me it is like a pitiless Eden this place, for see how serene it looks to the unadorned eye. And here you are above it, looking down for evermore—slipped from thy earthly bonds only to return a resting angel. Safe in your grave now, sweet sister, safe for evermore. Death has protected you from further desecration and will keep you now as one of its own. In that way, I suppose I am to envy you your death. For, who knows what awaits me—what pain and suffering, what great loneliness and failure I've yet to endure? But you've gone through that vale and beyond & in death, there can only be peace. As they say, *Rest In Peace*. I think it true, for nothing more can harm you where you are now.

O, I came this long distance thinking I'd write it all up quick and hasten back to New York and be done with this rustic place and its rustic people. That I'd make the city dwellers read how murder of a young and lovely innocent played out amid these hills. I'd make them see you as one of their own, and cause them to grieve for you just a little bit over their suppers, and realize how lucky they all were to be safe and far removed from this place. For you see, dear, dear Laura Foster, it's a writer's desire to make his readers feel the truest feelings about those they never met. And I wanted them to feel that way toward you—as though they'd known you, as though you were one of their very own.

But I'm not sure I can do it, for I haven't yet learned who murdered you. And without that secret told, the story is incomplete and you are incomplete and so am I. Most I've talked to say Tom Dooley did it. Others believe it was Cousin Ann who had a hand in it. Others still, conjecture that it could just as well have been the madman, Shinbone, or maybe even the self-righteous Grayson who struts about on his big horse. They tell me this bush here to the side of your headstone is laurel, and that one yonder is hollyhock, and somewhere back up in the undergrowth, I hear a trickle of water I suppose is as pure as was your heart. It is as though the very land itself weeps for you—for the injustice done you. And a greater injustice it will be if they hang the wrong man.

O, how I'd liked to had gotten to know you, to hear your voice, your laughter, to see the pert way your feet walked over this not so hallowed ground. Tom and all the others I've spoken to tell me what a beauty you were.

You are the missing witness to this *(his)*story, the one that will keep me from telling it the way it should be told. The one great injustice in life is that the dead cannot talk and tell us what we long to know: what those final moments for you were like, what went through your pretty little head. You cannot tell even who it was murdered you. And was it fear, or was it hope, or was it simply dreams that suddenly, in that last fateful minute, you knew would never be realized as the silver blade came plunging down?

Who could have been so callous as to do it, to put you here in this lonely place?

Who could be so callous still as not to confess it now?

Let me lay down here with you. Let me rest where you rest. Let me dream even one dream that is yours and I will come as close as I ever shall to telling the world about Laura Foster.

The scent of pine is sweet.

Earth, cool in shade.

My hat for a pillow, I lay my head upon the grave where you eternally sleep and close my eyes to the scented wind and try to connect somehow with what you were, what you now are.

For we are one, frail little sister—all of us who have come and gone and who are here now, connected by some invisible cosmic thread. And soon we who are here will be where you now are, in that great by and by—Tom and Ann and me, and all the others—the innocent and the guilty alike. And among them, rest assured, the one who is guilty of this thing will rest too.

But till then, I join you now, for a little while, here in this high place above the river that moves along, moves along as eternally as life and death itself—as eternally as great love.

Sleep now, and I'll sleep with you.

CHAPTER 34

The Testament of Augusta Keyes
I am the jailer, Keyes.

I drink some, yes. And I desire a woman's flesh when I can get it—I won't deny it. Look at me—a wooden leg and a belly grown big, but with a boy's heart inside me still. I'm not at the top of any eligible bachelor's list. And do you know what it is like to keep a man as you might a dog, in a cage, feeding him slops three times a day and carrying away his shit?

So it's a lonesome life for me, or it's none at all.

Jailer? Yes. But tell me how many professions are there for a one-leg man? I don't like it, but I don't have to like it.

O, I seen them come and go out of here: Drunks, thieves, murderers. I've looked into their eyes and saw in them what they didn't even see in themselves: that they were lost, hopeless, some already dead. I've kept them until they either paid their debt or got gone off to Statesville and hanged.

And when the cells are empty, I sometimes hear them walking around up there, the dead, anyway—their ghosts. Because this was the last decent place they lived before the hangman put his rope round their necks—this was the last oasis and that's why they come back and stomp around at night and I have to get good and drunk not to hear 'em. And I reckon old Tom up there will come back too and I'll have to hear him and get drunk not to.

O, I know what you're thinking there, Miss. You're thinking

315

I'm just like all these others you've talked with round here, these illiterates, and mush brains and inbreds. But you'd be wrong in thinking it, because I ain't like them.

I was growed up proper, with manners and respect for my elders and taught to read and write and was set to go off to college. I was even engaged to a girl whose father was a banker here in Wilkesboro. Pretty girl with strawberry red hair. I had the whole world by its scrawny neck. I was a baseballer—played the outfield and pitched. I was handsome. Look, look here at this photograph. That's me. That young, lean pretty feller. You wouldn't know it to look at me now. I had two legs and the world by its scrawny neck.

But you chop off your damn leg and see what happens to you, see how the world changes for you. All of a sudden people feeling sorry for you, people pitying you, people looking at you like you're some sort of queer thing—like you belong in the circus. All they see is that stump there—that's all they care to see. People don't look you in the eye when they talk to you, they look at that damn wood leg at the end of that stump. And suddenly you ain't got the world no more by its scrawny neck. You ain't got nothing.

And there goes college and there goes the banker's daughter and there goes everything you ever thought about getting. And so yes, I'm lucky to have me a decent job, meal money, a place to live, even if I do got to keep men locked up like dogs for it.

I seen both sides of the fence. You ever seen both sides of the fence? Because you sure don't look like you have seen even one side.

O, I was once fair and pert, a mighty fine man.
Then came the accident, the swift stroke of steel
That did me in, the thing least expected of all the
Things I could have feared. Just a blade of steel
Sharp and mean as the devil's teeth. All done.

Had Tom spoken much of his Laura to you?

All the time he spoke of her—*Laura Foster, Laura Foster.* I heard him some nights up there talking with her.

Laura, Laura . . .

Then answering, as though she was right there in the cell with him.

What is it, Tom? Tell me true.

Why I got the creeps listening to him talk and answer hisself.

Two years is a long time to be locked up.

I know it. They should have taken and hanged the poor boy after the first trial. But, Vance got him a second trial and that took another year and still they found him guilty. Tried twice for the same murder—but it sure don't matter to Laura Foster how many times they tried him.

What do you think of his guilt, Mr. Keyes?

O, I don't know there, lass. I learned to stop guessing whether any of them did it or not. I've not had a single one ever said he was ever guilty of anything—they're all innocent. I reckon Tom is too.

But in your heart do you believe . . .

Don't believe nothing anymore—stopped believing in things the day I saw my leg laying there chopped off . . . I drink and I whore some and I keep 'em like dogs until the law says what is to happen to 'em. It ain't for me to say a man's guilt or innocence.

What is the thing you remember most? I want to add it to the accounts.

The night before they took him on down to Statesville, I paid Nan over to the café extra to fix him a extra smart meal for his supper. I reckon he was due one, for they sure don't feed them nothing much down in Statesville. Guess they see it as wasted expense to feed a dead man.

I'm sure he appreciated the kindness.

I put a little dope in his coffee to make him sleep better and not be so worn out in the morning—it's a long ride down to Statesville.

Can I ask you something else, Mr. Keyes?

I guess asking's already out of the bag—go ahead.

If you hadn't lost your leg, what might you have become?

Lawyer, I reckon. Hell, I'da been a good one too, and might have even gotten old Tom off. So I guess you could say but for the missed swing of an ax forty years ago, a whole lot of us might have come to different fates—Tom included.

It is a lovely sentiment . . .

Ain't it, though?

CHAPTER 35

The Testament of Tom Dooley

Listen careful, Liza, for last night I had a dream. O, tomorrow they would take me to Statesville and maybe the dream meant something and maybe it dint.

A horseman rode alone across the top of storm-ravaged ridges, lightning and thunder shattering all round him. He carried a sword raised heavenward, the blade taking the lightning bolts one after another as the horse screamed—its scream like that of a woman terrified. I could feel the ground shudder, like I was standing atop a living thing trying to rise from sleep. The horseman rode to and fro and nothing could kill him, not even the lightning that struck his sword time and time again. I stood alone in the shuddering valley and watched until the horseman rode down off the ridges, his sword afire. He rode down on me and stopped just a breath away. I saw then that the horseman was Laura, her eyes all gone, her sword terrible and swift as it swung down on me . . .

I come awake like I was drowning . . .

O, it was just a dream and nothing real to it, as all dreams are, Tom. Why look, you're standing here real as anything . . .

I may as well be dead. I may as well be.

How can I calm you when I can't even reach through the iron lattice to stroke your cheek, to press my fingers to your trembling mouth? How can I calm you when I cannot even say soothing words to you, my tongue so useless? If I may have but one wish, dear God, let it be that for a single minute I can speak . . .

I hear the tremor in his voice and think any minute now he will break down, perhaps confess his sins, if sins they are. But instead he turns his face away, his hands clinging to the lattice of iron that holds him caged, that separates us one from the other. I see a transfiguration: from the living to the dead—the life visibly going out of him with each breath, and death settling in life's place. Then I see something I can only swear to and never prove: I see a blue aura surrounding him, a pulsating light like breath itself. It lasts only the time of several heartbeats, then is gone. I see him thus and wonder if I have been too long in this place of violent men and ghostly tales and strange lurking fogs. I do not know, I do not know.

Tom, I promise you I will write of these things as I've found them, without embellishment, without even judgment. For, I don't know what the truth is, and no one has told me, and I doubt anyone will at this point.

You think I done it, don't you, Liza?

I just don't know.

I guess I could say I did it, or I could say I didn't do it and it wouldn't matter none at this stage of the game, now, would it?

O, the truth we shared like an unhappy meal—Tom Dooley and me.

Listen, Tom, whatever confessions you feel you must make, might be best made between you and whatever god you may believe in. No, I don't think after two judgments brought against you by juries of your peers, it would matter much what you said. You know these people round here as well as I do. I doubt they'd believe other than what they already do no matter what you said . . .

They're good people, some of them, even if they are wrongheaded about me. But they're still my people. And I guess there's no getting around that.

I'd offer thee my hand, but the latticework won't let either of us do naught but touch fingers and so we shake like two proper souls at a tea—with the minimal of touching and I feel electric when your fingers touch mine and look deeply into your sorrowful eyes.

I cannot save him, I cannot save the one who would be my lover—and now, he cannot save me either.

Liza . . .

Yes, Tom?

O, nothing, nothing at all.

I'll stay as long as you like . . .

Would you stay forever and evermore?

Yes, forever and evermore . . .

No. You must go on now. Go on and leave me as I am . . .

And so I leave with the common unspoken knowledge between us that were it possible, I would bear his remains in a small sailboat and carry him far out to sea and offer him to King Neptune, for I know that would be his wish—to become a sailor, to rest for all eternity in the sea.

Outside the jail I see someone has planted flowerbeds— peonies and poppies and dahlias. They are like bright-eyed children kissing the wind. I turn one last time and look up and see a pair of eyes who have lost their light of hope and wave feebly, then turn away again.

O, love, that memory has not faded, will not fade.

Even as I watched them lower Billy into the grave, I thought of you and that moment I saw you waving so forlorn in the jail window, stone and iron between us and other untold forces.

★ ★ ★ ★ ★

Fini

★ ★ ★ ★

CHAPTER 36

Tom Dooley

I hear the thump of Keyes's wood leg on the stairs, coming, coming. I smell the plate of food: hominy and bacon and black-eyed beans and cornbread fresh-baked, still warm and coffee.

Tom . . .

I ain't hungry.

Best eat.

Why?

Because . . . well, because tomorrow they're going to take you down to Statesville. Dang it, I hate to be the one to tell you, but I reckoned you'd want to know. I had them cook you something special. Why, look, I even got you a slice of cherry pie . . .

Take it away.

O, Tom, you got to eat to keep up your strength . . .

So I'll be good and plump for the hangman?

O, don't be talking that away, Tom. Why anything could happen between now and . . .

Sure it could.

You oughter eat before it all grows cold . . .

Hand it on in then.

Now, you wouldn't try anything foolish, would you?

Don't know what you mean.

Like try and break jail on me, or something foolish like.

I'd never do nothing to hurt you, Augusta.

No, of course you wouldn't. Why, you wouldn't hurt an old one-leg

325

man now would you?

The pitiful fools we've become—far, far from the angels we began as . . .

Never hurt nobody . . . well, with the exception of the war, I reckon.

That's a good boy there . . . go'n eat your grub and drink your coffee. I'll bring you some more coffee if you need it.

Augusta . . .

Yes, Tom.

Would you go on out and ask Liza to come up and visit with me?

Liza?

She's been sitting out in the courthouse square all day.

Lord, why'd she do something like that hot as it is?

Could you ask her to come on in, I'd like to visit with her.

Sure, sure.

Thump, thump, thump.

I have no appetite, none at all. All day I have watched out the window toward the square where Liza sits like a stone statue, like something you might find in a cemetery—a resting angel waiting for the dead to speak to her. Well, I guess I'm the dead and it's only right I should speak to her. I know that last time she left, she left in haste because I ordered her to. But I can't stand to see her thus . . . out there in the courtyard alone waiting for something to happen to stir her from her patient rest. O, I should have known what true love was all along. But I dint.

I should finish up my writing, too. Hard to write with a rope around my neck, tell the world I'm finished—all done in . . .

I hear the heavy door downstairs open and close. The cornbread is warm and sweet in my mouth, but I have no taste for it. The coffee has a funny bite. Across the way goes Keyes—his wood leg tattooing out a sound on the cobblestones. He walks like he's riding the deck of a ship. O, the sea, the far, far sea—I won't ever go there now, unless . . .

She looks like a wilted flower craving rain from being out there in the sun all day, not moving, looking up here now and then. I've seen dogs wouldn't stick as long for their master as she has stuck for me out there in that square. What a sad child she seems. But what do I know about it, the heart of one so pure.

My hand finds the pen, the bottle of ink, nearly gone now, the last few sheets of foolscap. I guess it's my warning to finish up the story. For, Mizrus Boots died last Wednesday—Keyes said it was her heart when he told me the news. Poor, poor woman. Every time I think of her I think of the foul words Shinbone said about her. I can't believe him, not a single word. My hand moves the pen over the paper.

Our folly is near to us now. Is coming quick like labored breath upon us. Those we loved and those we said we loved will find us out soon enough. And those who hated us will rejoice in our defeat. Love and folly are but bride and groom in life's long and temperamental marriage. We survive or we divorce. Death comes quick. Strike me down, O Glory, in my vanity and let my bones wash upon the shore of lov'd ones' memory. And remember ye who survive, not so much my misfortunes or my folly, but those things I was to you who lov'd me, and whom I lov'd. A man is not but a mirror with many faces . . .

Door opens again. I hear Augusta speaking in that guttural tongue of his.

Right up here, Miss. Careful now not to trip on that loose stair. Most any day I aim to nail her down. Up you go—he's right up there.

I hardly hear her step at all and then suddenly she is there, in the small shadowy hall outside the bars—standing like a waif gone begging for bread.

Come closer.

She eases nearer.

327

Why'd you sit all day out in that hot sun?

The late afternoon light slips in through the side windows just enough to stroke her cheeks with the golden kiss of its ending.

She shrugs.

Surely it wasn't to see me, was it?

Her eyes clasp onto mine.

She nods. She takes the tablet from the pocket of her dress, the small worn pencil and begins to write.

I would wait forever to see you.

Why, when all is lost to me?

Because . . . because . . .

She takes a moment to breathe, her pencil pinched between her fingers.

Go ahead, take your time—why time is about all I got left to me. They say they will take me to Statesville tomorrow . . .

Scribble:

What for?

I want to scream *What for* but it isn't her who should carry my burden.

The light shifts downward, grows less golden. Shadows deepen and she seems to me the most vulnerable creature in the world. I see there in the shadows too, Laura lying quiet in the moss near the rotted log, the morning light playing out across the Irishman's field, the fog lifting up from the river like the breath of God. That morning so innocent I could not take a breath for fear it would crush me—death lying close by. Love gone. O, Laura.

To be hanged.

Her face crumbles and I think she will fall, but steadies herself.

O, it's true. They've made it true—my guilt. And now they must hang me for it.

She writes something, then takes the piece of paper, rolling it tightly, and passes it through the bars, but before I can read it, she puts a finger to her lips and waggles her head to tell me not to read it or say anything.

She comes so near I can smell the scent of her hair and it is like the fresh and blooming flowers there in the square where she'd sat all day.

The shadows encroach more still as though to devour her, us, everything. She places her face against the quilt of iron as though she is touching cheeks with a lover. She sighs, then rushes away, down the stair again. And in a moment, I hear only the yawning of the thick oak door accompanied by Augusta's heavy voice.

Well, good evening to you, Miss . . .

I shuffle to the only window afforded me and keep watch over the square until I see her going across it, hurrying along as though fearful night will catch her. The old lamplighter, Wells, going about lighting his lamps, barely turns a head as she hurries past—his work everything to him.

I watch until there is nothing but shadows, and the flickering of Wells's lamps dancing over the small patch of ground at the foot of each lamp pole. It is a night alive with shadows and small lights and empty spaces where once a girl sat all day under the hot sun.

I light my own meager lamp and sit on the cot where the few remaining sheets of my foolscap await the last words in me. My limbs feel leaden of a sudden. I sip the coffee to awake me; it does no good. I unroll the small bit of paper seeing still the startled eyes of the one who wrote it. I bring the paper closer to the lamp.

I love you, Tom. I shall always love you. Goodbye, my darling. Goodbye.

In these words burn the last flicker of true light. Beyond

them is only darkness.

Love seems as ancient to me as the time of Genesis.

With great effort I rise and go again to the window to watch outer darkness with its meager little dancing lights and announce my final testament to anyone who would listen.

I love you too, Liza Bouchard. As much as I have it in me to love anyone, I love you for your charitable heart and . . . and . . .

Then I retire to my cot again to write out of me the last words I have regarding Laura Foster and Ann Melton and Pearl and all the rest who were with me there in that valley of travail—in that Season of Sorrow—and are still there now, the living and the dead.

Elizabeth Brouchard

O, I could not stand those last minutes with him like that. I craved so to hold him, to kiss his dry sallow cheeks—kiss color and life into them again. Time and accusation had turned him from a boy into an old, old man in just the span of two years. Nightmares had tortured him and the light of day had tortured him and all the memories had tortured him.

But I could not torture him further by avowing my love in his presence.

And I'll never know the truth of what we could have been together.

And this is my one great regret in all of life—having not known true love.

I hope the children come early today & I hope they play well.

And I hope it does not rain in Paris

CHAPTER 37

Tom Dooley

Morrow arrives on a stiff wind carrying rain. In the not far distance I hear the whistle, then the huff of the train that will carry me down. I close my eyes and see the curious faces as they watch me shuffle aboard, ankles chained, wrists chained, armed men front and back.

Why, I wonder what that feller done?

O, why wonder, ain't it enough he done something.

Why, he's hardly more'n a boy.

Old enough to have done something to put him those chains.

Why, ain't it that Tom Dooley?

Don't look, don't look.

Rain sweeps the courthouse square and I see no Liza waiting for me this day. Rain makes the air gray and thick as smoke. I put on my shirt, pants, shoes—the onliest little pride I've left. My feet ache still from all the marching I did in that war. But if I had to, and they'd let me, I'd march all the way to Asia and never complain.

Rain drips from the trees gentle as a lover's tears.

O rain, carry me down.

Hear the door yawn open. Hear the voices of men, Keyes's mixed in with them.

He up there?

Yes, sir.

You want to go get him or you want us to?

I'll go.

No funny business there, jailer.

No, sir.

Thump, knock, thump, knock.

Hidey, Tom. They're here to take you on down.

I'm ready.

I sure hate to see you have to go, son.

I reckon I do too.

Scrape of lock as Keyes inserts *his* key and turns it—sound like a tooth being pulled out of its socket.

Do something for me, if you would.

Sure, Tom, anything.

Once I'm gone, give this to Liza Brouchard. Tell her I wanted her to have it. Tell her . . . O, just give it to her would you?

Sure, sure. I'll do it.

Tell her there may be more coming once I get down to Statesville, but I can't be sure they'll let me have any pen and ink and paper. So tell her I said wait to do anything with it if she's a mind to sooner.

I hand him the papers I've been writing, bound and tied with some butcher paper and a piece of twine.

You promise to give it to only her.

Yes, sir, I'm good for my word.

Well, then, let's get on downstairs and see what them fellers want.

Two men in rough coats, felt hats wet with rain. Must have come up from Statesville for they sure aren't locals. One of them is wearing a badge; both carry shotguns.

Chain him up, Albert.

The one hands the other his shotgun and takes from his coat pocket two sets of manacles and sets about *chaining me up.*

I feel good and fixed when he's finished.

Let's go.

The one wearing the badge does the ordering. The other steps in behind me, the badge leads me out. Even chained, being outside that jail for the first time in two years feels like freedom.

I lift my face to the rain and it comes down on me.

Move along there, bub.

The one in the back nudges me forward.

They get me up into a wagon. The one wearing the badge keeps an eye fixed on me while the other drives the team. The iron rims clatter on the cobblestone, down the street as we head for the train depot. A few folks stop and stare, letting the rain soak through their clothes as we go by. A few I recognize and one or two wave, and one old man with a white beard, his back bent like a fishhook from too much time on this earth, pauses and removes his hat and holds it over his heart. I see, then, it is Mr. Clements, who fit in the Indian Wars and understands what it is to fit in a war and survive it. I nod my head to let him know I appreciate his gesture.

Time we get to the depot, my hair's plastered down and my shirt is soaked through and so are my trousers. Rain drips off the hats of the men with shotguns. They don't seem to care none. Lift me down and I shuffle inside the depot and those waiting with tickets turn and stare—and some I know and some I don't. Nobody says anything. I don't say anything and neither do the men with shotguns. Instead, they take me on through and up the steps to a railcar and on down the aisle to the back where they sit facing me, me facing them.

You fellers must like this line of work I take it.

They don't say anything. I don't blame them.

Time passes timelessly. I remember when the mad preacher, Shinbone, said we were all timeless. Odd that I should turn my face just then, see out the rain-streaked window him standing on the platform amid clouds of engine steam. Shinbone is looking here and there, up and down the platform. His bramble of white hair hardly matches the nice suit he's wearing. Then I see that he is shoeless. I feel a sudden urge to tap on the glass to draw his attention, then think better of it. He is standing there in his madness and better he should have it to himself.

The engine's whistle blows sharply, then tugs against its cargo of humanity, the cars lurch one by one. The two men with shotguns brace themselves with their feet when the car we're sitting in lurches too. Fits and starts we lurch along and then we are gliding away, the clack of the wheels vibrates up through the floor, up through my legs, into my very blood.

O, carry me on down.

I watch what is familiar to me shrink away—this place I've known for two years now and that other place from whence I came and everything else that resides down deep in my bones. It all just shrinks away. I watch the wet trees nagged by the rain, the brick buildings of the town—the brick dark as old blood. I watch the rolling hills rise and fall like great green waves—cattle standing under their slick wet hides, old barns, lost dreams. All just shrink away.

Everything is sodden and dreamless to me. The one man guarding me snorts, the other cuts a chaw from a plug of tobacco with a Barlow knife, its bone handle worn smooth. I watch the dream shrink away while they snort and chew. Farther up the car I hear an infant cry.

In my mind I write my last will and testament.

To who it might concern. I've nothing to give, and no one to give it to. I spent my days gathering nothing, preparing only for life and not death. And now that death is near, I've nothing to show for the life I lived. For, how is it a young man can be convinced of his own mortality when all around him are only the days of his youth? No warning given. I went to war and came home again and that seemed to me enough contemplating death. So do not blame me for being so ill prepared, so inconsiderate, so full of folly. And when I sucked the marrow of life from the bones of others, it was sweet and addicting

and I never thought for once there would be an end to the feast. Now,
I see I was mistaken—that the end comes too soon, too quickly—like
a thief in the night. And even if I'd lived a hundred years, this death
would still have come too quickly . . .

The conductor shuffles down the aisle taking tickets, sees
me, sees the two men with shotguns, sees the chains round my
wrists and feet. The chaw freezes in his vein-splattered cheek.
His black coat seems too tight fitting, his cap too small.

You'd be the one I read about—Tom Dooley.

He says it wrong, a common mistake, but right enough that I
don't protest.

The man wearing the badge hands him three tickets.

Move along there, bub—official law bidness.

The conductor looks at each of them, then back at me.

You take care, son, in that sweet by and by . . .

He shuffles on calling—*Tickets! Tickets!*

I see wet pastures, a cemetery of stones like crooked teeth
gnawed through the earth, a church steeple rising from beyond
a hillock pointing the way toward salvation, I guess. I ask the
man with the badge what day it is.

Sunday.

Have you a wife and children?

He looks away, the other one looks at his shoes. I finish writing my will inside my head.

We are but children of the god who made us . . . no more, no less,
so I've nothing more to leave to anyone (having sent my ma my last
few things), and no one waiting to accept it. I gave love. I gave my
honor to a war that dint care whether I gave it or not. I gave my
friendship to them that deserved it. And now I'm all give out. That is
my last will and testament, for you who care to read it. Tom Dooley.

I feel pleased about the words and will write them down once
I get to Statesville. Surely there will be time before they hang
me. I think about you too, Liza, how I'd wished you'd been

there to see me off. But I understand why you weren't. It's okay. Everything between me and you has always been okay.

We travel far enough south that we ride out of the rain. Sun and clouds play tag over the fields and throw shadows over the distant mountains, then snatch them back again. And when sun struck, the mountains turn a hazy blue that feels like longing.

It's quit raining.

The men with the shotguns don't seem to care.

Carry me on down.

CHAPTER 38

Tom Dooley

Statesville don't look like much to me—quiet little burg with fine white houses on streets bearing oaks that throw shade for a man to sit under, for children to play under, for lovers to stroll hand in hand under.

I get taken down from the train, the steel rails still vibrating in my blood. Marched up the street, past the hardware store, past the barbershop, past the mercantile. I get marched up the street by two men with shotguns, one fore, one aft. Past the bank, a café, a bicycle shop. Always wanted me a bicycle. I think the men with shotguns have hearts tough as leather, tough enough to shoot me easy as they would a rabid dog should I run. Might be easier for me to get shot, unless their aim was off—high or low, then it could be brutal and they'd hang me anyway.

Women and their kids see me coming and cross the street. Men lean on streetlamps and spit and watch me marched by. I guess they seen it before—this being the hanging place. Get marched past a livery, a newspaper office, a funeral parlor.

Carry me down.

Stop me in front of a stone building, stone steps worn smooth in the middle, big oak door. This must be it, the hanging place. Quarry stone blocks three stories high couldn't blow it up with cannon if you had one and I ain't. Gilt dome atop some of it green from time, windows with bars lower levels. They march me in, the men with shotguns.

Man at a desk, bald, mole under his left eye like a raisin—long hall beyond.

Sign him in, boys.

Scratch, scratch goes the pen writing my name in a book with other names on red lines.

Consider him signed in.

Take 'em chains off.

I feel twenty pounds lighter with the chains shed.

Lead me down the hall; swing open a barred door.

Go on in, son.

Door closes. The three of them stand there looking at me.

You want me to fetch you a preacher or anything?

Bald man's got a high-pitched voice.

No, sir.

Polite boy, ain't he?

The men with the shotguns don't say anything. The three turn to go.

I'd appreciate a pen, some ink, a few sheets of foolscap . . .

The bald man blinks, the raisin under his eye leaps, settles down again.

Like to write out my last will and testament.

I'll see what I can do. Anything else?

No, sir.

Real polite young man.

There are no windows down in this place where they got me. It feels like gloom.

Carry me down.

Time passes. The bald man brings me a plate—cornbread not so sweet and moist as I like it, black beans, salted pork, coffee weak as tea.

You didn't forget my pen and writing paper?

No, I ain't forgot. Just ain't got around to it is all.

Turns to leave.

You know when it will be?

Soon as I get around to it is when.

No, I mean the day they set to hang me.

Friday, son. Friday's the day they set to hang you. Eight o'clock in the morning. We lucky, it won't rain. Hate a hanging in the rain.

There it is, the stated number of my days left on earth. I guess it was writ a long time ago in the heavens, the number of my days. Writ on the first day old time existed. I guess it is one less of God's great secrets he has to carry around with Him. I know I should try and settle affairs with Him, but I ain't sure how, or even if it matters. What if I get over yonder and he ain't there? What if there ain't no over yonder and all it is, is just black nothingness? Well, it could be worse. Burning in hell forever and ever could be worse. I lay me down on the cot, the wool blanket rough as grit. I try not to think of the number of days I got left. I try not to think about anything. Impossible.

Later still, the bald man returns and lights a lamp outside my cell and thrusts in pen, paper, ink.

You want anything else, a Bible maybe?

It ain't never made much sense to me before . . .

Maybe it will now . . .

Yes, maybe so.

Best get right with your savior, son.

I reckon.

That was a terrible thing you done, killing that girl.

I don't say anything. I've become like the men with the shotguns. I've become one of the lesser ones. I've become like Liza Brouchard—a mute.

Creps, the night man's coming on soon. You need something, just call out. He's a little deaf, but you call loud enough he'll come.

All around, I reckon the bald fellow isn't so bad, considering the line of work he's in.

Sometime during the night there is a ruckus. I have not been able to sleep, choosing instead to savor every moment left me. Even still, they go by quick. The ruckus is raised by a drunk man they've brought in and put into a cell across from mine. They shove him in roughly and he curses them, curses their mothers and curses their children.

The one I reckon is Creps rakes his wood baton across the bars.

You shut your yap, Mick, or I'll bust open your skull like a t'mater.

O, fuck you and yar ugly wife and all them ugly kids yar stuck in her and come out again ugly as sin.

I'm warning you!

Then the drunk turns and drops his pants and exposes his hams to the guard.

You stupid sot!

Creps goes out grumbling. The drunken man curses him all the way out.

Sees me.

Hey!

I don't say anything.

Hey, you. What they got yar in for?

I don't say anything.

Well, ain't this the goddamnedest thing . . . me, in with a mute!

In a few minutes the drunk is stretched out across his cot and snoring.

I don't want to sleep, but comes an hour I guess before dawn I cannot any longer stay awake.

First sleep, then the dream.

Girls in white dresses dancing upon crushed flowers—violets and roses and daisies—their pretty little feet white as alabaster. Hand in hand they dance and sing. They are the cousins, Foster—Laura and Pearl and Ann. They dance below me, reach up and touch my dead boots. I am strangled, dangling from a rope, but still can look down into their pretty faces. *Pretty Tom, pretty Tom, they've hanged you for what you did to us—ruined us every one, each in her own way. O, pretty Tom, look, see how he's become the pretty vine that hangs from the garden tree.*

I awake in coldness and write down the dream and everything that has happened to me since they took me from Wilkesboro. I want it all to be known, even the littlest detail—for my being here should count for something.

Hey?

The fella across the way, the one brought in last night, stands up against his bars like an ape. He is dark and squat and dangerous looking.

Say, you didn't see what them lads did with me fiddle, did you?

Fiddle?

I think I beat an engineer over the head with it in a fight last night.

That's no way to treat a good fiddle.

I know it ain't. But you get to fighting, especially over a garl, you're liable to use a fiddle over some feller's head or anything else you can . . .

So we started talking about fiddles and fistfights and women and he told me his name was Mick Kennedy and that he played music professionally in many of the saloons from here to Charlotte and on up to Virginia. I told him I was a musician too, but never got around to playing for money.

Why, money is the best thing there is to play for. Money and the pretty garls, of course.

I know it.

He asked me what I was in jail for and I told him.

To be hanged.

He asked me what I did for them to hang me.

Nothing.

I don't know if he believed me. I told him my name.

Why everybody around has heard of you, Dooley. Why there's even a ballad been writ about you and what you done to that garl up on that mountain.

Weren't no mountain and I didn't do anything.

Why, if I'd not busted me fiddle, I'd play the ballad for yar . . .

I heard my heart beating in my ears. He began to sing without encouragement.

O, they say poor Laura Foster went to her grave fair and pure. They say Tom Dooley loved her, but jealousy was love's cure . . .

His was the voice of a man who understood grief in a way that only certain men can understand it. I'd known many of the Irish boys during the war and they could all sing and weep and grow maudlin, especially when they sang about potatoes and hunger and true love lost. I called over to him to stop, for I didn't want to hear nothing about the events. But he didn't stop, for lost was he in his grieving ballad.

. . . and up there on that mountain, Laura sleeps all alone in a grave Tom Dooley made her, a grave as cold as stone, cold as a marder's heart they say!

Then he stopped and said he didn't remember rightly all the words yet and that each time he'd heard the ballad it had changed some; words were added and taken away and that he himself was now encouraged to complete it having met the real Tom Dooley. I told him it wasn't Dooley but Dula. He didn't seem to care the difference, said Dooley sounded better for the singing.

When will they turn you out, Mick?

He shrugs his broad sloping shoulders.

I've no money to pay me fine. I suppose tharty days is what I'll get this time. It's what they gave me last time.

In a way, he reminded me of Louis—the way he spoke, like a man going through each day for the very first time, as though he'd never lived any days before this one.

Were you in the war, Mick?

I was, Tom. But I'd just as well not speak of it and the terrible things I seen happen.

I felt the soldier's bond with him.

Can I ask a favor of you, Mick?

Sure, Tommy, me boy. Just tell me what it is.

Could you sing me the ballad again?

The slow version again, or the fast one? There's two you know.

The slow.

I lay and wept.

Elizabeth Brouchard

O, I've heard the ballad too. But I did not weep for sorrow as much for anger it had to be written at all.

I wouldn't be surprised they sing it still in those cold dark hills—my father's own tavern, late at night, the drunken sots.

But what would I know of cold dark hills?

For in the spring, Paris is charming and far, far away from cold dark hills.

CHAPTER 39

Tom Dooley

I cannot finish my story. You see, time and circumstance and the hangman won't let me. So I put down what I could, all that's in me. I wrote it down on sleepless, fevered nights by waxy yellow lamplight and by full moon's paler light, when there was a full moon and I could see well enough after they honored my one request to be moved near a window where I could at least see the stars.

Sometimes it is my hand does the writing and sometimes my hand is guided by what I can only guess as Laura's spirit. But whatever it is or was, whoever it is or was wrote it, it is an honest telling. That's all I can say. It is honest.

Mick.

Yes, Tom.

Will you do one last thing for me?

Certainly.

Will you see this gets mailed when they let you out?

Of course, lad.

In the morning they will hang me.

I know, I know.

You can have my Bible too.

You won't be needing it, but I can't say's I will either . . .

I've got out of it all I can. If I ain't got the necessary parts by now, it's too late.

The lord will be forgiving, you can count on that, me boy.

You think? Let's hope you're right then.

I seen it, lad.

You seen what?

The light of peace in dying men's eyes—men who never believed in anything, no kind of Jesus or Jehovah until the time came for them to pass over. I seen it a hundred times in the war. He's watching over you now, as we speak. He knows your heart, Tom. He knows when a heart's not strong enough to carry such burden. He knows forgiveness. He's pure love, Tom. Pure love.

The hammers of the carpenters still ring in my ears from earlier in the afternoon when they built my scaffold. I heard the carpenters laughing some, talking between blows, as though they were building a house. I guess they were—my house of inequity. Even Creps commented on it.

Fresh pine sawed at the mill, smells sweet as the piney woods they-selves. The square will be full tomorrow, Tom. You'll be the whole show!

I am no longer a man but a curiosity.

O, play your fiddle for me, Mick. Play it low and play it sweet. Play it sweet as those piney woods, sweet as wildflowers, sweet as a sweetheart's kiss.

O, wish that I could play for you, Tom. Wish I could play glory and freedom for you. Wish I could play you up a pair of wings to fly from this terrible place.

In the last hour I try and summon forth memories soft as a lover's kiss, and none with the sharpness of broken glass, or death to them.

Of these I write:

When I was a boy, I owned a tick hound pup I named Cicero. He was tan and black and could run three counties at the scent of a rabbit without stopping. I can't recall what happened to him. Like all other wonderful things, he was just gone from me one day.

I know now that the sounds I heard in my loft bed coming from below on those sharp cold winter nights were the hustings of my father working his politics on my mother for her love. These followed by her soft murmurings of consent. O, if I could have known such sweet and pure love . . .

Louis sits wrapped in his ragged wool blanket, his eyes tired with war, his mouth subtly set like the mouth of a Greek god. He is taut and beautiful as a girl. Our loneliness is soothed only by our shared desire not to die lonely.

Ann is naked, striped by slats of sunlight in an air dusty with the scent of dried corn. For moments at a time she is sheer pleasure and I dissolve into her until I am no more. This before foul reality shaped our sin.

O, frail Pearl lying upon my bed under heaven's moon, curled into me like a child asking me to take her again and again—and when I do, she still yearns for more and arches her back like a restless cat. Her hunger for me is unquenchable.

Laura . . . O, I can't think of her just in pleasurable ways. For death has tainted everything we were, every good memory is poisoned. And yet, I see her dancing in the rain, her hair wet and dark—her beauty greater than all women.

Of these, I loved her best.

I hear Cicero's baying off in the deep woods growing faint.

Sun settles beyond the blue ridges.

Darkness crawls down off the mountain slopes, slipping through the trees, coming near. A nightingale wings wildly across the black silver sky hurrying homeward. Silence follows the spilling ink of night.

Carry me down.

Footsteps coming!

Mick jerks his head round sharply, I do too.

Then our eyes meet across the span of life.

Goodbye.

Goodbye, Tom.

You won't forget?

No, I won't forget.

Well then . . .

It will be okay, Tom. Maybe an instant of pain, but that's all she'll be, and then you'll see glory. I wish I were going with you. I surely do . . .

My last words writ quick:

Dear Liza. Judge for yourself if the hand that could have writ this, this same hand that so truly gave the heart voice, could have harmed even a single hair on Laura's head? I was just a man in love. And this is what love's brought me . . .

Up the scaffold stairs I go onto the platform, the waiting hangman with waxed moustaches.

He fits the rope around my neck.

The old pastor steps close.

Is there anything you'd like to say, son? Confess? Any prayer you'd like me to pray o'er you?

No.

Then I hear as the crowd hushes, their faces turned upward, waiting, holding their breath and waiting just as I hold my breath and wait—Mick's keen Irish voice:

Hang your head low, Tom

Hang your head low.

Weep for your soul, Tom

Weep for your lover's soul

Fare the well, Tom

Fare thee well . . .

It is finished.

ABOUT THE AUTHOR

Bill Brooks is the author of over 40 historical novels, many of them Western Frontier. His novel, *The Stone Garden: The Epic Life of Billy the Kid,* was selected by Booklist as one of the 10 Best Western novels of the previous decade. He lives with his wife, Diane, in Florida after living in the Midwest and West.